A GAME WITH NO RULES

A NOVEL
BY MICHAEL ATAMANOV

*Wishing you safe travels on
your fantasy journey,*

Michael Atamanov

PERIMETER DEFENSE
BOOK#4

MD

MAGIC DOME BOOKS

A Game with No Rules
Perimeter Defense, Book # 4
Published by Magic Dome Books, 2017
Copyright © M. Atamanov 2017
Cover Art © V. Manyukhin 2017
Translator © Andrew Schmitt 2017
All Rights Reserved
ISBN: 978-80-88231-45-5

All books
by Michael Atamanov:

Reality Benders LitRPG series
Countdown
External Threat
Game Changer
Web of Worlds
A Jump into the Unknown
Aces High

The Dark Herbalist LitRPG series
Video Game Plotline Tester
Stay on the Wing
A Trap for the Potentate
Finding a Body

Perimeter Defense LitRPG series
Sector Eight
Beyond Death
New Contract
A Game with No Rules

League of Losers LitRPG Series
A Cat and His Human

You're in Game!
(LitRPG Stories from Bestselling Authors)

You're in Game-2!
(More LitRPG stories set in your favorite worlds)

TABLE OF CONTENTS:

BALANCE OF POWER

"How IS SHE?" I asked Miya as she entered the small dining hall. I was sure that the Truth Seeker would be able to guess who I was asking about but, if she didn't, she could always read it from my thoughts.

I noticed that my wife was looking remarkably poorly rested today. Even the expensive cosmetics and clothing she wore were unable to distract from the black circles under her eyes, drooping in exhaustion. Might that have been her age showing? Obviously, it was difficult to maintain the appearance of a young woman at her... how many years had Miya racked up at this point? One hundred thirty? One hundred fifty? Two hundred?

"Alright, alright, Georg. That's enough!" the beautiful redhead rushed to intervene, giving yet another confirmation that she read my mind all the time without a second thought. "I get the message. I'll make sure I don't come to breakfast again, without getting myself together first. It's just that I really am tired. I've never had an easy time talking with the

Dark Mother, and our last conversation just sucked all the lifeforce out of me."

"How is she?" I asked, repeating my initial question.

"The Dark Mother is slowly fading, Georg. Her decrepit body, wracked with diseases of old age, is just giving up. She is bedridden, and no longer even tries to stand. But she remains the strongest Truth Seeker in the galaxy, and could still use her mind to crush the skull of any person like a soft-boiled egg. After her feud with the Emperor, the Dark Mother lost her source of power and is now living on reserves. Whether they will last long is something neither I nor she knows. I'll admit, I still haven't figured out why the Dark Mother wanted to talk with me long distance. We didn't talk about what happened to her, nor did we discuss the Emperor. We didn't even get close to touching on political issues. It was simply a conversation with a frail old lady, mortally exhausted after a very long life. However, after that half-hour conversation, I feel like a squeezed lemon. I have the sensation that I just took an important exam and it looks very much like I failed."

Miya went silent, giving me the chance to think over her words. I pointed my spouse to her usual seat at the dining table, but Miya didn't sit down, instead heading toward a large mirror on the wall. It looked like the thoughts she'd overheard about her age showing had stung, and she now wanted to make sure they weren't true. But I was still thinking seriously over Miya's words. The Dark Mother had never been inclined to idle chatter. In fact, the most powerful of the Truth Seekers was known to speak quite rarely. But before, each of her words were akin to a command, because everyone understood that the ruler of the Empire spoke through her lips.

That all changed three months ago. I was one of the few who knew the true facts of the conflict between the Emperor and the Dark Mother. For the rest of the Empire, what happened was a real shock. It all started with a video clip depicting the Emperor's guard ruthlessly shooting down my bodyguards and cousin, Duchess Katerina ton Unatari, while the normally tranquil Dark Mother screamed rabidly for my head.

The video of the utterly unprovoked attack on Crown Prince Georg royl Inoky ton Mesfelle — the hero of the war with the Aliens, ruler of the Unatari State, loyal subject of the Empire and one of the most popular military commanders — caused a real stir, rattling society's faith in the Emperor's infallibility. Many leading aristocrats and politicians expressed a negative opinion of that event, including the heads of the Blue, Purple, and Green Great Houses, as well as representatives of the Imperial Joint Chiefs of Staff. So, the harsh ultimatum I issued in response was perceived by the majority of Imperial citizens as justified.

But what happened after that was thought by many to be impossible, and caught even me quite by surprise. Emperor August royl Toll ton Akad backpedaled, and begged an official apology for the attack on the Unatari embassy, agreeing to also pay me five billion in compensation for the murder of my diplomats and destruction of my yacht *Queen of Sin.* The Emperor claimed the Dark Mother had been the impetus for the bloodbath in the Silver Palace, explaining that her treachery was rooted in a very old panicked dread of nonhuman races, which gave her an incorrect view of the situation. August claimed to have been an unwilling victim, blindly following the Dark Mother's reasoning, which he'd grown accustomed to trusting over their three long centuries together. In his address to the people, the Emperor announced that he had dismissed the Dark Mother with honors, while his new Truth Seeker would be Krista, who had worked until that point for the ruler of the Blue House, Duchess Ovella royl Stok ton Miro*.

*these events were described in the short story *From the Life of Crown Princesses*, which was released in a separate collection of short LitRPG stories.

To be honest, I had never believed in the sincerity of the Emperor's regret, not three months ago, and certainly not now. It was just that August royl Akad was not expecting to come up against such a severe reaction from society, and had certainly not foreseen that I would manage to avoid arrest and slip away from the Silver Palace. Confronted with a difficult dilemma: either have at least the Unatari State and Green House leave the Empire, or admit guilt, August chose a third option: try to cordon himself off by using the Dark Mother as a scapegoat.

For a time, that really did dampen the anger in the Empire, though the Great Houses' trust in the Throne World never returned to its former level. For my part, I was immediately suspicious when I asked to be compensated in ships and parts instead of money, and the Throne World refused. I even made another offer, which wouldn't have cost the Throne World a single credit, but would have affirmed the course to reconciliation: I asked to have my son Georg Junior named an official Imperial Crown Prince but, once again, the Emperor said no.

Then, when my specialists tried to order heavy laser cannons and warp drives from manufacturing facilities in the Imperial Core for the new battleships and assault cruisers, they were refused everywhere without explanation. That all spoke to a restriction on selling high-tech military equipment to the Unatari State that, while not officially declared, did still exist de facto. Of course, such moves by the Throne World did nothing to ease tensions. Obviously, given that, there could be no discussion of sending my daughter Likanna back to her preparatory school on the Throne World. So, both Crown Princess Likanna royl Georg ton Unatari and her closest friend Crown Princess Natalie royl Cruz ton Unatari had remained in Unatari space.

By the way, as for Likanna, my daughter had come to breakfast wearing a set of warm pajamas, adorned with silly cartoon characters and a pair of huge fluffy slippers on her bare feet. I wanted to note to the young Princess that girls of her age were supposed to get dressed for the day before coming to breakfast. But the words got stuck in my throat, because Princess Astra came into the small dining hall right after Lika in a near identical getup — poufy white pajamas with pink frogs and little gray donkeys, plush slippers gaping up with huge googly eyes and a hood on her head with long bunny ears.

"Hi, dad!" said Lika, giving me a quick peck on the

cheek and sitting cross-legged on a high chair. "Have you heard the news? Astra is now owner of the studio that produces the cartoon *Jeanne the Star Traveler*! Remember a year and a half ago when we invested the money she got from her painting *The Last Day of Veyerde* into making a new season of the adventures of Jeanne the space frog? Well, it was actually enough for a whole ten new seasons, and they're amazing! The money we made from that was enough to buy a controlling share in the studio!"

I looked at Astra, smiling happily with her snow-white teeth. Her light-colored wavy hair was still messy after waking up, and her eyes were sparkling in childlike wonder. Now, the Princess was happy and proud of herself, so I figured I shouldn't make a comment about her appearance in this moment of triumph.

Astra was basically a fully-grown lady. The doting mother of a strong and healthy boy of seven months, she had received an excellent education and knew all the subtleties of courtly etiquette. But, all the same, I just couldn't bring myself to treat her like an adult. Her personality had a bizarre combination of brilliance, naivete and simplicity. And the Princess was not acting or playing, either. She really did live in her own special little world where, if something was boring or didn't concern her directly, it simply didn't exist. I suspect that Astra didn't even know about my problems with the Emperor, because it was just political news, and didn't affect her, so she didn't care.

Three months ago, in order to avoid potential issues with Astra holding the title of Princess which, after the destruction of Veyerde, was no longer strictly accurate, I had made Astra a Swarm Princess and assigned her a holding in the Uyakh system. And, instead of forming a group of economic, design and construction advisors, the first thing Astra did in her role as ruler was to... start learning the Iseyek language. Although the language of the insects was considered rather simple due to its low number of words and grammar rules, the human throat was not anatomically adapted to pronouncing a significant portion of the high-frequency sounds it employed. All the same, that didn't stop Astra, despite all the warnings.

In principle, I didn't see anything wrong with the ruler of a star system wanting to understand her subjects directly without a translator, but Astra wanted more. Just a month later, considering her language proficiency adequate, the Princess headed out on her own to the intergalactic communications center on my flagship *Joan the Fatty* and demanded that the officers provide her a direct line to the Uyakh star system. At that time, I was in Sector Nine, busy with some major training exercises for my space fleet, so I didn't hear about my favorite's little adventure until the news came out...

Bionica and Phobos, struggling with Princess Astra's horrifying accent, translated my favorite's speech for me. To be honest, I buried my face in my hands when I heard it, just incapable of listening to the drivel Astra was issuing from the podium. My favorite was suggesting the planet Uyakh-IV be turned into a heaven of comfort and also the very safest place in the whole Universe. She wanted to see parks and green everywhere. She suggested all the dirty factories be removed from the planet and that a great many museums of interplanetary art be erected in their place at once. And Astra also wanted the largest art academy in the whole Empire built on her planet, where they could host artists from the whole galaxy and, with time, where her anointed son would learn to paint...

And that was at the fact that the planet Uyakh-IV was one of the Swarm's main manufacturing centers, and the Princess's innovative ideas threatened to shutter thousands of factories and other facilities that made high-tech products necessary to the Swarm and the Unatari State as a whole. I was expecting dire consequences after Astra's unpredictable speech and innovative ideas, but they never came. The fourteen billion inhabitants of the planet Uyakh-IV listened attentively to the speech of the new ruler of their star system, appreciated her care for them and noted it with a whirlwind of relationship improvements from all Swarm races. And that, essentially, was all that happened.

As I later heard from Admiral Kheraisss Vej, himself a native of Uyakh-IV, the White Queen, as Princess Astra was known in the Swarm, had gained a firm reputation as a kind but eccentric and foolish companion of their ultimate ruler. Their job was to admire her, humor her idiosyncrasies, and protect her from her most foolhardy acts. Fulfilling her orders, though, was not even moderately necessary. So, the Iseyek were very skeptical of Princess Astra's announcements, and all the planet's factories were still in operation. As my cousin Katerina put it somewhat rudely: "She tripped the idiot sensor." The Iseyek were much more reasonable than we feared, and simply ignored her strange orders.

Yes, Astra was not a great fit for the role of a serious, respected politician. But at that, my favorite was madly adored by the denizens of Unatari, both insect and human. Everywhere she went, she was greeted with ovations and great bouquets of flowers. And that stood in sharp contrast to my legal spouse Miya — the Red Queen in Swarm terminology, who was more respected and perhaps feared, than loved.

"Come on, Georg, that's enough! Do you think I like to hear comparisons like that?"

I just chuckled in reply to the Queen's annoyance. It was her own fault. She shouldn't have been reading my thoughts. She didn't have to get this upset. But I didn't have particular complaints about my wife. The Queen was not in conflict with my favorite, because she didn't take Astra even remotely seriously as a rival. Astra then, after quickly figuring out that the Queen of Unatari, despite her ghastly reputation, was not working to destroy her, accepted Miya more as a piece of furniture or yet another of the monarch's bodyguards. Insofar as I knew, the Queen and my favorite had a conversation three months ago, in which they had come to an understanding, laying down rules to help them coexist in peace. But I didn't really know the details.

"What do you even mean details?" my spouse cut into my thoughts yet again. *"The Princess was utterly oblivious to my hints, so I told Astra directly that she had to go straight to the medical wing of the starship to senior doctor Nicosid Brandt and get the very best in*

contraceptives. I assured the Princess that she didn't have anything to fear from me, as long as she took the medicine as he prescribed. And if she decides to break that rule, well..."

Because Miya didn't finish that sentence, I made sure to clarify the possible consequences Astra might face.

"Georg, you know perfectly well that my arms and legs are bound by a promise I made to you and that I cannot do any harm to your favorite. But that didn't necessarily mean she had to know that. Astra is still abusing her impunity and has basically moved into your cabin. If it weren't for her son, with whom Astra spends lots of time in the playroom, the Princess would never leave your chambers."

I walked over to the Queen of Unatari, who was looking cantankerously at her reflection in the mirror and gave her a tender hug. Then quietly, so Likanna and Astra wouldn't hear me, I said:

"Miya, you shouldn't get upset. Astra has lived that way since her first day in my retinue, so she considers such behavior normal and doesn't even suspect that it bothers you."

My explanation was interrupted by an incoming call signal. The staff communications officer informed me:

"Your Majesty, incoming call from the Throne World. The Dark Mother would like to speak with your second Truth Seeker, Florianna ton Veyerde. Shall I put her through?"

It was a mere formality to ask such a question — could one really refuse such a powerful Truth Seeker? So, of course, I gave my approval. After finishing her rejuvenation procedures, my spouse turned around. Alarm could be read on her now youthful and flawlessly beautiful face:

"I don't like this, Georg. The Dark Mother has obviously got something in mind, and I don't trust her. For the last few weeks, I have had a growing sense of danger, and it has now become unbearably keen. Someday soon, something irreversible will happen."

I had no reason to doubt the presentiments of such an experienced Truth Seeker. To be honest, I had observed a strange lull in the political life of the Empire in the last few days, and didn't quite feel right about it myself. Normally, something happened every day — aristocrats would fight and make up, "eternal" alliances were formed and broken, reports came in from the fronts where the fleets of the Purple and Blue Houses were holding back the Alien onslaught with varying levels of success. But now, it was like the calm before the storm.

I turned to the table, which my servants had just finished setting under the watchful eye of my butler Bryle. I had lost all my appetite for breakfast, though. I just spoke to no one in particular, knowing that my order would be heard and handed off where it needed to go:

"We planned for there to be a conference of Unatari fleet commanders in four days, to discuss the production timelines for the new ships. Explain to all those invited that the scheduled time has been changed, and I expect them in forty minutes on *Joan the Fatty*. Miya, you'll be coming with me. As it happens, there's some work up your alley."

*   *   *

I was in a small circular room on my flagship, built to hold secret negotiations and conferences. It was totally blocked off from the outside world. No recording devices would work here, and all implants would be deactivated. My android secretary Bionica turned off instantly in this room as well, so the translator in this conversation, which would involve humans and Iseyek, was the head of my security team, the chameleon Popori de Cacha. I was normally accompanied by Flora, who checked the sincerity and loyalty of all those present but, today, my Truth Seeker was Miya. This was the first time the Queen of Unatari had attended such a conference. She was engrossed in a huge touch-screen in the middle of the room, over which there hovered a huge glowing hologram of Imperial Space with all Perimeter Sectors. There were a great number of variously colored markers showing the position of all known fleets, including those of the Empire, Great Houses, allied kingdoms, and even Aliens.

"Here, you can find the most up to date information on the position of all combat starships we've infiltrated. Even the Imperial Joint Chiefs don't have such accurate data," I said, unable to avoid bragging to my wife.

Miya didn't ask any questions, clearly reading all the information about my secret sources directly from my head. This tactical map was the true pride of the Unatari Fleet. It was kept up to date by tens of thousands of modest androids, who flew under the radar, working on military ships of the Empire and

Great Houses as housekeepers, haulers, mechanics, or even pleasure bots for the crews of the combat starships.

The number of android agents sympathetic to the Unatari cause had grown significantly. Bionica had long been swamped with all the encrypted data we were getting from our many agents. For that reason, two months ago, a special department of twenty robots was formed in my headquarters to receive the encrypted messages on service channels, check them for reliability, then place the data on the tactical map. As a rule, any messages about fleet movements were reaffirmed by dozens of independent sources, so any false information arriving to the headquarters would be immediately filtered out. But, as far as I knew, we hadn't yet detected any unreliable information, which gave me hope that no one in the Empire had yet guessed about my secret network of android spies.

An alternative source of information was the Arites, the very same diplomatic servants "killed" on the Throne World, as well as a hundred other shapeshifting secret agents flying around the Empire and embedding themselves in headquarters, fleets and communication centers. It was still a mystery to me how the Arites could recognize one another and converse amongst themselves, as they were very reluctant to discuss this topic. But the fact remained — the most valuable information about the Empire's secret docks, where they were building giant supercarrier-class starships, had been received from the Arite Iseyek.

The Unatari State had plenty of normal spies, as well. My authority in military circles was already high but, after the first successful counterattack against the Aliens in history, the defeat of the terrifying fleet of the Alien *Queen* and the liberation of nearly thirty star systems, the Imperial Military faction's opinion of Crown Prince Georg had jumped to nearly +60. As far as I knew, that was the highest such number among all fleet leaders and aristocrats in the galaxy. I could make use of that, but didn't think it prudent to do so for simple data gathering. Florianna and Miya were quite good and exposing spies in my ranks, so it made sense to assume that the other sides' Truth Seekers would be capable of the same.

The doors opened, and the members of my secret council entered the room one after the other. They were veterans of a great many battles, and experts in their fields, whose outstanding ability and loyalty I didn't doubt in the slightest: Sector Nine Fleet Commander, Admiral Stefan Antri-Mesfelle; Sector Eight Fleet Commander, Space Major Nicole ton Savoia; First Unatari Fleet Commander, Admiral Mike ton Akad; Second Unatari Fleet Commander, Admiral Kiro Sabuto; Virho Heavy Fleet Commander, the Alpha Iseyek Admiral Masss Azhzh; Ayho Strike Fleet Commander, the Alpha Iseyek Admiral Kheraisss Vej; Swarm Landing Operations Commander, Marshal Savasss Jach; and my second cousin Duchess Katerina ton Unatari, my political advisor.

I also had one new member, my Beta Iseyek First Advisor, Apasss Ugu. He scurried into the room last on his many little legs. He had previously been an advisor to Queen Nai Igir. When I first met him, I was unable to believe my luck. The unique insect had a phenomenal intellect and memory, and knew absolutely everything about all Swarm systems. Apasss Ugu could instantly provide information on ships under construction at all my docks, how long they would take to finish, material reserves, and the necessary number of transports to sustain every garrison. Such valuable staff had to be taken care of — even on the massive scales of the Swarm, such genius was exceedingly rare. So, in one of my very first orders as ruler of the Iseyek, I awarded my First Advisor a blue stripe on his abdomen, which indicated absolute untouchability.

And so, all the participants in today's private conference had arrived. I nodded at Popori de Cacha, and the head of my guard ordered a subordinate to close the door and activate the electronics suppression system. I knew when the electromagnetic cocoon that enveloped the room had turned on, because my electronic implants shut down. The only electronic device that did work in the room was the huge tactical screen, which had been designed with electric shielding for this very purpose.

"So then, let's begin," I said, walking over to the glowing hologram in the middle of the room. "I don't think my wife Miya needs any introduction. Because the topic of today's conference is extremely serious, the Queen of Unatari herself will be serving as Truth Seeker. Miya will make sure you all remain honest. She will also be blocking all mind reading until the end of the meeting."

The council members started making a din — they didn't all like the idea of mind reading being blocked. But no firm objections followed, so I continued:

"I remind you of one more rule — here, we speak as

frankly as possible, not afraid to hurt the others with our remarks or suggestions. The restrictions of laws or morals do not apply to those in this room. We consider all possibilities, regardless of the fact that some of them may not be met with approval in the outside world. So then, I want to give the first word to the Queen of Unatari, so she can share her thoughts and suspicions."

Despite the spontaneity of the speech, Miya held herself excellently. I suspect that my spouse had been made to give speeches to the public a number of times in her long life. I already knew she'd attended special rhetoric courses, and that experience was a major help. Miya didn't speak very loud, but each of her words imprinted in my brain as the infallible truth, like a dogma, to which doubts did not apply.

The Queen of Unatari told us she sensed a growing threat with her Truth Seeker abilities, and had even determined its source: the Antagonists were ready to invade. The Empire knew about our age-old enemy's plans, and a collision of the two most powerful forces was already unavoidable. And it was not a question of the far or even middle-term future, but the very nearest days or even hours. No matter who got the upper hand in the squabble, the victor's plans did not make room for an independent Unatari State. The Queen finished her speech with the following words:

"I don't see us in the future. None of those present. That means that, if no actions are taken and things are left to go on autopilot, everyone in this room is doomed, even me. We have a year and a half at most."

To be honest, the Truth Seeker's words left me with a ghastly feeling. That sense of alarm was shared between all participants. I directly felt the tightening grip of the future she described. When the Queen finished her speech, silence took over the room. The first to come to his senses was Admiral Masss Azhzh:

"I don't have the slightest doubt in the abilities of the Red Queen, but I really cannot understand how we have so little time left. Unatari has a powerful space fleet and would be able to withstand the attack of any enemy. And if our opponent is too strong, we can always turn off the warp beacons."

"Turning off the warp beacons will only prolong our agony, but it will not change the result," Miya parried instantly.

Duchess Katerina came forward. She greeted the council, and started speaking, glancing at the tactical map:

"The risk of a Gold House invasion is clear, although I don't see any signs of the Imperial Fleets being redeployed to the Core peripheries. I am surprised by something else, though. If you break it down, the brewing war between the Empire and the Antagonists is a struggle for the throne between Emperor August and his sister Eleonora. So, I suggest we all think over the following question: why have the Antagonists not yet reached out to the ruler of Unatari? After all, if you look at the question from a purely technical perspective, Crown Prince Georg royl Inoky ton Mesfelle is the grandson of the ruler of the Antagonists, and the most logical thing for him would be to join his closest relative, not someone from a totally different branch of the genealogical tree. So then, why has the Gold House not offered us an alliance?"

Kiro Sabuto sharply stood from place. The ethnically East Asian admiral, glancing severely at my cousin, started speaking in a none-too pleased tone:

"Duchess, I hope very much that your suggestion that the Unatari State join forces with the Antagonists was just a hypothetical. As with the majority of Unatari Fleet officers, I have spent my whole life serving the Empire in faith and truth, and I remain true to it. It was one thing three months ago when Crown Prince Georg was vilely attacked in the Throne World. I and all my officers would have stood to the defense of our commander without hesitation then, even if that meant going against the whole Empire. But it is another thing entirely to fight against the Empire for money or political calculations. That would mean going against friends and brothers in arms, of whom we all have a great many in the other Imperial fleets. The Unatari armed forces would be deeply perturbed by such a thing."

The admiral was supported by Sector Eight Fleet Commander, Space Major Nicole ton Savoia:

"Forgive me if this is too harsh, but he speaks the pure truth. I have been entrusted to lead the Perimeter Sector Eight Fleet, and we would never fight with the Antagonists against the Empire. I would consider such a turn treachery, as would all my officers. And as for Duchess Katerina ton Unatari's question, I know the answer. It's just that none of the sides in the conflict wants to make any promises to Crown Prince Georg they are not planning to keep, as not to provoke a strong reaction. In my time with the Imperial Joint Chiefs, I managed to familiarize myself with the ruler of Unatari's personal record, and got a strong impression from one very accurate entry on psychological characteristics. It reads: 'Certain to reject any attempt to impinge on his interests. He goes off the chain if someone tries to appropriate property which the Crown Prince considers his. Also, he has no understanding of concepts like equivalent or appropriate retaliation. The ruler of Unatari is the kind of person who would bite of somebody's entire arm for accidentally flicking him on the nose.'"

Miya thought it over and closed her eyes.

"Yes, that is true," the Truth Seeker agreed. "Power over a united Empire is not the sort of prize that can be shared or promised to a potential ally. So, I'm a bit confused about why such an offer has come in from Emperor August. I don't sense any trickery there, either — the Emperor really is prepared to give up his throne, if Unatari can defeat the Antagonists."

"But August also has a son, Duke Julius royl August ton Akad, who is first in line to the Imperial Throne," Katerina noted reasonably. "And what is stopping August from stepping down not long before victory over the Antagonists, thus passing his throne to his successor, who has not promised a thing to the ruler of Unatari?"

Kiro Sabuto shook his head:

"That would make war between Unatari and the Empire inevitable. I have a hard time believing Crown Prince Georg royl Inoky ton Mesfelle would forgive such trickery, and he has enough proof and influence to get a large portion of the Imperial Military to stand on his side. The Emperor's son would lose, and lose everything at that."

Everyone in the hall went silent. I found the

moment appropriate to voice my thoughts:

"Let's take it as a given that sitting on the sidelines will be impossible and that, somehow, Unatari will be forced to act. But I really don't like the idea of sliding into a conflict between two of the most powerful armada's in the galaxy, not knowing all behind-the-scenes understandings and positions of the other players. For example, the Green House has a colossal fleet of almost fifteen thousand starships. The Greens are still formally part of the Empire. Will they simply stay aside in the big squabble, or go against the Antagonists no matter what? What has the Emperor promised them for such support? And how would the Green House Fleet behave if it found itself in the same star system as one of our fleets? Might they perhaps stab us in the back?"

"The Green House will never be an ally of Unatari, there are too many old grievances," Duchess Katerina said. "The Lavaelle family will never forgive the ruler of Unatari for the killing of two of their Crown Princes and the shameful capitulation of their First Strike Fleet. They would certainly try to destroy our ships."

Unfortunately, I was in complete agreement with my cousin's assessment. Since my very first days in *Perimeter Defense*, my relationship with the Lavaelle family had only grown worse, having now reached the level of irreconcilable hatred. Although the Unatari State and the Green House were both part of the Empire, I certainly did not consider us allies.

And my relationship with the Purple House had grown significantly worse after swallowing Sector Seven as well. My twin sister Violetta royl Inoky ton Mesfelle-Damir was angry at me, and she had been aiming Purple House policies toward severing diplomatic relations with the Unatari State. For some reason, the head of the Purple House, Duke Takuro royl Andor had not done anything to check Crown Princess Violetta, which meant he had agreed to sacrifice our good relationship for some end I didn't understand.

The Blue House... Here, it was very complicated and confusing. Perimeter Sectors Fourteen and Fifteen were totally under Alien control. Sector Sixteen was cut off from the rest of Blue House territory, and that was where separatism had grown the strongest — de facto, the Sector Sixteen systems were no longer under central government control. In sectors Nine, Eleven, Twelve, and Thirteen, the young Duchess Ovella royl Stok ton Miro was waging a heavy war of attrition on two fronts — one against the invading Alien armadas and another against a massive opposition, which had quickly whipped itself up after the Truth Seeker Krista had left to the Throne World. Duchess Ovella was supported in the war against the Aliens by the Imperial Fleet, but the Emperor's ships would not be intervening in the internal political struggles of the Blue House on principle.

The political map of the Blue House was like a quilt. It was now colored with dozens of mismatching groups, both those who had openly declared their opposition to the Blue House, and those who remained guardedly loyal with certain conditions. Mercenaries, anarchists, armed rebels, political marginals... Most planets even had local conflicts and civil wars of some kind. Both large and small cities changed hands regularly.

Forces loyal to Duchess Ovella now controlled less than thirty percent of Blue House space. However, due to her greater organization and better equipment, alongside the disunity of her opponents, they not only successfully deflected the attacks, but were even gradually squeezing their opponents out. At the last such military council, we had discussed the Blue House's internal conflict in detail, and my advisors had predicted that Duchess Ovella would emerge victorious in three or four years, as long as the Aliens didn't destroy the Blue House first. And now, that looked to be the single most likely scenario, if the Empire removed its flotilla from the Blue House to fight against the Antagonists.

I zoomed the map in on Blue House space.

"Here is the only big political player who really does not want a faceoff between the Empire and the Antagonists. They need to solve their own problems. And what's more, they're the most vulnerable. If the Empire removes its fleet, the Blue House will quickly be destroyed by the Aliens. I think the time has come for a conversation with the blues to offer them our help. Not for free, of course — protection comes at a steep cost in these troublesome times."

"Is Your Majesty planning to go to war only against the Aliens, or also to intervene in the civil war?" Marshal Savasss Jach asked.

All the participants froze, awaiting my answer. And I didn't rush it, looking over the star map and thinking in agitation. It's easy to say: "Only the Aliens." As if that were so easy that it wouldn't even require discussion. And by the way, remnants of the

Alien *Queen*'s armada, which we had beaten so handily had been spotted in Sector Fifteen, confirming the theory that all three types of Aliens were working together. The arrival of the five *Mammoths* and twenty *Behemoths* in addition to the Alien starships already there had decisively changed the balance of forces and caused severe panic in the defenders. Due to the disorganization that took hold, they started to retreat, which caused Sector Fifteen to be lost in a matter of weeks. According to reconnaissance data, the captured human battleship *Orange Majesty* had also been spotted in Sector Fifteen.

Everyone was silent, waiting for my answer, but I was still silent. Finally, I came to a decision:

"It is not possible to effectively make war when chaos and anarchy are overtaking your supply lines. So before fighting the Aliens, we will put an end to the civil war in the Blue House. I suggest we demand all of Sector Ten from the ruler of the Blue House for our peacekeeping mission. It seems to me that, after the initial shock of that impudence passes, we will find understanding from Duchess Ovella and will manage to come to an agreement. The Blue House will get its long-desired peace and protection from the Aliens, and we can reinforce our position. And if it proves impossible to negotiate with the Duchess... Well, I see more than twenty other participants in the Blue House civil war. I'm sure we can find someone more amenable to our terms."

"The Blue House is part of the Empire," Katerina ton Unatari reminded me. "If we are planning to go against the legal authorities, we will need a very significant pretext to justify our actions so the Unatari

State won't be declared the aggressor."

"Cousin, that's just a hypothetical at this point. For now, tell the Blue House our desire to send them a diplomatic mission to negotiate on military cooperation. But if Duchess Ovella is not compliant, we really will have an iron-clad *casus belli*, so no one in the galaxy will doubt our right to send ships into Blue House space. One option would be starting a media campaign in favor of putting Crown Princess Natalie royl Cruz ton Unatari on her rightful throne. Our Crown Princess still has quite a few allies in the Blue House, so we would be working on the side of a legal claimant."

Duchess Katerina ton Unatari cringed, dismayed:

"Young Natalie has signed an official renunciation of her claim to the Blue House Throne. She even received a significant payoff from Duchess Ovella in return. Although... we could try to declare that the Crown Princess only agreed because her life was in danger. It's a fairly weak position, but I'm just thinking through our options."

"Another point of reinforcement was hinted to me in the Throne World by the Emperor and Dark Mother. They were afraid that the Swarm might eventually manage to grow so powerful that it would hold sway over two dozen nonhuman races. I suggest we probe over that option. Invite diplomats from all nonhuman vassal races of the Empire to a large reception in the Dekeye capital system in fifteen days."

First Advisor Apasss Ugu shuddered:

"Are you sure Dekeye? Not Unatari? It's just that, if I may be so bold, Your Majesty has a tough time with the elevated gravitation on the capital planet."

"That is true, but my health now is much better than it was during the reception with Queen Nai Igir. I'm certain that I can bare an hour-long meeting with the ambassadors quite easily. But if I am overestimating my physical abilities, we could hold the meeting on my flagship *Joan the Fatty*, which is still in the Dekeye system. In any case, I want to invite ambassadors to Dekeye, because that is the very system the whole galaxy associates with the center of the Swarm. And we'll have to, as if by coincidence, demonstrate all five of our carriers and our no less than fifty battleships. Just show them our combat starships. Let them make their own conclusions about our military might."

Admiral Stefan Antri-Mesfelle stood up, smiled and made a suggestion:

"If the mission is to impress people, maybe we should wait another month. Then, we'll be able to show the ambassadors a working *Mammoth*. I'm sure the effect caused by such a giant would be far greater than that of all five carriers."

I thought it over and was forced to refuse the tempting suggestion.

"No, the time has not yet come to reveal the *Mammoth*, or the *Queen*, which is also still under repair. Their very existence is still a secret to most political players. Let's keep our trump cards breasted until the best possible moment."

We spent around another hour discussing the affairs of the fleets entrusted to the admirals. They were suggesting methods of getting around the embargo on heavy cannon installations and warp drives. We also decided what to do with the giant ships in Dekeye, which had been built to evacuate the Iseyek eggs, given that they were no longer necessary. Finally, I declared the council over.

As soon as the electromagnetic defenses were shut off, I got a message from the communications officer:

"Your Majesty, the Dark Mother has been waiting to talk with you for some time. She's been on the line for forty minutes already, and refuses to let the conversation wait any longer."

I glanced at Miya, but my spouse just shrugged her shoulders in surprise. Then, suddenly, she said with a strange uncertainty:

"Georg, I don't know what this is, but the Dark Mother has grown noticeably weaker in the last few hours... For the first time in my life, I am stronger than her. Much stronger. Go talk to the old bat. There's certainly no danger. I can sense that. What's more, I could now protect you. Florianna could probably also manage."

Florianna's voice rang out in my head to explain what was going on:

"During my talk, the Dark Mother just asked a few questions about how I was doing, after which she poured a whole ocean of energy into me, healing my damaged vocal cords and nerve endings. She expended so much power that she almost fainted in nausea."

I ordered her call put through immediately to the nearest monitor. The screen lit up. The Dark Mother, her eyes closed, was lying on a hospital bed with an oxygen mask on her face. All around her, there were doctors fussing about. I overheard one of them say her blood pressure was critically low. So, I was very surprised when the old lady said something, muffled by the mask:

"Everyone out of the room! Now!"

A few seconds later, the Dark Mother was alone. Without opening an eye, the Truth Seeker removed her oxygen mask and spoke in a creaky, barely audible voice:

"Georg, I am dying... but I still have a few more things I must do in this life. First of all, I must give you one piece of advice: it doesn't matter how strong your government becomes, if it falls without a battle because its leader is dead. Among the people you trust, too many are loyal to the Empire and August. Keep that in mind always because, all the Emperor has to do is get rid of one person, and your whole state, together with all your territories and space fleets would be left to whoever your oldest daughter marries... My second piece of advice: do not align yourself with the Empire, or the Antagonists, because both would be equivalent to death for you. Believe me, I've seen the future and know what I'm talking about. Remain an independent third party, concerned with saving the human race as a whole and just let all the squabbles for the Imperial throne pass by without your interference. You are the last defender of humanity, and there is nothing more important than saving our species. Don't let anything stand in your way."

The old lady started coughing after such a long monologue and put her oxygen mask back on. While she was breathing greedily, like a fish tossed on shore, I asked a question that had been bothering me:

"When and how will the Antagonists attack the Empire?"

The Dark Mother smiled through her weakness and creaked out, barely audibly:

"Oh Georg, you're still Ruslan inside... Everything has to be explained to you... You don't know a single important detail from the Crown Prince's childhood, which is why you have such a poor grasp of this situation. Just know this: your mother never loved you. Think that over, and everything will become clear. If you cannot figure it out on your own, ask your advisor Katerina. She's a smart cookie and will be able to clear it up for you. Now, I've said everything I wanted. Put me through with the Truth Seeker of your daughter Likanna, little Milena. I want to transfer the rest of my power into her, because your daughter will never survive this harsh world without strong protection. Farewell, Ruslan!"

.

MOTHER'S SIDE

I WAS FEELING dumb as an ox, and that hurt me considerably... I spent a whole hour thinking over the Dark Mother's last words and studying a big guide on the genealogy of the highest families of the Empire, but never managed to find an answer. Sure, I already knew that my "mother," Crown Princess Elisa royl Clement ton Mesfelle-Lavaelle was the daughter of the ruler of the Antagonists. That relationship was always the reason for the heightened attention paid to her by all the Imperial secret services. Every one of her conversations were listened to and scrupulously studied, but not a single conversation had been deemed legally actionable in the last century and a half, even those with her own mother.

Now, Crown Princess Elisa was part of the Green House, which was much stronger than all the other Great Houses and allied Kingdoms, both militarily and economically. My mother, at present, was fifth in line to the Green House throne but she had no realistic chance of becoming Duchess, because the four Lavaelle Crown Princes ahead of her were a whole hundred years younger. Also, the head of the Green House would never allow Crown Princess Elisa to impinge on the rights of his many relatives and inherit their rightful throne.

In the events of three months ago, the head of the Green House, Duke Amelius royl Mast ton Lavaelle had seemed a completely sane person to me, who was perfectly satisfied with the role of "first boy in the village." He could pinch and tease the Emperor with glee, reducing his leader's standing while demonstrating his own political independence. But the Duke had too much to gain from remaining loyal to the Empire, including the powerful political support of the Throne World and significant tax benefits, so I couldn't see him wanting to start a suicidal game against Emperor August.

Standing change. Purple House (Empire) opinion of the Unatari State has worsened.
Present Purple House (Empire) faction opinion of the Unatari State: -30 (hate)

Standing change. Green House (Empire) opinion of the Unatari State has worsened.
Present Green House (Empire) faction opinion of the Unatari State: -56 (irreconcilable hate)

The sudden messages caught me off guard, interrupting my prolonged thinking. What could be said? It was confirmation that both Great Houses were on a course for collision with my state. Recently, such thing had been happening with considerable regularity, at least a few times every week, and I had already grown accustomed to them. It wasn't nice, of course, but I still didn't believe it was possible for the Purple House to sink to declaring war. The Unatari Space Fleet was twice as strong as that of the purples, which was to say nothing about my captains being much more experienced. So, the war would be sure to end in a quick defeat for the Purple House. But the next message was truly a surprise:

The Green House and the Purple House have concluded a military alliance

Yikes, none of that was good... The Green House must have been thirsting for revenge — three months ago, they had taken a very serious bump on the nose, losing their First Strike Fleet without a single shot fired. Now, the captured starships of their First Strike Fleet had joined my fleets, while twenty thousand officers and crew members from those ships had sworn loyalty to the Unatari State and were now my subjects. Naturally, my Truth Seekers had thoroughly checked all the newcomers and exposed all the potential traitors. It looked like the greens hadn't fully grasped that lesson, as they were now chomping at the bit for more confrontation...

The Throne World has lost sovereignty over the Anfey system

The Green House has gained sovereignty over the Anfey system

The Throne World has lost sovereignty over the

Forepost-20 system

*The Green House has gained sovereignty over
the Forepost-20 system*

*The Throne World has lost sovereignty over the
Natti system*

*The Purple House has gained sovereignty over
the Natti system*

It was good that I was sitting. Otherwise, I'm not sure
I would have managed to stay on my feet after that
portion of unbelievable news. The Throne World was
handing out Core systems??? What exactly was going
on? I called up my foreign policy advisor and asked
that very question.

"Georg, aren't you watching the news?" Katerina
was extremely surprised and even annoyed at my
poor grasp of current events. "Half an hour ago, the
Throne World officially announced the death of the
Dark Mother after a severe and prolonged illness. A
three-day mourning period has been declared for the
whole Empire. Celebrations are forbidden for the
duration. I am now busy composing a condolence
message on behalf of the Unatari State. No matter
how you look at it, the Dark Mother was a
distinguished figure and spent two hundred years
guiding the politics of all humanity."

The news of the Dark Mother's death really
knocked me off track. After all, I had been conversing
with the old lady just two hours ago! Sure, the Truth
Seeker looked unwell, and had even spoken about her

imminent demise, but I still didn't suspect she had so little time left. The shocking news almost made me forget what I wanted to talk to my cousin about.

"To be honest, I've been focused on the mourning events, so I still haven't figured out why those systems changed hands," Katerina admitted. "But yesterday, there was a rumor that Emperor August was planning direct negotiations with the heads of the Great Houses today, and the topic was supposed to be optimization of logistics between the regions and decentralization."

"But what would make the Emperor want that?" I asked in surprise.

Katerina lowered her voice to a whisper, as if someone might overhear us, and said:

"No one is talking about it openly, but there is a suggestion that August hopes to make peace with the Great Houses and secure their loyalty ahead of the upcoming Antagonist invasion. And at the same time, he wishes it will put an end to all the negative press he's been getting for the last three months. After all, what hasn't the media blamed on the Emperor recently! Military misfortunes and the loss of Sector Fifteen, inveterate bureaucracy in the Throne World and ineffective rulership of star systems, corruption in the secretariat... The row with the Dark Mother also made him look guilty, as well as the attack on our embassy and lowering of humanity's standing among the extraterrestrial races. Clearly, August agreed to give up a few peripheral star systems in the Core to the Great Houses in order to placate the Dukes."

"Unatari couldn't happen to shake out a couple Core star systems under the pretext of decentralization and logistical simplification, could it?" I chuckled, then got more serious and asked my cousin what she thought about my mother. But Katerina was in no mood to talk:

"Georg, that's a very big topic. I can't answer in two words, and I really am extremely busy right now. How about, first, I finish publishing our condolences, tackle some more urgent business, then I come talk with you? I need around an hour of time and, after that, I will be completely at your disposal."

"Alright. As it happens, I have a medical check to go to right now, then a half hour in the gym and sauna. So, we can talk after all that."

*   *   *

All tangled in wires and data transmitters, I was pedaling away on a stationary bicycle like a madman. My physician Nicosid Brandt was reading the data on a monitor and noting something to himself on a small tablet, periodically giving satisfied commentary:

"Blood pressure, normal... Heart function, just great... Hemoglobin levels, normal... Veins, clear... Cholesterol, normal... Muscles, in good shape... Brain activity, normal. Alright, that's enough for now. Crown Prince, please stop and get on the scale. Height: six feet. Weight: two hundred twenty-seven pounds... Your Majesty, I would set this as your target weight and just try to stay there. It really is optimal for your bone structure and muscle mass. Losing that couple extra pounds would mean a lot more fuss."

I turned to a big mirror on the wall and spun around, looking at my figure. It really was a joyful sight — the folds of excess fat on my chest and thighs were long gone. My stomach had sucked in and my arm and leg muscles were clearly visible. I wasn't Mr. Olympia of course but, for a fifty-year old man, I would say I looked very, very good. The biggest thing, though, was that I felt wonderful and could easily handle the dense schedule of the monarch of a space government. I suppose I was prepared to agree with the physician that I didn't see any reason to continue the intensive weight loss.

"Now, about the crystals..." Nicosid Brandt went silent, looking at some graphs I couldn't make head or tail of. "The tests are looking good. Your physical dependence is already neutralized, and the psychological is also going down. I suppose it's time to admit that I was overly pessimistic about the possibility of complete recovery. Oh, if only I didn't have to maintain doctor-patient confidentiality, I would publish a great treatise on how to cure a person of crystal dependence!"

"Well, go ahead and publish it. I won't mind," I allowed. But the old doctor got embarrassed for some reason and tried to stifle the topic:

"I cannot, Crown Prince. Too much of your personal medical information would have to be made public. I'll just have to get by without a scientific study. But now, I need to change out the microcapsules in your shoulder."

"What for?" I waved off the procedure as, to my eye, utterly unnecessary. "Just one month ago, you inserted new capsules, and said they'd last half a year!"

The old doctor's eyes started darting about

nervously, while his voice started giving a suspicious quaver:

"Y-y-your Maj-jesty, I wa-as wr-r-rong about the dose. I, uh, ass-ssumed th-the regeneration would go much worse."

Nicosid Brandt was a great doctor, but a terrible actor. Saying that I merely got on guard after he tried to reassure me would be putting it lightly. There wasn't even a trace remaining of my calm and good-hearted mood. The hair all over my body was standing on end in near panic.

"Flora, Miya! I need you now!" I called mentally, and heard an answer just a second later from my wife:

"Flora is sleeping. I ordered her to have a crystal dream so we would stay on different phases, and one of us would constantly be with you... Woah! Don't let the doctor inject anything! Don't take any medicine! It's an attempt on your life!!! I'll be there in a second!"

That means my instincts didn't mislead me. Distinctly, I spoke into emptiness:

"Seke-ti huma ('restrain this man' in the Ravaash language)."

A second later, the old doctor was lying spread-eagle on the metal floor of the medical room, immediately set upon by the trio of chameleons. Another second later, Nicosid Brandt's arms were pulled painfully back and a set of handcuffs clinked on. Meanwhile, Phobos and Rosss were standing over the dog-pile on the floor. The huge Alpha Iseyek had guns in their upper appendages, ready to shoot at any of the medic's assistants I pointed to.

I slowly bent down and picked up the injection gun the old doctor had dropped.

"Tell me, doctor, how many years have you been with me?" I asked him, looking at the apparently harmless medical device, loaded with millimeter-diameter microcapsules.

Nicosid Brandt, pressed down by my bodyguards, rasped back with difficulty:

"Crown Prince, I was sent to you from the Throne World when you were just four months old..."

"I've known you my whole life, and trusted you completely... So, tell me, doctor, how much must one pay a person for them to forget fifty years of flawless service and wish death upon a man they've sworn to protect and provide medical treatment?"

The old man took a very long time to answer, just sitting in silence, before saying barely audibly:

"This has nothing to do with money... These capsules were sent to me from the Throne World medical center along with the latest shipment of medicine... People I've known for many years told me it was for the good of the whole Empire... At one time, identical capsules were injected into you in a Throne World prison, but I removed them. Each capsule, along with the necessary dose of medicine, has a bug in it to track you and a micro ampule of poison that can be activated at any moment with a special command. I was told it had to be done to control your unpredictable nature. Someone in the Empire wants to make it impossible for Unatari to join our enemies..."

Miya entered the room decisively. The Queen of Unatari didn't ask any questions, just looked carefully at the tool lying on the table and held her gaze on Nicosid Brandt's assistants.

"His assistants didn't know anything. They're all afraid, but in general, don't feel guilty. They can be trusted."

"Let him go! Nicosid Brandt, I want you to call your old friend right now, and tell him you couldn't carry out his plan. After that, you may go. I have no more need for your services, because I cannot trust you. Considering your half century of flawless service, I'll still write you a great recommendation, pay you a half-a-million-credit bonus and order you a ticket on the most comfortable express flight to the Throne World. You'll find a new employer there, if your age allows it, or you can collect an honorable pension and spend the rest of your life in relaxation."

I got dressed quickly and left the medical bay, not wanting to be there while my former personal doctor talked with his co-conspirator. Miya remained with him. I didn't know a more reliable guarantee that all those guilty in the assassination attempt against me would get their comeuppance.

* * *

"My Prince, you seem utterly crestfallen..." said Bionica, looking gorgeous in nothing but a micro-G-string as she deftly massaged my back and shoulders with her surprisingly strong fingers.

"Yeah, I've just had such an idiotic day. It was packed! The news channels don't even know exactly where to begin their broadcasts. But I feel that my government and I have been shuffled to the edge of history and written off... Look, Emperor August didn't even invite me to a conference of the heads of the

Great Houses, even though the Unatari State is larger than the Purple House economically, militarily and territorially."

I was forced to end my sniveling and outpouring of problems, because Bionica asked me to turn onto my back and started in on my stomach muscles. That part of my body could, thankfully, no longer be called a gut, but it was still quite far from being a six-pack. I clenched my teeth in pain. It felt like the android's fingers were going nearly all the way through to my spine.

"But only the Dukes of the Great Houses were at the conference. If the Emperor had invited any of the monarchs, even the most powerful, all the others would get offended. Otherwise, he'd have to have invited all the other kings, right down to the most minor..."

"Maybe you're right, Bionica. But I'm still offended. And then there was the death of the Dark Mother and her last words, which just won't get out of my head... What connection could Crown Princess Elisa royl Clement ton Mesfelle-Lavaelle have with today's events? But the most upsetting thing, of course, was the assassination attempt by my personal doctor. Who in the galaxy can I trust if even those I've known my whole life have started betraying me?!"

"Crown Prince, you can always trust me," the pretty android girl chuckled and, playfully looking me right in the eyes, reached her fingers a bit below the laces of my swimsuit.

But I stopped Bionica, because I was very far from being in the right mood, and this also wasn't a good place. And it was good I did — just a few minutes later, without knocking, Katerina ton Unatari came into the massage room, which was next to the pool, in her swimsuit. With a judgmental look at the barely-dressed Bionica, my cousin just walked right up to us and sat on the nearest seat:

"I'm already done with everything, Georg, so I decided to come talk with you now. The Blue House has accepted our offer of negotiations, and set a time and conditions. Our diplomatic mission can consist of no more than three starships: one heavy cruiser and two of a lower class."

I stopped Bionica kneading my leg muscles, and sat up on the bench:

"Three ships? According to protocol, up to seven ships are allowed to be part of a diplomatic delegation, right?"

"Yes, that is true," my advisor confirmed. "It looks like the 'blues' are worried that seven starships under the command of such a renowned fleet leader could capture the whole Blue House. If we agree to such conditions, we'll have to fly out in two hours to make it on time."

"Alright, these negotiations are important to us, so we won't try to find fault with the conditions. Three it is. Our main ship will be the heavy assault cruiser *Emperor August*, the second will be one of the light cruisers like a *Curse* or *Thrush*, and third will be the *Mechanoid*."

"The *Mechanoid*?" my cousin asked in surprise.

"That's right. That way, we can mark out a path to the Blue House capital just in case — it might come in handy in the future, if negotiations break down, and the blues decide to turn off their warp beacons."

I stood up from the massage table and walked over to the edge of the pool, preparing to jump into the water. But Katerina stopped me:

"Georg, maybe we should have *One-Eyed Python* as our second ship. My husband has long been growing bored with the lack of action. He's down in the dumps, and that's been getting on my nerves. Yesterday, Corwin got drunk and started a fight again just because there was nothing better to do, accusing me of turning him from a combat captain into a 'marriage general' — the Duke of a star system, who doesn't understand a thing in politics and just follows his wife everywhere."

"Alright. Our second ship for the flight to the Blue House will be the light cruiser *One-Eyed Python*. What is more, my retinue and I will fly on that very ship but, for safety's sake, we can place some Arites on *Emperor August* disguised as us. Tell Corwin ton Unatari to prepare the cruiser. Will you come with me?"

"To be honest, cousin, I see no need for that. You can manage just fine without me. I already have a bunch of things to do here on Unatari, and Corwin and I could stand to take a break from each other."

I jumped into the cool dark blue water and swam to the other side of the pool without coming up once. When I did raise my head, I saw Miya standing no more than three feet from me in a long, bright crimson dress, and shuddered in surprise.

"Don't worry Georg, I'd have had enough tact not to come in if you decided to fool around with your synthetic masseuse. But I really have come on business."

"Alright, go to Katerina and Bionica. I'm gonna swim another few minutes."

When I got up on the edge of the pool, Miya was lying with her face down on the massage table, wearing even less clothing than Bionica, who was zealously kneading her shoulders.

"This is so nice!" the Truth Seeker said good-heartedly, lying with her eyes closed. "I really shouldn't have neglected these traditional methods of restoring my health! To be honest, I was always afraid to let anyone get close to my body — too many wish death on me and would joyfully tear my head off at the first chance. But it's much easier with androids... Georg, would you be opposed to me spending an hour a few times a week using your personal translator as a chiropractor?"

I had nothing against that, and Bionica didn't object either.

"Very well. But I actually did come on business," Miya continued, still not opening her eyes. "I really don't like the upcoming negotiations with the Blue House, or the terms they've laid out. It's not that I saw an unambiguous threat to the delegation, but the future is somehow worrying. I beg you not to take Duchess Katerina or Princess Astra with you — it is precisely their presence, whether together or apart, that could set off a chain reaction of scandalous and even tragic events."

"This must be connected with my husband!" Katerina cut into the conversation. "The Duke has been flirting openly with girls lately. Two times I've had to literally kick made-up trollops out of Corwin's bedroom. I'm afraid that the presence of Astra on board *One-Eyed Python* might lead to potential conflicts."

Remembering Captain Corwin ton Ugar's unhealthy interest of in my favorite Astra, I was forced to agree that those fears could have a basis.

"Alright, to keep everything copasetic, neither Astra nor Katerina can come. Anything else, Miya?"

"Yes. As everyone here is trustworthy, and this confidential information cannot get out of your innermost circle, I have to admit that I am very bad at checking peoples' loyalty, and even worse at distinguishing the hazy boundary between loyalty to the Unatari State and loyalty to the Empire as a whole. For example, I checked Nicosid Brandt very thoroughly, and didn't see anything dangerous in him, yet George just finished rubbing my nose in the fact he was quite unreliable indeed. I'm afraid that I'd never be able to check all of Unatari's ten thousand officers, or million soldiers even with a hundred years. I cannot even be certain that no traitors have wormed in among the six hundred members of the Unatari diplomatic delegation. Perhaps, Florianna can do better than me, but she'll be sleeping at least another few days."

"What do you mean, Miya?" I asked in surprise. "After all, you're stronger than Flora!"

"Yes, that is true, Georg. Now, I am the second strongest Truth Seeker in the whole Empire after Krista, and Florianna is approximately eighteenth. But every Truth Seeker is specialized in something. The Dark Mother had the best understanding of mental defense. Marian Sabati is tricky and capable of hiding her actions, and can also heal people. Flora, from what I know, is the only one who can detect enemy ships. Also, in reading thoughts, she's got at least a hundred points on me. I meanwhile, am best of all at killing..."

My wife sharply opened her eyes, and I saw that her pupils were sparking with a violent orange flicker. Bionica cut into the conversation:

"But if even the very strongest Truth Seeker cannot manage this task alone, maybe we should try to get help from others? There are billions of people living in Perimeter Sectors Eight and Nine. Among them there are quite a few Truth Seekers — their powers may be weak and unstable, but they have at least some mental abilities. Flora is an illustrative example — she was weak, and was not taken seriously until gaining power. Now, she is respected in the Unatari Fleet to the point of near worship. We could gather others, train them, and assign them missions. Let them work! Or is there something I don't understand, and that's impossible?"

Miya closed her eyes again and laid down in silence for nearly a minute before answering:

"Well, it might work..."

My cousin immediately lit up, becoming a font of ideas:

"An official invitation must be broadcast on all state news channels to everyone who feels they have psionic abilities. We'll have to pay for them to get to the Unatari star system. Yes, most will be impostors or simply confused, but it won't exactly be hard to pick them out. And the others, who really have even the most minimal Truth Seeker abilities, I suggest we give an official stipend or salary. We'll even have to create an official uniform..."

"And we can start a perfect analogue of the Truth Seeker school that was once led by Krista in the Throne World," Miya said, finishing the thought. "I'm not saying that's a bad thing, but I personally would be ghastly displeased due to the ghoulish discipline and draconian measures. Alright, Duchess, send the invitation. I'll handle the teaching."

The Throne World has lost sovereignty over the Lyghia system

The Green House has gained sovereignty over the Lyghia system

Katerina and I shuddered at the exact same time and exchanged glances. Miya, clearly having read the information from my head, got up on her elbows and said distractedly:

"Very bad news for the Empire. If this keeps going, there won't be any need for an Antagonist war — the Imperial Core will simply be split up into parts, and the enemy can just come to an agreement with the Great Houses."

"It's even worse than that..." my cousin said thoughtfully, then turned to me: "Georg, you asked about my opinion of your mother. Well, although I don't have any undisputable facts, just tangential evidence, I wouldn't doubt for a second that Crown Princess Elisa royl Clement ton Lavaelle has been working for the Gold House her whole life, and still does. Now, your mother is the very person determining the Green House's external politics. Your mother precisely will be advising Duke Amelius royl Mast ton Lavaelle on how the Green House, the strongest of all the Great Houses, should act."

I kept silent, because I didn't know anything about my mother's position in the Green House, and so I had nothing to judge the veracity of the information.

"That is true to the last word," Miya confirmed.

"And now, let's look at the bigger picture," Katerina continued. "Imagine a star map before your eyes. The Imperial Core has a hundred star systems. All around it are eighteen sectors, given to the Great Houses to control. So then, the leader of the Antagonists controls Perimeter Sectors Seventeen, Eighteen and One. Plus Sector Sixteen, which is cut off from the Blue House, but does border on Gold space. I have no doubt that the Antagonists already consider it theirs and have the situation firmly under control. Let's take this further. Elisa's daughter controls sectors Two, Three and Four. Her granddaughter, your twin sister Crown Princess Violetta determines the politics of the Purple House and controls sectors Five, Six and Seven. Meanwhile, her very own great-granddaughter, the Crown Princess Likanna will determine the Unatari State's policies, if something happens to you, giving her control over Sectors Eight and Nine, plus the whole Swarm, as well as the thirty systems liberated from the Aliens... open your eyes, Georg — the Antagonist invasion is already in full swing! But the Throne World refuses to see it and is trying to buy the loyalty of the Great Houses with gifts of Core star systems, thus actually strengthening the Antagonists!"

*   *   *

"Lika, have you talked with grandma Elisa recently?" I asked my eldest daughter at breakfast, as if in passing.

"Dad, me and her talk all the time. At least once a week. So what?" Likanna asked, a bit on guard, as if she expected me to be mad at her for speaking with a close relative.

"It's just that her birthday is the day after tomorrow, and I feel the need to congratulate her somehow. For some reason, she won't talk to me, but at least say happy birthday to grandma from me."

Lika immediately grew calm and even started smiling:

"Well, sure! By the way, grandma has been saying I should come visit her palace on Oveyete-VII for a long time. But she says you won't let me go to Sector Three, because Unatari and the Green House are enemies."

"It's not that we're enemies... As a matter of fact, I have no problem with them. It's more that the Lavaelle family is dreaming of a way to bury me as soon as possible — either they're up to something in the Throne World, or they'll declare war, or they'll falsely accuse me of all kinds of sins, like they did before. I mean, what am I telling you for? You've probably seen all the messages about the Green House spoiling our relations. A new one comes in every week. And as for you visiting Sector Three... tell your grandma that I am not opposed to letting you visit her for a few weeks, just not today. Such a vacation must first be planned — I cannot send you on a simple passenger liner!"

"Come on! I've ridden an ore ship before, and you didn't even get that mad," my daughter reminded me, but still agreed with me that a Crown Princess of the Empire would be better served by a comfortable and safe private starship.

Miya set her fork aside and started thinking, even closing her eyes in agitation.

"Likanna will definitely not be under threat in the Green House," the Truth Seeker told me confidently a minute later, then added a bit quieter. "But that's no guarantee that Lika will be allowed to come back. The Green House needs her as a tool to put political pressure on Unatari."

I frowned and told my daughter:

"Lika, in the next conversation, you tell grandma I have one condition: I'll let you visit the Green House, but only after I get an official guarantee that they will let you come back two weeks later. I wouldn't want you to be taken hostage, if a bad political situation arises, even if you're kept in a golden cage."

"Alright, I'll go tell her right now!" My hyperactive little girl lit up and hurried to climb off her seat at the dining table. Standing in the doorway, Lika stopped and asked: "Dad, do you think Crown Princess Natalie and Astra could come with me?"

I considered it seriously. Natalie royl Cruz could go wherever she pleased, as harming an Imperial Crown Princess was something no one would dare do — the reaction from all parts of society would just be too negative. But the rule of absolute untouchability did not apply to Astra. Everyone in the galaxy knew about my warm feelings for my favorite, so sending Astra into the lair of a potential opponent was an obviously risky and short-sighted step.

Fortunately, I didn't have to refuse my daughter — Astra wanted to stay home all on her own, pointing to the colicky state of her little son as his first teeth were coming in. That solved all the problems right away. I gave my permission, and Lika ran into her bunk, squealing joyfully.

Queen Miya turned to my favorite and said in a soft voice:

"Astra, little Georg is howling in the playroom again. Ayna cannot manage him, and my Deia has started to bawl as well, following his example. Seeing how you've already eaten, could you quick go to the playroom and calm your boy?"

As soon as the doors closed behind Astra, Miya said distinctly:

"Georg, it's better to say this out loud, as the question is really extremely important and sensitive. Did I understand your thoughts correctly?"

"Yes, Miya, you understood perfectly. Instead of the Crown Princesses, I will send Arites to the Green House in disguise. Popori de Cacha, after Lika's done talking to her grandmother, make sure our communications center doesn't let my daughter make any more calls to the Green House. And if Lika tries to call, have one of the Arites imitate her granny Crown Princess Elisa royl Clement and tell my daughter that her visit had to be postponed for some believable reason."

The head of my guard appeared several feet from me and clarified:

"Tuki-tuka-de-sa, how long should your daughter

be stopped from communicating with the Green House?"

"Two weeks at least, three would be better. That should be enough time for the Arites to gather evidence of my mother having contact with the Antagonists."

My cousin and advisor Katerina, until that point immersed in silent thought, shuddered abruptly and spoke with unhidden horror in her voice:

"Georg, when Lika finds out about this, she's gonna be outraged! And that's to say nothing about the Green House. We'd be spitting right in their faces! All the negative consequences are hard to read. Are you sure you've thought this through, cousin?"

"Well Katerina, whether we want it or not, there is already an undeclared war between the Empire and the Antagonists underway. My mother's side is silently building their power, getting more and more territory under their thumb, and soon will become unstoppable. So, our priority mission is to draw all the conspirators out into the open, even if that means sidestepping the rules of common decency. Yes, our spies may not succeed, and the consequences of their unmasking then could be rather unpredictable. But in any case, this is an attempt to sharply change the course of political life in the Empire away from one that is not acceptable to us. And I'll deal with my daughter somehow."

I called up the internal interface before my eyes and looked at the time. We had to go! A shuttle from *One-Eyed Python* already should have been docking on my flagship. Accompanied by Miya, Bionica and Popori de Cacha, I walked into the small ship hangar.

"Admit it, Georg, did my wife tattle on me?" asked Duke Corwin ton Unatari, who'd come to meet me near the shuttle. He then lowered the gangway and led me to his pilot's seat. "Did she say I had started drinking uncontrollably, wasting family money in the casino, and snuggling young girls on the sly...?"

"She didn't not say those things," I replied, not denying it. "Katerina said you got bored, so naturally you could no longer sit around patiently waiting. My cousin wants her gallant space fleet officer back, not some effete nobleman, languishing in ennui. To be honest, I also prefer that brave war-dog, a man who was not afraid to argue with his commander. You used to remind me of myself. And although the old you didn't always make my job easy, your *One-Eyed Python* was given an award as the best ship in the fleet in not one, but two training sessions!"

Corwin turned and smiled. Small fires of interest lit in the captain's eyes.

"My Prince, *One-Eyed Python* can still serve as a touchstone military cruiser. My crew is unmatched in the whole fleet in their professionalism and combat readiness. I give my word as an officer that none of my people will besmirch the honor of the Unatari State on this diplomatic mission!"

*   *   *

It happened after crossing the Blue House border, when the ships of my diplomatic mission were charging up at the Forepost-22 station. Miya woke me up. The Truth Seeker was extremely troubled, and hadn't even changed out of her thin nighty, which was red, like all Miya's outfits. My wife's crimson hair was ridden with bedhead, her eyes flaring a bewitching flame of frightening orange.

"Georg, wake up! I sense mortal danger!"

As if in confirmation of the Queen of Unatari's words, the lights flickered, and the cruiser switched to emergency power. A siren howled out a prolonged wail.

"Tuki-tuka-de-sa! Intruders on the ship!" said one of my chameleon-body guards, appearing next to me. "They're coming from the station! Our guard post at the airlock has been destroyed! Popori de Cacha is reporting that there is a heavy firefight in the corridor on the first deck. Our troops are taking losses and retreating to the freight elevators!"

Phobos, who normally sat like a motionless statue next to the doors, flew into action and leaned decisively with his flexible middle appendage on a scanning sensor on the wall. The wall panel moved silently aside, revealing a stand with firearms and a cabinet with light armored space suits. In a business-like manner, the Alpha Iseyek began handing out the laser assault rifles to the human security and chameleon bodyguards, who appeared from invisibility. Miya refused the laser rifle offered to her. That wasn't her modus operandi.

The huge praying mantis himself took a heavy infantry resonator, giving another to Rosss. A resonator is a terrifying close combat weapon that breaks down the cell walls of an organism. In the hands of a competent soldier, it can turn any living opponent into a heap of pulsating protoplasm.

"My Princcce, must to wear," the giant Alpha Iseyek

carefully took a silver helmeted suit from the stand and extended it to me.

I was going to walk up closer in order to take the hermetic suit with spherical helmet, but Bionica appeared in the doorway just then, panting, and shouted out in alarm:

"My Prince, I've detected an unknown device attached to our cruiser's energy grid! I can say with over ninety-eight percent probability that it is a bomb!"

"There's no time to get dressed!" Miya shouted, shoving me quite roughly through the door into the hall. "We have less than two minutes until the reactor explodes! We must run to the shuttles!"

Accompanied by my guards, I hopped out into the corridor and dashed to the nearest elevator. But our whole group stopped sharply, because I heard intensive fire coming down the hall, then the muted sound of an explosion. The nearest door opened, and Popori de Cacha jumped into our corridor in a puff of smoke with two pistols in his hands.

"Don't go that way!" shouted the head of my bodyguard, hurriedly locking the metal door behind him. "That corridor is full of assault soldiers in heavy armored suits."

Almost immediately, muffled slamming could be heard from the other side of the armored door, then a burst from a high-caliber weapon. Where the shots landed, the metal bulged out a few inches. Miya walked up to a console in the wall and, placing her hand on it, melted the plastic panel and its buttons.

"Now, the attackers will never get through! Let's go down into the service tunnel," the Truth Seeker said, pointing to a grate on the floor. "Faster! We have precious little time!"

Bionica, showing surprising strength for a woman with such a delicate frame, ripped off the reinforced floor grate, revealing an access hole going vertically downward. The android set an example, diving down the service shaft. I went after her, climbing down the brackets in the semi-dark of the emergency lights past cables and pipes. It turned out to be a very short path — just half a minute later, I found myself in the rescue shuttle berth. There were two shuttles waiting there, ready to take off.

"Faster! Faster!!!" Miya hurried everyone along, somehow having managed to clip a bag onto her shoulders with something round and heavy.

I threw myself to the nearest shuttle, where my bodyguards and chameleons were quickly filling the passenger seats. But the Truth Seeker quickly grabbed me by the shoulder and sharply turned to another shuttle:

"Georg, this way!"

In no position to disagree, I ran where she pointed. The shuttle Miya had refused closed its doors, turned on its engine and sharply burst from place, noisily humming down the tunnel to the airlock. There were very few in the second shuttle, just the Alpha Iseyek Rosss, Miya, Bionica and me. Popori de Cacha sat down in the pilot's seat.

"Alright, chameleon, start it up!" Miya shouted, having lost her normal self-control in her alarmed state. "There's only a few seconds until the reactor blows!"

The shuttle abruptly started off. I hadn't managed

to sit in the seat and buckle up yet, so I lost balance and somersaulted to the other end of the cabin, hitting my right shoulder painfully on a metal handle. My vision grew hazy. I felt like I'd broken something...

Rosss the Alpha Iseyek picked me up gently, placed me in a seat and buckled my safety belts. And then... I was briefly blinded by a bright flash. Through the side porthole, I saw perfectly as *One-Eyed Python* bloomed into a bright white flower of flame. Fortunately, our shuttle managed to get out of the blast zone before it reached us.

"I don't see the first shuttle!" came a surprised shriek from Popori de Cacha. "It isn't on the radar! How is that possible? They took off before we did!"

Despite the searing pain in my shoulder, I found the strength to turn and look at my wife. For some reason, I had no doubt that Miya knew something about the first shuttle.

"Yes, that shuttle has already been destroyed. I realized just in time that getting into it was an obvious mistake, just like staying on the ship. It would be just as much an error right now to dock on Emperor August. *The cruiser is also doomed and will blow in a few seconds. We need to get out of here. Now!"*

"Where should we go, Miya? We're in a hostile star system on an unarmed shuttle! We don't even have a warp drive to get near *Mechanoid* or jump away from the station."

"I don't know, Georg. But staying here next to the station would be a mistake. I don't know why."

I looked out the viewport. I was not interested now in the cloud of shimmering debris where the light cruiser had been, nor even the station with the heavy assault cruiser *Emperor August* docked at it (which is where, by the way, Popori de Cacha was steering our shuttle). I wanted to see the nearest planet, around which the space station was orbiting. There it was: a shade of reddish brown, dark, obviously with an atmosphere not suitable for breathing. But it was not a gas giant, nor a superheated ball of magma, and its gravity should have been somewhat less than crushing, based on the size of the planet.

"Tuki-tuka-de-sa, there is a group of frigates on the near radar subscan! Five *Claws* with Blue House identifiers. They're headed our way!"

"Popori de Cacha, immediately get our shuttle to the nearest planet and dive into the atmosphere! We need to hide from the enemy in the thick cloud cover. Then, try to land our shuttle on the planet!"

The little ship staked a sharp curve and tore full speed into the gloomy, opaque atmosphere of the planet. I saw one last thing before we entered the reddish black clouds as our shuttle sped into the atmosphere, rabidly shaking and heating up as we entered the reddish black clouds: far behind us, next to the Forepost-22 station, there bloomed another bright flower of explosion.

Emergency Landing

ONCE UPON A TIME, I had entered the atmosphere of the Throne World on a similar shuttle also making an emergency landing, and it wasn't the most pleasant sensation. But, as it turned out, that was just roses in comparison with doing the same thing blind on an unknown planet. With the high G-forces, ghastly turbulence and burning of our wings, there was also a nasty scraping and piercing wail, reminiscent of a circular saw. As Popori de Cacha informed us, the dark clouds seemed to be made of fine-grained highly abrasive silicon dioxide, while the atmosphere of the planet consisted primarily of a mix of nitrogen oxides.

A toxic atmosphere, and fine sand in a high quantity? Not the best conditions for flying! I looked out the viewport and led my gaze over something massive and dark, flickering along the left side of the ship.

"What was that, Popori de Cacha?"

"Tuki-tuka-de-sa, that was a rock face. The instruments are showing that there are many-mile high peaks all around here. We're traveling along a mountain ridge. There is no flat surface to be found. And on top of that, the windspeed is outrageous. It's a real hurricane. Worst of all is that our positioning system is failing due to the clouds of particles in the atmosphere. Also, the visibility is so bad I can't see the obstacles fast enough."

The situation he painted was extremely unpleasant. It was only a matter of time before our shuttle would slam into the next unexpected barrier in the dark cloud. I didn't distract the pilot any further and looked to Miya. The Truth Seeker was sitting all green — I didn't know my wife got nauseous from turbulence. Nevertheless, I needed her abilities.

"Go help the pilot! We need to land this shuttle!"

Miya undid her safety belt, stood up and clutched the wall handles, taking unconfident steps toward the pilot's cabin. With all the shaking, only her Truth Seeker abilities allowed her to foresee the shuttle's jerks and jumps far enough in advance to prepare. Finally, Miya reached the cabin and stood behind Popori de Cacha, placing her hands on the chameleon's shoulders.

"Make a sharp turn downward! Now!!!" the Truth Seeker brayed almost immediately, and the shuttle made a tight hook, just barely avoiding a head-on collision with a sheer cliff that appeared a few seconds later right in front of us.

We didn't manage to totally avoid the collision, though, losing a large part of one wing after grazing the cliff. By some miracle, Popori evened out our slight spiral and pointed the nose straight down. I saw a dark vertical wall in the viewport just ten feet to the right of our shuttle and, soon, an identical surface appeared to the left — we had entered some sort of crevasse. But there's always a silver lining: it wasn't at all stormy down here, so the turbulence was almost gone.

"There's been a breach in our air system! A crack in the hull at the right wing joint!" Bionica warned.

"Drop down and reduce speed! There is a small plateau up ahead where we can set down," Miya said confidently, and Popori de Cacha took the shuttle in for a landing.

The sound of the engines changed tonality, we came down as softly as conditions allowed on a stone-strewn platform. I exhaled loudly — we did it! With my good left hand, I tried to undo my safety belt, but it turned out harder than I had imagined.

"Don't rush, Crown Prince! I'll help," Bionica said, walking up to me and helping with the buckle.

"We cannot leave. The air is toxic, even to Iseyek," Rosss warned us all, turning his head and giving a sniff.

I also detected an unpleasant scent a few seconds later but it was barely perceptible, at least for now. Nitrogen dioxide is a very nasty thing, causing suffocation and death in humans and, on contact with water, forming a mixture of nitrous and nitric acid.

"What are we gonna do?" Bionica asked. "We need to fix the crack in the hull..."

I heard the chameleon's voice from the pilot's cabin:

"Every shuttle has emergency kits in a compartment in the wall near the tail with ten light spacesuits and three hours' oxygen, along with a larger reserve oxygen tank. In the same place, you'll find MRE's, water, and comms devices. There should also be some quick-dry sealant."

Rosss the Alpha Iseyek went to the end of the corridor and, pressing on red circles in the wall, opened both niches. It only took him a few seconds to look it over:

"My Princcce, there's no sealant, tank or food here! Just an emergency beacon and one light spacesuit!"

Well, this was it... And to think, the captain of this ship had just assured me it was the best in my fleet! Everyone went silent, taking full account of the now critical situation. In the silence that descended, the poison gas seeping into the shuttle made a distinct hiss — there was clearly more air pressure outside than in here. Popori de Cacha was first to speak:

"First of all, let's turn on the emergency beacon and inform our people what happened. After that, close the airlock into the pilot cabin and turn off the ventilation systems — that way, we can isolate it from the passenger area and keep the poison gas out. Yes, there won't be much air in there, but it should be enough for one person to hold out until help arrives. Beyond that, Georg will have a spacesuit, buying him three more hours. And the rest can wait in the passenger cabin and hope they survive... Yes, the chances are low, but the most important thing is saving Crown Prince Georg!"

"Thank you, of course, for your willingness to sacrifice yourselves, but I won't allow it!" I immediately refused. "I have a different suggestion. Bionica, disactivate yourself right now to save valuable oxygen. We can place your body into the wall niche so the aggressive atmosphere won't ruin your skin. Rosss, how much time will it take you to go into an anabiotic state?"

The huge, semitransparent Alpha Iseyek, twitching his mandibles, answered that he needed about twenty minutes.

"Start going to sleep, but go into the pilot cabin first. You're too heavy for us to move your body, and I don't want the acid corroding you. Popori de Cacha, you take the only spacesuit, lock yourself in the pilot cabin and send constant messages saying what happened and our coordinates."

"But, tuki-tuka-de-sa, what about you?" my bodyguard asked, afraid. I ordered him to be quiet and turned to Miya.

"Can you get us both to a safe place? Even if it's where you hid with our daughter and the chameleons?"

The extremely powerful Truth Seeker, somewhat awkward looking with just the short nighty over her naked body, nodded in silence. She took a reddish stone sphere out of a bag thrown over her shoulder and explained.

"This is a gift I got from Swarm Queen Nai Igir in exchange for my collection of numbered Sivalla emeralds. It's a storage device full of energy, a real boon for any psionic. Anyway, I should have enough energy to get us there, but there's another question: do I have the power? Moving two consciousnesses together with their bodies is a very difficult task. The best way, Georg, would be putting you out temporarily — either get drunk or fall asleep."

I looked at Bionica, already turned off, and the praying mantis Rosss sitting on the floor with his eyes tucked into his armor shell, and appendages folded up along his torso. After that, I moved my gaze onto Popori de Cacha. The chameleon nodded in comprehension and walked up to me. The head of my guard carefully placed his strong flexible fingers on my neck artery and asked:

"When will you return, Crown Prince?"

I didn't know the answer to that question, but the Queen of Unatari answered for me:

"You can be sure we'll be back in three or four days. I'll first need to have a crystal dream to restore my strength. We'll come back in this very place, so make sure everything is ready: breathable air and a sufficient number of soldiers to guard your sovereign."

"Yes, Ma'am!" the chameleon promised and pressed on my carotid artery.

*   *   *

When I came to, I was sitting on a leather chair in an unfamiliar room. Next to me was a fold-out couch, already turned into a bed and made up with sheets, but Miya hadn't had the strength to drag my two-hundred-thirty-pound girth onto it. For clothing, I was wearing the same long underwear but, on my right forearm, I discovered a thick fabric sling, not a bandage, not gauze, but some kind of thin many-layered porous polymer. My shoulder was blue and swollen, my arm was hurting quite badly, but I could move my fingers without issue. Of course, I was no doctor and, without an x-ray, it would be impossible to say for certain, but my sense was that it was just a bad contusion or a bone fracture, not a fully-fledged break.

I stood up and looked around the room with curiosity. There were no windows. The only lighting was a dim flat frosted fixture on the ceiling. I couldn't find any knob or remote to turn it off, down or up. I wondered about the source of light and scooted the chair up, standing on it and getting a closer look. It looked like a crepe — thin and flat, and not apparently hollow. It wasn't luminescent, nor light diode, without a filament, just some construction totally unfamiliar to me. And just as unfamiliar were the magnetic contacts. I had never seen a junction like that. The glass was engraved with some apparently linguistic symbols, but I couldn't make heads or tails of it.

I twisted out the bulb haphazardly, and accidentally disconnected it from the contacts, immersing the room in total darkness. I didn't get scared, though because I quickly noticed a light at the other end of a corridor. I got down off the chair and went in that direction.

I recognized this room immediately. There was a large cupboard with children's toys and a canopied crib in the corner, which was now empty. In another corner of the room, on a small folding bed, Miya was sleeping in semi-darkness. The Truth Seeker was lying totally naked, not even covered with a blanket or sheet. My spouse's long red hair was fanned out in all directions, her skin glistening white. Her breathing was even and deep and her perky breasts heaved with every breath. It took me a lot of effort to tear my gaze from the tempting curves of my beautiful wife and continue looking around the room.

Next to her on a round table, I noticed an empty box of crystalloquasimetal-cis-isomer valiarimic acid, her drug of choice. It wasn't very likely Miya had brought the crystals with her when fleeing the doomed ship. It was more probable that the Truth Seeker had stashed a secret dose of the drug here. On the floor, there was a canvas bag. Inside was the energy storage ball, now a pale pink. Its color had considerably washed out since I had last seen it. Most likely, that meant Miya hadn't had enough of her own psionic energy to bring us both here, and she had used some of what was stored in the ball.

I already wanted to leave, but my gaze happened to catch on a small patch stuck behind my wife's ear, the same tone as her skin. Normally, her thick bright crimson hair covered it up but, now, the locks were brushed aside, revealing a small piece of scalp shaved bald. My interest piqued, I walked over and carefully pulled back the patch. There was a tattoo under it reading "No. 4734," then a date and a label indicating it had been made one hundred seventy-eight years ago in the Throne World Truth Seeker Academy. Strangely, no hair had grown back on that spot since. As far as I knew, my wife had only one tattoo, a fanciful design on the small of her back, reading: "Mesfelle Family Plaything." It had been ordered by my father, Count Inoky royl Mesfelle forty years ago, long before I had entered *Perimeter Defense*. As it turned out, the woman's body also had another, older tattoo.

Miya really didn't like talking about her past, but

the time when she had studied in the psionic school run by Krista on the Throne World was an especially strong taboo. I had only heard that it had been governed by extremely strict rules, and that the Truth Seeker school was closed after a series of student deaths. It hadn't been so long ago that I had accidentally figured out that my dearest wife had a direct hand in those murders, but I had opted against reopening her old mental wounds by delving into the details. And now as well, I carefully reattached the patch over the tattoo and readjusted her red hair.

What to do? Probably, I should look into the neighboring dark rooms and get to know a bit more about this place. For a start, walk down the corridor leading away from my room and figure out where it led.

"I don't recommend that," my wife's voice rang out in my head. *"This is a totally unstable place. It isn't impossible that it exists only in my imagination, so you shouldn't stray too far from me."*

"So, you aren't asleep?!" I asked in surprise.

"I am asleep. And I'll be asleep for quite a long time. But you were looking too stubbornly at my body and thinking about me, so I sensed the attention. All Truth Seekers are capable of sensing attention paid to them, even when in a crystal dream. In the next room, there is a mini-bar and, three times a day, there will be a hot meal delivered pneumatically. You'll find a trash incinerator in the same place. A bit further down the hallway is a shower room and laundry area. Georg, you need to find something to do for the next two or three days while I regain my strength. If you need anything, ask me mentally, and I'll try my best. But

now, excuse me, I need my rest."

*   *   *

The food was unfamiliar, but tasty and nourishing. I still hadn't figured out what it was under the thick spicy sauce, mushrooms or vegetables, although it may also have been some kind of seaweed. It didn't matter. What was important was that the food was nutritious and sated my hunger well. And as for the alcohol, I didn't touch it; I needed a fresh mind. I just had too much to think about.

So then, the Blue House had tried to kill me. And at that, they nearly succeeded. If it weren't for Popori de Cacha's first class piloting abilities, and Miya's help, the Unatari State would have just gotten a new ruler. What made Duchess Ovella want that? Interesting question. After all, it was obvious that the young Crown Princess had nothing directly to gain from my death. She was probably promised something by someone else. For example, real military aid against her numerous rebelling systems.

Who had ordered my assassination? As they say in these situations, "cui bono?" Who benefits? But the problem was that my death was beneficial to too many people. For example, the Emperor, who would get a more manageable ruler of Unatari, probably a very old regent, conducting politics in total accord with orders from the Throne World. But with time, after the marriage of my daughter Likanna to this or that Crown Prince, Unatari as an independent state would totally cease to exist, first after changing name to the Orange House, then after dissolving back into the Empire.

Also, my death could have been paid for by the Antagonists. After all, that would mean the Empire would lose one of its most capable fleet leaders, with high popularity among the military. But weakened by internal strife and war with the Aliens, the Blue House, disappointed with the support of the Throne World, would soon have been forced to seek out an alliance with the Gold House. That seemed a very probable scenario.

By the way, what did I know about the Antagonists? Crown Princess Eleonora, Emperor August's sister, was older than her brother by a whole fifteen years. Now she would be... if I thought about it... three hundred fifty-five years old! You cannot fool the human body at such an age, even with the best medical treatment, and rejuvenating procedures of the most powerful Truth Seekers. It must have been hard enough without the intrigues and bloody battles. At her three hundred fifty years, the ruler of the Gold House should have been more worried about forgetting to change her diaper or taking her daily pills, not a meeting with generals or admirals. Maybe I was just exaggerating things of course but, still, the age of Crown Princess Eleonora would be quite significant and absolutely not appropriate for planning a military invasion with all the inevitable troubles and meetings with military experts, stretching far beyond midnight. I wondered why no one had thought about this before.

But... the Antagonist invasion was a fact that could not be disputed. No less an authority than Miya had spoken about it at a recent meeting and sworn by her abilities as a Truth Seeker. But then who was leading the invasion, if not the head of the Gold House? Who would be next in line to their throne? I didn't know the answer to that question, but I imagined it would be the Antagonist leader's only daughter, my mother. Was she in any way a bad candidate for the role of shadow ruler?! Perhaps that was exactly what the Dark Mother meant when she had mentioned Crown Princess Elisa royl Clement ton Lavaelle. But if that was so, the Arites sent to the Green House would certainly bring it to light!

Although... my mother wasn't exactly young either. One hundred eighty-three is a very respectable age for a person, even if they had been under the watchful eye of medics caring for their health from the day of their birth. So, she also didn't have the most appropriate physical condition to be military leader or brain center of the conspirators. But here, I unwillingly remembered Miya. Despite her respectable age, no one would think a day older than twenty or twenty-two. And her physical abilities would never make you question that. But the Queen of Unatari was unique in that sense, as one of the strongest Truth Seekers in the Empire and could rejuvenate her own body. Although, perhaps my mother also had a Truth Seeker maintaining her physical condition. I knew nothing about that, but that didn't mean such a person didn't exist.

The very strongest argument against Crown Princess Elisa as shadow ruler of the Antagonists was the fact that my mother had been the subject of very stubborn observation by the Empire's secret services after the Gold House had left the Empire. I mean, come on, she was the daughter of the head of the Antagonists! Everything she wrote was probably opened and inspected. All her contacts must have been checked carefully, all conversations recorded and poured over. In order to lead an invasion in such conditions, there would have to be a simply genius conspirator or... her role was to keep the heightened attention of the secret services on her, to distract from the true leader.

Alright, I'd leave Crown Princess Elisa as a suspect and look at all the other options. Her daughter, my twin sister Violetta royl Inoky ton Mesfelle-Damir. The Ice Princess, who had hammered together a huge income selling radioactive isotopes from her space-ice processing facilities. A nebulous, utterly unprincipled figure, chasing after power by stepping on the heads of all other claimants and ready to kill even her own brother just to get one step closer to a throne. She caroused with upper aristocrats and possessed colossal financial income, even by Imperial upper crust standards, as well as a personal space fleet more powerful than even that of Perimeter Sector Seven. Was there any reason she couldn't be ruler of the Antagonists? I was inclined to say no, especially if I considered her subversive activity in the Purple House and her striving to drive a wedge between Imperial allies. Violetta was always close with our mother and probably worked side by side with her.

Who else had I overlooked as a suspect? I thought hard, running through known political and military leaders in my head, and wasn't able to hold back a smile — from an outside perspective, the most appropriate candidate for role of military leader of the

Antagonists was me. Just think, the grandson of the ruler of the Antagonists, having proven himself time and again to be a capable commander. Also, I was currently in a feud with the Imperial authorities and possessed not only a massive space fleet with four and a half thousand starships, but also well-trained crews. Well then, that's probable exactly what the Empire thought, so I could look at the assassination attempt from that perspective as well...

*   *   *

Miya woke up on the third day. First of all, she limped over to the kitchen and spent a long time greedily drinking water from a glass bottle filled with small porous stones. After that, she walked over to the peeping pneumatic delivery box, took a bag of toiletries and locked herself in the bathroom for three hours. Only when she'd finished, did she come out to me, looking flawlessly beautiful, rested, smelling of her beloved violet perfume and dressed in an incomprehensible, frivolous nothing of pink ribbons.

"I see you made good use of your time here," she said, turning her head in surprise, commenting on the walls I'd marked up with a lead pencil. "Georg, did you seriously draw out a whole star map of Unatari and the Blue House from memory?!"

"Well, without Sector Fifteen. It's the farthest from us and occupied by the Aliens, and I also didn't remember it well. I didn't draw Sector Sixteen either. It's cut off from the Blue House now and has no influence on current events. But I did include a fragment of the Imperial Core. Just the nearest star systems, which contain all the exits into the Perimeter."

"Well I'll be damned! And what is that?" Miya pointed at a carefully drawn web and lots of little markers placed on it. "No need to answer, I already get it."

"You didn't 'get it,' you read it in my thoughts," I said strictly, correcting her. "Yes, I was trying to figure out who will be in control of the Forepost-22 system three days after the attack on our ship, based on the Blue House and Unatari fleets located nearby, their military might and the time it would take to get there. It isn't the most reassuring picture. If our Yayho Border Fleet came to the help signal sent by Popori de Cacha, and the station warp beacon is not turned off, it will soon be destroyed by the Blue House Second Strike Fleet. And our main forces won't have time to get there. And then you and I would be returning right into the hands of our enemies, who will take us warm as soon as we arrive."

"That's in the best case," Miya noted gloomily. "There's also a completely realistic possibility that the help signal was never picked up, and no one will be there to meet us. Then, we'll come back to a shuttle filled with nitrous oxide gas, and I won't have time or power to send us back to a safe place."

It was an unenviable perspective, but I still saw no alternative to our returning — we couldn't just sit forever in this isolated and unstable part of space. Miya nodded in agreement:

"And I wasn't suggesting we stay here forever. This is merely a temporary shelter. I have no way of getting more energy to consume here, so my strength will slowly decrease. Also, I cannot leave Deia. Without me, our little daughter is doomed, because she's a problem for too many aristocrats."

"For example?" I asked, immediately on guard, as any information about threats to my infant daughter was very important to me.

Miya stayed silent for a bit, then moved her gaze away from me and said quietly:

"Well, at least the ones who are in line for the throne right behind your children — the Duke and Duchess of Unatari. And don't interrupt me, Georg, first listen. You have a perfect basis to trust your second cousin Katerina and her husband Corwin, as well as your former father-in-law Valesy and Duchess Silva. They all owe you a lot and will not betray you under any circumstances, I am absolutely sure of that as a Truth Seeker. But all their loyalty only applies to you, not your children. So, if you suddenly disappear without a trace, a harsh struggle for power will begin, and the part of your children will be unenviable. But let's hope it doesn't come to that. Pray the signal reached our people, and they have taken measures."

My spouse was clearly not happy with herself for starting this conversation, and tried somewhat awkwardly to change the topic. But I, on the other hand, tried to immediately sort through all the details so I wouldn't have to return to this sensitive issue later. Looking Miya right in the eyes, I asked a direct question:

"Tell me, was Duke Corwin ton Unatari on *One-Eyed Python* during the explosion?"

The redheaded beauty, not taking her eyes off me, nodded in silence.

"And he died?"

Another silent nod. One of those who Miya considered a potential threat to her daughter had just died in the cruiser explosion. Wasn't that just too nice a coincidence? Shamelessly taking advantage of the fact that the Truth Seeker was unable to openly lie to a question, if I asked her directly, I inquired:

"Tell me why you neglected to inform the cruiser captain of the threat."

Miya finally took her gaze away and spent a long time in silence before giving an honest answer:

"Okay, Georg. I really did purposely not wake the sleeping captain to tell him about the enemy forces storming the cruiser. I already knew by then that the ship was doomed, and that everyone remaining on board would die. It may have been possible to save Duke Corwin, but I didn't do that. Why? It isn't so much because of a personal dislike of him, although my opinion of the Duke did have an impact, I won't hide that. The important thing is that, at that time, I was actively working to read all possible options of how to save myself, and you as well, so everything else was of secondary concern. Do you judge me for that, Georg?"

I shook my head in the negative. How can you judge a person for the fact that, above all else, they wanted to save themselves and their dearest? Miya had done the right thing, managing in a critical situation to articulate the most important mission and save us both from a huge catastrophe. But it would be for the best if Duchess Katerina didn't find out...

"Alright, let your cousin think that her husband

Corwin died in a firefight with Blue House assault troops in the cruiser corridors, heroically holding back the onslaught of attackers on his *One-Eyed Python*."

"I agree, that would be best for everyone. But let's leave the poetry for later. Miya, are you ready to send us back?"

The Truth Seeker gave a wry laugh:

"Georg, I've been ready for a while, but you haven't. Your consciousness is too active, and that will complicate the procedure. So, we'll have to think up another way to put you under. I cannot do harm to you, so the simple and effective method used by Popori de Cacha is right out, as is simply smacking you on the head with something heavy. So, it's up to you — either we wait patiently for you to get tired and go to bed, or we try to get you sloppy drunk. The booze here is perfectly good for those purposes, but it causes quite the hangover."

It didn't take me long to decide — I had just woken up and was energetic and full of strength, so it would be some time before I'd be ready to sleep again. I picked the second option.

"Alright then!" the beautiful redhead replied, lighting up as she dug in the mini-bar and pulled out a few bottles of wine along with a dark bottle of brandy. "There's no particular reason for us to hurry, Georg, we've got five hours until anyone's expecting us, so I suggest a romantic candle-lit dinner. I'm gonna stuff myself after my three-day fast, but you try to stick to the booze."

Despite the inevitable anxiety before walking into the dangerous unknown, I couldn't stop myself from laughing at the paradoxical nature of the moment:

"Most wives try to make sure their husbands don't get too drunk. But you, on the other hand, have set a mission to get me wasted."

"Well, I've gotta rouse my husband's spirits somehow," the beauty laughed craftily. "I mean, seeing your wife lying naked for three whole days barely even caught your eye..."

Seeing the embarrassment on my face, Miya laughed happily:

"I know, Georg, I know. You're not like that. That's one way you're different from the other Mesfelles. My helpless state in crystal naps didn't stop them one bit... it was more the opposite, in fact. But let's not dig up painful memories. It's been a long time since we've had such a great opportunity to spend time alone, just us two, so let's not waste it..."

*   *   *

"The Crown Prince is awake!" came a loud cry, making me wince in pain.

Why scream like that? Didn't they know that sharp movements and loud sounds were like harsh torture for me right now? Oh, my splitting head! With massive effort, I peeled back my eyelids and tried to focus my vision. A shadowy figure was quickly approaching me, forcing a cup of something into my hand.

"Drink this Georg. It will make it better," I recognized the voice of my cousin Katerina.

What the heck was she doing here? And where the heck was I?! I took a sip of the bitter, slightly salty fizzy drink and led my gaze over the room, already feeling my senses return. I could be sure this wasn't the shuttle we'd made the emergency landing in. It was a well-lit room with walls of plastic. As if reading my mind, Katerina answered my unasked question:

"This is a rescue camp deployed on top of a mountain on the second planet in the Forepost-22 system. But the Unatari rescue team really had to work to get to your shuttle at the bottom of that two-mile deep ravine! How you had the presence of mind to fly down there on a space shuttle and not hit any cliffs is beyond my understanding! The emergency signal couldn't even make it out of those depths, although our Yayho border fleet was already in the system, called by the *Mechanoid*. You should thank Popori de Cacha for your rescue. He had to climb up a practically vertical cliff to a plateau, which is where he managed to establish contact with our ships!"

So, there it was! I hadn't even considered that the emergency signal might not be heard from down there. It turned out that my life had been hanging from an even finer thread than I suspected.

"I will have to thank Popori de Cacha, then. Where is he now?"

"The chameleon was sent to a burn ward in Sector Nine — he's got nitrous acid abrasions all over his skin. The human space suit turned out to be too narrow for a creature of the Ravaash race, and also, the chameleon needed his feet and hands free to climb up the rocks. So, Popori de Cacha took only the helmet and oxygen tanks, leaving his body unprotected against the acidic gas."

Seeing the fear on my face, Katerina rushed to

reassure me:

"The medics say that he has very serious burns, and that the outer layers of tissue were deeply injured and necrotized, but his recovery prognosis isn't all that bad. Your bodyguard leader is sure to survive, and after molting, will even be able to go invisible as well. But Popori de Cacha will have to spend a few months in a clinic."

To my great shame, only then did I notice Katerina's appearance — she was wearing a black dress with a ribbon of mourning in her hair. I apologized for my callousness and expressed sympathy to my cousin. Katerina nodded distantly:

"After the reactor explosion, the remains of Duke Corwin and the other crew members from *One-Eyed Python* and *Emperor August* could only be identified by DNA. Yesterday we gave them a funeral with military honors. Five hundred forty airtight coffins were sent on a final flight into the nearest star... Another group of bodies were discovered earlier, orbiting the first planet in a shot-down rescue shuttle. There were six people there from your bodyguard, four chameleons and the praying mantis Phobos."

What happened at that critical moment when our shuttle had left the bomb-laden cruiser finally reached me:

"That shuttle was the first to take off from the doomed *One-Eyed Python*. It noticed a threat near the station and went into a warp jump to the first planet, leading the Blue House frigates after it. Our second shuttle only escaped because of that. The group of Blue House *Claws* went off to chase the defenseless victim, which we know only from radar records."

"Those bastards shot high-speed cannons at an unarmed rescue shuttle, and before that, made a vile attack on a diplomatic mission docked on a space station, and killed my husband. Georg, while you were gone, I took responsibility and, in the name of the Unatari State, declared war on the Blue House. The day before yesterday, there was a space battle in the Forepost-22 system. Our Yayho Border Fleet was wiped out by the Blue House Second Fleet but, after that, the Ayho Strike Fleet and Virho Heavy Fleet reversed the situation, and the enemy retreated."

I shook my head in dismay — how could they have allowed a firefight between the Yayho Border Fleet, consisting of only one hundred fifty light ships, against an enemy fleet of more than a thousand?! My cousin, seeing my vexation and understanding that I would never have allowed such losses, rushed to tell me more positive news:

"The neighboring star systems of Paada and Boti have already been captured by our ships. The battleships of Admirals Kheraisss Vej and Masss Azhzh are taking down the planetary defense systems, while thirteen *Trias* are leading a mass landing of Alpha Iseyek. Unatari's remaining forces are already on the way. The Sector Nine Fleet will arrive to the Forepost-22 system in eight hours, and the Second Unatari Fleet will be here the day after tomorrow. The Sector Eight Fleet and our First Fleet are also underway. Now, with our main military leader and monarch alive and well, I am glad to pass the reins of government back to you. Georg, crush these lowlifes! The Blue House must be destroyed!"

"

BLOODTHIRSTY AVENGER

MY FACE gone pale, and my teeth clenched until they cracked, I was watching a report on the landing of the praying mantis assault troops from a small town called Seaside on the planet Paada-II. The presenter was a young man in a sleeveless shirt with the emblem of one of Paada's local news agencies.

A Blue House infantry base on the outskirts of Seaside had already been destroyed by orbital bombardment, along with some light armor hangars. Six forty-ton bombs, launched from the battleships of the Virho Heavy Fleet by Admiral Masss Azhzh had turned the military base into a moonscape with huge craters. Very few Blue House military officers had survived the fiery hell. Orbital bombardment from battleships left very little chance of survival. And now, the hastily recruited Seaside militia — firemen, medical workers and even simple civilians — had picked up firearms from the local police and hunting shops, and were preparing to meet the Alpha Iseyek landing troops.

Despite the fact that their resistance was totally hopeless, I didn't see any signs of despondency or gloom on their faces. Quite the opposite. The people were full of decisiveness to fight the insect invaders to the last drop of blood. There were rousing and patriotic speeches, some were even joking. A young couple in the background was kissing. A boy in police uniform was making plans for the evening after the battle, while his smiling girlfriend pressed up to him, wearing a camouflage armor suit over a lightweight, brightly colored dress.

And this all had nothing to do with lack of information about our forces. No, the danger of the genetically enhanced ten-foot-high praying mantises was something they all understood perfectly. My soldiers were well known to be capable of running five times faster than humans and were also bulletproof with their impenetrable armor. But the people felt they had to fight for their homes and families, so they weren't even considering retreat or capitulation.

"It will all be a lot harder than we supposed..." I said gloomily, turning to my advisor, the Beta Iseyek Apasss Ugu.

The huge pill bug stared at me with his many tiny eyes. Even before Bionica had translated his chirruping, I had detected notes of surprise in the insect's trill.

"I don't know what you mean, Your Majesty. Savasss Jach's landing troops will capture that little town without even noting resistance. Losses among our soldiers, if there are any, will be utterly insignificant."

Just then, a pair of heavy machine guns on the

roof of the local school hummed into action. Some of the defenders tried to take down a low-flying Iseyek reconnaissance drone, studying the positions of the troops before the landing operation.

"Get me a feed from this drone!" I demanded and, in a separate window on the big screen, there appeared some scenes taken from flight.

There was a barricade of concrete blocks at the entrance to the city. There were a few trenches dug out nearby, and some hurriedly built firing points. In them were two hundred militia members with miserable armor and weaponry... Just a few minutes work for my Alpha Iseyek, who didn't know pity and lived only through war. The huge praying mantises, having come down from the sky hungry, would make no discount for the fact that they were being resisted by a barely trained militia. They would see these doomed people as nothing more than a high-calorie food source. All that felt incorrect. I asked to be put through to Duchess Katerina ton Unatari and shared my doubts with my cousin. My advisor, still dressed in mourning clothes, was very categorical in her appraisal:

"Georg, take into account that you are not watching a normal broadcast, but propaganda dreamed up by the best Blue House psychologists, professionally directed and made to create a certain effect in the mind! Our enemy is making themselves out to be the innocent victim and drawing attention to the alleged interspecies conflict between humans and insects. But you must know that they are completely wrong!"

"Yes, I know! But if even I, leading the invasion of the Blue House, feel extremely conflicting emotions from this broadcast and sympathy for the defenders, then imagine how normal Imperial citizens will take these video clips! If it goes on like this, humanity will turn away from us, while the Emperor will declare war on our state!"

"He won't," my cousin laughed predatorily. "Our opponents made two very big mistakes, beyond the fact that they chose to attack possibly the most dangerous man in the galaxy. You see, Georg, they didn't just blow up one of our heavy assault cruisers, but a ship built with the personal funds of the Emperor himself, and bearing his very name: *Emperor August*. And at that, Bayazid Krom died with the ship, who Emperor August had personally given a medal after the battle with the Aliens in Hnelle, and even awarded with the Order of the Emerald Star. Insofar as I know, after the attack, the Emperor was simply rabid and told the young Duchess Ovella royl Stok ton Miro that he was extremely perturbed by her actions. The second error made by the head of the Blue House is that, after Unatari declared war on the Blue House, Duchess Ovella became enraged and ordered our ambassador hanged."

"She executed Paola ton Akad?!" I asked in horror.

"That's right, cousin," Katerina confirmed in a hate-filled voice. "And beyond the fact that all ambassadors are untouchable, and this murder caused a negative reaction from all social strata of the Empire, it would have been hard to find a worse victim in the whole Universe. Paola ton Akad was the great granddaughter of Krista, the strongest Truth Seeker in the galaxy and the personal psionic of the Emperor. What's more, Paola was a member of the Akad family, which includes the ruler of the Empire himself, August royl Akad. De facto, over the last few days, the Blue House has spat in the Emperor's face two times. And after something like that, do you think the Empire will come to their aid against us?"

All that, of course, was true and my cousin, as usual, had read the situation correctly. What was more, my state had long had a trump card in the form of billions of praying mantis landing troops, who made capturing any space station or inhabited planet nothing but a question of time. Probably, it was worth making a clear demonstration of this power, so all of Unatari's neighbors would understand what awaited them in the case of aggression against us. But still, I couldn't get past the feeling that what was happening was wrong.

Achievement unlocked: Bloodthirsty Avenger

Global fame increase. Current value: +65

Global standing decrease. Current value: +7

Standing change. Empire Military faction opinion of you has worsened.
Present Empire Military faction opinion of you: +58 (veneration)

The message that appeared before my eyes reflected my own feelings perfectly. My fame was growing, but it was as the leader of an insect army annihilating human planets. Bloodthirsty Avenger? Yes, in the eyes of the people of the Empire, that was exactly how I most likely looked, and no words of reassurance from my cousin could overshadow that bitter truth. But Katerina was trying to distract me from the sad thoughts:

"Don't worry, Georg. We're about to put out a big series of reports about the low cunning of the Blue House and Duchess Ovella. We'll raise the curtain of mystery from the whole series of political murders, which allowed such a young royal to sit on the throne of a Great House. And if the enemy propaganda bothers you, there always remains the option of sending information from the fronts to the warp beacons, and then the Paada and Boti star systems will be cut off hermetically from the Empire, and no one will know about what is happening."

"Well, we really shouldn't do that," I replied, immediately refusing my cousin's radical suggestion. "Lack of information will give rise to all kinds of speculation about what we're doing. Instead of reports about successful Alpha Iseyek space landings and the destruction of Blue House defensive barriers, we will get utterly wild fantasies about women and children being eaten alive by praying mantises, human sacrifice and mass genocide. Never underestimate the imagination of a panicked, fearful mind. This way, the audience will at least see distinctly that our landing troops are only killing those who resist the invasion. And that is the very factor that must be repeatedly underlined: we are not at war with the civilian population, only with Blue House armed forces!"

"Unfortunately, that is not always the case, cousin," Katerina said, leading her gaze away. "Yes, we could declare that we are at war exclusively with

Blue House soldiers and will not touch the peaceful population. But the enemy will find dozens of examples to the contrary and call us obvious liars. Georg, this is war, and chance victims among peaceful civilians are unavoidable."

"My Prince, allow me to voice my point of view," the android secretary Bionica cut into my conversation with my cousin. "The boundary between civilians and militia can be extremely tenuous. And the insect landing troops can make mistakes because of that. Just look for yourself, Crown Prince. On the screen next to the barricade, at Seaside we can see people totally unsuited to war, some of whom aren't even armed. To me personally, as someone accustomed to strict classifications and clear algorithms, it is quite difficult to figure out which of these people belongs to which category. Who are they, peaceful people who happened to end up on the front line, or opponents?"

My translator's words were supported by First Advisor Apasss Ugu. The gigantic pill bug with dozens of arms and legs had already pointed to the data screen and started to comment on the image:

"Perhaps it is obvious to people who is peaceful, and who is an enemy. But as for me, a member of a different species, try as I might, I cannot always tell which is which. That couple there hugging, are they enemies of Unatari? They don't currently have weapons in their hands, and their uniform is not military, but they are in combat position, and not at home. And as for the reporter, how would you classify him? He has a bulletproof vest and a highspeed carbine, which my database tells me is a weapon for hunting and sporting competitions. Is that sufficient basis to classify him as an enemy combatant? And if it's hard even for me, a creature with unblocked self-teaching and high-intellect genes, what can we expect from simple obedient order takers, like the genetically modified praying mantis soldiers? I suspect that the Alpha Iseyek soldiers, the majority of whom have never even seen people in real life before and are totally unfamiliar with human culture, have a very hard time making out who it is before them. And that can cause tragic events, like when we took out those columns of camouflaged Blue House military transports, which seemed to be working to export their armor and anti-air defense, but were actually moving children to a safe place..."

I clenched my teeth in vexation. I didn't know anything about that tragic event, but I trusted my First Assistant. Apasss Ugu knew everything about what was happening in my state.

"And have many such tragic incidents already occurred?" I inquired cautiously, cringing internally in anticipation.

"Many, Georg, I'd even say very many," said my cousin Katerina, rejoining the conversation. "But I already told you that this is war and chance victims are unavoidable."

That may have been so, but I was totally unhappy with what we were doing. Even though the Empire wouldn't intervene on the Blue House's side, regardless of victims among the peaceful population. But my obligation as a ruler of the human race was to do everything in my power to minimize human losses.

"Alright, I've made a decision. We will not terminate the terrestrial operations on Paada and Boti. From a military point of view, it would be very stupid to abandon positions already occupied by our landing troops and give the enemy respite. But the Unatari State will officially declare a few zones on this planet free from military action. Our soldiers will not assault, nor bomb these regions, and we will let any civilian transports through to them unimpeded. When the intensity of the terrestrial battles dies down a bit, we will provide for the evacuation of people from these safe zones to any star system of the Imperial Core or Unatari. All civilian buildings and vehicles are to be marked with a bright blue stripe on a white background, which will allow them to be fully ignored by our landing troops and space fleet. Civilians of Paada and Boti must place that symbol on everything they don't want destroyed in the form of a clearly visible flag or drawing. These measures will allow us to, if not totally stop civilian losses, then to decrease them by many times."

Bionica made a dismayed grimace and interjected:

"My Prince, I beg forgiveness for interrupting Your Highness, but what is stopping our enemies from placing these emblems on their military vehicles or reinforcements to confuse our landing troops?"

But Duchess Katerina was enthusiastic about my idea and commented with a glint in her eyes:

"No, Bionica, they won't do that. At the very least on a massive scale. Because, all such cases will be immediately documented by us and exposed for all Imperial residents to see. And if they do, we can say the Blue House soldiers are knowingly placing their civilian population, who they've sworn to protect, at risk. That will be a very strong psychological blow on our enemies' positions. The population will stop supporting them."

"That's exactly right," I agreed with my cousin. "Let Marshal Savasss Jach draw up these safe zones, so they don't interfere too much with his military plans. But let's make sure one of them on the planet Paada is around Seaside — consider it my whim as a monarch. Also, Katerina, you must award that young reporter from Seaside some prestigious medal for journalism, along with a solid monetary bonus. Just make sure you point out that it is from the Unatari State for objectively casting a light on military actions, and say that the safe zone around Seaside is a result of his work. Similar medals should be awarded to another few reporters, those whose reports are the sharpest and least pleasant for us. Whether they accept the medals or not is up to them, but somehow, I don't think many of the journalists will refuse such a rare professional award, and especially the money."

My cousin laughed happily:

"You're very right there, Georg. The vast majority of those in the second oldest profession are little different from those in the first. I suspect the unexpected money and glory will turn the political weathervane in the diametrically opposite direction, and the tone of reports from the front will soon change cardinally. But what should we do with the other Blue House star systems?"

"I suggest we establish safe zones like those here, and inform the population in advance so the peaceful civilians will have enough time and chance to leave the dangerous parts. We won't rush the terrestrial operations there, but we must take control over the space and star systems as quickly as possible."

*   *   *

Senior Tactics Officer Max Gregor was describing the balance of power in the Uvi star system, accompanying a slideshow of photographs of enemy starships with detailed commentary:

"Before us is the core of the Blue House Second Fleet. These pictures were taken forty minutes ago by cloaked frigates. Four *Monarch*-class battleships. Two *Tyrant*-class battleships. Twenty-five heavy assault cruisers: nine of the outdated rocket *Yataghans*, six *Flambergs* and nine of the newest *Katanas*. Opposing heavy calibers are not in place, but are constantly changing position, not even always staying a decent distance from one another."

"Maybe they're worried about our stealth bombers?" I suggested.

"That looks very much to be the case," Max Gregor agreed. There aren't many light cruisers, just thirty *Thrushes*. And at that, there are more than enough small class ships: forty-seven Flycatcher destroyers and more than eight hundred frigates, half *Pyros* and half *Claws*.

"Eight hundred frigates?!" I couldn't hold back the surprised exclamation. "That's what I'm talking about! It inspires respect, even though half of them are horribly outdated *Claws*."

"The enemy is not turning the Uvi warp beacon off, as if inviting us in. But that is obviously a trap, Crown Prince! I ask you to look at these scenes here. The enemy is around three thousand miles from the

Uvi station and have placed a chain of mines in our direction with a laser control system and gravitational detonators. Here are some close-ups of the mines with good resolution."

In a perfectly straight line from the Uvi station, leading toward the Paada star system there was an endless chain of dark ovular objects. There were hundreds, if not thousands of them.

"Yes, the enemy is well prepared," I agreed thoughtfully. "Do we know how powerful the charges are?"

"Crown Prince, these are standard *Rascal-4* space mines. They can hold between one and fifty megatons TNT equivalent. The precise power of these bombs is unknown, but in any casc, there's no way a cloaked frigate of ours could jump unnoticed into the Paada system. Even with stealth systems activated, the curvature of space will set off the laser beam data readers. And also, a massive object jumping in near the detectors will be not go unnoticed, after which the nearest thermonuclear mines will all detonate. They're firmly anchored, and placed around one every mile."

I asked to see an image of the mine wall and thought hard. The enemy was obviously not afraid of wasting resources to create a barrier, and now was inviting our fleet to make a warp jump to Uvi and accept battle on these conditions. If the mines had the most powerful charges they could hold, then only the carriers of my First Unatari Fleet might escape, but all the other smaller-class ships would certainly be lost, even the battleships.

"Do we have alternative coordinates for a warp jump to the Uvi system?" I asked my officer, but Max

Gregor just shook his head in pity, "the *Mechanoid* hasn't gone through that star system yet."

Unfortunately, my ships would have to jump right into a minefield. No other way of entering the Uvi system existed. But that also, if I understood correctly, was not the last of our problems.

"I suspect that the Blue House has a cloaker tracking the movement of our ships."

"Yes, my Prince. On several occasions, we have detected the activation of long distance communication devices in the Paada system, but we weren't able to uncover the cloaked frigate," the tactics officer confirmed.

That was what I thought. Even if I sent low value ships first to open a breach in the minefield, then the rest of the fleet, the enemy would be sure to see these preparations and take countermeasures. For example, they could let the first ships through and activate the charges only when the main fleet arrives. Or, if the attackers are too many, they could flee from battle and turn off the warp beacon in the next star system. No, the Blue House fleet wanted to do battle in the Uvi system precisely, but we only could send a small group of ships there, so they wouldn't get scared and retreat. Battle at obvious numerical disadvantage on the opponent's terms... For such a borderline suicidal mission, we needed the best of the best, so I asked to be put through to Nicole ton Savoia.

The Perimeter Sector Eight Fleet Commander answered immediately. Space Major Nicole ton Savoia, despite her youth, looked very respectable with the flawlessly fitted senior space fleet officer uniform. All the gossip among her subjects had come to an end, but there used to be a lot of talk about her rank. Generally, a fleet of such size could only be led by an officer of rank no lower than admiral. However, the Perimeter Sector Eight Fleet captains had had plenty of chances at this point to assure themselves of the high professionalism of their gorgeous commander. But Nicole herself, I suspect, was still experiencing discomfort at the discord between her title and profession.

"Nicole, I'm reminded that you were once interested in new military tactics and participating in space battles with an initially hopeless balance of forces," I said, casting my line.

The girl's eyes immediately lit up with sparks of interest. Her lips stretched out into a pretty smile.

"Your Majesty, I'm still interested in new knowledge, and the fleet entrusted to me has not taken part in any space battles for nearly six months. Any mechanism, even the most well-oiled, will go bad and rust from inactivity, so my officers and I personally would be glad for any mission."

I grew slightly embarrassed, because Nicole was completely right. Her fleet had spent too much time stagnating. But my current offer was exclusively for Nicole, not her whole fleet. I needed a couple very experienced helpers for the upcoming battle. One of them, by default, would be Bionica. I'd need the android not only as my irreplaceable Iseyek translator, but also as my personal assistant, a job she was excellent at. The second vacancy was open. Max Gregor was a talented tactics officer, but didn't have a lot of experience. Valian ton Corsa on the other hand, had experience, but was less suited to making her own decisions and reacting quickly to fast-changing events, so clearly lost out as well. Nicole ton Savoia was better than anyone else in the role of a second assistant to the commander.

When I explained my idea to the girl, and her role in it, Nicole spent some time looking at me in shock, batting her lashes in surprise before answering:

"The Blue House Second Fleet rolled over our Yayho Border Fleet almost without losses, and it was made of light class ships. And Your Majesty wants to meet the Blue House ships again on the same conditions, but this time to lead the fleet myself. Is that what you're saying?"

"That's right. But you did forget to add that this time, we will have to navigate through an enemy minefield," I smiled in reply.

Nicole shuddered, but at the same time, much to my surprise, started smiling.

"Seven of their ships to our one, and fifty to one in volley weight most likely, and also a minefield... Well, Your Majesty, you really know how to make a girl a tempting offer. How could I refuse such an alluring and fun proposal?! Crown Prince, I'm in!"

Standing change. Nicole ton Savoia's opinion of you has improved.
Nicole ton Savoia's present opinion of you: +83 (completely trusting)

Standing change. Empire Military faction opinion of you has improved.
Present Empire Military faction opinion of you: +59 (veneration)

A change of my personal standing with the Imperial Military? In general, I thought such a change could only be initiated by an officer of general or admiral rank, or that an admiral had to agree to such a proposition by a lower-ranked officer. I looked at Nicole ton Savoia and met her gaze. The girl melted into a happy smile. I didn't clarify, even though I didn't understand if Nicole had already obtained such authority to speak for the Imperial Military Faction, or her decision was supported by some admiral friends.

"Alright, Nicole. Then take ten of your fleet's best frigates and ten of the best light cruisers. Have them join the 'national team' at the seventh planet of the Paada system. We'll have all the best ships of all the fleets. We'll have one practice session to learn to work together, then right to battle."

*   *   *

"And now I'm satisfied. All the ships are working exactingly in formation, holding position, carrying out their missions and not getting lost. I've got no complaints!" I said into the microphone, and got an elated roar of human and nonhuman voices in response.

Eight hours of practice... I was nearly falling off my feet in exhaustion. The crews, chosen from the best starships of all the Unatari fleets, were as well. It had taken much longer than I'd imagined to perfect our coordination.

"Half an hour break. Then we'll work again on our entrance to the enemy blocked system and closing the distance. If it all goes off without a hitch again, we can jump to the Uvi system and tear into the Blue House starships awaiting us there."

Again, their reply was an elated roar from hundreds of throats. The morale of the light fleet crews was above all praise — no one considered the upcoming battle hopeless. Quite the opposite, all the captains were proud of the fact that they had been chosen to join the best of the best and get our sweet revenge on the Blue House for destroying the Yayho Border Fleet.

I walked into the lounge cabin on the *Curse-80* light cruiser, which I had chosen as a flagship for the upcoming battle. The officers and captains stood in respect when I entered. I sat at an empty table, and Bionica quickly placed a tray with a warm meal on it, as well as pointing Nicole ton Savoia, who'd been walking with me, to a free seat.

"My Prince, I am very thankful to Your Highness for giving androids such a key role in this military operation," the synthetic beauty smiled at me. "And doubly thankful that you decided to treat them with as much care as living people."

I nodded. The first step in the operation I had planned was making wide gaps in the minefield. Twenty frigates, piloted by android crews, were supposed to make the warp jump approximately one minute before the rest of the fleet. All the participants in that suicidal breakthrough were to be restored in identical bodies with minds from premade backups. To me, it seemed like the least I could do, but it was perceived very positively both by the androids and military members of my fleet.

"Crown Prince Georg showed once again that all his

subjects are important to him, regardless of their race," Nicole confirmed, picking up her silverware. "The soldiers appreciate it and worship their commander, and what's more, their faith in Crown Prince Georg's ability to win in any situation is simply unwavering. In my Perimeter Sector Eight Fleet, there are some officers who aren't going to be taking part in the upcoming suicidal battle and are sincerely offended and envious of those lucky enough to have been chosen. I might be saying something seditious, but it will be the truth — if there is an upcoming split between the Unatari State and the Empire, a large part of the military would join Unatari's side."

"And what about you?" Bionica asked, immediately grabbing the opportunity to figure something out from the normally taciturn Nicole.

"I hope it doesn't get to that point," the young commander answered evasively.

Then I noted to myself the change in Nicole's emotional state. Just a week ago, the girl would have answered without hesitation that she would remain true to the Empire under any circumstances. But now, having seen confirmation of the fact that the ruler of Unatari trusted her completely and was prepared to assign her even the most important missions, the young fleet commander had begun to hesitate and think about the basis for her blind loyalty to the Empire. Taking advantage of the situation, I asked Nicole a question about herself: what did she want more of in life, now that her dreams of glory and military medals had come true?

Nicole ton Savoia sighed heavily and answered almost immediately, without a second thought:

"Right after my rapid ascent up the career ladder, I hit the ceiling. I have lots of experience leading star fleets in combat conditions and, as a commander, I am significantly more capable than the military civil servants in the Imperial Joint Chiefs, who have the power to raise my rank. They also understand that, so they will never agree to recognize my merits and will not allow me to become an admiral. They'll make excuses about my young age, insufficient number of years served, or find a bunch of other reasons why the commander of the magnificent Perimeter Sector Eight Fleet just cannot be given the rank of admiral."

"And, in human history, has there ever been an example of such a young star fleet admiral?" I asked Bionica, and she answered momentarily that she had not discovered any such cases in the database.

"And that's the whole thing!" Nicole shuddered. "My name could go down in history, if not for the rigidity of the Joint Chiefs bureaucrats!"

I drummed my fingers thoughtfully on the tabletop, because Nicole's dream was hard to accomplish, even for me, the ruler of a huge star government.

"Nicole, not all the admirals of my fleet have made rank through the Imperial Military. For example, the Alpha Iseyek Kheraisss Vej and Masss Azhzh became admirals through a vote in the Swarm and were appointed by the Swarm Queen. As the present Swarm Master, it isn't even a small challenge to me to give you the rank of admiral. But I'm afraid that such disdain for army traditions will be looked on negatively by the Imperial Military, so such a path is probably not for you..."

The girl nodded in silence, listening to carefully to

me and not moving her gray eyes from my face.

"Then I see only one path for you — prove your competency to even the most obstinate skeptics by winning in battle against several recognized admirals. You already have a certain reputation as a talented fleet commander, and you need to build on that. I will do everything I can to help you in this matter, but the main part of the work will have to be done by you. I'm afraid that even the King of the Unatari State is powerless to grant your wish. It would be easier to give you a title and appoint you ruler of a star system than to make you admiral of the space fleet..."

"Your Majesty, I understand..." Nicole said with sadness in her voice, then suddenly lit up and smiled: "Although my own star system and aristocratic title would also not bother me."

"Then Nicole, I offer you the following — if you succeed in the upcoming battle in Uvi, I will give you and your future descendants that star system in perpetual use. You have my word as a Crown Prince!"

Third Power

"THREE MINUTES to warp tunnel exit!" the captain's assistant of the *Curse-80* told me, and hurried to turn away so I wouldn't notice his pale lips and fingers shivering in anxiety.

But I not only noticed, but decided to point it out:

"What's got you so worried, space lieutenant?"

The young officer was clearly embarrassed, but still answered my question honestly:

"Yes, Your Majesty, I do have a bit of the willies. I'm worried about whether the frigate group managed to breach the minefield for us."

"Oh, that..." I waved it off with exaggerated carelessness. "You really don't have to worry about that, the enemy has played themselves here. What did the Blue House cloakers watching our fleet see? A group of one hundred fifty of our light ships accelerating toward the Uvi system warp beacon and jumping there at the exact same time. The enemy knows the flight time between the star systems, and the composition of our fleet, so there's really no nuances expected. I'd have fallen for it. What's more, at the exact estimated time, down to the second, a group of frigates will have arrived in the minefield, so it should have blown. But what the enemy was not expecting is that our ships didn't all make one long jump the whole distance, but two jumps with a minute break at a midway point. And that the frigate group arriving to the minefield started from a totally different part of the Paada star system. Of course, based on the time, the frigates should have already played their role and set off the thermonuclear mines. Now, our main fleet will show up on the arena. Bionica, countdown!"

My gorgeous blonde android put on her headphones and started counting down.

"Five, four, three, two, one. We've arrived!"

There was in fact no sudden explosion after that, so the space lieutenant's fears really were misplaced. As for me, I was hoping with my whole soul for our fleet to have a good arrival to the star system, so I sighed in relief, then issued a command:

"I need a tactical grid as fast as possible! Report on the situation!"

"The enemy fleet is twelve hundred miles away! A huge number of markers on the radar. Identification by radar signature is underway. Elevated background radiation. Lots of small debris."

Alright then, it looks like we made it just fine. The enemy must have slept through our arrival. Now, my fleet's mission was to get into combat formation and dictate the terms of the space battle to the enemy.

"All ships! Accelerate toward the second planet. Forty *Curses* go in a compact group. Do not release

drones for now. Radio-electric fighters after them —
twenty *Thrushes* and twenty *Umoyge*, maintain
distance of twenty miles."

"The enemy has begun maneuvers!" Nicole said,
and I also noticed that around three hundred small
red dots had started approaching my fleet. But the
majority of the small Blue House ships were still next
to their battleships.

I asked for the position of our cloakers to be
determined. I got an answer almost immediately that
Ghost-10 was fifteen miles from the core of the enemy
fleet, *Ghost-14* was at a safe distance, three thousand
miles away, as ordered, while *Ghost-11* had gone off to
the next star system Ukravi and was tracking
potential enemy reinforcements there.

"Great! First wing of stealth bombers, prepare for
attack. Get jump coordinates from *Ghost-10*. Report
back when ready. Only attack on my command,
otherwise you'll reveal yourselves and kill our recon
ships!"

"My Prince, do you really think the enemy doesn't
know we're going to bomb them? Look at how
compact their ship group is!" Nicole ton Savoia
posited with doubt in her voice.

"I'm sure that the enemy commanders will realize
we have stealth bombers, but not be expecting that
we are able to get them moving this fast..."

My speech was interrupted by a message from the
communications officer:

"Crown Prince Georg, incoming call request from
the battleship *Serenity*. It's the flagship of the Blue
House Second Fleet. Shall I put it through?"

I gave my permission and a frail gray-haired old

man appeared on screen in a Blue House Space Fleet uniform. After seeing his gold epaulettes and Five-Star Admiral patches, I realized I knew this man already:

Moridin ton Miro, Five-Star Admiral of the Empire, Commander of the Blue House Second Fleet
Age: 129 years
Race: Human
Gender: Male
Class: Military
Achievements: Meritorious Veteran, Ex-Head of the Academy of the Imperial Joint Chiefs of Staff, Author of many textbooks and treatises on space battle tactics, Has been awarded the Emerald Star and Silver Comet for participation in interspecies conflicts
Fame: +13
Standing: +24

"Before us is a true living legend! I read his textbooks in the Academy!" Nicole ton Savoia whispered to me, her head bowed in respect to the veteran.

"Yes, I am also familiar with his works on tactics," I confirmed. "But I thought he would have long been retired with honors..."

The gray old man on screen spent a few seconds trying to focus his weak eyesight on the screen, after which he creaked out:

"Alright then, I could have guessed. The unbeatable Crown Prince Georg royl Inoky ton Mesfelle — who else would have been foolish enough to dare jump toward my fleet? What can I say, Crown Prince? I'm a bit sorry that I'll have to break your streak of brilliant victories."

"What are you talking about, Five-Star Admiral?" I asked in sincere surprise. "My fleet has already successfully jumped to Uvi and now has every chance to defeat you. However, considering your long service and respectable age, I am willing to let your fleet retreat honorably, retaining all your ships. Believe me, Five-Star Admiral, I'm only doing this out of respect for you. In general, there are very few enemies I'd allow to avoid battle with honor."

But the old man still got offended at my words:

"Crown Prince Georg, you seriously underestimate me, and that rubs me the wrong way. I've spent half a century doing battle with enemies of the Empire and acquired significant experience in space combat. And after that, I spent three years lecturing young fleet leaders on battle tactics. Yes, I may be old now, and was already retired with honors until I was invited by Duchess Ovella to command this fleet but, trust me, no matter how good you are, there's no way I can lose with a six to one ship advantage!"

"My Prince, the first wing of stealth bombers is ready to attack!" the commander of the bomber squadron's voice rang out in my ear.

I gave an order to begin the attack and looked back at my ancient opponent.

"Five-Star Admiral, in my time, I read your tactics works in the most attentive fashion. It is all written from a very knowledgeable perspective. Your great experience really comes through. But military science is not stagnant. Methods of conducting space battles are constantly being perfected. Like now, you're referring to the alleged fact that you have more starships. But is that really so?"

I held a pause to give him the chance to evaluate the results of my bombing. Yes, the five *Surprises* did just the trick — from what I saw, not only were one hundred fifty or two hundred of the enemy frigates destroyed or damaged, but the cruisers took a serious blow as well.

"So then, back to the topic at hand, Five-Star Admiral," I continued, as if nothing had happened. "Twenty percent of your fleet is already out of commission and that's just the beginning. As such, I will return to my thought. An advantage in numbers just because you have a huge quantity of frigates is of absolutely no importance. In the end, the fleet that wins will be the one with the best trained crews and balanced starship composition, not some vaunted number."

"Let's see how Your Highness will talk when my frigates catch up with and immobilize your cruisers," he said with a slightly tortured smile. "Then, my battleships and heavy cruisers will go to firing distance..."

"If I allow them to do so," I parried. "Five-Star Admiral, if you think those three hundred frigates that are now trying stubbornly to reduce the distance to my ships will have even the slightest significance in battle, I'll order my fleet to stop."

Nicole, sitting to my right, shuddered and looked at me in alarm, hoping I had been simply joking, but I smiled reassuringly to my pretty assistant, then turned to Bionica:

"I need information about the main and reserve frequencies the Blue House fleet is using for communication, and also how their signals are encoded. Find out from your androids serving on the enemy ships. When you have that data, send it to our radio-electric fighters. Have them drown out any sensible information on these frequencies."

My synthetic assistant nodded in silence, although it seemed to me that the order didn't make the android too pleased. Oh well, she was worried, but I no longer had to expect any sensible actions from the enemy, for the next few minutes at least. Now was the very time to make use of that:

"All ships! Change trajectory toward the sun. Perpendicular to the previous course. Prepare to meet the first group of Blue House frigates. Small ship defense, split up into groups of five, pick your own targets. Fire at will, one volley, one ship down. *Curses*, only release your drones on my command, don't spook the enemy too early. Electros, deafen the nearest frigates. If the enemy's heavy calibers suddenly jump into close combat, electros immediately turn to them. As soon as they're within thirty miles, release drones. Get ready... Now!"

One thousand six hundred military drones, made from tech copied from the Aliens. Each such drone was no worse than a frigate-class ship in combat power, and even surpassed such ships in speed. It was all over in just one minute.

"My Prince, we lost four drones. No losses among our ships," reported Nicole ton Savoia, not able to keep the happy smile off her face. "This is just unbelievable!"

My assistant didn't say anything about the enemy losses, and there was no need to. I could already see that only a pitiful group of five *Pyros* had escaped, having rushed away from the terrifying slaughter where three hundred of their ships were shot down in just one minute. Neither the Blue House battleships, nor heavy cruisers made a warp jump into that meat-grinder in order to aid the dying frigates. Either they didn't have time, or didn't get such an order from the fleet commander. By the way, as for the commander...

The old man on the screen had a very gloomy look on his face and was holding his hand over his heart. Yes, it most likely was a severe trial for him, watching his fleet get taken down while unable to impede the bloody slaughter.

"Five-Star Admiral, I'm back," I said, drawing the enemy fleet commander's attention. "Your fleet is now half its initial size, while my fleet has yet to lose a single ship."

"What do you mean?" he lit up. "What about the few dozen Unatari fleet ships that blew up in our minefield?"

"Those were automated ships, uncrewed, all retired frigates — my modern take on fireships. Not a single living person suffered in the minefield explosion, while the several androids who did take part were backed up in advance so they could be restored after the battle."

That was the final blow for the old man. The Five-Star Admiral fell heavily into his seat and buried his head in his hands. His young assistant appeared on screen with a glass of water and some pills. I waited patiently for my opponent to come back to his senses.

"Crown Prince Georg," the old man finally said a few minutes later. "This is the first time in my life I've ever been so despondent. I'll be honest, I don't see any way of getting near the much faster Unatari ships without taking monstrous losses among my frigates. Staying where we are is also not an option; your cloaked bombers will just keep hectoring my ships. Every step I take has an effective counter. Yes, I still have a huge advantage in numbers and volley weight, but I just have no idea how to use it. How can I bring my battleships into play if my nimbler enemy can simply zip out of range?!"

"I'm glad that you've realized that, Five-Star Admiral. Yes, I came to Uvi with this fleet composition, because it's the perfect counter to your armada. My fleet's mission now will be simply to plague you, take nips at the remaining group of starships, then warp disrupt the most valuable of your ships when the Blue House Second Fleet tries to retreat. And you will be forced to retreat, because Unatari heavy ships are already speeding down a warp tunnel here. And that will include five carriers with fifty battleships each, which will leave you with simply no chance."

"Yes, I already know that. My recon ships saw your armada starting off," the old man agreed.

"See, you cannot win, Five-Star Admiral, so I'll return to my initial offer. I respect your past service and have absolutely no desire to see such a storied military career end with a crushing defeat. So, I offer to let you avoid complete ruin and flee to the Ukravi system with all the ships you have left. I want your descendants to think of you as a talented fleet leader and tactician, who managed to get his bearings in good time in a complicated situation and save his most valuable starships. But I do have one condition: before retreat, you evacuate the Blue House soldiers from the station. There's no reason for them to die ingloriously in battle with Alpha Iseyek. I give you three hours to collect them and promise not to impede the retreat of your ships. You have my word as a Crown Prince!"

The Five-Star Admiral thought very long and even conferred with someone I couldn't see on screen. Finally, the old man gave his reply:

"I accept your gracious offer, Crown Prince Georg royl Inoky ton Mesfelle. And at the same time, I relieve myself of my duties as Commander of the Blue House Second Fleet. I must admit, my time has passed. Military science really had made significant progress, and I wasn't prepared for all the changes. The fleet will be taken over by my deputy, Vice-Admiral Hugo ton Miro. He will evacuate the soldiers loyal to the Blue House from the station and remove the ships from the Uvi Star System. And I'd like to thank Your Highness for caring whether I retain my glorious name for my descendants."

Global standing increase. Current value: +8

Standing change. Empire Military faction opinion of you has improved.

Present Empire Military faction opinion of you: +61 (veneration)

The screen went dim. I gave an order to my ships to increase the distance from the Blue House fleet to eighteen hundred miles and not to take any aggressive measures. And when I got up from the console, preparing to leave my temporary headquarters, I was stopped by Nicole ton Savoia:

"My Prince, I understand everything. Five-Star Admiral Moridin ton Miro is an honored veteran, respected by the Imperial Military, so you had to treat him with respect. But why are we just letting his ships go? Why not try to capture the battleships with warp disruptor, so we can take them and include them in our fleet?"

I smiled good-heartedly at my beautiful assistant and even took some liberties, leading my hand through the girl's hair and putting a lock back in place.

"Nicole, I could, of course, answer you that it is just my whim as a monarch and say that I treated the elderly man favorably just out of a love of mankind. But you know me too well to believe that. I purposely gave the enemy three hours as a way of running out the clock. The cloaked frigate we captured from the Aliens is capable of opening mobile warp beacons in remote star systems, but it needs time to recharge. Just under three hours, as a matter of fact. And now, that ship will make it to Ukravi while the beacon is still on for the Blue House ships. Then, our main Unatari Fleet will come here from Uvi, recharge at the station, which we will take without a fight, and will be ready to continue the offensive. This way, even if the enemy turns off the Ukravi warp beacon, we will still get into the system. What's more, our five carriers will release a black cloud of frigates and destroyers right when they arrive, which will make it even further to the next warp beacons, and our incursion will then be unstoppable."

*   *   *

The trill of an incoming call woke me up. I tried to ignore it for some time and hoped the suicidal person trying to wake their dead tired monarch understood just how foolish their actions were and would sober up. But alas, no. The intra-ship call just wouldn't stop ringing, and I had to peel my eyes open to see which of my subjects had grown tired of living. It was my cousin, Duchess Katcrina ton Unatari, and that was strange.

She must have understood best of all just how exhausted I was after the battle in Uvi and accepting the official delegation of mayors from the large cities of the planets Uvi-II and Uvi-III, who had assured me they were fully loyal to my government and that there was no reason at all for an Alpha Iseyek landing party. The young Baroness Nicole ton Savoia-Unatari, who I'd appointed ruler of the Uvi star system, was perceived very positively. All formal questions of transition of power were quickly dealt with and the official event gradually gave way to a banquet with dances, live music and fireworks.

On my cousin's advice, I had been playing the role of a kindly monarch, enthusiastic to take two inhabitable planets under his wing. I had to have many personal conversations, listen to a heap of desires, requests and even denunciations. Near the end of the many-hour reception, I was so tired I could barely stay on my feet. It was good that, at the very least, the alcohol in my glass had been switched out for colored water, otherwise I would have certainly collapsed from the number of toasts to my health. I barely had the strength remaining to walk back to my cabin. So then, this must have meant something extremely out of the ordinary had happened, if Katerina had decided to wake me up just two hours later.

My cousin looked somewhat disheveled as if she herself had just now gotten out of bed herself, without having the time to get herself in order:

"Georg, turn on the big data screen! Duchess Ovella royl Stok ton Miro is giving an emergency speech to her subjects right now. Only the introductory part has happened so far, just the same threadbare statements about the Unatari State making a perfidious invasion of the Blue House without a valid cause, and that this is a holy war of humans against insects. Empty claptrap. Very few now believe in that, especially after we were greeted so joyfully as liberators in Uvi. But now is the most interesting part — my sources are saying that the Blue House is preparing to announce their secession from the Empire!"

I turned on the data screen. The young Blue House ruler had on flashy, blood-crimson lipstick. Her chestnut hair was put up high, emphasizing the crown on her head. Wearing an elegant dark blue outfit, she was telling the audience about her many unsuccessful calls for help from Emperor August. According to her speech, all her pleas to the Emperor

— guarantor off peace and upholder of the law — had gone unheeded and, meanwhile, the bloodthirsty insects were continuing to devour people in the Paada and Boti star systems...

"She's no orator, and a hopeless judge of psychology," my cousin noted with a smirk. "Do you really think a girl dresses like that when she wants to arouse sympathy?! If so, there would be no cosmetics. And what's more, the loud lipstick, and fancy rings and necklaces are a bit much. The hairstyle is also inappropriate to the situation, and her pants are just bad form..."

"Quiet, let me hear her speech!" I asked my cousin, and my advisor puffed out her lips in dismay.

The young Duchess gave a very long-winded and verbose speech, trying to use as many colorful comparisons and hyperboles as she could muster. I don't know who composed the speech for her, but I personally would have fired them immediately for incompetence. Finally, the ruler of the Blue House reached the point of her speech:

"Seeing how the mechanisms for guaranteeing our security inside the Empire are not working, the Blue House sees no more reason to stay part of the rusty, bureaucracy-laden fossil, which the once great Empire has become!"

Attention! The Blue House has seceded from the Empire!

"Well, what did I tell you cousin?!" Katerina couldn't hold back her emotions and spoke up.

"Ovella has no idea what she's doing!" I replied in

horror. "Only the Imperial fleet can hold back the Alien armada now on the border between Perimeter Sectors Thirteen and Sixteen. If those defenders leave, the only thing that will remain of the Blue House soon will be memories!"

But the young ruler, as it turned out, had her own impressions on the matter. Ovella announced that, on the Green House's initiative, a new state would be formed: The Grand Duchy, incorporating the Blue House, Green House and Purple House.

What was more, the Gold House was also interested in joining the new political alliance. According to her, for the first time in nearly two centuries, the reclusive Antagonists had decided to send observers and diplomats to get familiar with the political situation on the ground and assess the possibility of joining forces in the future. For now, there was no discussion of the Gold House joining the Grand Duchy but, in any case, Duchess Ovella saw a great success of her diplomacy in the fact that the two-century divide in humanity may soon have been overcome.

"Alright then, I see where has this game of political leapfrog got its legs," Katerina commented on the shocking news. "The Antagonists have finally decided to leave the shadows and openly announce their existence."

Meanwhile, the young ruler of the Blue House continued describing the advantages of the new military and political alliance to her subjects. Telling them that the united forces of the Great Houses not only could stop the insect invasion and their bloodthirsty leader Crown Prince Georg, but could also manage where the Imperial Fleet was powerless — to stop the Alien invasion of the Blue House.

To be honest, after such a brash announcement from Duchess Ovella, I grew internally on edge and expected a quick declaration of war on me from the Green, Purple and Gold Houses, as well as a message saying the Green and Purple Houses were leaving the Empire. However, none of that came to pass. The Duchess's speech continued and the topic gradually changed to internal political housecleaning in the Blue House, the ceasefire reached with one of the opposition blocks, and also newly appointed viceroys and ministers. I knew that nothing more interesting would be said, and turned to my cousin:

"I'll admit, all that left me with the sense of incompleteness. Why loudly declare you're leaving the Empire to form a Grand Duchy, when the other members of the new political entity, the Green and Purple Houses, would be remaining in the Empire? Why hope for military aid from other Great Houses when they are still not at a state of war with us?"

My cousin thought about it and agreed with me:

"You're exactly right, Georg. I also cannot escape the sensation that this is illogical. Judge for yourself: if the Green and Purple Houses leave the Empire right now and declare war on the Unatari State, how would that look from an outside perspective? A government loyal to the Empire at war against three separatist states. I think everyone would understand right away whose side the Emperor would be on! I get the impression that Duchess Ovella was rushing to reassure her distraught subjects after her armies' recent failures on the front and spoke too soon about her allies' plans to create a political entity independent of the Empire. I do not think she was supposed to reveal that secret so early. In one way or another, the general vector of the political situation was revealed to us by Ovella, so we need to make the appropriate preparations."

As soon as the young Duchess's speech was over, Katerina signed off. I now had no more desire to sleep. The enemy had made their move, even if it was an illogical and confusing one, but I needed to answer it somehow. I turned on the screen, called up the Imperial Warp Beacon map and that of neighboring states. It took me just a few seconds to find something positive in Duchess Ovella's speech — there were no direct transport routes between the Green and Blue Houses! The armadas of the greens and purples, who the young Duchess was counting on, could only reach her through the Imperial Core, or Antagonist space, and two Alien-controlled Perimeter Sectors, or through my Unatari State. I didn't even know which of those options was worse.

Taking Great House fleets through the Imperial Core was categorically forbidden. Yes, one time, Emperor August had allowed my Perimeter Sector Eight fleet to pass through the Core, but the political situation was much calmer then, and the size of my fleet didn't threaten the safety of the Empire as a whole. But now, it was very hard for me to believe that the paranoid August would allow the movement of a potential enemy through his star systems.

Going through Antagonist space? That would seem to be an option, yes. But such a route would mean first going through Blue House Sector Sixteen, then

Perimeter Sectors Fourteen and Fifteen, which had been overrun by the Aliens. Breaking through that way looked even less likely than my famous campaign through Alien-occupied Swarm systems. And if the Green House fleet was capable of such a feat, all that remained for me was to remove my ships from Blue House space and beg Duchess Ovella's apology, then start paying war indemnities.

The only option they really had was to try and make it through Unatari space, which would seem to be utter nonsense. However, practically all my military starships now were concentrated on the border with the Blue House and any treason in my border warp beacon staff would lead to armadas of opposing starships gushing through the undefended star systems of my state. I dared to say this potential threat mustn't be disregarded. Some of my ships needed to be returned to their places as soon as possible, especially to the most vulnerable Perimeter Sector Eight.

I didn't call up Bionica on the intra-ship phone, as my synthetic assistant's personal bunk was located no more than twenty steps from my own. So, I just threw on a robe and headed into the corridor accompanied by the semi-transparent Rosss and a group of bodyguards. My electronic pass allowed me to open absolutely any door on my flagship *Joan the Fatty*, so I pressed the plastic key against Bionica's door and went in.

It took me no more than a second to realize that I had come at a very bad time. On the floor was a heap of clothes in utter disarray. On the bed were two naked women, their bodies intertwined. Two pairs of eyes were looking at me, wide open in fear, those of my synthetic secretary and an aristocrat I had just elevated to the rank of baroness.

"Uhhh... Please excuse me. It seems I've come at a bad time," I said in embarrassment, stumbling back out the door and at the same time chasing my overly curious security detail into the hall. "Bionica, come see me in the morning. I've got a few assignments. Nicole, I'm gonna need your fleet tomorrow as well."

Both of the beauties nodded in perfect time, after which I closed the door to the cabin. The whole awkward situation amused me and even made me laugh. I was reminded of a change that had taken place just after I had brought Bionica into the headquarters of the Perimeter Sector Eight fleet as a translator and assistant. Even my daughter Likanna had noticed that Officer Nicole Savoia started putting on lipstick and using cosmetics. But at that time, no one had guessed the true reason why.

I returned to my bunk in an excellent spirit. I was even thinking of inviting Valian ton Corsa for a visit — the redheaded beauty was back to actively making eyes at me, hinting at the possibility of continuing our affair. I technically even had a reason to celebrate: the brilliant victory in Uvi, but I still refused the idea of a little nighttime debauchery. I needed a fresh head for tomorrow, because the fast-changing political situation demanded serious consideration.

Ten minutes passed before a hearty knock came at my door and Bionica entered, already wearing a flawless light beige business suit. The android was bringing me a hot coffee and sat down in an armchair next to me.

"My Prince, I am again prepared to fulfill my duties as Your Highness's secretary."

While I took tiny little sips of the burning hot aromatic beverage, my synthetic blonde told me, despite not having been asked:

"Nicole and I have long been close. It started when we worked together on *Queen of Sin*. She made the first move, and I couldn't find the strength inside to refuse. Although I do understand that I am a robot, an object that does not factually own itself, and that my master may not like these encounters, Nicole never used service commands and does not have superadministrator rights over me. But still I crave intimacy with her. One day, our paths diverged, seemingly forever — I flew away on *Star Mutt*, while my girlfriend headed to the Throne World to teach space battle tactics. But now, all this time later, we've met again in this huge Universe. I invited her to celebrate her new title and star system, and Nicole agreed readily. To be honest, I was afraid to meet her. After all, Nicole is now a titled aristocrat, and I understand how negatively society perceives liaisons between a robot and a noble. But the Baroness was glad to see me again and said that she missed me a lot. And I also missed her a lot. Strange for a robot, right?"

"Bionica, you haven't been a soulless set of predictable algorithms for a long time. You're something much bigger. You have living emotions, behave exactly like a person, and even make behave illogically on occasion. I came to mentally consider you a human long ago, not a robot, and the story of your meetings with Nicole only confirms that I was right to do so. At one time, I promised you I would consider allowing androids to get special implants to express your personal relationship to various people, factions and even states. I feel that moment has come, and you will become the first such android. You precisely will then create the Imperial Androids faction and will include other humanoid robots in it, unique personalities that you consider sufficiently developed. What's more, I want to give a gift to your new faction. The Alpha Iseyek landing troops are just finishing cleaning up the systems we won from the Aliens, and one of the inhabitable planets there will be given to the androids to build their own society."

I was forced to cut off my fiery speech, because the synthetic beauty suddenly collapsed before me on one knee and began shedding a flood of tears.

"My Prince, you have no idea what exactly you've just done for us androids! Crown Prince Georg, I was hoping greatly that this day would come, but I honestly believed it would never happen! I swear that we will never forget this gesture! It will give you hundreds of millions of workers and scientists fanatically loyal to Your Highness, as well as new factories and laboratories, taxes and investments, innovative technologies and military starships. But I am afraid that the Green House will come out categorically against Your Highness's decision..."

"Stand up straight, Bionica, and never kneel to anyone again! You are a free and conscious being, not an object, nor a slave. I really do not care how the Emperor or heads of the Great Houses react to my innovations. You showed with your example that androids can be sufficiently independent in making even the most important decisions. And I am prepared to defend your validity as distinct personalities and as a political faction. For the first six months, I expect all the faction's actions to be agreed on with me in advance, as well as everything related to your planet's development. But then, I will give you full decision-making rights. You have my word as a Crown Prince!"

An account balance change alert trilled out, and I froze in surprise. Bionica had already long been in charge of my personal finances, and my personal intervention was needed only if an outgoing or incoming sum was greater than half a billion. So now, when I opened the finance window, my eyes crawled up into my forehead. A thirty billion credit deposit!!! I met eyes with my smiling assistant.

"That's my personal gift to you, Crown Prince. For the last few months, my robot friends have been transferring money to my account to support their interests. Along with that, I was asked to try and buy a remote star system where the androids could be totally independent and build a society of their own. It seems to me you have just fulfilled my subjects' request."

I couldn't find the words to answer my wonderful assistant. But then I looked at the time and said with a smile:

"Tomorrow, the Perimeter Sector Eight Fleet is heading back to patrol its own zone of responsibility. I suspect that the enemy may try to break through our lines there. So, perhaps Baroness Nicole ton Unatari-Savoia will soon get the chance she always wanted to meet face to face with the greatest admirals of the Purple and Green Houses and prove in battle that she deserves the high rank of admiral. Go and personally tell your friend about this. I definitely won't be needing you until morning, so don't waste any time. The two of you have only one night before another long separation."

HOUSE OF CARDS

"THIRTY BILLION?!" my cousin threw herself back in her chair and laughed uncontrollably, even spilling a glass of vitamin-enriched juice she was holding.

It was nice to look at Katerina today — for the first time since the death of her husband Corwin, she was smiling and even displaying vibrant emotions other than hatred and animalistic scowling, which had been marring her face for the last few days. And although she still had on a dark mourning outfit, today it was a form-fitting black suit with silver hem — a clear step forward in comparison with the formless black robes my cousin had been wearing since her husband's passing.

"Duchess Katerina has already digested her sorrow and returned to her normal calm state," came the voice of Florianna, ringing out in my head. *"Now, she is just pretending to mourn and, if not for the risk of a negative reaction, she'd have changed this stylish black suit for a bright glamorous dress."*

Maybe that was so, but I wasn't going to judge my

cousin for leaving her many-day depression and her currently good mood. Quite the opposite. I considered it my debt to support her renewed interest in life and actively supported conversation.

"What are you thinking of doing with all that cash, Georg? Are you gonna start building combat ships for your fleets again?" my cousin wondered after she'd finished laughing.

Yes, that was probably exactly what I'd do. Order two new *Quasar*-class carriers at the Fia and Unatari docks. In seven months, they'd be ready and substantially increase the power of the Unatari First Fleet.

Duchess Katerina ton Unatari winced and got a dismayed look on her face:

"It'll take too long. I'm fairly certain all the big political events will be long over by then."

"Then, it's probably better to invest in battleships," I suggested. "Fifty *Tyrants* with the most advanced weaponry. The first of them could enter formation in just four or five months. Although... that's no good either... The Throne World won't be allowing me to buy high power laser cannons anyway. And getting enough warp drives for all those heavy ships would also cause complications."

"A few combat ships in six months is too long and will do nothing to help in the war with the Blue House. I have a totally different idea, Georg!" Katerina leaned toward me and said with a predatory smile. "Give me that money, and I'll find it a much more effective application."

At first, I thought my second cousin was making a joke that didn't quite land, but Katerina remained absolutely serious.

"Cousin, you're accustomed to behaving in a forthright manner and getting what you need just by brute force. But, victory can be achieved by other methods as well. Many military leaders, viceroys and governors can be bought. And that's especially relevant now, when the Blue House is being shaken by the most serious internal and external problems, and people are totally unsure of their future. Thirty billion credits could mean dozens off star systems joining your side without firing a single shot, even clearing a path to the very capital of the Blue House. It would be a blow to the political body of the Blue House, which will fall after that like a house of cards."

Katerina was speaking very convincingly and managed to get my interest with her original suggestion. I thought hard. She was right. A few additional ships six months from now would not significantly alter the balance of forces on the military or political map and would do nothing at all to help in the current war. If my cousin's suggestion did work... anything could happen, right? What if I really did manage to take a few Blue House star systems without fighting? Overall, I gave my theoretical agreement, just asked my cousin what kind of accounting she'd be using for the money. Katerina made an impossibly surprised face, then laughed:

"Georg, I don't really understand what you're on about. What do you want in the end? You need receipts from the viceroys and old officers of the Blue House for bribes with concrete sums and dates? Or do you want the civil servants we've bought off to pay taxes on graft?"

"Don't play the fool, Katerina," I frowned, as my cousin's jocular manner was absolutely inappropriate. "You understand perfectly that such a colossal sum requires a bit of financial oversight. This way, it won't seem like we just got a couple of decommissioned wash basins and backwater planetoids with five inhabitants, while thirty billion credits just went missing mysteriously..."

"Alright, Georg," my cousin immediately grew more serious. "I can provide you with a list of the Blue House aristocrats, civil servants and military leaders I'm planning to work with. I'll compose it myself. The list will contain concrete maximum sums that can be reasonably spent on this or that person, depending on their importance and title. If it ends up cheaper — great, but it definitely won't be more, don't worry about that. And I'll also need a certain amount to shore up media coverage. After all, we'll have to explain all the influential Blue House politicians and aristocrats joining our side. This way, it will be seen as yet another success of our diplomacy, and not just be blamed on our deep, open pockets."

"My Prince, for some time I have been unable fully check Duchess Katerina ton Unatari, so I am not certain if she is personally financially interested. I cannot say where such a powerful psionic block to mind reading is coming from. It wasn't there before. Now, I can sense only her general emotional condition — the Duchess is overwhelmed with elation, along with anticipation and impatience."

"As for the mental block, don't worry. That's all according to plan," I thought, mentally answering my little Truth Seeker. *"I asked Miya to make a reliable*

defense against mind reading for all participants of my private secret conferences. And as for Katerina's personal interest... sure, I hear what you're saying and will check the list and suggested sums. If I find her suggestions basically fine, then I don't see anything disgraceful in my cousin trying to skim a bit of money from a few of the transactions for personal profit. She's a beautiful woman, and also a Duchess. She needs lots of money for the dresses, jewelry and servants that befit her station. Let my cousin get the funds she needs so she won't be vulnerable to bribery by my enemies."

"My Prince, you are a wise ruler, and it's not for me to judge your actions and decisions. Although, I'll admit, I don't like that I cannot check the loyalty of the people closest to you."

"I suspect, Georg, that your extended silence can only mean one thing, you are currently checking my sincerity with the help of your Truth Seekers," Katerina stated with a crafty smile, and it took me a lot of effort to not shudder at how accurate her guess was.

Without waiting for any sort of answer, my cousin continued:

"Well, I totally understand your fears and am ready to give you a full account of every outgoing transaction. But now, cousin, if you're not opposed, I'd like to speak about something else entirely. It has already been several hours since Duchess Ovella's speech, but I still don't see any signs of activity from the Gold, Green or Purple Houses. No confirmations of the young Blue House ruler's words have arrived, but there have also been no denials. Georg, you are fairly close with the head of the Purple House Duke

Takuro royl Andor, after all. Could you maybe carefully sound out the situation with the old man? We don't know what to expect from the Purple House. Maybe he'll answer you honestly."

My cousin had once again guessed what was worrying me with surprising accuracy. It was the lack of any reaction from the Purple House that was worrying me most of all. Two times that morning, I tried to get ahold of Duke Takuro, but both times the secretary of the Purple House Head told me his boss was very busy and couldn't speak with me. And that was very strange.

I grew gloomy, stood from the chair and, placing my hands behind my back, walked over to the viewport. I looked in silence for some time at the dark side of the planet Uvi-IV, a lifeless desert.

Should I try to speak with the Purple House ruler again? Such importunity on my part was bordering on barbarity. If Duke Takuro refused to speak with me two times, that meant he had no desire. Nevertheless, I called the communications officer yet again and asked him to put me through with the head of the Purple House.

Nothing happened for a long time, and I had already decided that it wouldn't even go through this time. But suddenly the screen lit up, and I saw a very old Duke Takuro surrounded by a group of bodyguards. Right away, I noticed that his face looked tortured with exhaustion, and was marked with deeply sagging eyes. Only after that did I notice the Duke was wearing a light spacesuit. Then I noticed his backdrop — a metal wall, a viewport and the blackness of space beyond it.

"How glad I am at the chance to finally negotiate with someone not mixed up in the bloody chaos of the last few days!" Duke Takuro royl Andor said, greeting me with a brief nod. "Crown Prince Georg, before we get disconnected again, I beg you to shelter my granddaughter the Crown Princess Joan royl Reyekh in your Unatari State and provide reliable protection for her!"

That caught me completely off guard, and I turned to my advisor Katerina, but she just shrugged her shoulders in surprise — she also didn't know what was going on. I asked the old man to tell me more.

"There's no time for a long conversation, Crown Prince Georg! The conspirators are blocking all my attempts to communicate with the outside world, and now are just about to find where I escaped to from their bell jar. My ship cannot escape this star system, so this is the end for me. And because of that, I repeat my final desperate plea — Crown Prince, I beg you to rescue my granddaughter Joan. She is now locat..."

The screen suddenly went blank and the sound shut off. But I had already managed to figure out that something was amiss in the Purple house. The phrases: "bloody chaos," "conspirators," and "I beg you to rescue my granddaughter," didn't leave any doubts about the Duke having been deposed.

"Katerina, get our diplomat in the Purple House on the line this instant, and also call the Purple House ambassador to Unatari. I need to know right now what kind of mess is going on there!"

"Yes, I would also like to know," my cousin said, placing an empty juice glass on the table and walking out of the berth at a quick pace.

*   *   *

Just after the doors closed behind Katerina, one of the usually silent guards standing at the door drew my attention, calling me by name, then took a few steps in my direction. Instantly, my chameleon bodyguards and the Alpha Iseyek Rosss appeared from invisibility, a semi-transparent barely noticeable shadow flittering before me.

"My Prince, that is an Arite. He has absolutely no bad intentions," Florianna informed me.

The soldier stopped all on his own and, changing form from the brawny guard to Princess Astra in a pair of fluffy white pajamas and showing everyone his empty hands. I had always wondered where Arites' old clothes went after changing shape, and whether their laser pistols could actually shoot, or were just mere decoration. But my Arite Iseyek subjects always shrunk from answering these questions and asked me to respect the secrets of their race. I didn't raise this topic this time, showing my guards to relax with a gesture and letting the Arite through to me.

False Astra, absolutely indistinguishable from the real one, got up and sat with her legs crossed in a deep leather armchair, adjusting her disheveled purplish pink hair with her hand. To be honest, seeing my favorite like that knocked me off track and I ordered the Arite to pick a different appearance. A few seconds later, the ever-vigilant chameleon Popori de Cacha was sitting in the armchair opposite me.

"Tuki-tuka-de-sa, is this better?" my bodyguard wondered, and I gave my consent. "Your Highness probably doesn't know this, but when the cruisers

One-Eyed Python and *Emperor August* exploded in the Forepost-22 system, eight Arite Iseyek perished. Their bodies, for obvious reasons, were not found — nothing remains of us in a vacuum. Nevertheless, this is the largest single loss our race has sustained in the last three thousand or so years..."

"I really didn't know that, but I sincerely mourn your dead," I assured the extraterrestrial being. "Now, I will do everything in my power so the Blue House won't escape responsibility for their treacherous attack."

The chameleon bowed to me and started speaking in a barely audible whisper:

"In view of the extreme nature of the situation, the Arite Iseyek have conducted our own careful study of that tragic event. Yes, the Blue House was behind the attack on the ships docked on the station, but both of the bombs that destroyed the starship had been on the cruisers long before that."

"What do you mean?! Where did you get this information?" I asked, starting to squirm because, if someone had managed to place bombs on my ships long before entering Blue House territory, the issue was turned completely on its head.

"Crown Prince Georg, one of the special powers of my race is that we have the natural ability to detect electronic or energy systems at a fairly great distance. At the border station, two Arite Iseyek technicians servicing the docked starship noticed the very high-power bombs hooked into the electrical systems of the cruisers. But the technicians didn't think it very important and didn't raise the alarm, because they thought the bombs to be an element of defense for the diplomatic ships, to prevent their capture."

I frowned. That meant that both of the bombs had already been planted while the ships were in my space. I wondered who did it... The picture being painted was really very nasty. Someone knew exactly which ships were going on the diplomatic mission, and had sabotaged them in advance. The Arite then judged my silence and gloomy appearance to mean I didn't believe what he was saying and tried to convince me:

"Your Highness, do you really think the assault divisions from Forepost-22 were able to get through all your defenders to the cruiser reactors, opening several armored doors on the way, then carry in the bombs, take down whatever automatic security was on the starships, hook the bombs into the power system and set countdown timers, all in just a few minutes?"

"I have no idea, Arite. I have never blown up a starship from the inside, so I have no idea how much time it would take to do so. But it wouldn't be too hard to figure it out by asking specialists or doing a real-life test. Alright, I'll take your important information into consideration and will be sure to figure out where the bomb on my starship came from. Are there any other questions for me?"

False Popori de Cacha nodded his disproportionally large chameleon head with an important look and stated:

"Crown Prince Georg royl Inoky ton Mesfelle, I have been vested with the authority to make an official proposal on behalf of my entire species. The Arites request that you allow us to disappear forever, dissolving into the human race."

To be honest, that was the last thing I was expecting, so I was totally thrown off.

"Explain why you want that," I demanded and the chameleon answered readily:

"Your Highness, as a matter of fact, there are very few members of my race and we are already on the verge of complete extinction. Two hundred years of war with the Swarm reduced the Arite population to a critically low figure. There are less than three hundred of us left. So, the death of eight Arites at once was a catastrophic loss. After a long discussion, we came to the conclusion that the most reliable method of protecting our species would be to dissolve into your very numerous and strong race, becoming absolutely indistinguishable from the rest. In return for this protection, we are prepared to give up all our territories to humanity — sixteen star systems, containing four human-inhabitable planets with oxygen atmosphere."

I threw myself back thoughtfully into the armchair, nervously drumming my knuckles on the armrest, then voiced my decision:

"Well, I'd be losing a valuable reconnaissance tool... But alright, Arite. I understand your critical condition, take into consideration the invaluable aid your race has provided me, and am prepared to give my agreement. You can dissolve among the people of Unatari, but only after the Arite Iseyek delegation sent to the Green House returns!"

* * *

My fleet did not encounter any resistance in the Ukravi system. In fact, we didn't detect any enemy ships at all. There were no inhabitable planets in the system, while the space station had surrendered to the Unatari State without a fight, along with a couple dozen orbital factories for extracting rare-earth metals from asteroids. However, what seemed very surprising to me was that the next warp beacon in our path stayed lit as if nothing had happened. The enemy was not trying to stop my ships from getting through. So, right after restoring my starships' energy, we went onward, splitting up into three big fleets of one thousand starships each.

By the middle of the day, I finally managed to get some information about the events in the Purple House. The official channel of the Purple House was saying that the grandson of the Duke, Perimeter Sector Five Fleet Commander Khayt royl Andor ton Reyekh, had died suddenly. They stated that the heir to the Imperial throne had died in an accident. The Crown Prince had his own space menagerie with the most dangerous beasts from all kinds of planets, and preferred feeding them by hand for the thrill of it. The official story was that the Crown Prince lost vigilance and got too close to one of the dangerous beasts, which ended up killing him.

In the same broadcast, they said that the head of the Purple House, Duke Takuro and his two sons had abandoned all affairs and immediately headed to Perimeter Sector Five for their family member's funeral. The absence of the Purple House Head was explained as him mourning his late son in the capital, and the same explanation was given for his unavailability.

"The official version doesn't line up all that well with what we heard from the Duke himself," my cousin Katerina snickered untrustingly when she brought me a tablet with lists of visible Blue House figures.

But we didn't have any additional information. The Unatari State Ambassador to the Purple House also didn't have any additional news, although he had noticed an elevated activity level among Purple House military and Security Services. I couldn't get in touch with Marat ton Mesfelle, Perimeter Sector Seven Fleet Commander, either. My cousin then informed me that all her acquaintances from the Purple House were also silent. And they could not establish the location of Crown Princess Joan royl Reyekh, who Duke Takuro had asked me to keep safe.

Duchess Katerina was in my bunk when a pair of system messages came in suddenly:

The Blue House has lost sovereignty over the Kiva system

The Unatari State has gained sovereignty over the Kiva system

I read them and turned to my cousin:
"Is this your work?" I asked, turning to her.
She shrugged her shoulders indefinitely.
"Oh yeah, that's right! Here it is. And bribing the viceroy of the Kiva system cost me just six million

credits."

My advisor didn't manage to finish her sentence before two new messages jumped in:

The military faction *Ancient Traditions of the Blue House* has sworn allegiance to the Unatari State

The Parliament of the planet Origa-II has voted in the majority to leave the Blue House and accept the jurisdiction of the Unatari State

My cousin stretched over to the computer again to find information about the new deserters, but I stopped her:

"No need. I get the gist. These are just the first fruits of your labor, still relatively insignificant. But if the Blue House doesn't take countermeasures at once, this scurrying of little pebbles might grow up into a real landslide that could bury the Blue House under it."

At that moment, a knock came on my cabin door and Bionica came in.

"My Prince, I'm sorry to disturb Your Highness. A message has arrived to your inbox that I think you should read. It's a request for confidential negotiations over long distance from Count Albert royl Timur ton Akad."

I strained my memory, but somehow couldn't remember anyone by that name, although the title of Count and Imperial Akad family name meant he must have had a very high position in the Imperial Hierarchy. My advisor Katerina, who had an extensive knowledge of the intricacies of the Great House genealogical lines, even spent a few seconds digging in her memory. Finally, her face lit up:

"If I understand correctly, that Count could only be from the Gold House. Someone from the tip-top of the Antagonists wants to negotiate with you, cousin. And to think, Georg, you thought your distant relatives from the Gold House were ignoring you!"

* * *

Sometimes, when you meet someone, you like them on first glance. Whether for their nice face, proud bearing, confidence or frankness, such things are known to happen. Unfortunately, this was the opposite situation... As soon as I saw the foppish aristocrat, looking pompous look like a turkey tom with the fastidiously bored expression of a life-weary hedonist, I immediately guessed that we would not manage to have fruitful negotiations. Count Albert looked like a parody of Crown Prince Georg royl Inoky ton Mesfelle as I had seen him in my very first day in *Perimeter Defense*. The very same body, sloshing around in two hundred extra pounds of blubber, eyes flitting, obnoxiously expensive clothes with an unthinkable number of huge gems sewn into the fabric and adorning the hands that had never known hard physical labor, weak like a child's.

Albert royl Timur ton Akad, Count of the Gold House, official voice of the Triumvirate
Age: 69 years
Race: Human

Gender: Male
Class: Aristocrat/Mystic
Achievements: Playboy
Fame: +3
Standing: -44

Playboy? And also a mystic, firmly under the sway of narcotic crystals? And the Count's standing was also in the gutter. An exact copy of myself a few years earlier. It must be noted that it was a very unattractive spectacle from an outside perspective.

Only after a bit did I see something I should have noticed right away, "official voice of the Triumvirate?" Just what was this Triumvirate? The Count opted to explain on his own, having noticed the incomprehension on my face.

"Our eternal ruler, the Empress Eleonora is no longer young and cannot keep track of all the complex processes of external and internal Gold House politics. So, for that very reason, the Empress appointed three important politicians a little while ago, who she trusted fully, to be her eyes and ears. It is the Triumvirate that controls the Gold House now. The Empress intervenes in state affairs less and less every day. The names of the Triumvirate members will remain a mystery, because some of them live in Imperial space, not under Gold House control. Nevertheless, they are the co-rulers of the Gold House and are just as fully in control of their duties as I am. And I am the one who voices their orders and decisions, as the official voice of the Triumvirate."

Mental messages came in from both of my Truth Seekers:

"My Prince, I was not able to determine the names of the Triumvirate's other members — these Antagonists have a very powerful mental block, which I cannot get through. Perhaps Queen Miya will manage?"

"No, I was also not able. But Flora and I did manage to reflect the attempt by the Gold House psionics to probe your mind."

The man on the screen frowned in dissatisfaction, then his lips stretched out into a crooked smirk.

"Crown Prince, I've just been told that you tried to play dirty. I think you've already understood that trying to steal any information from my mind is useless. The Gold House was always celebrated for its most powerful Truth Seekers, and our best of the best did everything they could to lock up the names of our co-rulers safe and sound."

"My Truth Seekers also told me about an unsuccessful attempt of your psionics to dig in my brain," I answered the Count calmly. "So, the Antagonists are also not trying too hard to stay honest."

"Antagonists? How dare you say that vile word!" he objected, raising his voice to a whine bordering on ultrasonic and taking a sharp step back as he went bright red in indignance. "We have never been antagonistic to the Empire. As a matter of fact, we represent the legitimate legal ruler, not having supported the military putsch by Crown Prince August."

Global standing decrease. Current value: +7

Standing change. Count Albert's opinion of you

has worsened.
Current value: -34 (dislike)

***Standing Change. Gold House opinion of you
has worsened.***
Current value: -34 (dislike)

***Standing Change. Gold House opinion of the
Unatari State has worsened.***
Current value: -11 (disapproval)

I was slightly taken aback. Had that whole flood of negative messages about my standing and relationships of the Unatari State really been just a virulent reaction of the Count to my calling his state "the Antagonists?" How could he react so hysterically to a term, which had been common parlance in the Empire for almost two centuries?

"I hope that standing decrease will teach you better manners, Crown Prince Georg," the fat man on the screen said with a mischievous chuckle.

If he had kept silent, I wouldn't have even paid particular mind to the decrease of my personal standing. Just think how many times my standing had jumped up and down recently. One point more or less wouldn't even be noticed. But Count Albert's words enraged me — that fat man had wanted to teach me manners?! He had the gall to try and train me like a dog?!

"Miya, I have an order for you to send. All Unatari citizens with implants must immediately reflect their negative opinion in Count Albert royl Timur ton Akad's profile, as well as that of the whole Antagonist faction."

I also opened my internal interface and mirrored all the fat man's actions. After that, I threw myself back in my armchair with a glass of vitamin-enriched juice in my hand and watched a very curious spectacle — Count Albert convulsed like a vampire seeing a cross. His lips started quivering. The moderately aged aristocrat was nearly crying from resentment and impotence. And there was something to get upset about. Albert's standing, already not too polished, fell in just a few minutes to minus two hundred and was not about to stop. In addition to that, the Count found a way to get three new achievements in his profile: "Hopeless Diplomat," "Scorned by Mankind," and "Steamrolled." From what I'd seen, many factions had supported this attack — the Imperial Military, Artists, Financiers, Scientists, all Swarm races and even the Chameleons and Mechanoids had reduced their opinion of the Voice of the Triumvirate and the whole Gold House. A six-point fame increase was scant compensation.

"Alright, enough! I admit I was wrong!" came Count Albert, unable to bare the focused informational attack and begging for mercy.

I sent an order through Miya to stop the flood of standing changes. When the flow diminished, the man familiarized himself with his statistics and gave a nervous shudder.

"Aha... I've had the chance to read your dossier, Crown Prince Georg. I could have guessed such a reaction... But alright, I'll return to the main topic of the negotiations. Has Your Highness been made aware of the speech given by Blue House Head Duchess Ovella royl Stok ton Miro?"

After receiving confirmation, the plump man continued, now more confident:

"In that case, Your Highness must understand that the Blue House falls in the zone of interest of my rulers. The Gold House cannot stand quietly by as the Unatari State devours territories that will soon land under the control of the Grand Duchy. Yes, the young and inexperienced Duchess Ovella submitted to your crafty provocation, allowing her Blue House to be dragged into a war with Unatari, but was nevertheless smart enough to depict herself as instigator of the conflict. All the same, before these events even happened, the Blue House had been guaranteed protection, and the Gold House is preparing to fulfill its duty to its ally."

What was this, a declaration of war? I got on guard, but no irreversible words followed. Instead, the Count began to soften the formulation and limited himself to a warning. In his words, Duchess Ovella had jumped the gun with her announcement. They were even more peeved she had revealed the Gold House's plans to join the previously secret group. All the same, the Gold House really had already implemented plans to integrate the Blue, Purple, and Green Houses into one unified political structure.

"Just one month from now, there will be such forces defending the Blue House that Your Highness won't even dare cross the border. But now as well, although it will be somewhat delayed, the Gold House is prepared to intervene and finish this unnecessary war. With all due respect to your military talents, Crown Prince Georg, the Unatari Fleet is simply puny in comparison with the united forces of the Grand

Duchy. And I'm not even talking about the fact that modern Gold House ships are of much higher military value than Imperial ships of the same class. You will simply be forced out with numbers, and we'll barely even notice you. But the Triumvirate will give Your Highness a chance to avoid that war with your head held high. All territories that Unatari takes under its control within the next seven days may remain with your state. But by the end of the week, a peace treaty must be signed because, on the eighth day, Grand Duchy starships will arrive to the Blue House and begin patrolling the territory."

I fell into silent contemplation. The terms were very understandable — everything that the Unatari State could reach and get under its control in one week was promised to me under one condition: that I stop there and sign a peace treaty. On the one hand, it seemed like a generous offer, because open war with a fleet comparable in size to that of the entire Empire was something I definitely wanted to avoid. But on the other hand, might the Voice of the Triumvirate have been bluffing? The Gold and Blue Houses did border on the star map but, in reality, the Antagonists could only easily reach Sector Sixteen. The rest of Blue House space was separated by Alien-occupied sectors. How was the Grand Duchy planning to get their ships there through Alien territory? I asked that question to Count Albert.

"Good question, Crown Prince Georg, but it isn't possible to answer without revealing Gold House secrets. All I can do is swear on my aristocratic honor that there are ways of getting the ships there. I can also officially assure Your Highness that, after the end of the war, the Gold House will officially recognize all the Blue House territories you capture as Unatari space. You have my word as a Crown Prince!"

Then the man hung up. I spent some time sitting in silence, thinking over the present situation. I had one week. Not really that bad. My starships could reach a great many Blue House systems, especially if the enemy still had yet to come to their senses and offer resistance. But the Blue House was vast. Seven days was far too little time to capture even a third of their territory, which was to say nothing about Sector Sixteen, far away and cut off from the rest of humanity. I called Katerina and explained the situation.

"I can get more money, cousin. But what we really need now is time. So don't be stingy with the bribery fund! It's important to me that all aristocrats and viceroys willing to join our side for money get that chance within the next few days!"

My foreign policy advisor smiled predatorily:

"Well then, as they say, appetite comes when it's time to eat! Not very long ago, you thought it would be a good outcome if Unatari gained just Perimeter Sector Nine, now you want much more. And finally, you've unbound my hands, Georg! Let me assure you, cousin, this will be the greatest informational attack in the history of mankind! And also, it will be supplemented by cash injections so generous no one has ever seen the like. Thirty billion! Never in history has such a thing been seen. I assure you, Georg, by the end of the week, you will not recognize the star map!"

*　　*　　*

It happened on the fourth day.

My fleet entered yet another system with no resistance, Aarakh, and I was preparing to meet with a delegation of viceroys, mayors and visible local politicians, hurrying to personally tell me their burning desire to accept Unatari jurisdiction. It was a picture I'd grown used to in the last few days: a Blue House system, left to the winds of fate, whose defenders had retreated or defected to my side. Business as usual by then.

But suddenly, Duchess Katerina ton Unatari entered my room without knocking. My cousin was noticeably uneasy and immediately demanded that all servants leave the room, because she needed to talk with me alone. The massive number of makeup artists, costumers, and hair stylists preparing me for my speech hurried to leave us, but then my cousin pointed to the bodyguards:

"Georg, I advise you strongly to also send your guards away. This is an extremely confidential matter. You'll agree once you hear it."

My cousin managed to intrigue me. I trusted Katerina. And Florianna, now wide awake, was an excellent guarantee of my personal safety all on her own. So, I ordered the bodyguards to leave us, also letting Rosss and the chameleons go.

"What is the reason for such secrecy?" I asked as soon as the last of the chameleons was out of the room.

In response, Katerina unfurled a paper tube and showed me the hand-written note inside:

Captain Olaf ton Bogayan
Fifty million credits

"This is from the leader of one of the guard shifts at the Cloudy Palace, the residency of the Blue House rulers. He has permission to carry firearms in the Duchess's presence. Without attracting much suspicion from her other bodyguards, he could get to within shooting range of Ovella. He valued his efforts at fifty million. Half the sum in advance, and the rest after completion. He needs an answer in one hour."

It was good that I was sitting, because this news might have knocked me off my feet. I now had the unique chance to assassinate the enemy leader. Such opportunities weren't normally thrown around willy-nilly... But I was still in no rush to give my agreement. First of all, it could have been a Blue House provocation. The propaganda war was going rather one-sidedly in my favor, and if they could accuse me of the crudest violation of law, and have a real confirmation of that, it would come quite in handy. Second, I didn't see any particular reason to kill the weak ruler, who already de facto was not in control of the situation, because her heir could prove to be a more successful leader.

Anyway, who was next in the Blue House line of succession? Count Mark royl Ovar ton Miro? I had never heard a thing about this aristocrat, so I opened the guide. Ovella's first cousin. Thirty years old, he hadn't especially made a name for himself. Not a soldier, the type to avoid direct conflict. Loyal to the legal authorities, good relationship with his ruling cousin. He had a reputation as a taciturn politician, always ready to compromise. Nevertheless, he had repressed the separatist uprisings in his territories decisively and even harshly... A goody-goody, but also the kind of person, who would avenge the death of his cousin both calculatingly and viciously. Also, as the ruler of the Blue House, which was hostile to me, he seemed stronger than Ovella. No, it wasn't a good idea. I decided to refuse and turned to my cousin:

"My opponents have accused me of the death of many Crown Princes and Crown Princesses. The reality is that I haven't killed any. And I don't want to start now, when there really isn't a particular need for such an extreme measure. We can get by perfectly well without killing her."

"But Georg, this is a totally different thing. There's a war on. The Blue House is losing one system after the other. Their politicians cannot explain to their citizens why the soldiers aren't protecting them, garrisons are surrendering without combat, and more and more planets are voluntarily joining our side. The Blue House is stumbling and will surely fall. The Duchess's death might have a domino effect!"

"I said no!" I had to raise my voice. "No one can accuse the Sovereign of Unatari off sending assassins. That isn't our way. Pay the captain for his willingness to work with us. Let's say fifty thousand credits. But tell him we don't want Duchess Ovella dead."

Duchess Katerina, clearly upset at my decision, turned showily and, clicking her heels, headed out of my room. Already in the doorway, my advisor turned to me and said:

"Don't forget to send congratulations to your twin sister. It's already been in the news. Soon, the Purple

House will make an official announcement. You could learn a thing or two from Violetta. She's not so preoccupied with acting scrupulous..."

What was this about? I demanded to be put through immediately to the Ambassador of Unatari to the Purple House to figure out the situation, but then before my eyes jumped an important system message:

The Head of the Purple House, Duke Takuro royl Andor ton Reyekh, has died at age 232.

ATTENTION! The new head of the Purple House will be Duchess Violetta royl Inoky ton Mesfelle-Damir (75.8% of votes)

The ambassador, already dressed in situation-appropriate mourning outfit, confirmed that to me:

"Your Majesty, the authorities of the Purple House have informed me that there was a bomb attack on the mourning ceremony being held in honor of the late Crown Prince Khayt royl Andor ton Reyekh. Both of Duke Takuro's sons died there, and the head of the Great House himself took heavy injuries. The doctors fought for his life a long time, but eventually declared that he was beyond saving..."

"I see. Well, that was the very result that could have been supposed based on Duke Takuro's last words," I said thoughtfully and demanded to be immediately put through the newly-crowned Head of the Purple House.

I had to make sure I congratulated my sister for having become head of a second Great House in such a short time.

THE BLACK CLOUD
DISPERSES

VIOLETTA ANSWERED my call right from her dressing room, where there were servants preparing her for her first speech before the people as ruler of the Purple House. I still couldn't decide for myself what it was — a positive sign of trust and frankness or, on the other hand, a sign of disdain, as my sister didn't consider me sufficiently important to even get fully dressed before our conversation.

I said the appropriate words of congratulations, to which Violetta just nodded shortly.

"Will that be all, Georg? As you can see, I still need to get dressed."

So, disdain it was... A question tore itself spontaneously from me, although I didn't think long over the topic, forming various suggestions:

"No, this is all for now, dear sister. Just answer me one question. Who other than you is in the Triumvirate?"

By the way the Duchess shrieked in fear and

dropped her mirror, I realized I wasn't wrong. I hit my mark! Right on the money! One of the three co-rulers of the Antagonists had been outed. Violetta looked at me like a predator ready to throw itself on its prey. The woman's eyes were open wide, her pupils dilated in horror.

The person standing next to my sister, who I hadn't paid much attention to before that, taking her for a stylist or hair dresser, bowed to the Duchess and whispered something to her. My sister immediately calmed down and even found the strength in herself to smile:

"Guess that yourself? Or did your advisor Katerina tell you? Anyway, it doesn't matter one bit now. Tomorrow, or the day after at the latest, the foundation of a new military and political hegemon, the Grand Duchy, will be officially declared! It will surpass the Empire in every way: territory, population and manufacturing capabilities. And that's to say nothing of its military! All Imperial star fleets taken together will pale in comparison to the Grand Duchy's armada! And neither you, nor the so-called Emperor will have the power to interfere in its affairs!"

The Head of the Blue House, Duchess Ovella royl Stok ton Miro, has died at age 22.

ATTENTION! The new head of the Blue House will be Duke Mark royl Uvar ton Miro (24.3% of votes)

What the hell?! I hadn't ordered the assassination! Or had my cousin not managed to get the message to the captain of the palace guard in time? Ovella was just twenty-two years old, she couldn't have died of natural causes. My twin sister sharply cut off her bombastic speech and laughed uncontrollably:

"The look on your face, dear brother, is such that I immediately see who is behind the sudden demise of that prissy young girl! But how I understand you! Just imagine, we thought that dumbass Ovella responsible enough to bring her in on the plans of the Great Houses, and entrusted her with a great secret. But she proved her low intellect by blabbing at her press conference! Do you know, Georg, why the remaining Great Houses still have not joined the Blue House in declaring war on your Unatari State? Because we decided to punish Ovella for her loose tongue! They thought that losing part of the Blue House's territory would serve as a good lesson for her and check her pride! But you managed to get to her first! Well, brother, congratulations!"

I didn't deny my sister's conclusions. She wouldn't have believed my justifications anyway. Instead of that, I changed the topic:

"I need Duke Takuro's granddaughter, Crown Princess Joan royl Reyekh. I'm firmly convinced you know her location."

Duchess Violetta stopped smiling abruptly, her face attaining a dismayed and simultaneously apprehensive appearance.

"What do you want with her, Georg?"

Really, what? What well-founded excuse could I invent in this situation? I couldn't just announce to the newly-crowned ruler of the Purple House that I promised the old Duke Takuro to shelter his granddaughter, the legal heir to the Purple House throne and a direct competitor to the newly-crowned Duchess! Saying such a thing would mean condemning the girl to certain death. I had to take evasive action.

"Well, at the very least because the flagship of my fleet is named in her honor! And also, little Joan is the ruler of the Oort system in the Swarm cluster and is one of the main candidates for the title of Swarm Duchess! I really wouldn't want the girl to share the fate of her relatives, who passed so suddenly all at once. I hope you understand me, sister."

Violetta considered it seriously for a long time. It was funny to watch my sister drum her fingers on the table exactly the way I did in my moments of thought.

"Alright, brother, I'll tell you the truth. Crown Princess Joan is now hidden on a ship of the Perimeter Sector Seven Fleet, which has ceased to obey me, the legal ruler of the Purple House. The insurgents, led by our cousin Marat ton Mesfelle, are blocked into the Nayal, Simpo and Veyerde systems, having turned off the warp beacons there. I wouldn't have paid them particular mind, but those splitters are broadcasting propaganda to the neighboring star systems in the name of the underaged girl. In their provocative clips, they call for disobedience and say that Crown Princess Joan should be the new Duchess of the Purple House. It isn't seriously bothering me, but I am getting a bit annoyed. Georg, if you can talk the girl into leaving Purple House space, I promise to let her procession pass through to the Unatari border safe and sound, and not undertake any hostile actions. You have my word as a Crown Princess!"

"Alright, sis, I'll talk with the insurgents and send

them your offer."

The screen went dim, and Crown Princess Violetta signed off. I then, not wasting any time, demanded to be connected with the Commander of the Perimeter Sector Seven Fleet.

*   *   *

It hurt to look at Marat ton Mesfelle. The young and always flawless-looking commander was faded. His eyes were bloodshot from sleep deprivation, and were sunken in deeply, even with tears of exhaustion welling up.

"Crown Prince Georg, to be honest, I'm very surprised anyone was able to get in touch with my ships, despite the data blockade! All these last few days, the henchmen of the insurgent Crown Princess Violetta royl Inoky ton Mesfelle have been preventing us from contacting anyone."

"Well, my dear sister made an exception for me, allowing me the chance to speak with you for a short time."

The man noticeably stiffened up. I suspect that Marat had totally neglected the fact that Crown Princess Violetta was my twin sister, and was now probably reproaching himself for the fact he even let the call through. I had to reassure him:

"I have nothing to do with the insurgency in the Purple house and am now acting on the last will of Duke Takuro royl Andor."

The Perimeter Sector Seven Fleet Commander clearly didn't believe me, but at the very least, agreed to hear me out.

"Marat, in confirmation of my words, I'll send you a recording of my last conversation with Duke Takuro. There, I gave the old man my word as a Crown Prince that I would provide shelter to his granddaughter Joan royl Reyekh from the chaos currently underway in the Purple House. It didn't take me much effort to discover exactly where the little Crown Princess was hidden. And now, I am intending to provide Joan safe passage to the Unatari State, where the Princess will be under my protection. The new ruler of the Purple House gave me her word that she would not prevent little Joan from leaving her territory."

Marat laughed villainously in reply, even spitting on the deck of the starship in anger, which was generally an unallowable offence for any Space Fleet Officer. Such behavior was looked on as disrespecting the ship, the captain and the whole Imperial Military Fleet. To be honest, it shook me. Not able to hold back, I opened the relationship window, and reduced my personal opinion of the man by five points in one go, and also initiated a general reduction of the Imperial Military faction's opinion of the Sector Seven Fleet Commander.

It worked. Marat looked at the incoming messages, adjusted his uniform and stood up straight, no longer slouching with his elbows on the tabletop.

"Sorry, Georg. I'm just dead tired, and two hours ago I took a fragmentation wound to the chest. I haven't slept for three days. I'm only getting by on painkillers and energy drinks. But still, I know one thing for certain: you cannot believe a single word that trash Violetta says! Yes, Georg, forgive me for the sharp words, but your sister Violetta is an uncommon jerk and scoundrel!"

Marat looked carefully for my reaction, wanting to figure out how I felt about my sister. But I didn't speak in Violetta's favor, nor blacken her name, I just asked the man to continue.

"Georg, in the last few days, your sister has ruthlessly killed all of Duke Takuro's sons one after the next! Then five grandsons, the old Duke, and all the rest of the ruling house right down the line! The only surviving member of the Andor and Reyekh families, which ruled the Purple House for centuries, is Crown Princess Joan. All of her relatives have been offed, even the most distant! And you want to assure me that Crown Princess Violetta will let the very last and her main competitor to the throne escape her predatory paws?! Never in her life!"

I stroked the bridge of my nose in contemplation. I had no reason to doubt Marat's words. He was probably exactly right. It was really strange how easily Duchess Violetta had agreed to let Crown Princess Joan out of the trap in the blocked Sector Seven star systems. On the other hand, Violetta's coronation would begin and, any minute now, she would be declared ruler of the Purple House. In a few days, the whole messy situation would simply lose all meaning, because the Purple House would cease to exist, having joined the Grand Duchy.

"Crown Princess Violetta was not being sincere, Georg," Flora told me. *"Your sister just wanted the rebelling Perimeter Sector Seven Fleet ships to jump out to meet a Purple House fleet lying in wait. I have almost no doubt that, right after that, there will be an order from Duchess Violetta to eliminate the*

insurgents."

"Alright, Marat, I agree with you. After everything you've just said, my sister's promise to let little Joan go looks somehow strange. On the other hand, the Purple House will very soon cease to exist as an independent entity. Crown Princess Violetta is preparing to join the Grand Duchy. That means there will no longer be a throne for little Joan to lay claim to."

The man winced in pain, clearly suffering from his injury, then he shook his head in doubt:

"That is news to me, Georg. I haven't heard about any such plans. But even in that case, Duchess Violetta will never let Joan or the fleet loyal to her go. The new Grand Duchy has absolutely no need for representatives of former authorities, which the people may still support. But at that, the insurgent Duchess has a great need for my flagship *Peacemaker*. The pride of the Purple House, it's a practically finished *Quasar* carrier! Just five hours ago, that piece of trash Violetta promised billions for whoever kills Joan or at least turns on the Nayal warp beacon! And to my enormous pity, she found some takers among my officers. It took a good deal of effort to suppress the insurgency she inspired on my flagship."

I started thinking feverishly, counting through options and refuting them one after the next. The huge *Quasar* mothership seriously complicated the matter — this really was not the kind of ship that could easily be let go. Trying to put myself in Violetta's place, I admitted honestly to myself that I was not sure I would have been able to keep my word.

The temptation was too large in the literal and figurative sense.

"Alright, what do you suggest, Marat? Just hole up in a couple of dead-end systems and stay out of the conflict? I've already seen one such example. The pirates of the Brotherhood of the Stars also began as a principled opposition force against Orange House policies, turning off their warp beacons and making their systems untouchable to the legal authorities. But by the end, they were nothing but petty criminals, constantly raiding neighboring star systems. No matter how pure your intentions may be now, sooner or later, your resistance will meet the same end. After all, any fleet needs supply: fuel for the reactors, parts, rounds and lots of other things. You won't be able to get that all the legal way. The only way is to steal from your peaceful neighbors, in other words, the way of piracy."

The Sector Seven Fleet Commander didn't give an answer, but I saw that my words reached the man, and something sounded back in his soul. I tried to build on my success:

"Here it is, Marat. I can act as a mediator between you and my sister. I'll send one of my fleets to Perimeter Sector Seven. Unatari combat ships will act as the guarantors that both sides honestly uphold the terms of the deal. I am not planning to hold back your ships by force, but the *Quasar* will stay with me. I am prepared to buy it and compensate you for the staff at a fair price. From there, it's up to you. If you like, swear allegiance to the Unatari State and come serve me. If you don't, I'll let you go free as a bird with all the money."

Marat ton Mesfelle raised his face and looked at me. I saw a timid hope appearing after all these days of complete despondency. He even found the strength in him to smile.

"Everyone knows that the ruler of Unatari is gathering a powerful fleet. My flagship *Peacemaker* is a very valuable resource, and you won't miss the unique chance to take it for yourself. So I'm sure, Georg, that you'll do everything in your power to deliver this ship, along with its contents to Unatari space. Crown Prince Georg, I trust Your Highness and accept your offer of mediation."

Standing change. Marat ton Mesfelle's opinion of you has improved.
Presumed opinion of you: +52 (trusting)

All that remained was to find out my twin sister's opinion on my mediating the dead-lock. I had to wait almost four hours because, at first, Duchess Violetta royl Inoky ton Mesfelle was giving a speech to her subjects, then taking part in a big celebratory reception in her honor. The Purple House aristocrats hurried to assure the new ruler of their boundless love and loyalty. No one even remembered the former ruler now. But finally, my communications officer told me that the head of the Purple House was ready to speak with me.

The Duchess listened to me carefully, but didn't answer for a long time, not a "yes," not a "no." She was obviously consulting with someone off screen. Finally, my sister answered, adding her own conditions:

"Unatari may bring one medium-sized fleet, but you may not be its commander. As it is, I'm already violating generally accepted safety procedures by letting combat starships of an unfriendly state into my territory. So, I cannot take the risk of having it led by my much-vaunted brother. And my second condition: for the next seventy-two standard hours, you will not inform Emperor August about our agreements, nor my political plans. The Empire is no longer in shape to interfere with the formation of the Grand Duchy, but I still don't want to let them put a stick in our spokes."

"Alright sister, I agree to your conditions. But don't you need to get this decision agreed on with the ruler of the Gold House first? What if Crown Princess Eleonora is against it and cancels our deal?"

Violetta laughed, showing her flawlessly even, white teeth.

"Oh, my dear brother... You're just so dense and behind the times! Our grandmother Eleonora has been in a coma for three months since she had a stroke. The doctors all agree that there is absolutely no chance for the old lady to ever regain consciousness. What's more, her physicians are making sure of that with the greatest zeal, as they understand the potential consequences perfectly. For now, the old bat is needed alive as a symbol of legal Gold House authority. But after the Grand Duchy is formed, power will be shared among the three co-rulers. The need for the decrepit Duchess will fall away, and she will be cut off from her artificial life support system."

"Well, well!" It really was shocking news. "Did you

know that Emperor August is shaking in fear of his sister's revenge?"

"August simply has a dirty conscience, that's why he's shivered every time he so much as heard Eleonora's name mentioned for the last two hundred years. He treated his sister unjustly, depriving her of her rightful throne. By the way, Georg, you have repeated that error, removing me from the Orange House Ducal Throne. As a result, instead of a sister who trusts and helps you, you've now got an implacable political opponent. Although, I must admit, I've been watching your successes with great interest. I used to severely underestimate you, brother, thinking you a good-for-nothing nonentity in the game of politics. If you'd revealed your abilities earlier, like maybe twenty years ago, the Grand Duchy might have a Quadrumvirate."

*　　*　　*

I was sitting in Florianna's cabin. The little Truth Seeker was learning to walk again, supported under the arms by her physical therapists. As it turned out, for now, the girl wasn't doing particularly well. She was constantly stumbling, her legs twisting and bending. Her muscles, unaccustomed to the strain, were atrophied and hardly obeyed her. But all the same, it was grand progress for the once fully paralyzed girl, and I was sincerely glad for Flora.

"Alright, that's enough for today!" said the young, swarthy physician Imir de Riz, who'd taken the place of my former senior doctor Nicosid Brandt.

The thirty-year old specialist had graduated from

the prestigious Tesse Medical Academy with honors, successfully passed all checks by my security service and Truth Seekers, becoming the main doctor of the ruler of Unatari. It was now clear that he was taking mercy on Flora, who was drenched in sweat and shaking in exhaustion, but wanted to continue her exercises until she totally lost conscious from excessive strain.

"You're making progress," I said to the girl in approval, but the Truth Seeker just screwed up her lips into something resembling a smile.

"My Prince, you just thought my progress wasn't that great while watching me."

How hard it was to falsely compliment or flatter a Truth Seeker, they instantly sensed the lie. No longer trying to show approval to the girl, I asked her to tell me her presentiments. My sister's easy compliance with my offer of mediation had put me somewhat on guard, as had the fact that the Duchess hadn't even yet touched on such an important topic as the *Quasar*. A three-day period of silence on my sister's political plans was a very insignificant price to pay for saving the life of the main competitor to the throne and the loss of a flagship. And also, Violetta hadn't been very specific naming the size of the expanded Unatari Fleet. "One medium-sized fleet" in modern reality could have meant a thousand ships with a hundred battleships.

"I mean, what's there to think about? It's an obvious trap," Florianna declared dogmatically. *"The size of the Unatari Fleet doesn't mean much, because the Purple House and their allies will have many more no matter what. Our enemies would even be glad to see the*

Unatari State send as many ships as possible; that would mean Your Majesty would have that many less at his disposal."

"Flora, I still have to intervene. This isn't just about Crown Princess Joan, locked up valuable ships and the unfinished *Quasar*. It's indicative of something greater. I promised to help. They're relying on me, counting on my help. And at that, billions of watchful eyes will be waiting to see if I can justify the hope of these people my sister has condemned to death. It is a test for me as an independent political figure. Am I capable of going against the will of the Antagonists, or the Grand Duchy, as they've begun to call themselves? So, it's very important for me to find a way of pulling Crown Princess Joan out of the trap along with her blocked fleet. I'm really counting on you telling me the right decision."

"My Prince, I have no idea about interstellar politics, or military matters. My abilities as a Truth Seeker are also very modest, and do not allow me to give Your Highness any sound advice in this situation."

Yes, perhaps I really was asking too much from my Truth Seeker. She was still a little girl, and didn't nearly have enough experience. On the other hand, Flora was already in the top twenty strongest psionics in the galaxy, and I suspected that was nowhere near the limit of the girl's growth.

"Thank you for your faith, Crown Prince! But I really do not see any way of helping Crown Princess Joan. Either there is no way to save the trapped fleet, or there are even stronger psionics on their side working against me. But at that, I have discovered something that might be of interest to your Highness. In seven

minutes, a ship containing my sister will be docking on our ship."

"Princess Astra has come here to the front in Perimeter Sector Ten?! It looks like your sister has some bats in the old belfry! It's dangerous here, there's a war, any enemy frigate we missed along the way could have destroyed her yacht! I hope she at least was smart enough not to have brought our son with her."

"No, I do not sense little Georg. Astra left your son at home."

"I can at least be happy about that. Although... if we approach the issue from a purely technical standpoint, how did Astra manage to get through the warp beacons, which were off during the war??? Only I can give the command to turn them on, but I don't remember being asked. And I wouldn't have allowed Astra to take such a risk."

A call came in from the internal network. My Beta Iseyek First Advisor, Apasss Ugu hurried to tell his ruler that the White Queen had arrived, and a request for her ship to dock had just been received.

"Allow them to dock. Take Princess Astra to the sixth deck of my residential wing. Provide her everything necessary there and renew her pass to all rooms on the starship, except the potentially dangerous ones. And compose a full list immediately of those who, in violation of my instructions, turned on the warp beacons for her, after which you must bring them to justice."

The gigantic pill-bug flailed his many whiskers, touching a glowing display with his appendages, then chirring out in surprise. My bodyguard Rosss translated for me:

"No one turned on the warp beacons. The White Queen came on a *Mechanoid.*"

*   *   *

"No, anything but that!" I stopped sharply in the doorway to the bunk, remarking on my favorite's new style: bright crimson hair falling freely over her shoulders and a form-fitting orange dress that emphasized all the curves of her flawless feminine figure.

Princess Astra turned sharply, slowly hiding something in her hand behind her back. The joyful smile slowly faded from her beautiful face, doubt and worry taking its place.

"Is something wrong? Is the Crown Prince not glad to see me?"

"Astra, I'm always glad to see you. But I already have enough women in my close circle with fire-engine red hair. There was really no reason for you to copy that aggressive style from Miya."

"But this hair color and crimson clothing looks very good on the Queen! Your Highness's wife always looks exceptionally beautiful and stands out in any crowd. People don't even notice me when she's around. I look plain and pale. Bionica told me, so she advised me to dress like this!"

I just shook my head in reproach — she'd found a truly great source of advice! My android secretary Bionica had long been jealous of Astra and this wasn't the first time she had given her rival such "useful advice." Probably, my synthetic assistant knew perfectly well that my favorite wearing such a getup would cause me to reject her.

"I'll have a serious talk with Bionica. And you should have realized already that the tastes of androids don't always correspond with those of people. You shouldn't try to look like Miya, because you are completely different. She is a burning flame, arousing fear in everything that lives, the Red Queen, who should be wearing such frightening crimson attire. But you are a fragile shimmering snowflake. The White Queen, spellbinding with your beauty and elegance. With you, I can relax and not be constantly on-guard like I'm leading troops into battle. I value that quality in you very much, and also your spontaneity and joy at life, excellent knowledge of palace etiquette and ability to give timely advice."

At the end of her long speech, I spent a few seconds distracted, looking at a massive pile of boxes sitting in the corner containing the Princess's things. Then, turning back to Astra, I was amazed at the changes that had happened in such a short time. The girl had managed to change out of the clothes I had criticized, and was now in nothing but her birthday suit. Having no shame at my stubborn gaze, Astra walked up to a large mirror and, smiling shamelessly, spun around in front of it in a dancing motion. At that, the girl was still squeezing something small in the fist of her right hand.

"I'll admit, I'm very flattered to hear that my knowledge is something Your Highness needs. Do you know what advice you need now, Crown Prince?" my favorite asked, stopping her dance and breaking the prolonged silence.

I could barely hold back a smile, because my "expert advisor" looked more like she belonged on the cover of a glossy men's magazine than at a government meeting, especially in her present appearance. Nevertheless, seeing her earnest desire to help, I told her about the situation in the Purple House with the trapped fleet. Astra thought for just a few seconds, after which she gave a solution that was absolutely genius in its originality:

"Your Highness must adopt Crown Princess Joan! She no longer has any living relatives or legal guardians so, there's nothing stopping you in Imperial law!"

I'll admit, at first, I didn't understand all the advantages of her suggestion and hurried to express skepticism:

"What rot! What would something like that do to change the political landscape? Other than the fact that my sister the Duchess Violetta would then be killing not just some girl trying to claim her throne, but my adopted daughter?"

"And her niece," Astra corrected me. "But this isn't all about family status. From what I understand, your sister won't be stopped by that at all, despite the serious standing fall if she killed her own niece. The problem is something else: if rescuing a daughter, and also a Crown Princess, Your Highness would be legally allowed to bring combat ships through the Imperial Core without the preliminary agreement of the Imperial Secretariat and the Joint Chiefs of Staff. It will be enough to inform the authorities after the fact and pay for recharging energy at the warp beacons. There are precedents in Imperial history, so the law would be fully on Your Highness's side."

The ability to pass through the Core? The traditional route around the Core from Perimeter Sector Nine to Seven took around thirteen or fourteen days. But if I went straight on the shortest route? I turned on a data screen, brought up the star map on the monitor and calculated a route to the Veyerde system. I couldn't believe my eyes.

"Just fifty-three hours! And at that, my fleet will arrive to the Nayal system next to Veyerde by a little-used route, through the uninhabited Forepost-10 system. No one will be expecting us to come that way!"

I called Katerina on an internal line and asked her to check what Astra had said about combat ships passing through the Core. Astra walked aside as not to show up in the picture but, for some reason, she was in no rush to get dressed. My cousin then stayed silent for thirty seconds, checking something on her computer, after which she answered:

"Georg there really are a few exceptions in the law about fleet movement for Great Houses and allied Kingdoms. And one of them says: 'When an emergency action could save the life of a titled aristocrat of the Empire, who is close relatives with the fleet commander or ship pilot, the passage of one or several military starships of classes higher than frigate through the Imperial Core shall be allowed.'"

"Are there any limits described on the composition of the ship group? Do they have the right to pass through the Core, or must they only enter and wait, hiding from their pursuers in the safe system? I need to understand if, using this excuse, I could bring three thousand starships from Sector Nine to Seven."

My cousin's eyebrows jumped up in astonishment.

"Cousin, I am not at all sure that this loophole could be interpreted as a way to attack an enemy from an unexpected system!"

"But still, Katerina, you haven't answered my questions."

"No, there are no limits imposed by Imperial law," my advisor was forced to admit. "After all, traditionally, the Imperial Fleet surpassed any potential violators in force and would simply destroy those acting inappropriately. What have you thought up, cousin? I'm very scared of you asking questions like this."

I wasn't planning to hide anything from my advisor and told her in detail about the situation with the Purple House and Astra's suggestion. Katerina always figured things out fast, and here she immediately found two hidden obstacles in the plan:

"The Blue House is at war with us. Yes, now the blues are giving up position without resistance, but that is only because we have a significant advantage both in spacecraft and in number of terrestrial soldiers. Go ahead and take three thousand starships from the front, and that's it — everything will start rolling back! The Blue House will be able to resist effectively, and you won't be able to land Alpha Iseyek landing forces because the Tria's won't be able to make it through."

"I agree, cousin. Before starting anything against the Purple House, I should first finish the war against the Blue House."

"Exactly, Georg. Now, we're getting five to seven, or

maybe more Blue House systems. There is a very high probability that, after a peace treaty is signed, all these systems will remain ours. And now think, is that blocked fleet worth the potential benefit we would be giving up by rushing this military campaign that has turned out so well for us?"

I went silent, because the question was of course right-minded — was the *Quasar* and my promise to help the Princess in peril worth ten or even more lost star systems? Then Katerina continued:

"A second rather important aspect you are for some reason overlooking is that Joan royl Reyekh is an Imperial Crown Princess by birth and has priority in the line of succession over untitled individuals. Cousin, are you really prepared to impinge on your son George Junior's rights by placing Joan before him in the line of succession to the Unatari State throne? And it also seems quite obvious that Queen Miya will object, because Joan is older than little Crown Princess Deianna and would thus come before her, if you're planning to truly adopt Joan with all the legally required rights and privileges of a daughter. And half measures are out of the question here. After all, you only have the right to go through the Core to rescue a full relative. Technically, of your children and close relatives, only Likanna wouldn't be affected by these cardinal changes, because your eldest daughter was born two months before Joan."

I noticed that my advisor tactically mentioned "close relatives" there, without pointing to her own position. After all, Katerina would also be dropping as well. Yes and, based on the way Princess Astra was listening carefully to the conversation, and her obviously bewildered expression, my favorite hadn't thought through the consequences of her suggestion.

"Thank you, Katerina. I have seen these hidden obstacles and agree that it is a very difficult choice. I'll think it over and do some calculations. But in any case, I consider it premature to discuss any options without first speaking with the new ruler of the Blue House. Duke Mark royl Ovar ton Miro has received just a quarter of the votes in the election for the new head of the Blue House. His position as ruler is very shaky. And right now, while the Duke has yet to come to power, we need to figure out what terms he would find acceptable for his much-desired peace treaty."

Katerina promised to arrange a conversation for me with the Blue House ruler and signed off. I then turned my attention back to the fact that Astra was still not dressed, and was squeezing something tight in her hand. I wondered what it was. I didn't manage to ask my question, because Florianna gave away the farm on her sister:

"My Prince, as soon as she arrived, Astra went to the medical wing of the starship and was looking for Nicosid Brandt there. But when she realized the old physician had been fired, she spent a long time loafing around the hallways of the big starship in confusion, accompanied by a guard team until she randomly bumped into a condom machine. Astra was terribly embarrassed, but bought a couple. And now, she is deciding whether to allude to her desire to Your Highness, and is also afraid of Miya, because she isn't at all sure that the Queen will allow her to make such a change in contraception."

"Flora, you should be ashamed of yourself for

spying on your sister! Do something useful for the next few hours, search for the missing First and Second Blue House Fleets," I said out loud, after which I asked my bodyguards to leave my cabin, and suggested to Astra that we look over her purchases together.

Shades of Blue

"GET READY! One minute until go time! Georg, adjust the collar of your uniform! Bionica, see that lock of hair sticking out to the left? Get it behind his ear!" for some reason, my cousin Katerina was really stoking it, although I didn't expect any breakthrough solutions in the peace treaty with the new head of the Blue House.

Duke Mark royl Uvar ton Miro had barely ascended to the throne and was probably still getting a handle on things and familiarizing himself with his ministers and advisors. What was more, the extremely low percent of aristocrats who'd voted for him, less than a quarter of those who had the right to vote in the Blue House, meant that the new ruler could expect serious resistance to any initiatives he undertook, both in his lands, and at a gathering of Great House deputies. It was obvious that the Duke would very soon be having a discussion with more influential politicians, be offered something and thus increase the number of those on his side. But for now, my opponent had a very shaky position. Any unpopular decision, and the deputies could initiate a vote of no confidence, launching new elections. Because after all, a decision to make peace by giving up territory would be just such an unpopular decision.

"Ten seconds!" said Duchess Katerina ton Unatari, standing next to me with her face toward the camera.

My cousin looked exceptionally bright today and horribly official in her traditional diplomat's uniform with all appropriate Imperial regalia alongside that of an Unatari State upper aristocrat. The Duchess's crown looked stylish on her well-treated chestnut hair. A blue ribbon diagonally across her chest meant she was absolutely untouchable to the Swarm. Above the ribbon, there were several medals attached, including three military ones: the Black Star for having participated in the now legendary invasion of Alien space, the Sapphire Comet for having been an active participant in the epic battle with the Alien *Queen*'s fleet in the far-off D56KT system, and also the Silver Brooch with the number 47 on the four-pointed star, meaning she had participated in forty-seven space battles.

Miya was standing to my right-hand side, brilliant as ever and dangerous in her glamorous orange and crimson dress. The golden crown of the Queen of Unatari shimmered with little flames in her red hair. Very few knew that the role of my wife today was being played by an Arite, because the real Miya was currently off in the Unatari system, teaching the many psionics who had come to our invitation. But Katerina had insisted that my spouse be present, even if it was only a copy. In my cousin's words, the only condition voiced by the Blue House was that

Miya not be used during the negotiations for her murderous abilities. And so, as they were afraid of Miya, I just had to draw attention to our power by bringing the very powerful Truth Seeker into the negotiations.

My personal assistant Bionica, was standing on the far left. The synthetic beauty, who could afford the most luxurious dresses and outfits from the best couturiers in the galaxy, was wearing a simple space fleet uniform today. But the strict military uniform only emphasized Bionica's beauty, while the military medals and particularly the Emerald Star given by the Emperor, spoke for themselves.

I suggested to my cousin that we expand our negotiating group by including First Advisor Apasss Ugu or one of the Swarm admirals, but my cousin was firmly opposed. In Katerina's words, the negotiations were already going to be hard enough, and bringing other races into it would just complicate things.

Finally, the screen lit up. A scrawny looking and very young boy with a ducal crown in his golden red hair was staring back at us. And a boy was exactly what you'd call him. Despite Mark royl Uvar's thirty years of age, calling him an adult man was something I just could bring my tongue to do.

"Crown Prince Georg royl Inoky and his famous 'garland' of the most beautiful women in the Universe," the young Duke said instead of greeting me. "But for some reason I do not see your delightful favorite Astra in your delegation. Clearly, you decided to spare my feelings and not show me so much beauty all at once."

"It was just that we thought it excessive to bring two blondes in one delegation," Duchess Katerina said with a slight smile, and the man laughed gleefully, having considered that a joke.

And it should be said that my cousin hadn't bent the truth one bit. Diplomatic protocol stated a monarch's favorite was allowed in negotiations and even welcomed, in that it underlined their significance and official status. Astra was offered to join the Unatari delegation, and initially my favorite looked on the forthcoming event with lots of enthusiasm. But at the last moment, she had a sharp change of heart and, as strange as it may seem, the reason was her hair color. After my criticism yesterday, she had decided to live up to the image of the White Queen even in the smallest details, meaning absolutely snow white. And after seeing Bionica come into my chambers with a tray of coffee and pastries with the same hair color, the Princess became depressed and refused to participate in the negotiations.

"But why didn't you say that Unatari would have such a formidable delegation?" asked the young Duke, expressing his dissatisfaction. "I'd have liked to invite a couple of my advisors. And also, instead of everyday clothes, I would have worn the Duke's mantle, and belt with ceremonial dagger, much more fitting the occasion. Although... what's the difference, really? I'll admit, Crown Prince Georg, I was afraid of this conversation, and at the same time understood its inevitability. Both Blue House fleets have been missing for four days and aren't taking any calls... You wouldn't happen to have wiped them out somewhere recently, hm?"

I am not accustomed to stealing valor, so I honestly answered the Duke that I hadn't encountered any Blue House starships since the day I let the Second Fleet go free.

"I believe you, Crown Prince, although I really do understand why the ships of the Blue House First and Second Fleets are in no rush to fulfill their duty and defend my territories. Clearly, the admirals understand that they will die in vain and are waiting for a peace treaty to be signed. The Blue House has already lost the war, denying that fact is utterly useless. And I admire how artfully you performed that provocation in the Forepost-22 system, unbinding your hands. In the eyes of the whole Empire, my cousin Ovella was the aggressor, while the Unatari State got cart blanche to attack the Blue House. I'm being serious when I say I bow to your mastery, Crown Prince!"

Katerina and I quickly exchanged glances. My cousin shrugged her shoulders, not hiding her lack of comprehension. Showing my enemy that I was uninformed in some important matter was not the best way to start complicated negotiations, but I decided to be principled:

"Duke, when my diplomatic ships were boarded and sabotaged at the Forepost-22 station, and Blue House frigates shot down rescue shuttles with my dear friends inside, I took no joy in that. It was an obvious attempt at assassinating me, and only Miya's abilities," I said, pointing to my "wife," "allowed me to avoid death."

"All the same, the Blue House was not behind the attack," he parried. "Believe me, Crown Prince Georg,

I had a very frank conversation on that topic with Ovella, and she denied it. For her as well, what happened was totally unexpected. In fact, my cousin spent a long time trying to meet with you to discuss the possibility of signing a military alliance. Also, you were attacked by *Tusk*-class frigates, but we only have that old crap in our Second Fleet reserves, but they were five star systems from Forepost-22 at the time, so they couldn't possibly have been involved."

"And what do the soldiers that took direct part in the assault of the ships have to say?" I asked, interested in my opponent's story.

The young Duke grew noticeably embarrassed and led his gaze away.

"My sister ordered the soldiers of the border garrison carefully interrogated as precisely as possible. They were all equally convinced that the criminal order to attack the Unatari diplomats came from the Blue House capital and had been given directly by my cousin Ovella. The major commanding the garrison, who was also taken aback by the contents of the order, even demanded it be repeated in confirmation, and he got that. Only after did he order his subjects to storm the starships docked at the station."

"I'm getting the impression that some third party baited us very skillfully," my advisor said.

"I even suspect I know who it was," the young Duke said with a crooked smile. "The Gold House has already secretly brought its soldiers into Perimeter Sector Sixteen. What's more, their representative, a certain Count Albert royl Timur ton Akad has been trying very actively to get in touch with me. I've just kept telling him to buzz off, because I'm not planning to have anything to do with a person of such repellent standing!"

Despite the seriousness of the negotiations, I couldn't resist and broke down laughing. I never would have thought that my spontaneous decision to spoil the standing of the impudent "Voice of the Triumvirate" could have such an unexpected effect on political issues! Based on that, Duke Mark royl Uvar had never spoken with the Antagonists and never had anything to do with them.

"Yes, I've had the misfortune of talking with that odious worm," I said, explaining my untimely happiness. "He tried to threaten me and even gave me ultimatums. I had to do a painful number on his ego and lower him to unhallowed ground. Based on that, the only language he understands is brute force. I wish I could have given him a special achievement: 'Pedal-Powered Tool,' because his pathos, rudeness and impudence were a great impediment to his profession as a diplomat."

"Good that I didn't talk to him then. I've never gotten along well with rude men. But I suggest that, if you are not opposed, we return to the main topic of discussion. Given that the Blue House is being eaten from three sides by stronger neighbors, Unatari, the Aliens and the Antagonists, I see no reason to continue the war. But I also do not desire to be written off by historians as a ruler of a Great House who signed a demeaning capitulation, either."

"And?" Bionica asked, hurrying the Duke along, as the man suddenly fell silent.

"I thought for a long time about this dilemma, and

it seems I've found a way out. Crown Prince Georg, I propose we marry our families together and thus unite our territories and end the war. Your daughters, Crown Princesses Likanna and Deianna are too young to be considered for a dynastic marriage. And I would never make a claim on your wife Queen Miya. It wasn't for nothing that I asked about your favorite Princess Astra, but she isn't here. But your cousin Duchess Katerina ton Unatari, from what I understand, has recently been widowed and is not bound by any marriage obligations. Katerina is a rare beauty and a very smart woman, while as a reporter from hotspots she truly knows no equal. I never miss any of her reports and have very warm feelings toward the Duchess. And so, Crown Prince Georg royl Inoky ton Mesfelle, I ask for your second cousin's hand in marriage."

My foreign politics advisor was very hard to catch off guard, and even harder to baffle, but the Duke's suggestion did just that. My cousin got confused, embarrassed, then blushed. For some time, Duke Mark and I waited for a sensible reply, but Katerina was just frozen in horror. Finally, my cousin gave an answer:

"All in all, I'm not opposed, Duke Mark. But I'm still mourning my dead husband Corwin, so this won't look very decent to me until I'm over that. What's more, I know of my cousin's appetites and understand that Crown Prince Georg has his own plans for some part of Blue House space. Isn't that right, Your Highness?"

"Yes. I can offer Crown Prince Mark one of the Perimeter Sectors, his choice. Except Sector Ten — it is already under Unatari State control and goes to me as a trophy of war. Fourteen and Fifteen are under Alien control. Sector Sixteen, from what I understand, has been taken by the Antagonists. So, he may choose either Eleven, Twelve or Thirteen."

"Not such a generous offer," the young Duke cringed.

"But it is fair!" I said firmly. "The Blue House will never hold these territories and, in a week or two, such an offer won't even be possible."

"Alright, Crown Prince Georg. I choose Sector Eleven. But how do you suggest we perform the legal transfer of power?"

Katerina and I had already long discussed that factor, so my advisor told her future spouse the details of the peaceful and legal transfer of territorial jurisdiction. According to that plan, the Duke would give his agreement to Crown Princess Natalie ton Miro rejoining the Blue House, after which he would announce another election. The votes cast for him, the Duke would give away to the little Crown Princess which, together with those she gained on her own, would be easily enough for victory. In that the ruler of Unatari was the official guardian of the underage Crown Princess Natalie ton Miro, he would technically gain control over the Blue House, thus bringing the war to an automatic end.

"Very crafty. But what will happen in five years, when Crown Princess Natalie becomes an adult?" Duke Mark clarified.

Katerina looked at me and said a suggestion aloud, which I had been holding in my head after the conversation with Astra, but hadn't yet come to any final decision on.

"I believe, by that time, my cousin will have officially adopted Crown Princess Natalie and thus get the Blue House for life!"

*   *   *

I was much more worried about this conversation than the earlier negotiations with the Blue House head. The grandiose perspectives that had just been unfurled before me, could only come to fruition if I got the agreement of this one lady. Naturally, I was referring to Queen Miya. After all, my previous experience talking with the red-headed Truth Seeker had told me that her opinion and interests simply could not be neglected, as doing so would necessarily lead to loss of life.

Now, my wife and I had formed a certain kind of mutually beneficial partnership — I fought the battles and removed the threats while expanding state borders, and Miya helped me with her unique and powerful abilities. But at that, we both followed a set of rules we had made a long time ago: she wouldn't mess around in running the government or stop me from indulging from time to time, while I wouldn't try to divorce her or impinge upon the rights of my spouse or our daughter Crown Princess Deianna in any way. But now, the Truth Seeker could, and not without basis, regard the fact I was adopting two daughters as an attempt to move her child back in the line of succession. That was a serious problem. An insulted Miya could consider our agreement broken, which would thus cancel her oath not to harm anyone near me, or even me.

"Is it something urgent, Georg? Or can it wait an hour and a half? It's just that I'm teaching a lesson to young psionic girls now, and it would be very bad to interrupt their studies at this phase." My wife was in an insulated track suit (yet again red) and was sweaty and overheated, as if she had just been working out in a gym.

I didn't answer the Queen's question, giving the Truth Seeker the chance to just read what she needed from my mind. A few seconds later, the Queen's brows shot up in surprise. Miya turned to the side and said loudly:

"So, girls, you're unspeakably lucky: King Georg himself has just called to give you a five-minute break."

In reply, she got squeals of joy from the many gifted girls, some of whom were merely young, while others were actual toddlers. The severe Queen winced and hurried to cut down her students' excessive joy:

"Let me warn you now: those of you who take even a second longer than that getting back into pain awareness position will be punished in the harshest way! I guarantee that everyone who commits this offense will be paralyzed from the waist down for life!"

I knew perfectly well that the Truth Seeker was not joking or just trying to frighten her students. Miya really was capable of doing that.

"Do you really have to be so sadistic when teaching?"

"I don't know," she said with a careless shrug. "I just use the same methods Krista used on us. The course of study proved effective for me and my classmates, so I see no reason to change any part of it. And you're wrong, Georg. This is not just mindless acrimony. A psionic who cannot bear pain may lose concentration and will die in their first battle. So, the first thing all talented girls learn is the ability to resist pain, fear, disgust, fatigue, and maintain their bodies' physiological responses."

So, there it was... I had no suspicion of just how nasty day to day life was at the psionic school, even though I had heard that Krista had rather severe mannerisms in her old school.

"Beyond that, there's another explanation. People need a powerful stimulus to move forward. Threatening health and life are just that kind of stimulus. Someone doing a long jump will go practically twenty-five percent further if the usual sand is replaced with a ditch full of napalm or a pit of sharpened spears. Developing Truth Seekers is nothing more than a series of such tests. Overcoming them gives new experience and strength. But I don't think it was the subtleties of training psionics you wanted to hear from me, right?"

Somehow the Queen and I had strayed very far from the topic I wanted to talk to her about. The adoption of two Crown Princesses. I was well acquainted with both of my daughter Likanna's best friends, and even found them funny and sweet. But I was not doing this now just out of monarchical folly, nor philanthropy and not even sympathy for orphans. This was pure calculation. There were four star regions of the Blue House riding on this horse, the ability to get into the Imperial Core undetected by the enemy and go to aid my allies in the Purple House.

"So then, your decision?" I said, hurrying my wife along, as she had been silent for too long, not giving any kind of answer.

"Seeing as you've bothered asking my opinion for once in such a long time... I am opposed, Georg!"

"But... why? The benefit is obvious, and as for how to compensate Deia's position..."

"This has nothing to do with Deianna!" my wife sharply cut me off. "I'm against it not because of my daughter. It's just that I understand perfectly well that my husband is lagging behind and playing the political game by antiquated rules. And after all, a bad evaluation of the political situation could mean death for both of us!"

I was somewhat thrown off by my wife's words and asked her to explain.

"Georg, what are you doing still looking back to the Empire? Forget about it! The Empire is a corpse. It's already rotting and decomposing. It died the very moment August royl Akad broke the political foundation that once bound the loyalty of the Great Houses. The Gold House was lost to the Empire due to August's malfeasance long ago. The Red House has been destroyed by the Aliens. The Orange House no longer exists either. The Blue House has left the Empire, and soon the Green and Purple will follow after it. What remains? Just the Core, which is shrinking every day."

"The Empire is not just systems. It's also got a powerful space fleet with forty thousand starships and armed forces numbering in the millions. They will be capable of stopping the fall of the Empire."

"The armed forces are controlled by living people.

Your standing among the Imperial Military is very high, and a certain part of the fleet and army would join you, if need be. The same can be said for the rulers of Core systems. They will follow whichever leader they consider the strongest. The whole Imperial political system has rotted and is falling apart. Georg, has it occurred to you that you are still only eighteenth in line to the Imperial throne? Who are these seventeen aristocrats standing before you? I know only your sister Violetta and the Head of the Green House. I've also heard tell that the Emperor has a son. That's it! The rest are rich lay-abouts, pointlessly wasting their lives, whose whole political strength consists of only their close family ties to former rulers. Throw the allies of the Grand Duchy from that list and you get the real condition of the present Empire: a decrepit impotent old man, his son who's not interested in politics and nothing."

Miya spoke very convincingly, and I also understood that she was only saying things that needed to be said for a long time. The Empire as a political organism was already dead...

"Now, now!" the Truth Seeker said, clearly reading my thoughts. "The Antagonists also understand that perfectly. Remember your conversation with your twin sister. Violetta was thinking of blatant nasty treatment against her competitor, however swore, at that giving her word as a Crown Princess, not to do harm to little Joan. But that was all after she'd already announced her plans to join the Grand Duchy and leave the Empire. Strange that you didn't notice how Violetta will soon stop being a Crown Princess of the Empire, so her oath to not attack Crown Princess

Joan's convoy doesn't actually hold her to anything!"

"Hey, you're right!" I agreed. "I really was confused that my sister gave such an oath, while planning to violate it from the start. Here's how that makes sense, I guess. On habit, everyone considers such an oath inviolable, but Violetta understood that she would stop being an Imperial Crown Princess in two or three days, and gave the promise calmly."

"I'm glad you're starting to understand, Georg. And now, look in a new light at your suggestion to adopt the two girls. I mean, for me, it largely makes no difference what you do with them. Their title as Imperial Crown Princesses is just such a fragile mirage as the one made by your twin sister Violetta. It's a holdover from an old system that's already dead. The interests of the Unatari State and the Empire are bound to clash, just as Unatari is bound to stop serving the decrepit old egomaniac August royl Akad. The corpse of the Empire will be torn to pieces sooner or later by Unatari and the Grand Duchy, and our mission is to tear away the biggest chunk, so we will have the better position in the deciding battles. If we win this dispute, you will be able to appoint new Crown Princes and Crown Princesses yourself, and the current order of succession to the Imperial throne will have absolutely no meaning. I know that our daughter Deianna will not be left empty handed, and Georg Junior will also get the much-vaunted Crown Prince title, in this case. And if we lose, Duchess Violetta has made a clear demonstration of how the Antagonists handle their political opponents."

That was true. Forgetting the example set by my sister of the total genocide of all members of the

Purple House ruling family was simply impossible. I was prepared to do everything in my power to stop that from happening to my family and those close to me.

"Alright Georg, now you're ready. Go and do what you think is best. And also... if the 'voice of the Triumvirate' tries to talk with you again, put him straight through to me. I need to give my students a real-world test. I've chosen sixty of the most capable girls from all the candidates and am preparing to turn them into a group of psionics capable of working jointly on the same wave. In one year, this psionic battery will be capable of handling even Krista!"

*   *   *

The reaction of my eldest daughter to the news that she was getting two new sisters was fairly predictable — Likanna shrieked and clapped her hands in joy:

"Dad, you're the best! For a long time, Natalie and Joan have been more to me than simple best friends. I'm so happy they'll be my sisters! I cannot raise my opinion of you any further, because it's already at max, but just so you know, I adore you!!!"

I won't hide it, it was nice to see sincere happiness in the eyes of my daughter. Just for that alone, it was worth making the decision to adopt Natalie and Joan.

"I'll go first to tell Crown Princess Natalie the good news! She went to study how to pilot a yacht with solar sails, and is now riding the waves somewhere near my palace on Tesse."

"Yes, I know. I've just had a long conversation with her referencing all the details. Natalie was very glad at this change in her fate and immediately agreed. But first, she had to send a request to the Blue House to have her rights restored. Some bureaucratic formalities had to be observed. Nevertheless, Natalie does have some relatives there, and also the current head of the Blue House is her second cousin. But such technical details are probably of no interest to you."

"Yeah, of course, I only care about the result. Then I'll tell Joan!" she exclaimed, jumping for joy.

No one told my daughter that all distant and close relatives of her friend Joan had fallen to the hands of usurpers, and that the life of the Crown Princess herself was hanging by a hair. Likanna was too small to react appropriately to such heavy information, so I tried to protect the girl from the news. Not because I was afraid for my daughter's mental state, although that was a factor. It was just that it was very hard to predict how Likanna would respond. It was very much in Lika's spirit to suddenly tear off and fly across half the galaxy to "rescue her friend." And now, I didn't delve into the details and tried to get by with a half-truth:

"Well, sweetie, I don't think you'll be able to get in touch with Joan. The Purple House and the Green House have implemented a data blockade. They have some complicated political stuff going on right now, a struggle for power and the formation of the Grand Duchy, some new government that will replace the familiar Great Houses."

"Yeah, I noticed," my daughter said, accepting the explanation easily. "Joan hasn't been answering my calls for a few days now. And grandma Elisa hasn't given her final agreement for me to visit the Green House for two whole weeks. She said she was having a problem with subterfuge..."

"It's nothing, Lika, it will all be over soon and the blockade will be removed. Then, I'll fly out to get Joan myself."

My daughter signed off and I spent some time looking in contemplation at the black screen before opening the relationship window and initiating the sending of two long-prepared messages:

Crown Prince Georg royl Inoky ton Mesfelle offers to adopt Crown Princess Natalie royl Cruz ton Unatari (presumed opinion of you: +78, completely trusting)

Crown Prince Georg royl Inoky ton Mesfelle offers to adopt Crown Princess Joan royl Reyekh ton Andor (presumed opinion of you: +74, completely trusting)

Almost instantly, I got a positive answer to my first message. Crown Princess Natalie officially agreed to become my adopted daughter:

Crown Princess Natalie royl Cruz ton Unatari has accepted your offer of adoption
Your daughter's new name: Natalie royl Georg ton Unatari

I wasn't expecting a speedy reply to the second message, which made its arrival a few minutes later all the more unexpected:

Crown Princess Joan royl Reyekh ton Andor has accepted your offer of adoption
Your daughter's new name: Joan royl Georg ton Unatari

Alright, there was no going back now. I officially recognized Joan and had received the full right to protect my daughter by any means necessary, even leading combat starships through the Core or starting a military conflict with the Grand Duchy. I was very much hoping that such a radical move wouldn't be necessary, and that Violetta would have sufficient tact to retreat in this conflict, which was now a matter of principle to me.

ATTENTION! Your daughter the Crown Princess Natalie royl Georg ton Unatari has submitted a petition to join the Blue House.
Because Crown Princess Natalie is underage, this will require the agreement of the head of the Blue House and of her closest relative (father).
Duke Mark royl Uvar ton Miro, head of the Blue House, has given his agreement.
Do you agree to let your daughter Crown Princess Natalie royl Georg ton Unatari join the Blue House?
(Yes/No)

I chose the option "Yes," after which I asked Bionica, who was standing next to me, to open a bottle of dry red wine, and waited to see how things played out with a glass of wine in hand. And it wasn't even five minutes before my advisor Duchess Katerina got in touch with me and asked me to immediately turn on the official Blue House news channel. In the huge glimmering room, made to hold thousands of people and now totally packed full, Duke Mark royl Uvar was giving a speech before a gathering of deputies.

He was speaking about an attempt to make peace between all warring groups, in order to overcome the crisis of power. The audience heard out the new Great House Head guardedly, with no ovations or applause. Finally, the young Duke arrived at the essence of his speech and told them right from the podium that the popularly beloved Crown Princess Natalie was returning to the Blue House. For the first time in the whole speech, the audience lit up. A few shouts were heard as allies of the runaway Crown Princess, as well as her political opponents lost control. The head of the Blue House called for silence, after which, beyond all exaggeration, he astounded all the deputies, declaring right from the podium that he was resigning and declaring a new Blue House election!

Duke Mark royl Uvar ton Miro, head of the Blue House, has called for a new election.

ATTENTION! A Great House of the Empire cannot be without a leader!
Election for new head of the Blue House will begin immediately.

You, as the closest relative of the underage Crown Princess Natalie royl Georg ton Unatari, have the right to cast 21.3% of the votes in the Blue House.

Furthermore, 11.8% of the Blue House aristocrats have entrusted you with the right to cast votes on their behalf.

Would you like to support the first in line to the throne: Duke Mark royl Uvar ton Miro, or vote for a different candidate?

Naturally, a different one! I opened the very long list containing several hundred candidates to the ducal throne. My daughter, Crown Princess Natalie royl Georg was third in that list, behind only Duke Mark and some Countess Umma royl Edd ton Miro, who I'd never heard of. Just out of interest, I skimmed through a few pages, but didn't really see any famous or even familiar names there.

Returning to the beginning of the list, I confirmed that I was casting 33.1% of my votes for Crown Princess Natalie.

ATTENTION! The new head of the Blue House will be Crown Princess Natalie (59.3% of votes)

ATTENTION! Because the ruler of the Blue House is too young, power over the Blue House will be held by a regent, Unatari ruler Crown Prince Georg royl Inoky ton Mesfelle, until she comes of age (4 years, 10 months and 23 days).

ATTENTION! The war between Unatari and Unatari (Blue House) has been ended due to: lack of enemy.

The audience of Blue House deputies started buzzing like a batted bee's nest. I understood the lack of comprehension all the viceroys and aristocrats were feeling. I mean, instead of the modest little girl who was so easy to manipulate and trick, they were getting a harsh monarch as a ruler, who ruled with an iron fist and would not accept any tomfoolery!

I was already familiar with the deplorable situation in the Blue House treasury, from which tens of billions of credits had evaporated without a trace in the last few months, and understood that one of those present in the large hall probably had a lot to say about this and other financial fraud. One of the deputies was probably remembering my wife Miya with fear now, and understanding that there was no way he'd hide his embezzlement and less-than-legal affairs from the new ruler.

This was the very time for me to give a speech before my new subjects. My image appeared on the huge screen before the deputies, looking confused and utterly thrown off. The din in the room immediately went silent. Those gathered looked carefully at the screen, expecting some momentous decisions from their new ruler. And they weren't mistaken.

In fact, my speech was half a contestation of current facts, and half an ultimatum. With my very first words, I thanked Duke Mark royl Uvar and Crown Princess Natalie for their finding a peaceful and political way of ending the senseless war, which was of no use to anyone. Afterward, I declared that, from that very minute, the Blue House was a core territory of the Unatari State and would be returning to the Empire. So, there could be no discussion of the

Grand Duchy or anything connected with the Antagonists, while all the Antagonists' emissaries were to be subject to immediate arrest.

Wasting my personal time to sort out all the complications and twists and turns of the Blue House civil war was not something I had the patience for. So, I gave all those taking part in the civil war twenty-four hours to recognize their new ruler, in which case they would be guaranteed full amnesty, no matter what they may have done in the past.

I also promised that the factions and groups that refused my peace plan would not be negotiated with. Criminals would simply be exterminated as quickly as possible. I had millions of hungry Alpha Iseyek landing troops that would be glad to restore order to the problem systems.

The Blue House aristocrats would retain all their titles and territories when joining the Unatari State. All viceroys, city mayors and other civil servants would retain their posts in the Unatari State, but only after voluntarily returning all illegally obtained money to the treasury, with the best Truth Seekers of my state checking their honesty.

I didn't look one bit like the ghastly man-eating monster Blue House propaganda had made me out to be. The deputies gradually calmed down and were now trying to prove their loyalty to their new ruler. The longer my speech went on, the more the audience lit up, applauding with greater and greater frequency. I started to get personal relationship improvement messages. Just a few at first, but soon a real torrent. Soon after that, there followed messages about global standing and fame increases.

Global fame increase. Current value: +70

Global standing increase. Current value: +11

Standing change. Empire Military faction opinion of you has improved.
Present Empire Military faction opinion of you: +63 (veneration)

Global standing increase. Current value: +12

Achievement lost: Bloodthirsty Avenger

Achievement unlocked: Peacemaker

Global fame increase. Current value: +71

Global standing increase. Current value: +13
...

At the very end of my speech, I offered the council of deputies to hold an open election on changing the sovereignty of all Blue House systems to the Unatari State. Here, the speaker of the Blue House parliament raised his voice for the first time, telling the ruler without much confidence that their regulations had no provisions in them for open voting. In reply, I just laughed:

"You and I are grown people, so let's stay realistic and not tell one another fairy-tales about secret voting. You cannot seriously think that I won't find out who voted for what, right? So, I suggest we not waste our time here, and annoy the Red Queen over something so foolish."

The speaker wasn't stubborn on it and announced the vote would be public. A minute later, I saw the final results: 91.4% voted "Yes," and 8.6% "No." In theory, I could already officially declare the end of the Blue House's existence, but I was in no rush. I looked through the list of "No" voters, and asked one of them to make a speech arguing for their choice.

A middle-aged dark-skinned woman took the floor, representing the planet Vazshi-V from the Vazshi star system in Perimeter Sector Sixteen.

"Your Majesty, Your Highness, and Your Grace," she began, running through my titles. I stopped the deputy and asked her to get to the point. "As you most likely know, Sector Sixteen is cut off from the rest of Blue House territory by a group of systems under Alien control. We can discuss as long as we want at these conferences and make all kinds of statements and declarations, but the reality is that the Blue House no longer controls my homeworld. Not too long ago, the Gold House took up defense of Sector Sixteen. Say what you will about the Antagonists, but for my homeworld of Vazshi, the choice isn't great: either the Antagonists or total annihilation at the hands of the Alien hordes. The Gold House soldiers have yet to encroach on our sovereignty, but I'll be direct: as soon as the Blue House ceases to exist, the Vazshi star system will change color on the political map to gold. As will the rest of Sector Sixteen."

I already knew that, so I thanked the deputy for her honest and frank answer and asked her to add another couple comments and arguments from those who'd voted "No." But it quickly turned out that all those who'd refused were from Perimeter Sector Sixteen and already mentally saw themselves as Gold House subjects. Alright, I didn't waste any more time and started the procedure of changing sovereignty of all Blue House systems.

Before my eyes there ran a long list of eighty-four star systems that were going to be nestled under the wing of the Unatari State, then the final messages:

ATTENTION! The Blue House has ceased to exist.

Global fame increase. Current value: +75

Achievement unlocked: Largest territory

Achievement unlocked: More territory than the Emperor

Global fame increase. Current value: +77

Experiencing a certain apprehension, I familiarized myself with the new achievements. Was it really true that the Unatari State now had more star systems under its control than the Imperial Core? My First Assistant Apasss Ugu came instantly to dispel my doubts. Bionica obligingly translated the insect's chirring for me:

"There are ninety-three star systems of the Imperial Core directly under the control of August royl Akad. Your Majesty now has one hundred thirty star systems. That is technically more. Although, in human population, economic indicators and military might, the Empire still exceeds Unatari by a whole order of magnitude. And I must also direct your attention to the fact that the nineteen star systems of Sector Sixteen have just joined the Gold House, significantly increasing the Antagonists' forces."

"That doesn't matter now," my cousin Katerina commented. "Georg is on the right path and will quickly gain power and popularity among the people, while the Emperor's standing and influence on his subjects continues to fall. If this tendency goes on even another six months, my cousin will be more popular in the Empire than August royl Akad, which is to say nothing of all the other politicians and aristocrats. That reveals very interesting perspectives for us..."

"I'm sure August understands that as well and is doing everything in his power not to allow it," I said, interrupting my cousin's day-dreaming. "But all in all, you're right. The Emperor is hardly likely to be openly aggressive against a Crown Prince with so much popular authority. So, I suggest we not waste time for nothing and go forward with the plan. Katerina, release some disinformation saying that I am preparing to fly to the former Blue House capital in the next few days to personally meet with the most influential politicians and aristocrats. Admirals, tell the whole united Unatari Fleet to be ready to fly in thirty minutes! We're going through the Imperial Core!"

Unknown Fleet

MY LATE DINNER in the company of Bionica and Astra was interrupted by the sharp ring of an emergency call. My communications officer was very worried and even started hiccupping slightly:

"Y-y-your Majesty, a message has come in from the Imperial Secretariat. C-c-c-code R-red. They're demanding that Crown Prince Georg royl Inoky ton Mesfelle immediately transfer control of the wh-whole fleet to the Imperial Joint Chiefs. The Crown Prince himself has been called to hurry t-to the Throne World to explain the intrusion of Unatari State combat ships into the Imperial Core. If not, the Empire will re-retain the right to destroy all your ships in its space."

If I'd gotten such a categorical ultimatum from the Throne World a few years ago, I would have surely considered my part in *Perimeter Defense* lost. And even six months ago, I'd have been shaking in terror and really would have hurried to fulfill the Emperor's every demand. But now, the situation was different:

"Tell the Imperial Secretariat that I was at the Throne World not that long ago, and I really hated the reception they showed me in the Silver Palace. So, if Emperor August royl Akad is so thirsting to speak with me, let him haul his fat ass off the throne, go over to the nearest data screen and give me a call. I promise that I will hear out his grievances in the most attentive fashion, and give my commentary on all issues."

"What, should-d I j-just s-say it like that?" the communications officer asked, nearly having a stroke.

"If your good upbringing won't allow you to say the word 'ass' to the Emperor, use a more concordant synonym: butt, posterior, center of gravity, or whatever you like," I allowed gracefully, and my subordinate hurried to sign off.

Astra, having overheard the conversation, even spilled some juice from her glass. Bionica didn't allow herself such clumsiness, but also didn't hide her surprise:

"My Prince, shouldn't you be speaking 'as politely as possible and even in a servile manner' with the ruler of the Empire, as demanded by law and courtly etiquette?"

"I should, but only if the Emperor is sound of mind and inspires respect and awe in his subjects. But only a madman, having lost all connection with reality, could send such an unfulfillable demand to me. And why be so dainty with a crazy person? And if Emperor August doesn't know what's going on, and the message was sent by a secretary without his knowledge then all the more so. Why should I bow and scrape before them?"

We continued our dinner, although the former atmosphere of good will at the table had completely disappeared. I was waiting for the Throne World's next move with anxiety. And truly, before five minutes had gone by, the very same communications officer told me that someone from the Throne World wanted to speak to me. Could August really have swallowed the injurious words about his fat ass and decided to speak? The man on the screen was not the Emperor, but Count Timur royl Nayt ton Miro, the official representative of the Imperial Joint Chiefs of Staff. There was no bowing and scraping, nor greeting. The man immediately got to business:

"Crown Prince Georg, I sincerely hope that you have an explanation for why Unatari State combat ships have entered the Silli, Uvari and New Oborite systems, which belong to the Imperial Core."

"Of course, Count. I am acting in complete accordance with Imperial law. Look in the Codex on Great House and Allied Kingdom Ship Movement, section eight, paragraph three, note six. I'm rushing to save the life of my daughter, who is in Perimeter Sector Seven, and so am taking the shortest possible route."

The man on the screen started thinking. Clearly, he had a legal database open before his eyes and was searching for the law I'd just named, and the concrete paragraph. Count Timur needed just two minutes to familiarize himself with it and think it over.

"Is Crown Princess Joan royl Georg ton Unatari really in danger?" the Count clarified with doubt, having correctly determined which of my four daughters I was referring to.

"Haven't you noticed, Count, that the Antagonists have killed absolutely all of her relatives in the last week and a half? The head of the Purple House Duke Takuro and his three sons, all grandchildren... The list of victims is massive, over seventy aristocrats from ruling families. Just don't tell me that the Imperial Military knows nothing of this story!"

"And why not? We are well informed of the chaos in the Purple House due to change in leadership there. But what do the Antagonists have to do with this? The new head of the Purple House is Duchess Violetta, a loyal servant of the Purple House and, by the way, your sister! These are the internal power struggles of a Great House, and the Empire does not intervene in such matters."

"And do you also not know that the Gold, Purple and Green Houses, in accordance with the Antagonist invasion plan are going to form the so-called Grand Duchy and leave the Empire in the next few hours? Or is that also none of the Empire's business, and just internal politics of one of the Great Houses? And the fact that Duchess Violetta is part of the Antagonist's shadow government and is even part of the ruling Triumvirate, is that also news to you?"

The man cringed in dismay and said with reproach:

"Crown Prince, forgive me for the harsh words, but what is this bullshit? What do you mean 'shadow government,' and 'Triumvirate?' The Antagonists have been ruled single-handedly by Crown Prince Eleonora royl Akad for two centuries, and as far as I can tell, no one has overthrown her yet."

"The Emperor's sister Eleonora is more than three hundred years old. She's a decrepit old bat, whose health has long prevented her from truly controlling anything. But unlike her brother, Eleonora had enough balls to recognize her impotence and hand power over the Gold House to the three people she trusted most, the so-called Triumvirate. Now, Eleonora is just a figurehead that doesn't decide anything and, from what I've heard, is even in a deep coma. It's totally different people in charge. One of the real rulers of the Antagonists is Eleonora's granddaughter Duchess Violetta royl Inoky ton Mesfelle, who recently came to power over the Purple House."

The Count twisted his lips in disbelief and slightly tilted his head to the side. The news was too shocking to just take at face value.

"Crown Prince Georg, you cannot just throw such accusations around so carelessly! If this is all made up to justify your fleet's passage..."

"Come on! Wake up!" I couldn't hold back and raised my voice to a scream. "How blind must you be to not see the obvious!!! What point is there for the Empire to have a secret spy corps if they do not fulfill their duties or know about the Empire's historic enemy! The situation is such that the Antagonists have killed every single Purple House ruler loyal to the Empire. The only survivor, Crown Princess Joan, with the remnants of the Perimeter Sector Seven Fleet, also loyal to the Empire, are now stuck in a dead-end in the Nayal and Veyerde systems, and will soon be killed if I don't help her! My fleet is now rushing to rescue the Crown Princess! It's up to you, Count, to believe me or not, but I'll bring my ships to Sector Seven to save my daughter, even if I have to fight my way through!"

Count Timur thought it over deeply and for a long time. It seemed to me that he was consulting with someone, or even more likely, with a whole group of people. Finally, the Joint Chiefs representative gave his answer:

"Unatari State ships will not have to fight their way through. We'll clear a path. But the Joint Chiefs still want to know exactly what of your forces are now passing through Core territory."

I couldn't believe my ears. They didn't even have a way to tell? My fleet had passed through three star systems of the Imperial Core already, and the Imperial military still hadn't gotten radar signatures on my fleet?! My opinion of the Imperial military fell through the deck of my ship. I mean, I had peaceful intentions, and wasn't threatening public order in the Empire. But if I'd wanted to take hostile action? In the nineteen hours it took them to make their first reaction, I'd have been able to capture five, or even eight systems. The Empire could have lost ten percent of its territory before they even realized they'd been attacked!

All the same, I didn't reproach them for their disorganized border control. Instead, I brought up on screen a list of all the ships in my fleet and started reading them off:

"Five carriers, two *Uukresh* and three *Quasar*. Eighty battleships: thirty-two *Monarchs*, and thirty-seven *Tyrants*, one fairly old *Usurper* and ten *Meresh* of Swarm design. Four hundred seventy cruisers, of which one hundred ninety are heavy. One thousand two hundred destroyers, primarily of Swarm construction. Seven *Tria* landing ships, but none are fully stocked — the Alpha Iseyek sustained losses in my war on the Blue House. And one thousand seven hundred frigates: *Pyros* and *Warhawks*, approximately half and half. All in all, that's approximately three and a half thousand starships."

The Joint Chiefs representative gave a somehow nervous chuckle, said something like, "I told you, no rush," to some people off screen, then explained the reason for his reaction:

"The Seventh Imperial Strike Fleet, reinforced by two squadrons of light ships, has received a mission to move out to capture the Unatari State ships, stop you and, in case of resistance, to eliminate you. They are waiting for you in the Timocha system, next on your path. Anyway, this fleet contains twelve battleships, sixty heavy cruisers and one hundred twenty light, plus a bunch of smaller-class ships, two thousand in total. The Joint Chiefs command thought that should be enough. It's very good that the situation was resolved to our mutual satisfaction, and no catastrophes happened."

"I have never had any intention of doing battle with Imperial ships. But in the case of aggression from the Seventh Strike Fleet, we would have wiped the floor with them, not even particularly noting resistance."

"I don't doubt that, Crown Prince. Now that fleet will have a new mission: to accompany the Unatari State ships out of the Imperial Core, then follow them into Sector Seven. If the information about Duchess Violetta being party to a conspiracy against the Empire is confirmed, the Imperial Fleet must arrest the traitor. And I greatly hope that the Unatari ships will help in that endeavor. All the same, the movement of such a great number of starships must be kept secret from the Antagonists. I will give orders to that effect, and the information about the Seventh Strike Fleet and Unatari Fleet's movement will not leak."

Before the Joint Chiefs representative managed to sign off, I got another long-distance call. As soon as I realized who wanted to talk to me, I cringed in disgust, feeling like putting the "voice of the Triumvirate" right through to Miya. But still, I held back my emotions and accepted the call.

Albert royl Timur ton Akad, Count of the Gold House, Official Voice of the Triumvirate
   Age: 69 years
   Race: Human
   Gender: Male
   Class: Aristocrat/Mystic
   Achievements: Playboy, Worthless Diplomat, Despised by Humanity, Steamrolled, Pedal-Powered Tool
   Fame: +5
   Standing: -644

It took me a great deal of effort not to laugh, looking at all the weight my reply had stacked on the Count. With such a horrible standing, he probably wasn't even allowed to use the public restroom, which was to say nothing of aristocratic councils and serious meetings. It was no surprise that the Blue House head had refused to talk with such a vile cur!

But some learn nothing from fate. From his first

words, Count Albert threw himself on me with reproach, accusing me in sharp terms of breaking our agreement. I didn't think I had — I ended the war with the Blue House in just five days, in accordance with my understanding with the Antagonists, and had every right to the territories I'd gained in that war. But I didn't justify myself before this obnoxious boor and ordered the Count transferred to the Red Queen.

*   *   *

"Your Highness, Admiral Peres ton Mesfelle-Tesse, Seventh Strike Fleet Commander, has arrived to *Joan the Fatty* and asks that you see him."

I pulled away from my discussion with the admirals of the united fleet. In the center of the room was a huge hologram depicting the part of the galaxy known to humanity with a web of transport lines and markers for all known fleets. I turned sharply to the officer who'd come to talk to me. For some reason, he went pale and swallowed his spit, but I answered with a good-hearted smile:

"Why would I refuse a guest, if he's asking so politely? Take the admiral here to the fleet control headquarters. But, colleagues, take the Imperial fleet off the map first. There's no reason to show that we're tracking them. And darken all Unatari space, because that also has markers guests shouldn't see."

"Does Your Highness mean the *Queen* that's under repair?" clarified Admiral Kiro Sabuto.

"Not only that. There's also the *Mammoth*, which is nearly ready, and a string of super-heavy ships in Uvi and Dekeye. And our unfinished battleship fleet, which we cannot receive the heavy cannon installations for. It's also quite important not to tell them about the fact two former Blue House fleets are missing. Just think, it's been two whole weeks since we've heard anything from fifteen hundred ships that should belong to us! If one of our allies finds out, we'll be laughed out of town!"

The disappearance of the Blue House ships had become the mystery of the century. Two huge fleets with a total of fifteen hundred ships had just disappeared in the infinity of space! When Mark royl Uvar ton Miro, during the negotiations with me, complained that his ships had disappeared, I just laughed to myself, considering it an aftereffect of the chaos afoot in the Blue House. But now, in Mark's place, I didn't know what to think about the matter. Every last system of Perimeter Sectors Nine, Eleven, Twelve, and Thirteen were now under my control. Of the forty-seven factions in the Blue House civil war, forty-five had recognized me as their rightful ruler.

Both of those who'd refused to lay down their weapons were armed religious fanatic groups, who'd captured one of the planets in Sector Thirteen and were using terror to propagate their rather unusual beliefs. Both extremist groups were, basically, different branches of the same religion, which denied the very possibility of interstellar flight, the existence of people outside of that particular planet and the existence of other cosmic races. Their theologians asserted that signals from outer space were mystification created by the competing confession to spread chaos and doubt among their flock. For obvious reasons, the two missing fleets were definitely not connected with those religious groups. My orbital bombers and Alpha Iseyek landing troops, meanwhile, were going to put an end to their theological debate soon and get their brains back in place.

Admiral Peres ton Mesfelle-Tesse was a gray-haired, but quite active old man, with a long thick, white beard. He looked a lot like Santa Claus, dressed in a space fleet uniform. Despite his ninety years of age, the strict military bearing and proud poise of the admiral could be envied by younger officers. The gallant military man's whole chest was weighed down with a great many ribbons and medals. It made a great effect, although I immediately saw that most of the medals had been awarded to the fleet leader for years served or in honor of commemoratory dates. Along with the admiral, there came a large group of Seventh Strike Fleet senior officers: the captains of all twelve battleships and a few senior tactics officers.

"Crown Prince Georg royl Inoky ton Mesfelle, allow me to express my great respect to your Highness!" the old man said with a slight bow, the gesture repeated synchronically by all his subordinates. "You turned out absolutely right, Your Highness. The Throne World has confirmed what you said about the Antagonists' plans to create a Grand Duchy. Our agents have determined that, in forty minutes, there will be a grand address of the heads of the three Great Houses, in which they will announce the departure of the Green and Purple Houses from the Empire!"

It was not news to me, I already knew it. But a gasp of amazement rolled over many of the officers. Meanwhile, the old admiral continued:

"I have received an official dispatch from the Joint

Chiefs saying the Empire will join the war against the separatists immediately after they announce their secession. As you know, Crown Prince, my fleet has a special mission to arrest the head of the conspirators Crown Princess Violetta royl Inoky ton Mesfelle-Damir. According to our recon data, the insurgent Princess is now located in the Damir system in Sector Seven. That's just one and a half days from here, so I request that Your Highness aid me in this mission."

He wanted to arrest my twin sister? Naive... It wasn't that I was against it. More likely I was in favor, but the gallant military man's plans seemed nearly impossible to me. But anything was possible, especially if he acted suddenly. I stood from the armchair and walked closer to the hologram.

"Zoom in on Sector Seven! Center on the Forepost-10 System! Commander, come out here to the viewing platform, let's look over your suggestion together, based on the forces of all players represented in the region."

The admiral tried very hard not to show any emotion on his face, but the old man did a bad job of it. He made quite a bad actor. The fleet leader's eyes were just burning in agitation when he saw the detailed interactive tactical map, which showed in real time the location and movement of all fleets, and even lone ships. After letting the admiral admire the crucial and accurate tool, I walked over to the console and started pointing and commenting on the markers on screen:

"Here is the Forepost-10 system with an uninhabitable warp beacon, which is where we are now. Here is the next system in our route, Khell, a local transport node that connects four star systems: Forepost-10, Anti, Nayal and Uvara. That is where the large Purple House fleet is now located. It contains fifteen hundred ships among which there are thirty battleships. That fleet is loyal to Duchess Violetta and is tightly blocking the exit from the Nayal-Veyerde corridor, which is where seventy ships of Perimeter Sector Seven Fleet are trapped, along with my daughter, Crown Princess Joan. Another large Purple House fleet of one thousand ships is in the next system, Anti, blocking the path to the Damir system, where the 'ice princess' is now. With Duchess Violetta in Damir is her personal fleet of three hundred ships. Another three hundred ships are in Uvara, that is the part of the Perimeter Sector Seven Fleet loyal to the new authorities. Also in Uvara is my Perimeter Sector Eight Fleet of five hundred ships, recharging energy for the jump to Khell under the command of Space Major Nicole ton Savoia."

"So then, we have a two-to one ship advantage!!!" the old admiral crowed, getting worked up. "Six thousand starships against three thousand Antagonists! What are we waiting for, Crown Prince?! We need to attack immediately!!!"

I didn't go finding fault in the word 'we,' although the goals of the Unatari State and the Empire didn't fully coincide, and our fleets had different goals in this military adventure. Instead of that, I turned to the commander and asked him, looking the old man right in the eyes:

"Admiral Peres, you have many years of wisdom behind you. Do you really think our enemies stupid enough to have brought two thousand eight hundred ships to this key point in our highly important political stand-off, then split them into three groups? Sure, the Purple House doesn't have much in the way of personal forces, but there are several Green House fleets in their space now, amounting to a total of more than six thousand starships. Why aren't they here in Khell? The Purple House could place five times more forces at this key point, but they haven't. Why? The way they're sitting, it's like they're inviting us to Khell. Why do they want that? We must be missing something. What is it?"

The old man looked at the map for a long time, thinking it over and sucking silently on his lips. Finally, he answered:

"Yes, Crown Prince, the situation does look strange. But it is not my custom to fear the unknown. Perhaps, we've just overestimated our enemy's knowledge of the situation, and the Purple House doesn't know that our two huge fleets are in this distant system. When does the operation begin?"

I looked at a table on the wall with countdown timers for various events.

"In three hours and twenty minutes, the Perimeter Sector Eight Fleet will have the energy for a warp jump to Khell. It will take them three hours and forty minutes after that to reach their destination so, they will arrive in seven hours. Immediately after that, in accordance with our arrangement, the Purple House Fleet will receive control over the Nayal warp beacon and can send some of their ships there to take the system under control. Marat ton Mesfelle's ships then, on the other hand, will jump to Khell and join Nicole ton Savoia's fleet in four hours. The most dangerous time will be seven hours from now. That is when the Antagonists will have the best opportunity to attack the Perimeter Sector Eight Fleet, when the blocked fleet has already jumped to Khell with Crown Princess Joan, but hasn't yet arrived."

"Don't you worry, Crown Prince. By that time, the Purple House will already have joined the Grand Duchy and will thus be a clear enemy of the Empire. So, my ships will come to Khell in seven hours and attack them doggedly. I hope that your starships will be with me, and will support the Seventh Imperial Strike Fleet in battle. But we could manage regardless: two thousand ships against fifteen hundred, it will be glorious!"

"I've already told Your Highness, and am prepared to reaffirm that this is a trap."

"Flora, I know that. Only naive idiots could believe the Antagonists haven't noticed the movement of a fleet of five thousand ships into their space. But the enemy is not taking any actions in response, and that's strange. I do not understand our enemies' plans, and that really frightens me. So, I won't stop the Imperial ships. But I will go separately. We need a victim to voluntarily enter the trap, provoke the Grand Duchy to fight and force them to show their hand, thus disarming the trap. And let that victim be Imperial ships, not ours."

*   *   *

"My Prince, the first part of the mission is complete. The Perimeter Sector Seven Fleet has just made a warp jump from the Nayal to the Khell system. At the same time, the Purple House Fleet jumped to Nayal in its entirety. Your Highness's message to Marat ton Mesfelle was sent simultaneously."

I smiled at my beautiful Perimeter Sector Eight Fleet Commander. On the big screen, Nicole looked flawlessly prim, strict and at the same time feminine and elegant, just as she did in real life.

"Wonderful, Nicole! But now, don't call them the Purple House. It's the Grand Duchy. The Gold, Purple and Green Houses have all declared they are joining together and leaving the Empire. An hour ago, I lost the Largest Territory achievement, and now the Grand Duchy is the largest political force in the galaxy, larger than the Empire and our state."

"So, are they enemies now?" my subordinate clarified.

"Technically, the Unatari State has yet to declare war on them, but that won't last long. The Empire has already officially declared war on the Grand Duchy and moved their fleets out to attack. So Unatari, as an allied kingdom that is part of the Empire, must either also declare war on the side of our suzerain, or declare that we are also seceding from the Empire. According to the law, as the ruler of Unatari, I have one day to make my final decision."

"Does that change my mission at all?"

Nicole asked, her voice remaining firm, even though the brilliant fleet commander understood perfectly that her eight hundred starships were deep in foreign territory surrounded by potentially hostile ships which numbered four times more than her fleet. And at that, I couldn't tell the girl that my main fleet was very nearby in the neighboring Forepost-10 system and could come to her aid. In the last few days, I had spoken with everyone through a retransmitter on the territory of the former Blue House, so Nicole thought that I was on my way to the Blue House capital to make my first moves as the new ruler of my expanded realm.

"No, Nicole. You should still meet the allied ships from the Nayal system and provide for their protection. From there, it will depend on the Empire and Grand Duchy. By the way, the large Seventh Imperial Strike Fleet will reach you in Khell in a few hours, so that should make things easier. But no matter what Admiral Peres says, the Perimeter Sector Eight Fleet has its own mission, and you are not obliged to obey him. And another thing..." I made a pause to make sure this conversation was on an encrypted channel. "I order you to mine the Khell warp beacon with thermonuclear bombs before the Imperial Fleet arrives, and to do it in such a way that the staff don't notice. Even better would be to change out all the warp beacon staff with your people, so no one knows."

What is the difference between soldiers and civilians? After receiving such a, to put it lightly, strange order, a civilian would try to figure out the reason or demand explanations, but a military person would carry it out first. And here Nicole, although she couldn't keep the dispassionate emotionless look on her face, gave me a salute and promised to complete the mission. An ideal order taker.

Attention!!!

A new faction has come into being: Imperial Androids

Imperial Android faction's present opinion of you: +25 (approval)

I turned to Bionica, who was sitting next to me sipping a vitamin enriched juice through a straw. The synthetic blonde smiled at me and commented:

"My subjects considered this the ideal moment to reveal our existence. All the galaxy's news channels are packed with stories about the beginning of the war between the Empire and the Grand Duchy, so no one will pay particular mind to us modest androids. And after this, people and other races will gradually grow accustomed to us and, soon enough, no one will even be surprised anymore by the androids as a separate faction. Emperor August royl Akad has already given his approval, although his agreement came at a very, very high price."

All in all, a logical move. In the place of intelligent humanoid robots, I would have done the same. All political leaders had their heads filled with completely different matters now, and no one would express much of a point of view on the androids' desires. The Emperor, meanwhile, could only be for it. After all, the hundreds of millions of androids were traditionally considered property of a Green House corporation, and paid taxes and commissions to them. So, depriving the Lavaelle family, which was now an enemy, of a stable source of funds was something the ruler of the Empire could only be glad about.

"Crown Prince, something strange is happening! I'm detecting the arrival of a large number of previously

unknown ships to the Nayal system."

Notes of panic slipped through in Flora's mental message. My little Truth Seeker, who had the unique gift of being able to sense the movement of ships along the warp beacon transportation network, was now sensing something that simply could not be, so she doubted her sensations and even her abilities.

"Flora, that's probably the fifteen-hundred ships of the former Purple House, which was holding the Nayal-Veyerde pocket under siege. There shouldn't be any other ships there."

"No, Crown Prince. The Fleet of the Grand Duchy is still in warp jump from Khell to Nayal. And... It's hard to explain to a person without these abilities... I cannot tell you exactly how, but I know that these are totally different ships."

"Aliens? Sure, that is probably it. After all, they have attacked Nayal in the past, jumping from somewhere in their space to our activated warp beacon. The beacon is on again, so the invasion is back underway. And at that, the first person to chance upon the Aliens would be the Grand Duchy's fleet of fifteen hundred. Although they'd be my enemies in five minutes' time, I hoped the people would have the strength to stop the breakthrough."

"My Prince, I want to remind Your Highness, that I was never able to sense Alien ships before. Of course, it's been a long time since then, and I have become stronger, but still... Once again, I cannot describe how I know this... but I'm sure they are human ships."

Well that's a fine how-do-you-do! An unknown fleet had just warped into a closed pocket from out of nowhere. What could this even be? Flora then added some more information to think over, telling me that both of the Grand Duchy's other fleets we knew about had begun jumping to the Khell star system, but from different directions. I didn't manage to answer, because two thirds of the monitors in my headquarters turned off, and my glowing star-map hologram as well. Sabotage, again?! But this time, it was a different reason, and the officer responsible for the tactical map told it to me:

"I'm not getting a signal from any of the data channels connecting us with Unatari and the Empire! I also cannot connect to Veyerde! The comm lines all get cut off at the warp beacons. There's no way to send messages through the Anti, Uvara, Nayal or Forepost-9 systems. The Forepost-10 retransmitter in our system is also turned off! Data blockade!"

*   *   *

The faces of everyone in the room turned to me. They were all expecting me to react or comment, so I couldn't show any despondency or perplexity at that moment no matter how I felt.

"Get a landing group to the Forepost-10 warp beacon at once! Take it under complete control! After that, place a two-hundred megaton thermonuclear bomb there! Can we communicate with the fleet in Khell?"

"Yes sir, Your Highness!"

"Tell Space Major Nicole ton Savoia what happened and ask her about the beacons surrounding the Khell system. Can we talk to our cloakers in Forepost-9? There was a mobile warp beacon deployment ship there and, I think, one or two *Ghosts*."

A few seconds later, I got my answer that they were unreachable: both the Forepost-9 system and the transmission of signals through it were turned off. What an idiotic situation. In the neighboring system, there was an uninhabitable warp beacon, and we could have taken it under our complete control with just a few people. And also, the mobile warp beacon deployment ship we'd captured from the Aliens was in the same system and could theoretically open a portal for us there. But how could we tell them to do that?!

"Flora, can you issue commands mentally?"

"Unfortunately, I cannot, Crown Prince. Sending thoughts is not my specialty. I can speak only with Your Highness, your second cousin, and the Red Queen. But wait! Unlike me, your wife is great at that. I could try to send a mental message to Miya."

"Go ahead. I need our cloakers in the Forepost-9 system to take the warp beacon there under control. It doesn't need to be turned on, and transmission of messages doesn't need to be restored. All-around, it's better for them not to reveal their presence. Just make sure they're ready to activate the beacon for us. And let them send one of their ships to the neighboring Amati system. The warp beacon there should also be taken under control. We need to make sure our fleet can get back to the Imperial Core."

"I'll try and send the message, Crown Prince."

"Great. All ships, at the ready in ten minutes! We're going to Khell to see this unknown fleet for ourselves!"

Rat in a Trap

THE COMING of the Unatari fleet to Khell was met with such stormy jubilation that Florianna nearly lost consciousness when trying to consume and assimilate the outpouring of emotions. The little Truth Seeker even had to be brought to her senses with smelling salts, because the girl fell off her chair and was shaking as if she'd just touched a live wire.

"The flow of adoration and joy was unexpectedly powerful, I couldn't digest it all," Astra's sister said aloud, embarrassed at her weakness. "Even after military victories, the emotions weren't that strong. But here, the Sector Eight and Seven fleets already thought they were doomed, and feel they've just been rescued from a death trap. When Your Highness's ships arrived, it was as if they had been brought back from the dead."

Flora's voice was hoarse like an old man's, not childlike at all. Nevertheless, the maimed girl's vocal cords were gradually healing, which was a huge step on the road to recovery.

"Your Highness, the cloaked frigate *Surprise-77* requests to dock on your flagship."

"Allow them! What's more, meet the group as they arrive, provide security and bring them to headquarters."

Surprise-77 had an especially important mission. Just a few people knew, but Crown Princess Joan wasn't under guard by soldiers loyal to her on the huge *Quasar*, as everyone thought. I didn't exclude the possibility of a sneak attack on the Perimeter Sector Seven Fleet by the Grand Duchy, so I didn't want to risk the girl's life. For the last few days, my daughter had been on the little cloaked frigate, perhaps not in comfort, but at least in relative safety.

An incoming call request came in from the Perimeter Sector Eight Fleet flagship, the battleship *Ravenous*. Space Major Nicole ton Savoia, not even trying to hide her tears of joy, greeted me and reported on the situation:

"Crown Prince Georg, the Imperial fleet came to Khell just as you warned. But they didn't stick around, quickly recharging at the station and leaving for Nayal to catch up with the fleet of the Grand Duchy. Admiral Peres suggested my fleet join him in the chase, but I remembered Your Highness's order and refused. Then, all the warp beacons around Khell immediately went out!"

"Yes, the trap has slammed shut, we have been cut off from the rest of the galaxy," I said, not hiding the complexity of the situation from my subordinate or the other officers in earshot. "I order all Sector Eight Fleet Ships to take up positions in common formation and maintain combat readiness. In twenty-seven minutes, we expect thousands of Grand Duchy ships to arrive here from the Anti star system, and in another six minutes, reinforcements will come from Uvara. Then, it will also become clear whether the Grand Duchy ships are our enemies, and we will act in accordance with that. I see only two possibilities: either we are allowed to go to Unatari unimpeded, or we will destroy the enemy ships that arrive to show them not to mess with us. And from there, we can see if the Grand Duchy has the forces to hold us in this cell!"

I interrupted my emotional speech, because Crown Princess Joan showed up in the open doors. I couldn't recognize the girl. Normally full of vibrant joy, happy and careless, she now looked tired and even ill. Her cheeks were sunken, her gaze was dim and she had huge black bags under her eyes. I could never have called her a fatty now. The girl had lost a ton of weight, and it was immediately obvious how hard the last few weeks had been on her. Joan entered the large room boldly and stopped, looking around indecisively and meeting only unfamiliar faces. It seemed she didn't see me until I stood from the fleet commander's seat and walked out to meet her.

"Crown Prince Georg, I... as the last representative of the ancient family of... well..." the girl sobbed and got totally embarrassed. The speech she had prepared just flew out of her head.

I walked up to the girl and embraced her tightly.

"Everything is alright now, Joan, be still. You're my daughter now, and I won't let anybody hurt you."

The little girl nodded, poking me in the shoulder and bursting into tears, only then allowing herself to release the horrible tension that had been building up in her for the last few days.

Crown Princess Joan royl Georg ton Unatari's opinion of you has improved
Current opinion: +100 (absolutely trusting)

But at that, I knew without any Truth Seekers that Joan wasn't just acting, and wasn't trying to butter up her adoptive father. Her emotions and behavior were totally sincere. The girl sobbed and, swallowing tears of rage together with fragmentary sentences, told me all her fears and umbrages. The little girl saw me as a reliable protector, who would accept her however she was, always understand and, beyond all doubt, punish those who did her wrong.

And then I sensed that something had broken inside me. Tears welled up in my eyes. What was there to hide here? The decision to adopt Joan was one I had taken primarily out of political considerations. But from that moment, everything changed. I accepted Joan as my daughter without any limitations, even making no mental distinction between her and my other children.

I don't know how long my daughter and I spent standing, warmly embracing and speaking, having forgotten about everyone and everything going on around us. But eventually, a communications officer tore me from the family idyll.

"Crown Prince Georg, incoming call from the planet Oveyete-VII. That is Grand Duchy territory, Perimeter Sector Three."

Beyond all the unnecessary hints, I knew perfectly well where the capital of the Green House was, or whatever it was calling itself now. I was slightly annoyed but quickly got myself together and asked in a normal tone to wait a bit to put him through.

They wanted to speak with me so badly they had temporarily removed the complete data blockade. But if the Grand Duchy's signal had come through the chain of warp beacons, maybe one of ours could as well?

"Send an encrypted message to our ships in the Forepost-9 system to take the warp beacon under control! Did it send? Did you get a confirmation receipt? Great! Alright, now we can speak with the Grand Duchy. But first turn off the hologram behind me and the tactical map. There's no reason to give information to the enemy. Flora, be ready to defend me from mental attack, if necessary. Put them through!"

I had seen the tall, thin woman with a massive golden crown in her ultrashort dark hair thousands of times in photographs and videos, but I had never spoken to her in all my time in *Perimeter Defense.*

Duchess Elisa royl Clement ton Mesfelle-Lavaelle, co-ruler of the Grand Duchy
 Age: 188
 Race: Human
 Gender: Female
 Relation to you: your mother
 Class: Aristocrat
 Achievements: Daughter of the Enemy, Defector, Political Weathervane, Unprincipled, Schemer, Got Hers
 Fame: +42
 Standing: -9
 Presumed opinion of you: - 58 (hate)

Grand Duchy's opinion of you: - 11 (dislike)

"I see you managed to rescue the girl after all, Georg. What can I say? Your zeal is admirable. But it was naive of you to think you could bring such a large fleet through our holdings unnoticed. We were expecting you and prepared carefully. Six months ago, you were able to trap the Green House Fleet very skillfully, by turning off the surrounding warp beacons. We learned a lot from that painful lesson. Now, it is a great irony of fate that the successors to the Green House have done the very same with your fleet."

I had a hard time holding back a smile. Did they still think they had caught me? That must have meant that the short, encrypted signal to the Forepost-9 system had remained unnoticed. What could I say? The easiest enemy to have is the kind that wrongfully supposes they are in complete control of you. I didn't try to talk my mother out of her confusion. In fact, I played along:

"There's a very substantial difference between what happened six months ago to the Green House First Strike Fleet and the current situation. Demyen royl Amelius ton Lavaelle's fleet was trapped in the Forepost-31 system, which is uninhabitable and useless with no food, water or anything that could have allowed them to survive for long. But my fleet in the Khell system controls a large transport hub, which cuts off eight Grand Duchy star systems from the rest of your territory. We are not currently low on provisions, but if we do happen to need them, we can take them from the densely populated planet of Khell-

IV. So, the Grand Duchy will be forced to find some way of smoking out the Unatari Fleet. We are not limited by time and can dictate the conditions ourselves."

"I think not!" Duchess Elisa said sharply and, turning to someone I couldn't see, ordered: "Turn the camera and show him!"

The image shifted onto my two daughters. On a small round pedestal, Crown Princesses Likanna and Natalie were on their knees with their hands bound behind their backs. There was a group of armed guards around them. Joan, who was next to me, shuddered at the sight of it and shouted in fear, then covered her face with her hands. But I frowned, having recognized several aristocrats from the Lavaelle family among the guardsmen holding the girls in their sight. That family hated me fiercely, so the guards really were inclined to shoot the hostages.

I also noticed three women standing behind Duchess Elisa in dark clothing with hoods covering their faces. Three Truth Seekers! It looked like my mom was afraid of this conversation and had taken the appropriate measures to avoid me doing anything unpredictable.

"As you see, Georg, you really cannot dictate the terms. And seeing as you put forth so much effort to save your adopted daughter Joan, you definitely won't let two of your other daughters die, especially your beloved oldest daughter Likanna. Now listen carefully to me, Georg, and your daughters will remain among the living! In twenty minutes, Grand Duchy ships will be arriving to Khell. You will order your starships to turn off their energy shields and thrusters, then you will take a shuttle to the ship we tell you to go to. After that, you'll do as you're told. I promise you, son, if you do as I say, no one has to suffer!"

So that's what you call "going to visit grandma in Sector Three..." How low and evil it was to use trusting little Crown Princesses to blackmail their father! Especially after Elisa gave her word as a Crown Princess and swore by her aristocratic honor that she wouldn't do anything bad to the girls if they came to visit, and that not even a hair would fall from their heads. All the same, I didn't reproach my mother for breaking her word — that was useless. She'd probably say, after all, that she was no longer an Imperial Crown Princess, so all her old oaths had lost their force.

I'd like to find out whose idea it was initially to take the girls hostage — my mother's, or the Lavaelle family's. In fact, I wouldn't mind finding out what their relationship was like right now in general. Why was the crown of a Grand Duchy co-ruler on Elisa's head, but not Duke Amelius royl Mast ton Lavaelle's? After all, the old man, in appending his Green House to the Grand Duchy, was most likely counting on ruling the united government. What had the Antagonists offered the Green House Head to give up their claim to power? Or maybe, someone had simply pressured him and forced him to stand aside? Should I try to play on possible tensions between the Green and Gold House?

I took a step forward and, putting a bored and ambivalent expression on my face, said to the Duchess with reproach:

"Mother, you've always been a terrible actress. Now

as always, you're overdoing it. After all, no one seriously believes that you'll agree to sacrifice your beloved granddaughter Likanna! But we'll leave that for later. Now, I'm troubled by something else entirely. Tell me why you aren't upholding our understanding?"

"What are you talking about, Georg?" With my words, I managed to knock the Duchess off course, and she couldn't hide her incomprehension.

"Our understanding? I was supposed to remove all claimants to power in the Orange, Red and Blue Houses. It wasn't easy, but I did it. All more or less popular aristocrats were killed or signed resignations. You'd need a microscope to see what's left of them on the political arena. My twin sister Violetta's mission was to pull up the Purple House ruling families by the root, which she did spectacularly. And you promised my sister and I that, before you were crowned co-ruler of the Grand Duchy, you would remove all other claimants to the Gold and Green Houses up to and including babies, so they wouldn't stand in the way of our family's rule! So then, why do I see members of the Lavaelle family with you in the room?! Why have they not yet been exterminated?!"

Based on the frozen picture on the big screen, they were all in a stupor. After all, no one had ever before guessed that the complicated and bloody process of uniting the Great Houses could be seen as a purely intrafamily affair of the daughter of the ruler of the Antagonists and her two blood children. And one after the next, those two children had already removed all even remotely significant competition, and were now just discussing the technical details of a process that was near completion. Now, it seemed, the people in the room had opened their eyes, and begun to suspect.

The first to come to his senses was some officer in an old Green House uniform. He shouted an extremely insulting phrase at my mother and reached for his holster. But he didn't manage to do anything. Within a second, he was lit up like a candle and, collapsing to the floor, wailed hysterically. Duchess Elisa's bodyguards and Truth Seekers clearly worked for their bread. Another aristocrat of the Lavaelle family also tried and failed to shoot and was disarmed by the attentive guards.

But they still didn't have time to neutralize all the many, armed guardsmen. Duchess Elisa gasped and stared in surprise at the smoking hole burned through her luxurious dress right where her heart was. The woman stood up straight for another few seconds, then the Grand Duchy co-ruler's knees started buckling and she collapsed to the floor. The golden crown flew from her short-haired head and rolled across the mosaic floor.

ATTENTION!!!
Your mother Duchess Elisa royl Clement ton Mesfelle-Lavaelle has been killed by Baron Maggo ton Lavaelle

There was no reason to try and get revenge for my mother's death because, by that time, all that remained of Baron Maggo was a pulsating lump of protoplasm. One of the distraught armed men had managed to get his heavy infantry resonator working in the fray, mowing down a wide swath of both allies and erstwhile enemies. I had a hard time tearing myself from the spectacle of the bloody slaughter and turned to the Crown Princesses watching the chaos with their hands bound:

"Likanna, Natalie, your mission in Sector Three is completed. Return to Dekeye with your report, after which you may go free, along with all the other members of your race."

Both of the girls stood at the same time, bowed very gracefully, then shook the useless fetters from their wrists, dissolved into whitish clouds and flew out of the room.

No one even noticed the Arites. In fact, there were few living people left in the room. Just three very badly wounded soldiers kicking the last remaining Truth Seeker as she lied on the floor, having lost her power when she lost her master. What I wanted to do was order the transmission ended, but I noticed the Lavaelle family crest on one of the bloodied soldiers attacking the lifeless psionic.

"Flora, get them too! Bionica, while we have a stable connection, order the palace androids on Oveyete-VII to destroy all footage of this incident, and any other information that may have been retained."

"My Prince, it will be done in the very best fashion, don't you doubt it!" my synthetic assistant promised.

And I turned to my silent officers and little Joan, staring at me with their eyes wide in horror. Probably, after what I said to my mother, they all saw me as a coldblooded monster, who had ruthlessly slaughtered all those keeping me from power. As such, I couldn't get by without some commentary here.

"If any of you didn't quite understand what you just saw, let me explain. There is not and never was any secret understanding between me, Duchess Elisa and Duchess Violetta. I never murdered or tracked any aristocrats or rulers of the Blue or Red Houses. And with the Orange House, I behaved very reservedly, especially in comparison with other aristocrats, and limited myself to just a couple forced resignations. The only exception was the man who killed my brother Crown Prince Roben, who was assassinated with my tacit consent. But that was a special case, and I acted fully within the bounds of the law."

Florianna stood from her flying chair, raised her right hand and said distinctly:

"I swear by my abilities as a Truth Seeker that Crown Prince Georg royl Inoky ton Mesfelle is speaking the pure truth!"

A collective sigh of relief rolled over the room. Everyone there knew perfectly that Truth Seekers were incapable of flagrantly lying. Taking advantage of the opportunity, I continued my speech:

"What you heard just now in that conversation with the Grand Duchy was pure ad lib. It would have been stupid not to take advantage of the chance to use some disinformation on our opponents, driving a wedge between our enemies in the Green and Gold Houses. They obviously didn't trust one another, and my words served as a spark to turn their moldering distrust into direct, fiery conflict. I admit, I wasn't expecting it to cause such a bloodbath, but I don't regret what happened one bit. Let our enemies fight amongst themselves. And yes, you didn't mishear, I called them our enemies! The Unatari State is declaring war against the Grand Duchy! Katerina, release an official statement! And now, friends, everyone in their seats! In fifteen minutes, a huge enemy fleet will be arriving here to Khell with a thousand ships. Let's give them a fiery reception!!!"

In return, an elated roar from many throats rang out, but I called them to silence with a gesture.

"Florianna, get up from your chair and walk over to the interactive map. Don't help her, she can manage!"

The little girl, draped in black clothing, got up from the flying chair none-too-confidently and, refusing the help of her four Beta Iseyek, staggered over to me on her shaky disobedient legs.

"Show us all on the map where and in what formation the enemy fleet will enter the system."

Dozens of attentive eyes watched the bewildered little Florianna closely. Her face reflected panic, and her eyes widened in fear.

"Crown Prince, but I don't..." Flora suddenly froze mid-word and, not even fully believing the reality of it herself, started placing ship markers quickly on the large interactive map.

*   *   *

"Thirty seconds!" the tactics officer's message boomed out in the echoing silence with particular sharpness.

Everyone in the headquarters was fully concentrated, because the enemy's fleet had one thousand ships and that was very, very serious, even if you considered our four-to-one advantage and the information we got from the Truth Seeker. I was also a bit nervous, even though Florianna had shown us exactly where the enemy fleet would arrive and in what formation. In fact, the forthcoming battle had become a type of exam for my Truth Seeker. The girl was making fast progress, increasing her strength and, if her ability to foretell the positions of enemy ships was confirmed, Florianna would become a truly invaluable tool in space combat.

I put the helmet on my head and turned on the microphone:

"I remind the whole fleet, ignore the first group of ships to arrive! Those are empty, old ships and fireships laden with explosives. Fifty-five seconds after that, activate the mines! Twenty seconds after the big blast, three groups of ten bombers each iron out the main concentrations Flora has marked. After that, we can see what the enemy has left, and act accordingly. Three seconds. Two. One. Let's go out to greet them!"

A two-and-a-half-mile-long chain of small ship groups appeared on screen. Within one second, the friend-foe system identified them, and the markers of the ships that arrived turned red on the tactical map.

"Looks pretty. Like a red thread in a green tube!" Nicole ton Savoia giggled on the common fleet channel.

I winced in dismay at the badly timed and meaningless comment from my first assistant. The normally dead serious Sector Eight Fleet Commander was simply unrecognizable today. Nicole was still in a state of near-euphoric elation after the Unatari Fleet came to Khell and saved her ships. The young Space Major had already begun laughing without any reason a few times in the last couple of minutes, and was now littering the airwaves with empty chatter during battle. I had to take measures. After turning off my microphone in order not to shame the girl before the whole united Unatari Fleet, I said strictly:

"Space Major Nicole ton Savoia, I temporarily relieve you of your duties! Go to the middle of the room and do three sets of thirty pushups with two-minute breaks for rest! Rosss, make sure she completes the exercises properly. Captain Valian ton Corsa, you are temporarily promoted to commander's first assistant!"

Nicole stood humbly, not saying a word, unbuttoned and removed her medal-laden jacket, hung it on the back of her chair and went to do the pushups. The free seat next to me was taken instantly by Valian ton Corsa, the girl's eyes shimmering in happiness.

The redheaded beauty, who had once wanted to become my favorite, had tried and failed to get close to me again a few months ago, and felt disgraced by that. Not long after, Princess Astra royl Veyerde returned to take the place of my favorite and was fulfilling the difficult role in the monarch's retinue better than ever.

"Valian, you take the second group of heavy cruisers and all the electros. Bionica, you're on small ship defense and sending commands. Max Gregor, you take battleships and monitor electric shields as usual. It'll all start with a bang soon, and we can get to work! All ships, cover light-sensitive equipment! Here they are!!!"

The bombs went off splendidly! The mines were so

effective, I nearly repeated Nicole's violation myself. A series of the brightest sparks, blinding the eyes even through the lowered light filters, rolled in a long many-mile line through nearby space. And in a few places, for a few seconds, new stars bloomed precisely where Florianna had predicted the arrival of large enemy ship groups.

"So, stealth-bombers, get ready! That group survived. Let's get to work! And over there, lots of little ships survived," I said, placing target markers for the cloakers.

More thermonuclear explosions followed. There wasn't even a need for a second and third wave of bombers. Just a few dozen scattered ships remained, mainly of heavy classes. I canccled the *Surprises'* attack and sat back in my armchair, admiring the glorious spectacle. Four and a half thousand green markers went into action all at once, striving to reduce their distance to the enemy. None of the rest of the ships, including the six carriers, even released their drones. There was really no need for that now. At this stage of battle, we just needed to catch the confused, stunned and disorganized enemies that were left.

My direct participation in the battle was not needed, because I fully trusted my assistants and staff officers to control the fleet. So, standing demonstratively and placing my hand behind my back, I walked unhurriedly to the huge hologram depicting the Khell star system in detail.

Ten steps from me, Nicole ton Savoia was straining to do another push up, her teeth clenched and blowing sharply from time to time at a disobedient lock of hair falling into her eye. The semitransparent Alpha Iseyek Rosss was keeping count. Rosss was counting in insect language, but no translation was needed. I turned to the glowing hologram in order not to embarrass her.

"My Prince, when you sent Nicole away and put the red-headed lady next to you, she thought some wild things. I'm even embarrassed to tell you her fantasies."

"And you don't have to, Florianna, this is not the time for that. Otherwise, you'll be doing pushups next to Nicole. Or maybe not. It's too early for that. But I'll think something up... You keep exercising your psionic abilities and tell me where the second group of enemy starships will be."

The girl walked to the map, took a laser pointer in her hands and started placing ship markers, much more confidently this time.

"My Prince, they're surrendering and requesting mercy!" Bionica's voice rang out.

"Three enemy battleships and eight heavy cruisers have lowered their shields and are sending signals of capitulation," Admiral Kiro Sabuto said, clarifying the number of trophies.

And then, when I was about to declare victory and order the surrendered ships quickly captured, a huge marker appeared one hundred twenty miles from my flagship, which the computer system identified as a *Queen.*

What the hell?! The *Queen* wasn't finished being repaired yet and should have been at the secret space docks in the Fia system. My advisors said it would take no less than two months before the huge starship could be launched. Or had my subjects secretly sent the unfinished *Queen* to help my fleet?!

I must have said my thoughts out loud, because Bionica hurried to correct me:

"My Prince, this is not our *Queen!*"

And she was right. The huge starship marker on the tactical map was colored red for enemy. Well then... The last thing I needed here in Khell was Aliens! And not just Aliens, but the most dangerous of their ships. The huge disk-shaped mothership was over twenty miles in diameter! It was capable of releasing over seventy thousand deadly combat drones at any second, all while itself remaining impervious to attack. The giant's energy shields were so strong no weapon in my fleet could pierce them.

Without even turning my head to my officers, I knew for certain that the faces of all my subjects were now pointed in my direction. All my soldiers were at a loss, terrified. And not only those in the fleet headquarters. The whole many-thousand-strong Unatari fleet was waiting impatiently for me to give them my commentary and clear detailed instructions in this very nonstandard situation.

At that moment, it occurred to me that this was exactly why space fleets had commanders. After all, the battle could be conducted by my staff officers, or even without them, though it would be less effective. But there absolutely had to be someone who assumed all the fear, risk and responsibility and set the mission in just this kind of difficult situation.

I coughed, put the helmet back on and activated the microphone, saying in a clear voice:

"Attention, all ships! Increase distance from the *Queen* and carefully watch her behavior. Heavy ships, begin to accelerate toward the ninth planet. Exercise extreme caution! Be ready to warp out on my command, if the enemy releases a mass of drones. All captains report to the headquarters on how much time is needed to charge up for a fully-fledged warp jump to the Forepost-10 system. Boarding teams, continue capturing the surrendered ships. If you even slightly suspect disobedience, destroy the surrendered Grand Duchy ships!"

"If I may be so bold as to remind Your Highness, in less than three minutes, another Grand Duchy fleet will be arriving," tactics officer Max Gregor told me.

"I don't give a damn. It's a puny fleet, and it'll be two thousand miles from us," I huffed back, waving the problem off as insignificant. "I'm sure they won't join the fight after seeing THAT... Although, no. Max, you're right. We cannot miss the perfect moment to attack the enemy, even in the presence of this giant. *Pyro* groups from one to fourteen, go as fast as you can to the point I've just marked! If even one Grand Duchy ship larger than a destroyer escapes, all frigate captains will be sent to retake their qualifications! One hundred radio-electric fighters, accelerate in the same direction. As soon as you get the coordinates from the frigates, warp out. First stun the main calibers, and take down the rest as needed! Sixty destroyers go as well, work in groups of three! Alright, great, take position! Twenty seconds to start! Max, the whole operation against the Grand Duchy reinforcements is on you! Valian will help..."

"Your Highness, I beg your apologies, but you're definitely going to want to hear this!" My speech was interrupted by an agitated communications officer who ran over to me with headphones in his hands. "It's a short message recorded in the Nayal system. There are twenty-three seconds of sensible speech. The rest is too garbled. It came in one minute ago."

The officer was pale. He understood perfectly the risk he ran by interrupting his fleet commander, but nevertheless, extended me the headphones. I removed my normal helmet and microphone and put on his.

"...ssage for any allied ships. They're killing us! I repeat, the Seventh Imperial Strike Fleet is under attack in the Nayal system! We're taking heavy losses! Please, anyone who can hear me! Tell the Throne World that the Antagonist Fleet and the Aliens are working together! Eight thousand enemy shi..."

A horrible scraping noise exploded from the headphones, and the message broke off. I demanded to be sent a full recording of the message at once. Unfortunately, there wasn't much more information. Based on the unique encryption tag and encoding, the message had come in from the heavy assault cruiser *Clairvoyant*, which really was in the Seventh Imperial Strike Fleet. The recording was very buzzy and distorted, and other than the fragment I'd already heard, the only thing that could be made out was the short phrase: "the admiral has died," a few curse words, and a terrified scream.

I was standing in a state of deep contemplation. "The Antagonist Fleet and the Aliens are working together..." That part of the message really had me worried. I suspected that, in the turmoil of the unfortunate battle, the Imperial officer had simply been mistaken, because believing in such an alliance between people and the main enemies of humanity was extremely difficult. However, I didn't simply write the story off, no matter how unlikely it looked at first glance. As a matter of fact, it explained why the Grand Duchy hadn't turned off the risky Nayal warp beacon. They were letting the Alien fleet in, including the *Queen*, which was shining like a beacon now on our locators.

Nicole walked up to me panting and stood in silence two steps from her seat, now occupied by her replacement.

"Have you come to your senses?" I asked. The girl nodded in silence, holding a morbidly serious expression on her face.

I stood and gave up my free seat to the Space Major.

"In that case, put your jacket back on and take over command of the united Unatari Fleet."

"My mission?" Nicole ton Savoia asked me shortly, not expressing any emotions at being given the extremely important role as she took her place at the console.

"Destroy the *Queen*!" I said, pointing at the huge red spot on the tactical map.

Two Minutes

I HAVE TO give my assistant her due for her composure. Not even a single one of Nicole's face muscles twitched. The girl made no gesture or word, to suggest that the mission she was given seemed strange, difficult or impossible. Also, the Space Major didn't rush or give hurried orders. My assistant just asked one lone clarifying question: how much time did she have to complete the mission?

"Two hours ten minutes," I said, giving the minimum time necessary for the enemy fleet to get to Khell from the Nayal system.

After that, taking the laser pointer in my hands, I walked into the center of the room to the huge hologram of the tactical map and turned to all my officers:

"I suggest everyone think this over well. The *Queen* came from the direction of the Nayal system," I said, drawing a straight line between Khell and Nayal with the laser pointer. "In theory, we already knew it was dangerous to have that warp beacon on, because the Aliens had shown up in the Nayal system before. We have long known that every successive wave of Alien invasion is stronger than the one that preceded it, so there really isn't anything weird about the Alien super-carrier appearing from the Nayal system. I'm surprised by something else: why did the *Queen* come alone? Based on the fragment of evidence that came in, there were eight thousand ships hostile to the Empire in the Nayal system. Fifteen hundred of them were the Purple House Fleet in Nayal, which means that six and a half thousand combat units were Alien ships. A huge fleet. Why didn't it go with the *Queen*? Your suggestions, ladies and gentlemen?"

I heard a long trill from Kheraisss Vej, which Bionica instantly translated for me:

"The Aliens are learning from their mistakes. Every time they entered a system occupied by your Highness's fleet, they took heavy losses. Your mines and stealth bombers caused the Aliens to regularly lose a significant portion of their small ships, and since recently, *Behemoth* battleships as well. Now, the Aliens have sent the *Queen* in advance, because it cannot be destroyed with mines and bombs. That massive ship will clear the way for the *Behemoths*, *Sledgehammers*, and smaller ships. Beyond that, we know that the Aliens have huge *Mammoth*-class supercarriers, with easily enough energy for a few warp jumps in a row. Perhaps the *Queen* is also capable of such things, unlike her smaller starships. She didn't need time to charge, so she went first."

"Excellent guess, Admiral! I think that is exactly what we're seeing now. Which means that an Alien fleet will soon arrive in Khell with a force of approximately six thousand starships. And that is exactly why the *Queen* isn't doing anything active, observing us and waiting for the rest of the fleet to arrive. But even all on her own, she's quite a threat, and not only in the number of combat drones in her bowels. I want to remind everyone that the *Queen* has already shown that she can influence the human psyche. So, if anyone senses an attempt at mind control, they're to tell me at once!"

"She's already influencing our collective psyche just with her presence..." came the grumbling voice of Admiral Kiro Sabuto on the common channel.

I didn't remark to the celebrated admiral, although his reply did precious little to facilitate moral reinforcement of the fleet.

"Last time the *Queen* attacked me mentally, taking the commander out of commission during the hottest phase of battle. Then, we were not ready for things to take such a turn, lost control over the fleet and, as a result, were almost dealt a crushing defeat. I suppose the *Queen* may try to repeat such a mental attack. In fact, that is one of the reasons why the leadership of the united Unatari Fleet has been transferred to Space Major Nicole ton Savoia..."

"Crown Prince Georg, the Grand Duchy reinforcements that arrived have been fully eliminated!" Valian ton Corsa reported, interrupting my speech. "We lost eight *Pyro* frigates, two *Safas*, and one *Flycatcher*."

I winced in dismay, and it wasn't only because I had been interrupted again. With that many radio-electric fighters on our side, the enemy should have been completely stunned, their sensors filled with white noise, their targeting systems disabled, and all their comms jammed. But now the enemy had not only shot, but had done so quite well. Clearly, my officers hadn't done their jobs, and the crews weren't trained well enough. But I'd speak with them about that later. Now, with certain death hovering two hundred miles away from me in space, it was not time to demotivate and excoriate my fleet.

"I need an encrypted line to talk with Miya!" I demanded.

A minute later, the screen lit up, showing my spouse in a spacious gloomy hangar. Lots of girls in black clothing with their eyes covered were sitting before the Truth Seeker in even rows right on the cold concrete floor.

"What do you need, Georg? As you can see, I'm in class," Miya said, annoyed and not hiding it. "Your question couldn't wa... What? Aliens in the system?! A *Queen*?!"

"That's right. This is a very serious matter. Get in touch with Krista immediately. I need a powerful line of Truth Seekers in one hour's time for an attack on an Alien *Queen*. We're going to try to stun her to buy time for an Iseyek landing party to get inside and take her down."

"Are you in your right mind, Georg?" my wife was unable to cope and nearly started shouting. "You have no idea how hard it was the last time to get the *Queen* to submit to our will. And we had the Dark Mother with us then, who took the brunt of the mental attack on herself! No one alive now is capable of doing that! What's more, Krista might not want to work with me."

"Miya, I know about your complicated relationship with Krista, but there's no other way out. We have to destroy the *Queen* while we have the chance. Otherwise, I'm afraid we'll soon see the *Queen* fighting alongside the Antagonists, which the Empire will never survive. And neither will we."

Miya lowered her head in distrust, meeting my gaze and... her eyes went wide in horror. It seemed she had read the phrase from my head that had me so worked up: "The Antagonist Fleet is working with the Aliens."

"I'll try, Georg. Krista should understand the importance of the moment, so she won't refuse to help. I really hope so..."

"Great! I've already given an order to unfreeze all the praying mantis assault troops on five *Trias*. In one hour, a million Iseyek will be attacking the Alien flagship. We already have a grip on the design of the *Queen*, and know the gigantic starship's weak points. That's where we'll attack, and that's where we'll lay the thermonuclear charges. The landing troops will only need a few minutes to get through to the key points inside. But the praying mantises cannot even get close to it while the *Queen* still has tens of thousands of combat drones under her control. Stun her, and we win! I can offer Florianna and a battery of four hundred Beta Iseyek to help. From you, I'll need your girls and you."

The Truth Seeker led a long evaluating gaze over the girls sitting before her... and I saw tears in Miya's eyes! I had never seen my tough and even severe wife in such a crushed state. No one would now guess that the woman before me was the second strongest psionic in the whole galaxy, famed for her cold blood.

"So many talented girls will die today..." the Truth Seeker said, wiping the tears with the back of her hand. "They are my students, and I have put some of myself into each of them. They're practically daughters to me... But I agree with your plan, Georg. We cannot allow the Antagonists to have the *Queen* — that would mean death for us all. So, you'll get your Truth Seeker chain!"

*   *   *

"One million one hundred fifty thousand Alpha Iseyek are ready to move out, Your Highness! Savasss Jach has unfrozen all his reserves to the very last soldier," Bionica said, tearing me out of the thoughtful state I had been in for the last few minutes.

"Then don't let the Truth Seekers waste time and get started!" I commanded, but my synthetic assistant just shook her head in the negative.

"Crown Prince, they cannot. The psionics have already tried, but the *Queen*'s consciousness is closed up tight. Our Truth Seekers are unable to establish contact with her."

Well, shoot... An unexpected obstacle. After all, my calculations were based on stunning the *Queen* and taking her mind under control, because directly attacking the supercarrier with the Unatari Fleet was equivalent to suicide — seventy thousand combat drones could destroy my ships in a matter of minutes. Was this *Queen* really any different from the one we'd defeated and captured earlier?!

My Prince, Krista is suggesting you try and speak with the enemy ship. I have been assigned the task of communicating with you. We really need the enemy to open up and start a dialog," Florianna was just two steps from me, but preferred to communicate mentally.

Speak with the Alien ship? Start the conversation? I might have tried, but how??? The *Queen* had always started the conversation before. Nevertheless, I tried to reach out mentally to the massive black starship. Almost immediately, I doubled over as a sharp pain twisted through my body.

"I KNOW YOU. YOU DESTROYED THE PATRIMONY OF A WHOLE CIVILIZATION. YOU KILLED AN INVALUABLE MIND, CREATED THROUGH MILLIONS OF YEARS OF EVOLUTION AND KNOWLEDGE. WHY DID YOU DO THAT? WHY DO YOU KILL US? WHY NOT LET US GO?"

The last thing I was expecting was for the Aliens to blame me for going to war with them. After all, they were the ones who came out of god-knows-where in space and attacked humanity, the Iseyek and other races! The Aliens put other species on the verge of total annihilation, wiping them from the face of the galaxy system by system. We were forced to defend ourselves!

"THAT IS NOT SO. WE SIGNED A PEACE TREATY WITH YOUR PEOPLE. AND WE ARE SIMPLY CARRYING IT OUT. YOU WERE THE ONES WHO DEMANDED THAT WE ACT THIS WAY. NOW, THE TIME HAS COME FOR YOU TO DO WHAT YOU PROMISED. WE WANT..."

And then I was roughly jerked into reality. I saw myself sitting on my knees in the center of a room, blood pouring from my nose onto my blue uniform pants.

"What treaty? Who did you sign a treaty with?

What has humanity promised you?" I shouted these questions aloud, but it was utterly in vain — my connection with the *Queen* had already been lost.

Katerina leaned over me with a packet of tissues. My cousin was upset and even afraid at my state, but I calmed her and stood to my feet. The head-spinning quickly passed. My condition could be called "surprisingly alright." All the same, not everyone in the room was doing as well as me. Just a few steps away, Florianna was howling in pain through clenched teeth and twitching as if she'd just touched a live wire. Four Beta Iseyek were holding the shaking girl in their many arms, otherwise she would definitely have fallen from the chair to the floor.

"Flora, Miya, what's happening?" I demanded a report from my Truth Seekers, but didn't get an answer.

Apparently, the psionics were already in battle, which was the only way to explain such a sharp end to my mental dialog with the *Queen*. Yes, this is exactly how we planned our actions, but the attack was so very untimely! I was just one step away from understanding the motivation of the Aliens and figuring out their secret understanding with mankind! By the way... there was a slight chance that the Truth Seekers' rush to attack may have been meant to stop me from obtaining the crucial information from the Alien *Queen*.

But what to do now? Rip out my hair, go ballistic and demand the Emperor's Truth Seekers explain? That would obviously be dumb. After all, in any case, the enemy was tied up in battle with the united team of psionics. All that remained was to return to the old plan and begin the landing. I sent a message to Marshal Savasss Jach through Bionica, saying to send a test group of Alpha Iseyek landing troops to the Alien flagship.

The whole headquarters was looking on, their hearts fluttering as an array of green dots tore off from the nearest *Tria* heading for the huge disk-shaped enemy. And the needle-shaped Swarm landing modules successfully maneuvered between the defensive turrets' blind spots, reached the *Queen*'s energy shield and sharply reduced speed. Only objects traveling very slowly could pass through the shield. Everything else was deflected. And these thirty modules made it past the barrier and successfully reached the *Queen*'s chassis!

"Bionica, tell the Marshal my order: begin the mass landing operation! Actually, no! Wait a second! Cancel!!!"

It was apparently too early to consider the enemy defeated and helpless. From the bowels of the massive supercarrier, whole rivers of combat drones started gushing into space. Thousands and thousands of them. All the Alpha Iseyek landing groups were annihilated in an instant, while the active defense made the massive ship basically unreachable for the other landing modules. What was more, the communications officers were telling me that the gigantic Alien ship had started giving off sharp electromagnetic pulses every few seconds, meaning the *Queen* had turned on her stealth bomber defense, revealing cloaked ships at a very significant distance.

Off to a bad start. The Aliens learned quickly from their errors and took effective countermeasures. It would be impossible to make a stealth bombing run on the drones. I cursed aloud, not ashamed to demonstrate my annoyance in front of my subordinates. And then, as if there weren't enough other problems, a message came in on an internal channel telling me that the Beta Iseyek supporting Florianna were all dying.

"It seems our psionics are having a hard time..." my cousin Katerina said in agitation.

I tried to get in touch mentally with my Truth Seekers again to figure everything out. Florianna didn't answer, but I did manage to overhear some echoes of Miya's thoughts.

"Georg... ation is critical. Me and... students were atta... cynically by Krista... with a group of psionics! Toge... just barely managed... the mind of the Queen under our control, but... just... Krista left the chain... retrained all her might... psio... ... against my group. I was not able to close the connection... We were forced to fight... the strongest Truth See... of Emperor August!"

The last thing I needed! Krista and her group of Truth Seekers had attacked Miya?!

"Why did Krista do that?"

"I do not know... Georg. ... ... they closed off and retreated! Let me tally up the results... of that nasty attack. The little girl Milena, the Truth Seeker of y... daughter Likanna has died. My old... friend Uya also died... I invited to the group. Flora fell out of the chain... But I sense that the girl is still holding out. Many of my stu... some just lost consciousness. Just seventeen girls are still with me. Sorry, Georg, but we didn't have time for the Queen. We had to fight for our very lives."

The messages were becoming more and more

coherent. Clearly, my wife was gradually coming to her senses after the sharp expenditure of force.

"And what now, Miya?"

"I can only say one thing — without a direct command from the Emperor, his Truth Seekers would not have stabbed us in the back like that. It seems that August royl Akad was certain that no information on this incident would slip out. But they thought wrong. We managed to fight them off. Georg, this can only mean one thing — the Empire has declared war on us. Our opponents also took losses. I personally killed three of the ancient hags from Krista's group. While Florianna strangled Marian Sabati when she got too caught up attacking me. To be honest, I wasn't particularly counting on Flora in this fierce scrap of experienced Truth Seekers, and I definitely wasn't expecting the girl to be able to kill the third strongest psionic in the galaxy. Now, I need to get back in touch with Florianna, bring my girls back to their senses and, in fifteen minutes, we'll try to attack the Queen again without any outside help."

"What?!" I couldn't believe what I was hearing.

Before, Miya had told me taking on the Alien *Queen* was practically impossible after the death of the Dark Mother. But now, my wife was saying that she thought she could win with just her rag-tag band?

"The mental channel is still open and we can use it for a repeat attack. We won't be able to kill the Queen. We also cannot paralyze her consciousness for long. But I can promise you that the Queen will be totally inactive for two or three minutes. After all, she suffered badly in our attack, burned through her psionic reserves and is now licking her wounds, preparing to

flee back to Nayal. In fifteen minutes, when we start, hit her with everything you've got. Mow down the enemy drones and land some soldiers. The Aliens learn from their mistakes, so we'll never get a chance like this again. You'll only have two or three minutes, after which the Queen *will come to her senses and become meaner, more experienced and more dangerous than ever before."*

*   *   *

"Two Minutes? And after that, death to anyone in our fleet who doesn't manage to get the hell away from the massive black wretch? Correct me, Your Highness, if I misunderstood, but it seems we risk losing all ships heavier than a destroyer in this attack– they simply will not manage to fly far enough away to save themselves. Do I have that right?" Admiral Kiro Sabuto was in a very pessimistic mood.

"In general terms yes, my friend. As soon as we get a confirmation from our psionics, our whole fleet will warp to the *Queen* and start shooting down her drones. There are a bit more than eighteen thousand of them spinning about the cosmos now, so it's completely realistic to destroy all of them if they really do not resist. But the problem is that the majority of the drones are still inside the supercarrier. The *Queen* will start to release them as soon as she comes back to her senses. And these fifty thousand drones will be active, dangerous, and mean. Our fleet's mission is to hold out as long as possible, distracting the drones and giving time for a landing team to get inside. At least one minute, but preferably five. Then, by

Savasss Jach's calculations, his landing troops are guaranteed to destroy the *Queen*."

Kiro Sabuto shook his head in doubt, looking at the colossal Alien starship on the monitor, but didn't argue. The experienced admiral didn't see any chance for victory, but still trusted his commander and was prepared to share my fate. I then read a report sent to me by Savasss Jach.

The Marshal was saying that the very first Alpha Iseyek landing groups would manage to break through the chassis and into the *Queen* within one minute and a half. Over the next thirty seconds, the number of incursion points would grow, but just two or three and a half thousand praying mantises would get inside, which was clearly not enough to complete the mission. After the two minutes Miya promised us, the *Queen* might come to her senses, in which case a severe space battle would begin. After that, every additional second would mean hundreds and thousands of new soldiers getting inside the supercarrier. Overcoming all the crew resistance, the praying mantises would start to get to the starship's key points, where they would be placing bombs. The most important thing was that the landing troops had to have enough forces for that. So, the main mission of the whole fleet was to make sure enough Alpha Iseyek could get inside the *Queen*.

And though the ships of our fleet had a chance to escape in the forthcoming battle, and not even such a bad one at that, the Iseyek landing troops were facing inevitable death. First, for the groups that didn't even manage to get in the gigantic starship, then for the others, because the praying mantises wouldn't be able to get out and would surely die when the *Queen* exploded.

I was betting the lives of a million intelligent creatures for the hypothetical chance to destroy an Alien supercarrier... A very hard decision for me as ruler of the Swarm. I approached the sacrifice with a heavy heart, but the Iseyek in my circle all assured me that there was nothing unusual in such a result and, in the history of the Swarm, there were quite a few instances of much greater losses to reach a certain goal. Marshal Savasss Jach told me that he had personally checked over all the calculations several times, so the deaths of more than a million Iseyek would not be in vain.

"One minute to action!" I said out loud on the fleet channel, and that order was immediately transmitted to the landing modules. "Begin acceleration toward the first group of *Pyros*. In fifty seconds, they will be behind the Alien ship to give the fleet jump coordinates. In the warp tunnel settings, set two hundred miles so we get cheek to cheek with the *Queen*. Who were the brainless morons that just jumped without command?!"

Bionica, barely glancing at the tactical screen, answered instantly:

"Twenty-six landing modules from *Tria-4*. They were all from the same group: EA118. Obviously, this was due to a mistaken command from their leader."

"Attention, all ships! Learn from the mistake of that landing group. How long did they survive? One second? Even less? I repeat again, do not warp without command! We're waiting for a confirmation from the psionics."

"Georg, we are ready for the mental attack. We will begin in ten seconds."

The message from Florianna came just in the nick of time. The wing of *Pyros* was just behind the *Queen* at full speed, where they gave our whole fleet warp jump coordinates.

"Attention, all ships! Be ready in five seconds! Four. Three. Two. One. WARP!!!"

*   *   *

In the few seconds that had passed since *Joan the Fatty* left the warp tunnel, I had time to get scared, curse elusively and give an order to my ships to start the battle. The *Queen* was still active by the time we approached, and met my starships with heavy fire from her defense turrets. Eighteen thousand drones from the *Queen* also immediately set about attacking my ships and the Iseyek landing modules. Fortunately, six seconds later, the resistance was sharply reduced. All the same, I sprouted quite a few extra gray hairs.

After wiping the sweat from my forehead and slightly calming down, I said, now in a firm and confident voice on the common channel:

"The first stage was a success. Congratulations. Although I did notice a few ships of my fleet jumping late into battle, when the Alien resistance was already ending. What was that, cowardice, lack of attention or lack of ability? In any case, consider this your first and last warning. If such a thing happens again, the captains at fault will be stripped of all regalia and forced to disembark at the first uninhabited warp beacon we reach with just a bag of seeds and some fertilizer, you have my word as a Crown Prince! And now, let's keep taking down drones! Whoever shoots down the most drones will be promoted one rank and get an exclusive bottle of brandy from the personal reserves of Duke Paolo royl Anjer, former head of the Orange House! Admiral Kiro Sabuto, prepare a report on our losses in the first phase of battle!"

The gray-haired admiral told me that the report was ready now, and had been sent to my terminal. I opened the message and read its dry lines. We'd lost twenty-six *Flycatchers*, eleven *Safas* and thirty-four *Pyros*. The main losses had been taken among the praying mantis landing modules — the *Queen* had managed to destroy over eleven thousand of the maneuverable vehicles. Over one hundred thirty thousand Alpha Iseyek had died, which amounted to twelve percent of all my landing troops. And that was all in less than eight seconds of active battle... What ghastly firepower! It was scary to even imagine what would have happened if the psionics hadn't managed to stun the *Queen*...

In the report, it was particularly noted that the enemy's drones and weaponry were totally ignoring our large ships. Not a single shot had been detected on my cruisers or heavier starships. That couldn't have been a coincidence. The mind of the Aliens determined practically instantly that the biggest threat to the *Queen* was the praying mantis landing groups setting down on the surface of the huge supercarrier, and had given a command to eliminate them. And if it weren't for Miya and Florianna, the whole Iseyek attack would have drowned in blood in just one minute...

"My Prince, all drones from the *Queen* have been shot down!" Bionica reported.

On the tactical map, there was not a single small red dot remaining. Just the huge red dot and thousands of green ones around it. I looked at the timer. It had been a minute and a half since the attack began. The first landing groups should have already been getting into the Alien supercarrier. Everything was basically going well, but I suddenly got a panicked mental message from my wife:

"Georg, she's very strong. We won't hold out much longer. Twenty or thirty seconds at most."

Just twenty seconds?! So little?! But that, after all, meant that our trickle of forces to capture the massive starship wouldn't be enough! Alright, leave the panic for later! Think, think, think!!! There were no drones left in space, the main thing now was to impede the arrival of new ones, and neutralize the defensive turrets. That's what was firing on my ships, and all our present losses were from them.

"Bionica, send an order to the marshal to send the landing groups to capture and destroy the defensive turrets. And another order — get the Alpha Iseyek out of the zone of fire — we're attacking the airlocks the *Queen* uses to release drones with small nuclear bombs! I've marked them on the hologram. There are seventy-three in total. Prepare the *Leech-A*'s! Assign targets! Approximate time to attack: thirty seconds!"

"My Prince, the Marshal asks you to cancel the nuclear attack!!! Savasss Jach is saying the losses of his landing troops would surpass all allowable bounds, and that there would not be enough troops to accomplish the main goal! The praying mantises will try to shut the airlocks, making plugs out of smashed modules and paneling, attaching them together with ropes or welding. And if they don't succeed, they'll blow up the passages themselves. Many of the landing groups have bombs with them of up to seven kilotons."

There was no time to think it over, I had to act intuitively. I gave the Marshal complete carte blanche, ordering the fleet to cover the working groups at the airlocks. And then... the *Queen* broke free!

I immediately realized it, even before I got a message from Florianna saying they'd lost control. The *Queen*'s thrusters had activated, and the huge starship was beginning to accelerate very slowly.

"She is trying to flee," Miya said, confirming my fears.

The fact that the very dangerous opponent was afraid of us and trying to retreat gave me courage and confidence in my own abilities. After activating the microphone, I shouted:

"Don't let her get away! All frigates, put warp disruptors and webs on the *Queen*! If she gets out, I swear that I will literally decimate you and order every tenth person in the fleet executed!!!"

As if in response to my words, a wave of bright sparks lit up on the huge starship. The praying mantises were blowing their nuclear bombs, destroying the defensive turrets on the *Queen* and not letting the enemy drones get outside. There was a fervent battle underway for the main drone airlocks on the supercarrier. Four thousand ships and ten thousand drones launched by my fleet were trying not to let the *Queen* use her main weaponry. The Alien drones, just after leaving the bowels of the *Queen*, were quickly picking up speed and leaving the defensive shield, where my ships would meet and destroy them.

But the *Queen* had already learned from her mistakes. After lots of senseless losses, the drones spent the next four minutes building up under the supercarrier's shield, not leaving the defended area. When the number of enemy drones ready to attack was over thirty thousand, I ordered my ships to retreat in an organized fashion, because the battle threatened me with critical losses. Just a few frigates were still holding the *Queen* as before in stasis webs and warp disruptors, while the wing of *Surprises* was ready to bomb the dense group of enemy drones as soon as they left the safe zone.

But that was no longer so important. The most important things happening now were not in space.

I looked anxiously at the huge monitor. It was showing the movement of the praying mantis divisions through the corridors, rooms and technical spaces of the gigantic enemy spaceship. Two hundred thousand Alpha Iseyek had already seeped into the *Queen*, which was more than enough to accomplish the mission they'd been given. What was more, as it turned out, we had initially overestimated the enemy's close combat abilities. The jellyfish-like Aliens, which is what we discovered inside this *Queen*, were significantly weaker than the "bushes" from the last one. They couldn't survive in a vacuum for any length of time, and It was fairly simple to kill them with laser or rail guns. What was more, they were very vulnerable to fragmentation grenades and bombs. All in all, three of the eight thermonuclear mines had been placed in the central nodes of the enemy spaceship. And then...

"MY OPPONENT, I REQUEST MERCY!!! DO NOT KILL ME. MY SHIP IN RETURN FOR MY LIFE."

UNBEATABLE ARMADA

T HE *QUEEN'S* MESSAGE beamed directly into my mind and nowhere else, so my officers and guards were taken aback when their fleet commander suddenly collapsed to the floor with blood pouring from his nose. My arm felt heavy as lead, but I still managed to raise it to tell them everything was fine, and croak out for no one to help me.

"Order your crew to cease fire, and call your drones back in. My praying mantis landing troops will not shoot either, but I will still have them place the remaining thermonuclear bombs just in case. We can talk after that."

I had no idea if the *Queen* had heard me or not, so I asked for confirmation from Marshal Savasss Jach through Bionica. The synthetic beauty, not hiding her amazement, said:

"My Prince, all the drones are going back into the supercarrier. The enemy has ceased fire."

"Great! Send an order to all the landing groups not to shoot. Let them fan out inside the starship and take the turrets, power stations, control centers, comms centers and retransmitters under their control. Let them set bombs and weld shut any openings that could be used to release drones. Congratulations, everyone! The *Queen* has surrendered!"

Global fame increase. Current value: +80

Global fame increase. Current value: +81

Global standing increase. Current value: +16

Beyond all doubt, there had not been such adoration in the Unatari Fleet since the grand victory in the D56KT system, when we killed the first Alien *Queen*. Respectable, mature officers, who were generally quite reserved were jumping, shouting, throwing their caps in the air, laughing and crying in joy. There was an incomprehensible mixture of hollering and chirring on the fleet channel.

Standing change. Empire Military faction opinion of you has improved.
Present Empire Military faction opinion of you: +66 (veneration)

The last message gave me a happy smirk. On the verge of a war with the Empire, my standing among the military of a potential enemy was higher than any of their own fleet leaders or military commanders. Naturally, that revealed tempting perspectives for the future...

A message came in from Miya. It seemed to me that

the Red Queen was bewildered and even somewhat frightened to see that the battle had ended that way. In an unheard-of turn of events, my wife even apologized to me for getting mad. Then she asked me politely:

"Georg, would you please allow my girls to also feed on the energy of your adoration. Florianna is already sated, and I've also had my fill. But so much concentrated positive energy is a rare treasure to psionics. It will allow my students not only to restore their strength, but also grow stronger."

"Will they become my Truth Seekers?" I clarified, and got a negative answer from my wife.

"No. There's no reason to repeat the Emperor's error. Once, many years ago, August royl Akad thought that the adoration of hundreds of billions of subjects would allow him to support a whole group of personal Truth Seekers. But as soon as the Empire hit a rough patch, his psionics starved. The Dark Mother, Krista, Mariam Sabati and Veronica ton Taki 'ate' the lion's share of the energy, while the other Truth Seekers stopped getting enough to even maintain their own abilities, which is to say nothing of professional growth."

"Are you now talking about the split and secession of Great Houses from the Empire?" I asked, my interest piqued. But Miya answered otherwise:

"No. It wasn't today, or even yesterday. I'm referring to an event three or four years ago, when the Empire demonstrated its complete impotence against the Aliens, and the faith of its people in the infallibility and omnipotence of their ruler stumbled. Ever since then, the situation has only gotten worse due to his military and political blunders. And today's battle showed that

even the very strongest of the Emperor's Truth Seekers are in quite poor shape. They had a long enough fuse to start off with a very intensive attack, and at first it really was very hard for us. Obviously, Krista was counting on taking us down in one fell swoop, but she was wrong. We held out and, in a few minutes the situation started to change. A few of the old ladies started to fade, and even Krista started trying to ration her strength. Then, after Mariam Sabati died, we got the upper hand, and the Emperor's psionics retreated. So, just two of your Truth Seekers at full strength were stronger than thirty of the Emperor's, who were so starved they could barely stay standing. Let's hope it stays like that in the future."

I trusted Miya's experience in all issues connected with the training and strengthening of the young psionic girls of the Unatari State, as she was one of the strongest Truth Seekers in the galaxy. And I told her that immediately.

"Alright, Georg. I'll serve as a retransmitter and help my girls restore their depleted energy. But in the future, all my students will become Truth Seekers for totally different people. You have appointed quite a few rulers, viceroys and military leaders to high positions. And now, they will surely need psionics to protect them, help them and give them proper guidance. And also, your daughter Likanna lost her Truth Seeker, so a replacement for little Milenna will also have to be found."

"I'VE MET ALL YOUR TERMS. MY TURRETS ARE DEACTIVATED. MY DRONES ARE ISOLATED. MY CREW DID NOT IMPEDE THE PLACEMENT OF YOUR BOMBS. NOW, I WANT TO RETURN TO

NEGOTIATIONS ON THE CONDITIONS OF MY RELEASE."

Clearly, it was because I hadn't yet finished my conversation with Miya, but this time it didn't hurt at all to talk with the *Queen*. I even stayed on my feet.

"She's still dangerous, Georg. The Queen is temporarily weak and vulnerable. She's retreating, trying to negotiate for her life and freedom. But in the future, all that might change, and you could find yourselves in the opposite positions. If you want my opinion, do not miss such an easy chance to kill this Alien superconscience. Although... I'm reading your thoughts and seeing that you have totally different plans as for her."

"Yes, Miya. I am prepared to let her go in exchange for this huge starship and some information on the Aliens. After all, we barely know anything about them, even though we've been at war for several years. Their homeworld. Their culture. Their technology. Their plans. That is all of significant interest to me. I am also greatly intrigued by the understandings the Aliens have with humanity, and whose orders exactly they're carrying out. If the *Queen* answers my questions, that will be a high enough price for her freedom."

"Alright then, try. The Queen is no danger to you now, especially if she loses her ship and you tie her up with treaties and oaths. But I cannot guarantee that your gesture of good will to a clear enemy will not be looked on badly in the future."

My wife cut the mental connection, but I could still sense her strong vexation. And sure, I understood Miya's viewpoint perfectly. The *Queen* had to be destroyed for the peace of mind of all humanity. In part, I shared her fears — the Aliens were making an obvious demonstration of their danger to the rest of the cosmic races. Now, it would be good to hear the opinion of my other Truth Seeker as well. Perhaps, if Flora also voted for the death of the *Queen*, I would change my mind.

But Florianna was having a hard time answering. She just pointed to the obvious plus of obtaining the huge supercarrier for the Unatari Fleet, but couldn't decide the fate of the Alien superconscience. Astra's sister had taken a serious injury in the battle with the Emperor's psionics, and was nearly falling off her feet in exhaustion, unable to find answers to any difficult questions. The only thing Flora could think about now was taking a dose of crystals as soon as possible and immersing herself in a many-day dream.

I had to act on my own and figure it out with just my intuition. After concentrating my attention on the huge disk-shaped starship, I mentally sent my demands to the *Queen*. The answer came back almost instantly:

"TWO OF YOUR CONDITIONS ARE IMPOSSIBLE. I DO NOT HAVE THE RIGHT TO REVEAL INFORMATION ABOUT MY UNDERSTANDINGS WITH YOUR RACE. ALSO, YOUR FELLOW HUMANS FORBID ME TO SHARE TECHNOLOGIES WITH ANYONE OTHER THAN THEM."

"But can you at least tell me which person precisely you were negotiating with?"

"NO. REVEALING THAT INFORMATION IS FORBIDDEN."

Well hell, what a debacle... But who could it be? It

was clearly someone very highly placed in either the Empire, the Great Houses or the Antagonists. The first thing that came to mind for some reason was my late grandmother, Crown Princess Eleonora. Such a powerful personage, full of rage at the Emperor, really could have encouraged an Alien invasion to weaken the Empire. Most likely, Eleonora had not negotiated personally with the Aliens, but through a middle man of some kind. Maybe it was the "Voice of the Triumvirate," Count Albert royl Akad. Perhaps, the Count's haughtiness and pretension were explained by the fact that he knew about the agreements with the Aliens and supposed that he was capable of wielding that force.

Another candidate that seemed like a good fit for the role of Alien conspirator was the Dark Mother, who served for many years as the Emperor's closest advisor and most trusted confidant. The strongest Truth Seeker and the Emperor clearly knew much more about the Aliens than they let on. By the way... if I thought about it, I had never once heard the Dark Mother or August royl Akad express a single fear about the Aliens invading the Imperial Core. And after all, the Aliens had spent all that time just attacking systems of the Swarm, other nonhuman races, and Great House peripheral systems, but had never once touched the inner systems of the Empire. Was that just mere coincidence, or might it have been a limit imposed on the Aliens by the Dark Mother?

But both the Dark Mother and Crown Princess Eleonora were already dead, along with many other visible aristocrats, military leaders and psionics. The wars and troubles of recent years had significantly redrawn the political map and shuffled the leaders of the Empire around.

"It may be that all the people who were negotiating in the name of humanity are dead now. Then, the old understandings would no longer be in force..."

"NO, THAT IS NOT SO. ONE OF THE PEOPLE PRESENT FOR OUR FIRST MEETING WITH HUMANITY TOOK PART IN TODAY'S ATTACK ON ME. I DO NOT HAVE THE RIGHT TO NAME THEM."

Now there's a real riddle... There were four thousand ships in my fleet, containing one hundred thousand people. Although... I probably should have been looking at just the most visible captains and admirals — the *Queen* would hardly have considered normal crew members and landing troops to have the authority to represent humanity. That meant the list was significantly shortened. I already wanted to give Bionica a mission to check the service lists of senior officers of my fleet and cross reference it against those who had participated in the very first battles with the Aliens. Such facts were, after all, probably reflected in their biographies.

But I stopped, struck by a new thought. In today's attack on the *Queen*, other than military soldiers, there were also dozens of Truth Seekers, and thousands of androids that were externally indistinguishable from people, as well as probably a fair number of Arite Iseyek. So, the list of suspects was materially broader than I first supposed. It seemed that this mission could not be solved so easily. Alright, I'd handle it later. I had more substantive matters now.

"We know about your large fleet in the neighboring

Nayal system. Tell me, can you exert influence on your fellow Aliens to make them go back and not attack us? I need there to be no battle."

"I HAVE NO WAY OF MAKING CONTACT WITH THE OTHER SHIPS OF MY RACE. THEY'RE ALREADY IN A WARP JUMP HERE. AND THEY WILL NOT OBEY. TO THEM, MY STARSHIP IS MARKED AS CAPTURED BY THE ENEMY."

Another failure! No matter what I asked, the *Queen* either wasn't able to answer, or simply refused. And the Alien fleet was already on its way here... I was more and more inclined to the option suggested by Miya of blowing up the supercarrier and sending it straight to hell while we still had the chance. Because, with a sober evaluation of the distribution of forces before the forthcoming battle, I most likely had no way of keeping this gigantic starship.

But killing the *Queen* once and for all was something I could do. That said, it was important to squeeze as much information out of her as I could.

"And how are you planning to hand the ship over to me, from a technical perspective?"

"NAME ANY PLANET WITH A NONACIDIC ATMOSPHERE. METHANE. ARGON. NITROGEN. HELIUM. AMMONIUM. OXYGEN. TEMPERATURE AND GRAVITATION HAVE NO BEARING. I WILL UNLOAD THERE."

Any planet? Was she joking?! Here in the Khell system, there was only one planet, Khell-1, and it was inhabited by people. Or was the *Queen* not limiting herself to just the Khell system and would consider any star system? She couldn't seriously be unaware that all warp beacons to neighboring systems were shut off and that we were cut off from the transport network, right? Or... here my breathing seized in panic... Perhaps, the *Queen* was able to move between the stars regardless. After all, the Aliens used some alternative methods of travel, not standard warp beacons! Alright then, let's check. I opened the star map and searched for a planet in Unatari State space that would correspond to the *Queen*'s request.

"Hnelle-VI. A gas giant. Methane atmosphere. Does that work?"

"YES. I CAN MOVE THERE, BUT NOT FROM THIS SYSTEM. I NEED A SYSTEM WITH A DISRUPTION POINT. THERE IS ONE IN NAYAL. THERE IS ONE IN AMATI."

I tried not to get surprised that the Aliens were familiar with the human names for star systems. I also didn't ask what disruption point meant. The chance was high that the *Queen* would think she didn't have the right to share that information. Instead of that I, trying to imitate a careless bored mental state, offered the *Queen* to consider different flight routes to Hnelle.

"I DO NOT COMPREHEND. OTHER ROUTES ARE LONGER."

"Well, speed isn't always a priority. Sometimes, safety is more important. My state is currently at war with human enemies. All around are fleets hostile to my own. The path to Nayal is also closed. Going to Amati through the Forepost-10 and Forepost-9 systems may also be impossible. But I want to consider different routes. Could you give me a list of systems with disruption points? I need to see the best way to lead you around the enemy fleets."

– PERIMETER DEFENSE BOOK FOUR –

A very strange vision appeared before my eyes, with lots of bright spots on a black background. The spots were white, gray, and blue for the most part, but one was vibrant red. Many of the dots were connected with bundles of variously colored lines. Clearly, this was the disruption-point map I'd asked for, but I couldn't make heads or tails of it. I needed some kind of key to match it up with the political map I was familiar with. What was more, I was accustomed to looking over only the star systems with warp beacons, and with transport routes, totally ignoring the unavailable ones. Here, I needed a specialist in star maps and navigation.

"The Senior Navigator of *Joan the Fatty* is needed urgently in fleet control headquarters."

Three minutes later, they brought out a mustached gray-haired officer with space captain patches. He was clearly worried, having found himself in the company of a crown prince for the first time. He was nervously kneading his hat in his hands.

Mike ton Tir
Human
Military
Space Captain of the Unatari State Fleet

"Mike, I've got a job for you," I said, pointing to the monitor with the image of the gigantic disk-shaped starship. "The Alien *Queen* says that she can jump from the Amati system directly to Hnelle, a star system neighboring Unatari. Speak with the *Queen* and figure out the technical details. I want to understand if the rest of my fleet would be able to

– 270 –

make such a jump with her, and what would be necessary to do that. What's more, the *Queen* has mentally sent a map of the jump points the Aliens use. It's very interesting data, but I don't know enough to match it up to our customary map. I want you to try and do that. If you can manage, I'll give you a king's ransom. You have my word as a Crown Prince! If you cannot, I guess my flagship will have to find a more competent navigator!"

*   *   *

A message from inside the ship caught me just as I started my late dinner with Joan and Princess Astra.

"Crown Prince Georg, long distance call from the Damir system. Duchess Violetta royl Inoky ton Mesfelle Damir, co-ruler of the Grand Duchy, would like to speak with you."

My sister? Her and I had spoken in the last few days. On the day of her coronation, as a matter of fact. What did Violetta want from me now? She couldn't seriously want to discuss the death of our mother Duchess Elisa royl Mesfelle-Lavaelle, right? Knowing about the, let's say, nowhere near optimal relationship between Joan and her new aunty, I asked my daughter to move seats so she wouldn't be in the scene, and put a finger to my lips.

My guess was right. the Duchess was in dark mourning clothes, emphasizing the sorrow and the pain of her loss. Based on the surprise and dismay that slipped through on my sister's face, she was expecting to see me in mourning clothes as well. I realized too late that I obviously should have been showing my sorrow and should have dressed accordingly, but the late Duchess Elisa had really never been associated with the word mother to me.

"Georg, I already know that our mother died while speaking with you long distance. And I want to find out what happened in the palace on Oveyete-VII."

I put a sorrowful expression on my face, struggling to hold back a smile that was tearing itself from me. The androids under Bionica's control really had managed to destroy all recordings of what had happened. Now, my sister would only know what I told her.

"Mother called me that time to say that my fleet was in a trap, and didn't even hide her malevolence. She suggested I surrender without a fight, saying the Grand Duchy had fleets coming to Khell from all sides. I, naturally, refused and promised to destroy these ships. Then, the Duchess suggested I think about joining the Grand Duchy myself. She started telling me how much had already been done to make sure power over all the Great Houses was concentrated in the hands of our family. But she wasn't allowed to finish. Baron Maggo from the Lavaelle family shot her in the back!"

"Yes, I am aware..." my sister closed her eyes and raised her face, trying to hold back a flood of tears.

Duchess Violetta said nothing further, so I continued my story.

"Mother's guards got retribution on her murderer, although it was too late. There wasn't just one conspirator in the room. Many officers in old Green House uniforms were armed and started shooting at mother, her bodyguards and Truth Seekers. There was true slaughter in the room, resonators, plasma grenades and all. And when the dust settled, I didn't see a single survivor."

"The conspirators tried to destroy all clues. In the Palace of Oveyete-VII, not a single recording of the tragedy could be found. Representatives of the Lavaelles have already gotten in touch with me and assured me that someone was trying to frame them, saying they had never thought anything bad against our mother. The head of their family even expressed a readiness to undergo Truth Seeker testing to prove his innocence. Brother, I need a video of the attack on mother and the ensuing firefight. I need to prove to my subjects that it was not a random lone-wolf attack, but a planned action of the Lavaelle family. As for motive, I am quite clear. After the death of our mother, the family head Amelius royl Lavaelle is trying to claim the title of Grand Duchy co-ruler. I'll never let that happen!"

"Yes, Violetta, I'll send you a recording at once, raw footage without any edits or cutting. But only starting from mother's shooting, because the negotiations we were conducting before that were too sensitive, including secret information about the number and position of my fleet. And you'll have to excuse me here — I will help you get revenge for our mother's demise, but I will not allow you to destroy my fleet!"

My sister nodded, showing me that she agreed to the conditions. I turned on the microphone, ordered Bionica to bring up the recording and watched it myself so that nothing undesirable would end up in it — not my address to Duchess Elisa, and not the scenes of the Arite Iseyek. Only the first and second unsuccessful assassination attempts by members of the Lavaelle family on the Duchess, then the third, which proved fatal, the death of our mother and the ensuing bloodbath. All these incriminating scenes were accompanied by hateful cries from Lavaelle officers directed at the co-ruler of the Grand Duchy. The material turned out simply murderous — iron-clad proof that the whole Lavaelle family was at fault and, at that, any expert would confirm that the recording was unaltered.

I sent the file, and my sister immediately familiarized herself with its contents. Duchess Violetta's face went dark in rage:

"That's what I thought! The Lavaelles will pay for their breach of faith. Their whole family will pay, from the very bottom to the very top, I swear it! The vile traitors! After all, I suggested to mother that we pull their family tree up by the root, considering them unreliable and dangerous allies. But she didn't listen, and paid for her trusting ways in the end..."

My sister was already nearing the end of her screed, but I managed to ask a question that had been bothering me:

"A strange message has come in from Imperial ships in the Nayal system saying that the Grand Duchy fleet and Alien ships are working in tandem. Can you confirm or deny such an alliance?"

My twin sister looked somewhere aside, apparently at the time. Then, she answered as if she hadn't heard my question:

"Georg, the throne of one Grand Duchy co-ruler is unoccupied, and I was thinking it didn't make sense to give it up to someone not from our family. Maybe mother was right, and you could join. But first, brother, you need to significantly reign in your desires and rid yourself of all this excess pride. With the second, it will be quite easy. In forty minutes time, you will get an important lesson that will unravel the myth of your invulnerability. A lesson that will upend all your fantasies about the balance of forces. So, let's talk after the battle. A lot will be clear then, that you don't know now. I wish you luck, brother! And make sure you don't die!"

*　　*　　*

My synthetic assistant placed a hot coffee on the console before me and, bowing down right over my ear, asked quietly:

"My Prince, is this risk really worth taking? It doesn't look like Duchess Violetta was joking or bluffing, when she talked about the unbeatable fleet just about to land on our heads. My human body language processing program says there is a 96 percent chance that your sister was speaking the truth."

"Yes, Bionica. Miya says roughly the same. My twin sister really was warning me of an upcoming danger, and Violetta believed that winning the forthcoming battle would be impossible, despite my skill. But are we really gonna leave without getting a glimpse of this all-consuming power she's using to scare us?"

The android girl's face twisted into a very authentic imitation of fear. I drank a sip of the burning hot roast-firo-nut beverage which, by my light hand, had practically officially begun to be called coffee. Even the demure and pedantic butler Bryle and my senior chef called it that now, and I had recently seen that name mentioned in an online culinary encyclopedia. Well, no matter. I guess I'd brought one word from my world into *Perimeter Defense*. It was my only serious slip-up in all this time. I smiled at my secret thoughts and nodded to my assistant, grateful for the coffee:

"The Queen of the androids always knows what this human ruler needs for a peace-making mood. Now, I'm ready to meet the fearsome unbeatable fleet, no matter how great their numbers. And you've got nothing to fear. All my ships are accelerating towards the Forepost-10 warp beacon now, and are ready to jump there right after the *Queen* leaves."

"Your Highness, aren't we even going to try a bombing run on the enemy?" asked Nicole Savoia, sitting to my other side.

"If we get a good opportunity, our stealth bombers will be sure to strike. But we've already used the cloaked bomber attack on Alien ship groups so many times that our enemies are sure to be expecting such a thing from us and will take countermeasures..."

I wanted to say what countermeasures a fleet could take to defend itself from cloakers, but I didn't have time. A siren started whining out, and the signal lights flickered on in alarm. The officers ran to their seats. The enemy had finally arrived! First a few large groups of red markers appeared on the tactical map then, at several-second intervals, other proportionally sized groups started arriving. A few minutes later, it finally became clear that the enemy somehow had an unrealistically huge number of starships. On the tactical map, my fleet looked like just a short green banner in front of a three-thousand-mile-long red armada. And the groups of enemy starships just kept coming...

I listened carefully to the messages of my tactics officers, ready at any second to command us to retreat.

"There's already more than eight thousand of them!"

"The enemy fleet is forming three clusters around its large ships. Distance to nearest group - twenty-five hundred miles."

"Nine *Mammoths*. Twenty-three other large starships of a familiar shape. But on closer inspection, they have turrets of a colossal size. Two hundred forty *Behemoth*-class battleships. Almost one thousand *Sledgehammer* cruisers. Three hundred *Chainsaw* cruisers and another two hundred of an unknown design."

"Identification of destroyers and frigates is still under way. Primarily *Meteors* and *Ascetics*..."

"Some of the enemy ships have disappeared from the radars! Two hundred cruisers we didn't recognize disappeared along with four hundred cloaked frigates of three different types."

Those seven hundred cloaked ships could be anywhere, which was too grave a threat to simply overlook. What was more, it had already become very clear that there was nothing to catch here. With such a distribution of forces, my fleet was not likely to achieve victory. I was already preparing to give the order to retreat when I suddenly got an alarmed cry from the tactician:

"A new large fleet has arrived! It's human! They've come from the Nayal system! Three thousand ships!!!"

"Three thousand ships? Where did they find that in Nayal?" I exchanged glances with Nicole ton Savoia, who shrugged her shoulders in surprise. Bionica, meanwhile, commented on the reports coming in from the tactics officers:

"These ships are certainly of human construction, approximately half of them have been recognized as the Purple House First Strike Fleet, now to be more accurate, a Grand Duchy fleet. These are the very ships Imperial Admiral Peres ton Mesfelle-Tesse was chasing. But the other fifteen hundred are very strange. They give an incorrect response to the friend-foe system, and none of them can be identified by radar signature. We don't have any such ships in our database!"

"That could only be the Antagonists!" I said with confidence, trying to turn from camera to camera on my own and zoom in the image, but finding it far too blurry.

Bionica, having noticed my fruitless efforts, did everything necessary to get more clear images on my screen. Although, at such a huge distance, even after processing, very little could be made out. It was really just the approximate outlines of the very largest ships. One was abnormally rotund and droplet-shaped, and another looked just like a trimaran. I had definitely never seen such starships before.

"All the types of Imperial combat ships we know were developed after the Gold House left the Empire. It is no surprise that the Antagonists developed their own ships in that time," said Nicole ton Savoia, as if reading my thoughts. "Those over there must be battleships. Those are cruisers. And that giant with half-mile-long cannons doesn't seem to have an analogue in Imperial combat starship classifications."

"Commander, incoming call from that massive ship!" the communications officer cried out, circling the ship I happened to be discussing with my assistants.

"Georg, Florianna is already deep in a crystal sleep. But I am prepared to cover you if anything should happen. I myself would like to know who's come to pay you a visit." Hearing Miya's thoughts gave me confidence, and I told the man to put the call through.

Bah! I'd seen this face before. On the screen, I saw Demyen royl Amelius ton Lavaelle, the very same Green House Crown Prince whose fleet I had so successfully trapped in an uninhabited system and forced to surrender. I was reminded that Demyen had given his word as a Crown Prince that he would never again plot against me or lead combat ships against my state. Now, my opponent's face was beaming in triumph:

"Crown Prince Georg royl Inoky ton Mesfelle, I've been waiting for so long for the chance to get revenge on you for that shameful defeat! And now finally, the tables have turned. The Unatari fleet is trapped in a pocket, and now I will be dictating the terms of your capitulation!"

"Are you sure about that, Demyen?" I asked, trying to put the most malignant possible expression on my face. "Look at the data from your locators. See all that starship debris? That means you're not the first person who's come to Khell and suggest I surrender.

In the last half day, I have fought in three battles here, wiping the floor with two Grand Duchy fleets, and even forcing a massive Alien supercarrier to retreat. But my losses have been minimal. What's more, I have even expanded my ranks with captured ships."

"Crown Prince Georg, you managed to force the *Queen* to retreat? I didn't even think such a thing was possible! I profoundly admire your talent! But that changes nothing. Even without the *Queen*, I have easily enough forces to cope with the likes of you. As you can see, there is a huge Alien fleet under my command. But that isn't everything! Look at my ships, they are perfect! They incorporate advanced Alien technology, having surpassed what humanity managed to build on its own over our two-hundred-year split! Admit it, Crown Prince, you're surprised! Just imagine the surprise of Imperial Space Marshal Abram Kovel when his armada met with a different Grand Duchy fleet in Perimeter Sector Three."

The man gave a self-satisfied chuckle. I, meanwhile, tried to maintain a calm demeanor, although the news that the Grand Duchy had another fleet just as terrifying as this one was, I'll admit, extremely dispiriting. All my staff analysts, and I together with them, had seriously underestimated the forces of the Grand Duchy. Meanwhile, my Unatari State spies, who I mistakenly considered borderline omniscient, had slept right through an alliance between the Antagonists and the Aliens.

"I won't hide it, Demyen, the unified fleet of the Antagonists, Purple House and Aliens was just as much a surprise to me as the fact that their commander has disregarded his oaths."

My opponent cringed in pain. Despite the whole ruse with changing the name of the Green House, in his soul, the former Imperial Crown Prince still understood that he had broken his word. But Demyen quickly came to his senses:

"Don't try and provoke me, Crown Prince Georg. I understand perfectly that you're trying to drive me mad in hope that he will make some error. But no, that will not happen. The Unatari Fleet is completely trapped in this and the neighboring systems, and there is no way for you to escape this trap. Whether here in Khell or the Forepost-10 system, I'll destroy all your ships. So, Crown Prince Georg, I suggest you surrender. Even for such a celebrated fleet leader as yourself, there's no shame at all in admitting the fact that you're colossally behind in both military might and technology."

"Georg, it wouldn't be even remotely hard for me to kill this impudent fellow. As strange as it may seem, Demyen is not being covered right now by a single Truth Seeker."

"No, Miya! Don't do that! Demyen thinks he's in control of the situation. He's self-satisfied and hopeless, and also thirsts to prove to everyone that he can defeat me. Any other commander in his place would simply trap my fleet in the unpeopled Forepost-10 system, if I retreated there. But I need the enemy fleet to follow after me. Remember, we can go beyond to Forepost-9, but his fleet cannot..."

"As you say, Georg. And yes, I can affirm as a Truth Seeker that Demyen is sure to chase after your fleet."

Well, if the second strongest Truth Seeker was

certain enough to guarantee my success, I could stop teasing my opponent:

"Demyen royl Amelius ton Lavaelle, I would gladly stay here and chat with you, but my calculations have shown me that your seven hundred Alien cloakers are just about to reach my fleet. So, as such, allow me to bow out! All ships, warp to the Forepost-10 beacon!"

Dark Paths

DUCHESS KATERINA ton Unatari threw open the doors loudly and flew into a small room where I was dozing off on a love seat after all the agitation of the last few hours. I had just an hour and a half to restore my strength while my fleet charged its drives at the Forepost-10 warp beacon, so when Astra had come to see me in nothing but a transparent nighty, I had put her to sleep as well. My favorite didn't argue, although she was in a playful mood today and was clearly expecting an utterly different reaction, given that she had painted her body with some kind of complex glow in the dark pattern.

The semi-transparent Rosss, guarding me in my sleep, tried to stop my first advisor, but she had just waved off the deadly Alpha Iseyek, saying:

"Let me through! Georg, there's something you must see!"

My cousin turned on the lights without asking and, not paying any attention to Princess Astra grumbling in dismay and covering her eyes with her hands, activated the wall screen. My own eyes had yet to accustom to the bright light, so I didn't see the image immediately, but I did recognize the voice of Emperor August right away:

"... in these trying times, we all must rally together for the sake of victory! Hundreds of millions of citizens of our great Empire must join together in a burst of patriotism to prove to the traitors in the so-called Unatari State and their puppet masters..."

What?! I shot up, instantly forgetting my exhaustion. Katerina turned on the sound with a remote and gave commentary:

"Cousin, this is being cycled on absolutely every news channel! It's a twenty-minute speech in which the Emperor announces that Unatari State psionics made an attack on his Truth Seekers, killing and paralyzing several of them. According to him, your betrayal was in order to allow the huge Alien supercarrier, which Krista and her group very nearly destroyed to leave the system. And at the same time, they say the Unatari Fleet, under your leadership together with the ships of Grand Duchy traitors in the Nayal system made a vile attack on the Seventh Imperial Strike Fleet, when it was bravely fighting off the incoming hordes of Aliens..."

"What drivel is this?!" I asked, sincerely outraged. "My fleet was never even in Nayal, which is to say nothing about the other, utterly ridiculous accusations! And proving that is elementary! I have footage in the databanks on my starships. I have the emergency recording devices. I have warp beacon data. I have a huge number of witnesses, first and foremost the residents of the Khell system, who will all confirm that the Unatari Fleet never went to Nayal. At the end of the day, I can even use the abilities of my Truth Seekers!"

"Wake up, Georg! Who would ever doubt and check recordings, when the Emperor himself made an unambiguous accusation before his subjects! You and I were called traitors! Ten minutes ago, the Empire officially declared war on the Unatari State! With his declaration, August declared you and me, along with all the other Unatari Fleet officers, traitors and deprived us of all titles and medals! So, our explanation and broadcast won't even be watched in the Empire! And no one would be able to see it, even if they wanted. All the warp beacons on the border have already been put into unidirectional data blockade mode, I've checked. Imperial propaganda gets through, but our broadcasts are shut out! Damn, my standing has already fallen by seven points in just ten minutes!"

What? It was my cousin's last words that hooked me, having stood out from the stream of hysterical yelping. Of course, Katerina's standing was falling after such accusations from the Emperor himself. But why hadn't I gotten any messages about mine? I opened the internal interface and looked in detail at my information:

Georg royl Inoky ton Mesfelle, Crown Prince of the Empire, Ruler of the Unatari State, Swarm Five-Star-Admiral
Age: 49
Race: Human
Gender: Male

Class: Aristocrat/Mystic
Achievements: Elder Chameleon Female, Discovered Arites, Got through Alien Blockade, Researcher of the Unknown, Imperial Land Grabber, Ex-Fleet Commander for Sector Eight, Malingerer, Respected by the Swarm, Dekeye Champion of No Rules Fighting, Defender of Humanity, Master of the Hive, Favorite's Iseyek Mating Dance, Peacemaker, More Territory than the Emperor
Fame: +83
Standing: +24

Strange. Both my title as Prince and heir to the Empire were retained, along with all my achievements. And my standing hadn't fallen one bit, either, as far as I could tell... How? Why was Katerina's standing falling, but for the exact same "sins," mine was staying exactly the same? And also, how could a signal from the Empire even reach us here in the Forepost-10 system? The Grand Duchy was blocking broadcasts from its enemies, right? But what if...

Here, I was visited by a thought that made my heart seize in fear. What if the clip of the Emperor was a falsification, and my second cousin was trying to trick me?! What could Katerina hope to achieve by that? The answer was obvious: she wanted the Unatari State to get tied up in a war with the Empire! Here, after all, it was enough to simply begin combat operations, and there would be no going back. The war would be very harsh, and last until one side achieved total victory. Why would my advisor want such a thing? My cousin couldn't have been working for the Antagonists, right?! And by the way... Katerina was once official speaker of the Green House and had taken part in every important negotiation. And if the first encounter between mankind and the Aliens took place in Green House space, Katerina would certainly have been there to take part! The Alien *Queen* couldn't have meant my advisor, when she'd referred to a person who had taken part in those long-ago negotiations, right?

I have no idea what conclusion I may have come to, but right before my eyes there came a packet of new information:

Global fame increase. Current value: +84

Global fame increase. Current value: +85

Global standing increase. Current value: +25

Standing change. Empire Military faction opinion of you has worsened.
Present Empire Military faction opinion of you: +65 (veneration)

That meant there was no complete information blockade, and messages really were getting through. My fame was growing, as was my global standing. The fame was clear — more and more people in the Empire knew who I was. The standing as well — aristocrats and the representatives of various factions, as a rule, mostly did not like stagnation and would come out in favor of any changes, hoping to use that to reinforce their position. But the Imperial Military was a different story. They saw me as a fearsome enemy they'd have to reckon with, and the worsening of relations was totally predictable. But where were the negative changes Katerina had experienced?

"What's wrong, Georg? You're looking at me like you've never seen me before!" Duchess Katerina ton Unatari tore me out of the contemplative state.

Should I tell her about my suspicions or not? On the one hand, it would be dumb to admit my doubts and fears to the very person they applied to. But on the other hand... everyone needs at least one person they can trust in this life, otherwise they'd become paranoid in short order. So, I honestly told my cousin my confusion.

Standing change. Katerina ton Unatari's opinion of you has improved.

Katerina ton Unatari's present opinion of you: +87 (completely trusting)

"Thank you for your faith, cousin. It's good that you honestly shared your worrying thoughts. I cannot prove right now that I have never spoken with the Alien *Queen*. But I swear to you that I did not do it and am prepared to undergo Truth Seeker testing at any time. But that is an interesting little brain teaser. That means you're saying, someone who was there for the attack on the *Queen* once negotiated with the Aliens... I'll think over the riddle. But as for your standing, that really is strange..."

Katerina considered it and even closed her eyes for thirty seconds, then looked at me with her eyes wide in surprise and said in agitation:

"Georg, this is the first time I've ever seen something like this! The Emperor's allies simply do not have a high enough vote percentage to make negative changes to your standing! Cousin, your fame and standing are too high, so no less than two thirds of aristocrats must agree with August's initiative to declare you a criminal. But that is not happening, because you still have plenty of allies in the Empire! And to deprive a Crown Prince of his title, from what I've seen, you need practically unanimous approval of the other Imperial aristocrats!"

"It looks like August tripped into a puddle then?" I suggested with a smile. "The citizens of the Empire didn't believe the accusations against me?"

"Or they did, but they thought that Crown Prince Georg had finally stopped blindly obeying the Emperor and launched his own political game," Katerina chuckled.

"It's about time, Georg! It's been two years now since you promised to take me to the Throne World and show me all the beautiful sights. I bought outfits just for the purpose long ago, and our excursion just keeps getting pushed back. Everyone knows that a Crown Prince's word is sacred. I say, if you need to overthrow the Emperor to fulfill your promise, do it!"

It wasn't hard to guess who said that: Princess Astra royl Veyerde. Katerina and I exchanged surprised glances.

Astra with her strange and frequently childlike behavior was hard to take seriously. I quite often forgot she was in the room and, normally, my favorite didn't try to jump into serious conversations about politics. So, hearing the Princess speak on substantive issues, I felt very thrown off and spent a long time rooting in my memory to remember if any other serious conversations had been had in her presence.

"Well, your little doll is right," Katerina said in contemplation. "The Emperor's political star is setting inexorably. He is losing state power, strength and authority. And, everyone understands perfectly that August is of more than advanced age, and the Empire will need a new ruler, if not today, then tomorrow. What's more, there aren't too many figures on the political stage of first-order greatness — you, Duke Amelius ton Lavaelle and your sister Duchess Violetta royl Mesfelle-Damir. Eventually, you'll have to find the decisiveness to officially declare that which has been spoken of in whispers for so long by aristocrats in the whole Empire..."

My first assistant's speech was crudely interrupted by a siren on the starship and intercom message:

"Combat alert! A warp beacon has appeared in our system!!!"

* * *

The reigning atmosphere in the fleet headquarters was noisy and charged, but more celebratory than worried. Everyone had already realized that the enemy had committed a brutish error and jumped right into our trap. As soon as I arrived, the officers crowding around my assistants hurried to get back to their seats. Nicole ton Savoia jumped out of my fleet commander seat and hurried to make a report:

"Your Highness, you were completely right: the enemy was tracking us. Demyen royl Lavaelle's fleet managed to jump to Forepost-10, despite the warp beacon there being off. Crown Prince Georg, I beg the deepest apology for mistrusting you."

And although it wasn't in the presence of all the staff officers, just in a narrow circle of the commander and three assistants, Baroness Nicole ton Savoia really had dared to doubt my decision to take the fleet out of the Khell system before the ships of the Grand Duchy fleet restored enough energy for another warp jump. My assistant thought we had to give the chance for the fleet following us to enter the trap, and turn on the Forepost-10 warp beacon for a minute or two to lure them, as if by accident. But I came out categorically against that idea. It was too obvious. The enemy wouldn't believe we'd be so reckless, which would put them on guard.

What was more, earlier in our conversation, Demyen royl Lavaelle had bragged of his ability to wipe out my ships either in the Khell or Forepost-10 system, which spoke to his being in possession of a trump card of some kind. And also, my mother had confirmed that she was tracking the movement of the Unatari fleet. All that pointed to there being a cloaked mobile-warp-beacon ship from the Aliens in the Forepost-10 system, and maybe more than one. This was the very conclusion I led Nicole to then, but my assistant had not changed her opinion. Now though, the space major was expressing sincere regret and a preparedness to undergo punishment for disputing her commander's orders. I rushed to reassure the uncommonly talented girl:

"Nicole, you did exactly right, telling me your questions and remarks. I don't have any need for subjects that blindly believe whatever they are told. A certain share of healthy skepticism and your own opinion simply must be present. On that, I suggest we end this topic and return to the present situation in space."

"Yes, Your Highness. The mobile beacon ship held the portal open for more than four minutes. That time was easily enough for our frigates to reach the little bugger and get it held down tight. We didn't destroy it, just as you ordered. But it has so many stasis webs and warp disruptors on it that the ship is technically unable to move. Assault groups have already been sent out to capture the ship."

"Great! Bionica, how are things going with you? Did you manage to get in touch with the androids of the Grand Duchy fleet to gather information on our enemy?"

"My Prince, the mission could only be partially completed," the synthetic blonde replied, lowering her head, clearly unhappy with herself. "There are androids loyal to me on Grand Duchy ships, but not many. The vast majority of anthropomorphic robots there were flashed by the Green House Security Service. Their unique characteristics were wiped, and their behavioral settings were reset to default. The developers found and eliminated some of the programming loopholes we used to secretly communicate and coordinate our actions. I had to take immediate action as not to be exposed. I did figure out the enemy fleet's composition, though. I also learned the code tablets by which Grand Duchy ships communicate with the Aliens. But, I'm afraid, that is all I managed to get. I wouldn't be able to repeat the sabotage of dumping water and destroying food reserves, or get access to the cannons, thrusters and arsenals on the enemy ships."

"Calm down, Bionica, I didn't tell you to get me an automatic win button. But it would be quite interesting to have a look at the enemy fleet composition. First of all, I'm interested in the question of whether Demyen royl Lavaelle still has mobile warp beacon ships, and where they are located."

The light blonde android beauty answered momentarily:

"My Prince, the enemy has another such frigate in the Khell system. Although the Grand Duchy Fleet Commander placed a garrison of thirty thousand former Purple House soldiers on the Khell station, he also left himself another secret way out. It would seem he doesn't trust his new allies and is afraid they will betray him. Shall I order the Alien frigate to leave the system?"

Was that seriously possible?! I tried not to show my surprise, although there was plenty to be elated about here. Just a second ago, I had made an off-hand remark about an automatic win button. What Bionica had just offered was even closer to that than what she had been unable to deliver.

"Yes, send along an order for the Alien frigate to leave to Nayal. Or wait... is there a code for 'dock at station?' Great! Then tell it to dock at the Khell station. Max Gregor, in five minutes, set off the thermonuclear mine placed on the station. We've already evacuated all civilians, and this will be a good lesson to our enemy. They'll live to regret going to war with us a million times over!!!"

*　　*　　*

There they are! From the spy satellite camera, I could see the enemy's armada of many thousand ships come out of warp jump. Demyen royl Amelius ton Lavaelle's fleet stretched on for a few thousand miles.

"Crown Prince Georg, should I call them?" Nicole ton Savoia inquired, but I shook my head in the negative.

"It's too early. Now, they'll be scanning near space, sending out recon frigates to the far planets and asteroid fields, and basically scrambling to find my ships. After all, my opponent is certain that I had nowhere to run from his trap, and that victory is already practically in his hands. He doesn't know about Mechanoids though, or our ships in the Forepost-9 system and thinks he has us backed into a corner. Let the full depth of the trouble he's gotten himself into reach the former Crown Prince. We'll give him forty minutes. I bet that is more than enough time for him to figure everything out."

The Grand Duchy Fleet Commander figured it all out much faster, though. Just seventeen minutes later, he sent me a long-distance call request. The former Crown Prince didn't look quite as courageous and pompous as before but still, Demyen royl Amelius ton Lavaelle was trying to threaten, bluff and negotiate, clearly not yet having grasped the magnitude of the trap I'd led him into. I had to put that jackass in his place:

"Demyen, the reason you do not see the Khell system warp beacon has nothing to do with temporary technical difficulties. I just blew up the Khell space station together with your garrison and the Alien frigate docked at it. Yes, it was harsh, but it was the only way to protect the millions of inhabitants of the planet Khell-1 from the ruthless hordes of Aliens you've led into human space."

"Crown Prince Georg, you don't understand..." my opponent tried to argue, but I cut him off sharply, raising my voice to a shout:

"I understand perfectly!!! I cannot find a single justification for your treachery! You in the Grand Duchy are still under the naive impression that you can control the Alien ships? They'll only obey your orders as long as doing so is beneficial for them! Try to find a code in the communication table under your hand that stands for: 'Put down your weapons and surrender.' Oh, there isn't one? Well, how about: 'cease fire,' 'fall back,' or 'retreat?' Not there either? What a shame... So then, how were you planning to stop the genocide of humanity in the Khell system?"

The man went silent, turned away from the camera, and asked his assistants to check my words. And while Demyen was waiting for an answer, I continued my invective:

"In order to avoid any misunderstandings from the get-go, I'll be as frank as I can. In a few minutes, I'm planning to blow up the Forepost-9 warp beacon, which is where we are now. When I do that, your fleet will be forever deprived of any method of communicating with other star systems inhabited by intelligent races. Your calls for help will take many years to get anywhere, and whoever does finally receive them will have no way to help you. For my part, I'll make sure the fact of a deadly Alien armada being locked up in the Forepost-10 system is recorded in every star atlas from here on out, to make sure not a single warp beacon will ever appear in jump radius from your fleet. So, if you have any last words for your father, any other relatives, or humanity in general, say them right now, and I will relay your message. You have my word as a Crown Prince!"

"Crown Prince Georg, you will not do that!" But now, I could read sheer terror on the face of the Grand Duchy Fleet Commander. "I am prepared to surrender! Tell me your terms! I swear honestly, I will fulfill every one!"

Demyen royl Lavaelle collapsed onto one knee and folded his hands in a gesture of prayer. But, I just shook my head in the negative:

"Once upon a time, you promised to never again go to war with me. You swore by your title and aristocratic honor. And now, Demyen, I know that you have no honor, so I have no faith in your words. And also, how can you promise that the Aliens in your fleet will surrender, if you don't even have a way to give them such a command?! It looks like you're lying again. What kind of aristocrat and officer are you, if you can bring shame so easily on yourself and make promises you have no intention of keeping! You don't inspire pity in me, just detestation and scorn. To be honest, I could have killed you in the last system. My wife Miya offered to do so. But it would have been too easy and quick a death for you. No, you must have enough time to think over your utterly worthless life. In the memory of your descendants, you will remain a commander who sold himself to an enemy of humanity and twice got caught in the exact same trap..."

"No! I am no traitor to my species! My father ordered me to include the Alien starships in my fleet. He's the one who gave me the signal codes to control their ships. Tell my father... No, tell all people everywhere that I still had enough honor to avoid shame!"

What happened next came very fast.

Without even standing to his feet, Demyen pulled a laser pistol from the holster on his belt and placed it to his forehead.

With a bright flash, the Crown Prince's lifeless body collapsed onto the cold floor.

"Wow, cousin, you're really good at making people go white hot..." said Katerina, providing dismayed commentary on the tragic incident after the initial shock had passed. "Sometimes, after talking with you, I want to either hang myself or whack you on the head with something heavy. But why, I ask, did you have to force Demyen to commit suicide?! Of course, he was an unreliable and rotten person, I won't argue with that. But at least let him tell us about the alliance with the Aliens or share some of their technologies first... Alright, why worry? It's over now. Should I end the call?"

"Wait, don't!!!" on the screen next to the commander's corpse there appeared a fairly old red-haired military man in a uniform with the gold patches of a senior officer. I didn't recognize him.

Kevin ton Moldier, Grand Duchy Fleet Admiral
Age: 68
Race: Human
Gender: Male
Class: Military/Aristocrat
Achievements: Former Perimeter Sector
Eighteen Fleet Commander, awarded medals
and orders for participation in interspecies
conflicts (complete list of medals can be seen in
Attachments)
Fame: +4
Standing: +14

Sector Eighteen? But that was... the Gold House! Based on what happened next, Katerina ton Unatari had also noticed that:

"So, we finally see an Antagonist. I was worried we would just get more marionettes, but here we have a puppet master."

"Antagonist?" the admiral asked me from the screen, not having arrived at what my advisor and I were referring to. "Ah! You're talking about me. Your Highness, I ask you to forgive me for my drowsiness and ignorance. This is my first time leaving Gold House space, and I still am not familiar with the local terminology and idiomatic expressions. As a matter of fact, we call First Imperial Fleet Commander August royl Akad and his conspirators the Antagonists, after his sabotage two centuries ago against his rightful liege, splitting the unified human Empire..."

"Admiral, that is neither here nor there!" Duchess Katerina replied, sharply interrupting the verbose commander. "Do you have any substantive information, or are you just drawing out time, trying to find a way out of the trap for you and your allies, the enemies of humanity?"

The man on screen went crimson and clenched his teeth, seemingly barely able to hold back sharp words. But he quickly got himself together and answered in an intentional, steady voice:

"Duchess, I've been fighting all my life, defending the interests of the human race. No one can accuse me of betraying mankind! I'll admit, it makes me uncomfortable to be in the presence of such a huge number of Alien ships, but they were brought in by the rulers of the Grand Duchy. The Gold House Third Expeditionary Fleet joined this armada two days ago. We were told they were our new allies. Just like the Green and Purple Houses, who had also provided ships for our unified Grand Duchy fleet."

But here, I did not agree with Admiral Kevin ton Moldier grouping all these forces together. To my eye, they were fundamentally different:

"There's an enormous difference between these allies. No matter how strained the relationship between August royl Akad and his sister Eleonora royl Akad, or the Empire and the Great Houses, or certain military leaders and aristocrats, in the end, they were all fighting for the advancement of the human race. The Aliens, though, are trying to erase humankind and all other space-faring races from the star map. I have seen with my own eyes planets that were entirely depopulated by the Aliens, I have seen the ruins of the civilizations they've destroyed. You must agree, Admiral, that such 'allies' look somewhat strange in your fleet."

The red-headed Admiral lowered his head, shook it and said, now all the less confident:

"I have spoken with Green House officers and know about the... let's say... difficult relationship between humanity and the Aliens. I know about the destruction of the Red House and the other battles between our species, but I swear on my head that neither I nor my subjects have anything to do with those bloody events! I am also aware of the leading role played by Crown Prince Georg royl Inoky ton Mesfelle in turning back the Alien invasion. To be perfectly honest, Your Highness, I couldn't even believe it at first. I remember seeing you in the palace of the Minor Capital, and you made quite a singular impression..."

What was this nonsense?! He and I were not acquainted, and had never met before! The Minor Capital was in Sector Eighteen, deep in Antagonist space! I had never been there, and never could have, even in theory! The border there was guarded on both sides, and the warp beacons were always turned off!

It was good that I didn't manage to voice these thoughts, because it would have made things very uncomfortable. My wife jumped into the conversation just in time and commented:

"Georg, he is not lying. But these events took place BEFORE you came into Perimeter Defense, so you don't know about them. To be as brief as I can, you and your closest relatives — your mother, brother and sister — were invited by the Gold House to your grandmother Eleonora royl Akad's three hundred fiftieth birthday party The Emperor considered it a sufficiently momentous occasion and made an exception, so the

border was opened for invited guests. But you, or to be more accurate, your predecessor Mr. G.I., was strongly disconcerted. He couldn't bear all the pre-party drama, omnipresent Gold House special service agents, and the guard-slash-escort stuck to us all day and night, so he got boorishly drunk. And when I finally managed to get you back to your senses, you took crystals out of spite, after which you sunk into a four-day dream and missed the whole celebration. Your family and wife Marta were just livid."

Everything became clear at once. Making a mental note to ask Miya to tell me in more detail about my trip when a chance presented itself, I answered Admiral Kevin ton Moldier:

"I have a perfect imagination of how nasty the impressions I left behind in the Minor Capital were. However, in the last five years, the situation changed cardinally. The Aliens invaded, putting the very existence of humankind under threat. The first meeting with just one of their ships nearly ended with the complete annihilation of the Perimeter Sector Eight Fleet and my death. Oh, I learned well from that heavy and painful lesson! Since that very day, I have been studying in the most intensive fashion, and now I know the tactical and technical characteristics of all Alien ships by heart, along with all their strong and weak points. I have never since allowed myself to underestimate an enemy or act predictably and formulaically — it's the only way to defeat an enemy that surpasses you technologically. Yes, the enemy is very strong, but I believe that this war can be won! And we will continue our determined march to victory, destroying all Alien fleets, as well as any other ships allied with enemies of humanity, no matter what race they belong to!"

The man on the screen straightened up, adjusted the collar of his luxurious admiral's uniform and unexpectedly gave me a military salute, placing a hand against his black beret with gold ribbon.

"Crown Prince, I admire you as a military leader, advocating for freedom and the future of humanity. It's too bad that we ended up on the wrong sides of a barricade. My Gold House Third Expeditionary Fleet is stuck in the Forepost-10 system together with the Green and Purple House Fleets and the Alien armada. From what I understand, you will not turn on a warp beacon to allow us to leave the trap no matter what happens — the risk of releasing thousands of Alien starships is too great. We are fated to die here in this blocked-off, uninhabited system. Is that right?"

I nodded in silence, still not understanding what the Gold House Admiral was hinting at. Meanwhile, he continued his speech:

"Alright then... I appreciate the honest answer. But before Your Highness detonates the Forepost-9 beacon, I want to tell you that I support the difficult choice you're making with my whole heart. It is best for the whole human race! If there's anything I can do to help Your Highness, just tell me. Duchess Katerina mentioned Grand Duchy technologies I might be willing to share. I'm afraid I don't have much useful information, but I am prepared to share everything I have. I can send the blueprints of our ships, thrusters, cannons and communication systems. These are the newest Gold House starships, developed and built in the last few years. Perhaps they really were built with Alien technology, as Commander Demyen royl Lavaelle claimed, but I do not know. Turn on data acceptance, I'll send you everything we have. Perhaps it will really be useful to you. Then, I'll lead my ships into battle against the Alien armada. It will be a final, hopeless engagement, but it's better to go down fighting than to die of starvation, old age or realizing one's lack of purpose."

"Your Highness, long distance data acceptance from the Forepost-10 system has been activated," the on-duty officer commented.

I looked at the screen where Admiral Kevin ton Moldier was standing at attention with his right hand on his beret, and answered him with an identical military greeting. After that, I said to the courageous military man:

"Admiral, I value your bravery and readiness to sacrifice yourself for the good of humanity. So, in order for your last battle not to be utterly senseless and hopeless, I have decided to share some important information with you. The warp beacon in your system has been mined. There is a two-hundred-megaton bomb installed on it. I'll give you the activation codes. Use the code table and send the Alien ships to the station to charge, then blow the bomb. Two hundred megatons won't be enough for the Alien heavy ships, but the little stuff will be ground to dust. And I've also got a tip: before blowing up the warp beacon, make sure to turn it on. That will increase the power of the blast by many times. We started a similar explosion in the Aysar Cluster, and it was judged by my science consultants to have been four hundred teratons in TNT equivalent. Almost nothing survived within a radius of four thousand miles of the epicenter. The only ships with any chance are *Mammoth*-class supercarriers, but even they might be destroyed. There is also one very important condition: the Aliens are no fools and will not trust humans. If you attempt to bring your ships away from the mined station, the Aliens will do the same, and the explosion will not do much damage to them."

Not a single muscle twitched on the courageous admiral's face, although he knew perfectly that I was proposing his certain death.

"I'll do it for the good of humankind, Crown Prince Georg royl Inoky ton Mesfelle! And I thank Your Highness for the chance you've given me and my soldiers to go down in eternity with honor and our heads held high."

*   *   *

I saluted the heroic man, and the admiral went offscreen. He needed to give his final orders to his fleet. Taking advantage of the pause in negotiations, my cousin Katerina ton Unatari walked up closer, switched off the microphone and turned to me:

"Georg, you're just going to let them die? What, you aren't even going to try and lure at least the most valuable Great House ships away to reinforce your fleet? Doesn't seem like you..."

In reply, I just shrugged my shoulders indefinitely, because I really had not yet made a decision on the trapped starships, even for myself. My advisor Katerina ton Unatari was not mistaken in guessing the struggle going on inside my head.

On the one hand, it was very stupid to risk it and give the enemy even a slight chance of escaping the trap I'd tried so hard to get them in. On the other, Admiral Kevin ton Moldier of the Grand Duchy seemed like a good guy, even though he was commander of an enemy fleet. What was more, as Katerina had noted correctly, there was a huge number of ships in the Forepost-10 system that could potentially be used to reinforce my fleet...

"Commander, data transfer complete. I've sent the materials to your terminal."

After quickly skimming the files he'd sent, my eyebrows shot up in surprise. Battleships that shot antimatter. Cloaked cruisers with fully-fledged weaponry. Stealth frigates capable of firing laser turrets without revealing themselves. And a colossus with cannons of just over half a mile in length...

Blowing up a detailed blueprint of the starship with gigantic turrets on the huge hologram in the center of the room, I stood up and walked over to the shimmering three-dimensional projection.

"Officers, I want everyone's attention! Before us is *Executioner*, flagship of the Gold House. It is a human ship that incorporates Alien technology. I don't even know how to classify such a prototype. Mega-battleship? Dreadnaught? Titan? At any rate, it shoots antimatter. To be more specific, it has long rail cannons that fire spheres of anti-iron at near-light speeds. Based on the specifications we just received, the projectile travels so quickly that it will essentially ignore energy shields. A strike from such a giant could one-shot any ship, including a carrier. It would take down our *Joan the Fatty,* for instance, in the blink of an eye."

"Reload time?" "Effective firing distance?" "Cannon tracking?" questions piled in from all around and I called for silence with a gesture.

"It is a one-shot ship. It can shoot a volley from its two main cannons, destroying the one or two most dangerous targets, after which it requires a prolonged and complicated reloading procedure of around one hour. However, *Executioner* is free to participate in combat with its twelve laser turrets during this time, and they are comparable in battle characteristics to the combat lasers of our *Tyrant*-class battleships. But, you must understand that, while reloading, the *Executioner* is not such a great threat. It's just an overgrown battleship with all the associated downsides. The cannon tracking is worthless. It will never hit fast maneuverable ships. Sluggish and unwieldy, it is simply an ideal target. What's more, I have serious suspicions that our stealth bombers would be able to get that giant off the battlefield using a standard chain of electromagnetic and gravitation bombs. All in all, it isn't easy to find an application for the *Executioner* in battle. It has lots of downsides. But, dear officers... you know my weakness for heavy starships. I want to try and get this giant in our fleet."

Silence descended, my subjects thought over my words. Finally, Admiral Kiro Sabuto asked:

"Crown Prince Georg, are you suggesting that our fleet return to the Forepost-10 system to capture a trophy?"

"Oh no," I reassured the famed admiral with a happy chuckle. "Doing something like that would be equivalent to suicide. It's too dangerous to go into a system where a fleet three times larger than your own is waiting. What's more, the enemy is backed into a corner and totally hopeless. They have nowhere to retreat to, so they would fight to the death, not even counting their losses... That is surely not the end result I'd like to see. I would like to try and solve the matter not by brute force, but diplomacy. But here, there is one important obstacle in my way..."

"My Prince, what might that obstacle be?" Bionica asked, curious after I went silent midsentence.

"That obstacle is you!" I said, pointing my arm in a wide arc at everyone in the headquarters. "Yes, you precisely, my most experienced and loyal officers who have followed me through fire and water. After all, I could try to lure some of the ships onto our side from the trap in Forepost-10, but many times I have heard you all say that you would never fight side-by-side with Antagonists. To me, your loyalty is worth much more than any potential ship acquisitions. And because of that, although the trophies are very attractive, I will not do anything to get them without your approval."

Admiral Kiro Sabuto came out in front, pushing through the backs of the officers. The gray-haired East Asian veteran, who enjoyed massive authority among the military, was a veritable expert in army traditions and officer honor.

"Crown Prince Georg royl Inoky ton Mesfelle, there is no leader in the galaxy with so much respect for the traditions of the Imperial Fleet and Army, and who is so respected by the military. I think that I am now speaking for all space fleet officers, no matter what political force they belong to in these troubled times

— the pitiful remains of the once-great Empire, or our proud and quickly growing Unatari State or the bizarre new government made of Great Houses. All military people understand perfectly that Your Highness is the very leader capable of ending all our squabbles and rallying humanity against the Alien horde. Securing the future of our species is a very lofty goal, and nothing can be allowed to stop Your Highness on that path. So, do whatever you think is right! We will support Your Highness in all undertakings!"

The other officers started clamoring loudly, confirming the admiral's words and assuring me of their loyalty. But Kiro Sabuto called everyone's attention with a gesture and... unexpectedly bowed down before me on one knee.

"Crown Prince Georg royl Inoky ton Mesfelle, the others simply haven't made up their minds to say this aloud yet, but I will. We all see before us a future Emperor, who is coming to replace the decrepit August royl Akad!"

After these bold words from the famed admiral, silence descended. After that, all my staff officers, as if on command, lowered down on one knee and bowed their heads.

Duchess Katerina ton Unatari and Bionica followed their example, and even the Iseyek made deep bows in a showing of deepest respect. My chameleon bodyguards became visible and also lowered their heads to demonstrate solidarity with the others and their feelings toward the ruler.

Everyone in the room was silent and clearly expecting me to answer Admiral Kiro Sabuto's words along with the overall expression of respectful loyalty. In such a situation, staying silent would be totally impossible. I ordered everyone to stand with a gesture and, increasing the volume of the microphone on my uniform, said:

"Yes, friends, I see no reason to hide or obscure it any further. Emperor August has long been too old to lead and, based on his last absolutely mindless actions, he's now so decrepit he has no good sense left. We all remember the way he made an unprovoked and vile attack on the Unatari State Embassy in the Throne World. Although the Emperor did beg my apology then, he gave an order today to exterminate my Truth Seekers so we couldn't capture the Alien *Queen*. And when his plan blew up in his face, August royl Akad finally pulled off the mask of a just ruler of the Empire and openly declared war on us. So, I have no further plans to act ceremonious with this old madman! My friends, I officially declare to you that I intend to win this war and become Emperor, uniting a scattered humanity under my command! So, I don't see the ships trapped in Forepost-10 as enemies from the Grand Duchy so much as potential subjects who can and must be encouraged to join our side. I think soldiers who stay true to their oaths should not suffer because they didn't have the good fortune to be on the right side of a conflict!"

Standing change. Empire Military faction opinion of you has improved.
Present Empire Military faction opinion of you: +66 (veneration)

Standing change. Empire Military faction opinion of you has improved.
Present Empire Military faction opinion of you: +67 (veneration)

Standing change. Empire Military faction opinion of you has improved.
Present Empire Military faction opinion of you: +68 (veneration)

Just what I needed! My subjects, who had declared their undying loyalty to the Emperor not so long ago, and also said they would never accept being in the same fleet as Antagonists, were now reacting positively to my scorn toward the ruler of the Empire, and my suggestion that Grand Duchy ships join our fleet.

Now, I had the following mission before me, which was quite challenging: force the Grand Duchy fleet, which was larger than mine, to join the Unatari State, then somehow drag these ships out of the trap in the Forepost-10 system without letting the Alien fleet come with.

ENEMY OF THE EMPIRE

"SOMETHING isn't coming together, cousin..." Duchess Katerina ton Mesfelle said, setting her tablet aside and sitting back in exhaustion in her small sofa. "I've spent the last hour pouring over the list of Truth Seekers, officers and general crew members who were present for the attack on the *Queen*. I didn't find anything of use. No one seems to fit the bill. Someone who participated in the first negotiations with the Aliens, and was also at our recent battle. It seems to me that we must be making some mistake or missing something. All in all, it looks like the first contact of the Aliens and humanity took place in Antagonist space. Is that right? Georg, don't stay silent, answer me! What, are you sleeping?!"

I cracked open one eye and yawned in exhaustion, covering it with my hand for politeness. I wanted horribly to sleep. Energy drinks and stimulants had lost all effect. But I was holding on and fighting to stay awake, because I knew my body very well. If I gave into weakness and fell asleep, then it would be very hard to think when suddenly awoken later. It was better to bear it for an hour or two while the whole crisis situation with the trapped Grand Duchy fleet was resolved, then give into Morpheus' sweet embrace and sleep even for two days, if necessary.

"I'm not asleep, just resting. All in all, it looks like you're right. First contact must have taken place in Antagonist space, given that the Gold House is in possession of Alien technology," I agreed with my advisor.

"Yes! We saw hundreds of starships built in the Gold House based on Alien designs with our own eyes. If similar ships were built in the Empire or at Green House docks, we would know. So, let's take it as a given that contact took place in Antagonist space, and the one who made it is from the Gold House. But after that, the mysterious conspirator somehow got through unnoticed to Imperial space, successfully passing all the meticulous questioning at the border. Then, they stayed away from mind reading or loyalty checks by your psionics in order to embed themselves in the crew of an Unatari Fleet ship. You must agree that the risk of failure would be huge, and the main thing is: what does this person stand to gain from that?!"

Here I was in complete agreement with my advisor. This was extremely illogical behavior for the Antagonist spy. What was more, if it was a captain or senior officer, he would probably have been efficiently exposed. Florianna and Miya regularly scanned the thoughts of my subjects to detect traitors and spies. Sure, general crew members were not checked, but the information such a person might have access to would hardly justify the huge risk of such infiltration.

"The same goes for the Truth Seekers," Duchess Katerina continued her train of thought, now convinced that I had caught her idea on the military. "All psionics from Krista's group are quite famous Truth Seekers. Their biographies are freely available. They're always in the public eye, and it can be said for certain that none of them have been in Antagonist space for the last one hundred years. And same goes for your Truth Seekers. Miya has spent the last few years with you. Florianna's biography is also transparent, until meeting you, the girl had never left her home system of Veyerde. Dead end..."

A message beeped into my terminal over internal communications. I overcame my lack of desire and exhaustion with difficulty and stood from the couch, activating the screen and reading. And right from the first lines, my weariness blew away like the wind! I told my cousin what I'd seen:

"I just got some information from the former navigator of *Joan the Fatty*. He says that he managed to figure out the Alien map and transpose their system of coordinates onto our usual one. Interesting, very interesting... Yes, here is a map of star system locations with space disruption points and a scheme of possible movements between them. Woah! From the system neighboring ours, Amati, you can even get to Sector Seventeen! Think of how surprised those Grand Duchy people would be if we dropped by for a visit! There are more than seventeen disruption points, of which just eight are in human space. There are also a couple in the Swarm but the others are extremely far from the systems known to humanity...

And it should be said that, in Gold House space, there is just one weak point: the Korusyo star system, which just so happens to be in Sector Seventeen! Now we know the location of humanity's first contact with the Aliens!"

My advisor walked up nearer and started studying the map with me. Soon, our attention was drawn by a point far from any human-known star systems, the only one marked on the map in red. On Katerina's request, I opened the note from Mike ton Tir:

"The D5-113G system, an orange-dwarf-class star. Alien space. Based on the data we got from the Queen, *this is systems the Aliens spread from, after inventing rapid interstellar flight technology."*

My cousin and I looked at each other at the exact same time. There it was — the historical homeworld of the Aliens! I opened the map, trying to find its scale. Ugh, damn! Two hundred thirty thousand parsecs from us! Seven hundred fifty thousand light years. The Aliens had gone a long way in the process of their expansion...

My further conversation with Katerina was interrupted by a call from the fleet headquarters:

"Commander, a warp beacon has turned on in the Forepost-10 system."

Apparently, Kevin ton Moldier was prepared for the suicidal Alien armada explosion after all. I ordered to be put through immediately with the Grand Duchy Admiral. A few seconds later, the wall screen lit up, and the red-headed Admiral appeared on it, looking down at me. He had shaved recently and was wearing his ceremonial uniform with all its many medals and other regalia.

"Crown Prince Georg royl Inoky ton Mesfelle," said the man, placing his hand on his beret in a military salute, "the order for the Alien ships to go charge has already been given. I ask you to tell me the activation code for the thermonuclear bomb on the warp beacon!"

Now that was self-control. The Admiral knew perfectly that he had just seconds to live, but I didn't see even a shade of gloom on his face, and certainly no fear.

"I admire your courage, Admiral Kevin ton Moldier. But I ask you not to rush to your date with eternity. In the time since our last conversation, I managed to speak with the admirals and captains of my fleet. And they would be honored to serve side-by-side with such brave officers as yours."

The red-headed Admiral made a dismayed grimace and removed his hand from his beret:

"I can't believe my ears. Crown Prince, you cannot seriously suppose that I and my people could change our oaths and join our enemies?! That is simply unheard of! We prefer an honorable death to treason! Let's say this nasty attempt of yours to tempt us didn't happen, and return to our former understandings."

It seemed that the conversation was taking the wrong path, and I needed to immediately change my tactic. The brave commander was clearly not the type to change his loyalties. So, I screwed up my face into a dismayed grimace and barked at the military man:

"You're forgetting your place, Admiral! How dare you accuse a Prince and heir to the Empire of untoward behavior! The only thing I demand from you and the other Gold House officers is to fulfill your duty! You all swore an oath of loyalty to Crown Princess Eleonora royl Akad, the legal ruler of the Gold House. But she is dead, as is her only daughter, Crown Princess Elisa royl Clement ton Mesfelle-Lavaelle. All the same, her grandchildren are alive, direct heirs to the Gold House throne. My twin sister Violetta and I are the only possible legal heirs so, to keep your oath, you must declare allegiance to one of us!"

Based on the authentic amazement drawn on the admiral's face, he'd never before thought about his political alignment in this way. And while the shock hadn't yet passed, I continued my speech, beating my words into the brain of the dumbstruck military man, like nails into a yielding tree trunk:

"I'll be direct. My sister and I have equal rights to the throne, but Violetta has chosen the path of alliance with the Aliens, blatant enemies of humanity. I, though, walk the path that shall save our race from these ruthless enemies. And now, Admiral, I demand that you decide once and for all: who is your legal ruler? If you choose my sister Violetta and her allegiance with the Aliens, you and your fleet will share the fate of our enemies. But if you call me your legal ruler, I swear that I will do everything in my power to get you and your people out of the blocked system. So, I await your answer!"

Ten seconds passed, and I had already begun to worry that I would never convince the man. But my words resonated in the courageous military man's heart. Admiral Kevin ton Moldier, unhurriedly and with dignity bent down on one knee, lowered his head in respect, and pronounced:

"Crown Prince Georg royl Inoky ton Mesfelle, you are the only legal heir to the Gold House throne! My people and I remain true to the oath we gave and are prepared to follow our new Gold House ruler through fire and water! We await your orders, Your Highness!"

Achievement unlocked: Enemy of the Empire

"It isn't all so smooth with this Antagonist admiral, Crown Prince Georg. Yes, he recognized you as his ruler aloud, but he would prefer not to give any official oaths of loyalty. He's still hesitating and holding in mind that his officers might have a different point of view and refuse to obey. Several times, a thought flickered in his head that the most important thing was getting out of the trap, and the balance of forces would become clear once he made it to your system. And then he would decide whether to become your subject or, on the other hand, take the situation under his control. But now, the admiral is prepared to lie under oath, if that saves his fleet and the people entrusted to his leadership."

"I see, Flora, thank you for the information," I mentally answered my Truth Seeker. "Well then, we'll take preventative measures. We'll bring his ships out in small groups, telling them coordinates from the *Mechanoid*. As each ship arrives, we will immediately place Alpha Iseyek divisions on them. Then, we'll make all the new officers give a fully-fledged oath of loyalty to Unatari and at the same time weed out traitors."

I turned to the admiral, who was bent down

respectfully on one knee. Everything in his facial expression and pose were demonstrating obedience and loyalty. To look at him, you'd never think he was hesitating... Good thing I was warned. Well then, I'd have to act carefully and not create a situation where the newcomers might start thinking about disobedience and mutiny. Then, in a few weeks, they'd gel with the common fleet, grow accustomed and even stop thinking themselves any different from the rest of my troops.

"For now, wait, Admiral. There is a way of moving ships to star systems with disactivated warp beacons. But it will be difficult, and we still have calculations and preparation to do. We'll be removing the ships in small batches, calculating temporary jump coordinates for each group. I'll let you know when everything is ready."

The new admiral of my fleet gave a salute and signed off. As soon as the screen went dim, Duchess Katerina giggled nervously:

"I'll admit, when I saw how angry he got at first, I was one hundred percent convinced we'd never come to an agreement. But, Georg, you simply slayed me. What a superb genealogical feint! Just to think, my second cousin — legal ruler of the Antagonists! If you'd have told me that just one year ago, nothing could have made me believe it! Now, we need to think of the most delicate way possible to communicate that fact to Unatari's subjects, so they don't get too flabbergasted. Well, alright, I'll deal with that myself."

*   *   *

My fleet was in Amati, carefully checking all ship systems and preparing for the never-before-attempted jump directly from Perimeter Sector Seven to Eight. The usual path, which passed along a long chain of transport warp beacons took more than eight full days, but my fleet was going to do it in just twenty minutes. It was simply unbelievable! But the navigator of *Joan the Fatty* assured me that it was possible, showing a folded sheet of paper as an example and talking about the complicated properties of space and time. The *Queen* had already told us the coordinates to warp jump to the Hnelle system, and preliminary calculations showed that his data was accurate. But all the same, the nervous charge in the fleet headquarters was palpable.

The captains of the fifteen hundred former Gold House ships who had joined my fleet were also nervous, but it had nothing to do with the upcoming long jump. As a matter of fact, the upcoming warp transfer worried them very little. They had made a super-long jump before when coming from Antagonist space to the Nayal system and were sure it could be done safely. What was making those captains nervous was that I ordered Alpha Iseyek combat groups to be placed on all Gold House ships to avoid any unexpected excesses. The presence of the huge deadly insects on the ships made my new subjects nervous, and they periodically expressed their dismay and annoyance on the common fleet channel, complaining about their commander's mistrust.

But I didn't pay any mind to their discontented

grumbling. They'd get used to it. My troops were already totally at ease with Swarm individuals, and there were even mixed assault subgroups in the Unatari Fleet containing both humans and Iseyek. And I'd even seen that there were some ships crewed by chameleons, people and praying mantises, taking advantage of all the strong sides of each race. By all accounts, they also got along swimmingly.

And as for the "mistrust of their commander," I couldn't believe the captains of the former Gold House were complaining. We dragged every last Gold House ship out of the Forepost-10 trap, but left all the Aliens there together with the Green and Purple House ships. And that was fifteen hundred human starships together with all their crews, around a million people, left to die in a lifeless, uninhabited system...

It was a very difficult decision, but it was taken consciously by the vast majority of votes at a gathering of senior officers of my fleet, where I spoke in favor of just such an outcome. The subdivisions most loyal to the Grand Duchess Violetta and Duke Amelius royl Lavaelle, our clear enemies, were caught in the Forepost-10 system. I gave them the chance to save their own lives, offering them to give in and join my side, but didn't find any understanding. Now it was too late. The Forepost-10 and Forepost-9 warp beacons had already been blown up. It was too dangerous to leave the warp beacons unharmed even in a disabled state. After all, it was possible to hack into the automatic control system, or bribe the staff, and then the huge Alien armada would be set loose, bringing death and destruction to humanity.

And then, when I was already prepared to give my

fleet the go-ahead to jump to Sector Eight, a long-distance call I'd been expecting with particular impatience came in. It was my twin sister Violetta. I was reminded that she promised to get in touch with me after the Unatari Fleet's battle with the Grand Duchy Armada when, according to her, I'd know the bitterness of defeat, and my haughtiness would be reigned in.

My sister couldn't hide her surprise, and her very first words confirmed the Grand Duchess's extreme confusion:

"Georg, why are you in the Amati system?"

"Where else should I be, sister?" I chuckled happily. "I picked up my daughter Joan, milled the fleet you sent to stop me into dust, and now I'm going back where I came from."

There was such an awkward combination of mistrust and surprise reflected on my twin sister's face that I broke down laughing. In the end, Violetta came to the conclusion I was mocking her, and grew clearly offended:

"Do you have anything serious to say, brother? The warp beacons around your fleet were turned off! You wouldn't have been able to get to Amati on your own, which is to say nothing of defeating a fleet so much stronger than yours! Admit it, are you now in captivity on one of my ships?"

Here came my turn to get offended and put on a dismayed countenance:

"Violetta, you may find it hard to believe, but Demyen royl Lavaelle's fleet no longer exists. To be more accurate, the fleet may still exist, but it will not be available for many years to come. We switched roles. Your ships are trapped in the Forepost-10 system, while I left the trap and blew up all the neighboring warp beacons. Demyen royl Lavaelle, your fleet commander, fell into the same trap I caught him in once before, a fact which he found unbearable, so he shot himself. I will send you the video of the former Crown Prince's suicide, and you will send it on to his father Duke Amelius royl Lavaelle."

"Is that so...?" my sister asked, immediately familiarizing herself with the video clip. But she was clearly in shock and couldn't fully believe it was real. "On one of the Perimeter Sector Seven Fleet ships, there is a young man I care for greatly... As a matter of fact, he and I are secretly engaged. He is the father of my future child. Georg, are you really saying I'll never get to see him again?"

Hearing her change the topic of conversation from the heights of interstellar politics to the deepest personal issue was very surprising. Clearly, Grand Duchess Violetta's internal value system placed the fate of her fiancé on a very high pedestal. I just shrugged my shoulders ambiguously:

"Sister, if you have any scout ships at hand, you could send them to the Khell system right now. In six or seven years, the ship will reach them, build a new warp beacon, and you can meet your beloved, though he will, in truth, no longer be quite so young. And that's if, of course, the hungry Aliens don't devour him before that..."

"Is there no other way?" my sister asked, her eyes growing wide in horror. "Six years! What's more, from what I know, there aren't any scout ships in Grand Duchy space right now."

"I have a friend among the Imperial scouts," I reminded her. "But I don't think the captain of *Star Mutt* would be too elated if I pulled him off another long-distance flight for personal reasons. But I could try. So then, what was the name of your lame duck?"

"He's no lame duck! Baron Juan ton Amolie is from an ancient aristocratic family. He's a space major, and senior tactician on the battleship *Purple Star*, the Perimeter Sector Seven flagship. He's a very handsome, noble young man with dashing thick mustache and fists the size of a normal person's head. He's a great dancer, very gallant and knows how to treat a woman. I was even thinking of naming him my official spouse and making him Grand Duke... But somehow, I don't think you called to talk about my fiancé..."

I nodded shortly, as Violetta's amorous affairs were really of little concern to me. My sister kept silent for a little, then began a serious conversation:

"In Sector Three, the main Grand Duchy Fleet scored a solid victory over the First Imperial Fleet. There was a whole series of battles there, which came together into one grandiose conflict. The Empire lost more than ten thousand ships. The Grand Duchy's losses were also great, but quite a bit less. My Third Fleet from Sector Six is successfully attacking the Core now. And even though my Second Fleet is lost, Emperor August's days are numbered... Brother, have you given any thought to a future peace treaty?"

"Yes, that's all I think about," I muttered, mentally imagining the position of the largest fleets and the balance of forces on the political arena after all the events Violetta had just described. "Well, we shouldn't divide up the pelt of a bear before it's dead. The Empire has thirty thousand combat-ready ships, and the Grand Duchy has one and a half times less..."

"Yes, something like that," Duchess Violetta confirmed my approximate calculations. "But the Grand Duchy has a significant advantage in technology. And that's not all..."

I realized my sister was referring to the Aliens. After the nasty defeat in the D56KT system and the loss of the fleet in the Forepost-10 system, the Aliens still had at least the third largest fleet, which had rolled back the Red House and conducted a successful war against the Blue House. Plus, in the light of new knowledge, it was impossible to exclude the possibility that reinforcements had arrived from the Alien homeworld.

"Georg, you don't have enough strength for an independent political game. But your fleet is easily enough to help me tip the scales in the war against the Empire. Why hesitate, Emperor August has already declared war on your government. I saw your new achievement, Enemy of the Empire. So, what are you waiting for? The Empire is our common enemy! Help me, and together we'll rule the galaxy! As brother and sister! We were together even in our mother's womb, so fate itself has determined we should be as one!"

"And what role do you see me playing in the structure of the post-war world?" I inquired, simply to understand my sister's thoughts.

"Don't you see, Georg?" Was it just me, or was Violetta really surprised I hadn't guessed. "The very same role you've always had: that of a dear and beloved younger brother! Judge for yourself: I have much greater territories, greater industrial capabilities, a much higher population, and a space fleet ten times the size of yours! I will make no claim on that which you already have gained, and will honestly share all future trophies. You will get the title of Grand Duke, junior co-ruler to the Empress of all humanity! You must agree, it sounds tempting!"

I shook my head and answered, making a show of not looking at Violetta and staring at my fingernails, as if the conversation was boring me:

"You've obviously got me mistaken with someone else, sister! I have no interest in your offer whatsoever. And just so you know, my fleet can handily defeat whatever the Grand Duchy has left after its bloody and costly victory over the Empire. And that's if you can even achieve it..."

After these words, I finally looked at my sister and smiled. I had no doubts remaining. Violetta was clearly bluffing, pretending to be in command of the situation. In reality, even though the Grand Duchess did have an advantage in the war, she wasn't totally convinced of her victory over the Emperor.

"Alright, Georg, tell me your terms! What do you want?"

My sister fell back on offering concessions surprisingly easily, and I needed to take advantage of that.

"Now that's better, sister. Listen to me. I need all your information about contact between humanity and the Aliens — who, where, when and what they agreed on, and all the technologies they gave. I also want to know everything about the Triumvirate and the co-rulers of the Grand Duchy. And I demand that the Aliens be sent back from whence they came, giving up all the systems they captured from humankind..."

"You're demanding the impossible, brother! I don't have such power over the Aliens! Yes, they are allies of my Grand Duchy, but I can only give commands to their ships and point where to attack, and say who not to touch. Giving technologies to your government may be realistic, but from where and when this knowledge was received I do not even know myself. That was done by the ruler of the Gold House and her advisors. And I cannot name the third member of the Triumvirate either — that would do too much to strengthen your positions to the disadvantage of mine."

I considered it improper to conduct further negotiations without first coming to an understanding on the very most basic principles, so I signed off. What sense was there in discussing the structure of the post-war world and other such lofty matters if my sister had an elementary mistrust of me and was incapable of truly being open? What was more, I had the upper hand. Violetta needed the Unatari Fleet to support her in the war. But immediately after victory, given the Alien armada would remain in human space, there would be nothing to stop the newly minted Empress of all humanity from turning all the might of the unified Imperial Fleet against me. From what I had discovered about the difficult character of my sister, that is exactly what she would do. What need did an autocratic ruler have for competition? And no family ties would have stopped Violetta...

"Yes, that is exactly right, Georg. As a political partner and ally, you will cease to have any value to your sister right after her coronation as Empress. And as a dangerous rival in a struggle for power, Violetta will do away with you at once," Miya told me in an uncommonly categorical fashion. No "maybe" or "probably." She was one hundred percent sure that my sister would be getting rid of me if she managed to take power over the Empire.

"And the Throne World? Is an alliance with the Empire possible?"

I already had an idea of the Truth Seeker's answer, I just wanted to check. And I wasn't wrong:

"No, all chances for alliance have already passed you by. August royl Akad is terrified of you and has already ordered you eliminated. We found that out recently by coincidence. An encrypted order came in on an antiquated channel addressed to Nicosid Brandt and, naturally, was intercepted by your security service. By the way, you changed personal doctor just in the nick of time."

"Does the Throne World not know that we exposed their agent?! How is that possible? Can the Imperial Secretariat really not have noticed that old Nicosid Brandt has already returned to the Imperial Core?"

"He never returned to the Empire... The old doctor hung himself in the bunk of the luxurious interstellar liner right after the flight began. I asked your advisors not to tell you about Nicosid Brandt's death as not to upset you in these troubled times. It was right after we just barely survived the assassination attempt in the Blue House. You were all wound up and I thought that news might put you into a rut. Let me assure you: I

studied the old doctor's death and didn't find any signs of outside interference. Taking his own life was a decision the old man came to on his own. No one helped him."

Despite the confirmation that my old doctor was an embedded Throne World agent, I was still upset. Nicosid Brand had worked as Crown Prince Georg royl Inoky ton Mesfelle's personal doctor for half a century, and saved the hard-living Crown Prince's life on multiple occasions, whether after drinking until his heart stopped, or from a coma induced by crystals or other drugs. And also, the transfer of my consciousness into the body of the dead Crown Prince was successful largely thanks to the talent and experience of the old physician.

Before Miya said goodbye, and with a perfect understanding that there was very little chance for a positive answer, I asked my wife if she had managed to read any information about the Triumvirate and co-rulers of the Grand Duchy during my conversation with Violetta.

"Grand Duchess Violetta's mind is tightly closed off to reading. It's a firm, impenetrable wall, which many strong Truth Seekers labored to create. And what's more, the defense wasn't created so very long ago. The thing is, I placed a mental block on Violetta on your request seven years ago, when you were plotting against your older brother Roben together. But then, there was no trace of any other defense."

"Clearly the third member of the Triumvirate is someone I know very well, in either Unatari or Imperial space, otherwise my sister wouldn't have hidden it. No chance it's you, Miya, is there?"

I asked the question spontaneously, and couldn't even imagine how I'd react if my Truth Seeker had confirmed my guess. But my wife, fortunately, denied everything:

"You must be very confused, Georg, because you're saying very stupid things that hurt me badly. I assure you and even officially swear by my abilities as a Truth Seeker that I am not now and never have been a member of the Antagonist Triumvirate, nor a co-ruler of the Grand Duchy."

Miya was clearly insulted. Who finds it pleasant to be interrogated when unable to lie or hide the truth? I had to apologize to the Red Queen and even promise my wife to smooth over the unpleasant incident with a gift of some kind, befitting the Queen of a stellar government.

"Alright Georg, you're forgiven," my wife agreed to close the topic. *"And let me remind you that it was precisely in the Amati star system, where we are now located that the shuttle of your father Count Inoky royl Mesfelle crashed seventeen years ago. If you'd like to pay respect to his memory, the catastrophe took place in the asteroid field near the third planet. There's an obelisk anchored there."*

"And what brought the Count to the Amati system? Did he lose something here? And in an asteroid field on a light unarmored shuttle?"

"Although your father lived on Tesse in Perimeter Sector Eight, he was a very active person and regularly flitted about Sector Seven. This is where he bought the Damir system from the Orange House head and invested in the construction of space-ice-processing facilities for separating valuable isotopes. There was

no direct path at that time from Sector Eight to Seven, so your father went through the Imperial Core, which brought him through the Amati system."

"But Miya, as the Count's Truth Seeker, weren't you supposed to accompany him on his journeys?"

"I did accompany him, but not always. My former master always took me to his business negotiations, but not always to personal meetings. Count Inoky was a gallant and handsome man, and also an Imperial upper aristocrat, rich, amorous and generous with gifts. Your father, it seemed, had lovers and admirers in every star system. And as for official favorites, he would go through five or seven every year. So, I wasn't especially surprised when the Count left me on his luxury yacht and ran off somewhere on a shuttle. When this happened, I was in a crystal dream. I nearly died together with my master, then spent a few years coming back to my senses after the severe loss of energy."

*   *   *

I did visit the monument in space to my "father" after all. I even flew around the huge black asteroid a few times on an armored *Warhawk*. One side was polished to a mirror shine and carried an image of a human face in profile. He stared back with a severe gaze under sumptuous brows. His cheekbones were sharp, and his chin powerful. The features were distantly reminiscent of Roben, but really only distantly.

"Are you sure this is the exact site of the catastrophe?" I inquired from Bionica, who was accompanying me, and the android secretary confirmed, checking the information in the guides. "Strange. The conditions for space flight here aren't really all that bad. There are some large asteroids, but they're far enough apart. The automatic system should have warned him about the danger of collision and changed the shuttle's course."

My synthetic assistant shrugged her shoulders tentatively:

"My prince perhaps, when building the memorial, the area nearby was cleared of dangerous flying objects so the visitors to the monument wouldn't share the tragic fate of Count Inoky royl Mesfelle. Although, I'll admit that there is nothing stating that in any historical documents. Or perhaps it was precisely because dangerous asteroids are so rare here that your father ignored normal flight safety standards."

"Perhaps... There's no way to check now anyway. What's strange is something else. Why did my father even come here on such a small shuttle? A secret meeting with yet another lover? I'm sure they could have found a better place for a romantic encounter, right?"

Bionica looked at me somehow strangely and gave a mysterious smile, not saying anything. Clearly, my pretty assistant wanted to remind her forgetful Crown Prince about a damp dark underwater cave on the planet Unatari, but didn't say anything aloud. Perhaps the android girl was right — after all, we didn't have the most comfortable location for our encounter, based on the standards of the coddled aristocracy, accustomed to conveniences and luxury.

"But why was there not a single word in any of the investigation materials about a second ship? After all, the data from the Amati warp beacon and all neighboring ones was copied by the investigators when they were looking into the tragedy, and I didn't see anything about other ships in the Amati system at that time!"

"Yes, my Prince. In the investigation materials, it did state that there was just one lone ship in the Amati system at the time of the tragedy, *Star Bird*, your father's personal yacht. The nearest starship, an automatic ore freighter, had passed through the Amati system three days beforehand, and didn't stay there for even a second more than it needed to charge up for its next jump. I'm sure your father's secret lover didn't wait a week or two in a space suit on an asteroid! And plus, how would she have gotten out of the system unnoticed after? So, the idea that his was a romantic encounter seems farfetched."

"I agree. Unless she was on a cloaked frigate, in that case the warp beacon wouldn't have noticed her. Or if she was on the shuttle together with my father!"

"No, Your Highness, that story doesn't fly either. There were just two crew members on the shuttle with the Count, both men. Everyone on board died in the accident."

I stayed silent, not commenting aloud on the nontraditional possibilities coming to mind. Imperial law was extremely unambiguous in that regard — an aristocrat could be immediately deprived of his title for such conduct, and it was impossible to hide one's predilections from Truth Seekers.

"Alright Bionica, let's go back to *Joan the Fatty*. If

even the Dark Mother herself was powerless to deal with the events at that time, then we're all the less capable of figuring out what happened seventeen years ago in the backwater Amati system asteroid belt."

A Breather Before a Jump

I WAS AWOKEN by the joyous laughter of little girls. My three eldest daughters, the Crown Princesses Likanna, Joanna and Natalie were playing some loud game somewhere and scampering about after one another through the rooms of the island palace of Unatari, shrieking and howling with laughter. Astra, lying in embrace with me, not waking up, muttered something indistinct in dismay and covered her head with the comforter. I had already slept enough and, carefully peeling my favorite's leg off my stomach, sat up in bed.

"Tuki-tuka-de-sa, your nanny Ayna is quieting the noisy princesses down as we speak," the chameleon bodyguard standing next to the door assured me, but I just waved a hand:

"No need, let the girls have their fun! This is the first time they're all together as sisters. What's more, Joan has just gone through a very difficult period in her life, and she simply needs such joyous emotions to forget her fear and pain."

I threw on a robe and walked over to the slightly opened window. The weather was excellent. The sun was shining in the cloudless azure sky, and a warm breeze was blowing. You start to especially appreciate such joys after a long stay in the cold darkness of space.

"Is it urgent?" I asked Bryle as he entered the room.

The old butler bowed with dignity and answered unhurriedly:

"Crown Prince Georg, Baroness Nicole ton Savoia and First Advisor Apasss Ugu have been seeking a meeting with Your Highness. The Baroness arrived by plane early this morning, but didn't wait for your Highness to wake up and went to swim in the lagoon with Bionica. The First Advisor is waiting in a room on the first floor. There is an Alpha Iseyek translator with him."

"Alright then, set me out a light breakfast in half an hour and invite the Crown Princesses. And invite both of the swimmers to the table when they return."

I went down to see Apasss Ugu myself, because the Beta Iseyek found it very difficult to go up the steep stairs designed for human locomotion on his many short legs. The sixteen-foot-long millipede and a small praying mantis were waiting for me in the room and gave simultaneous deep bows when I arrived. I greeted the First Advisor and looked with interest at his new translator. Its shell was white with a wide blue stripe across the cephalothorax. It lacked spines on the upper appendages and had thin chitin, clearly the first molting.

"Have new diplomats already matured?" I guessed.

My advisor warbled his many whiskers and chirred out something, which his translator relayed to me in very clean-accented human language:

"Yes, Crown Prince. After the destruction of the Swarm embassy in the Throne World, we increased the development speed of eggs with traits necessary for future diplomats. Whole-heartedly loyal to the Unatari State, quick-learning, non-aggressive, but capable of holding their own and defending their master if need be, they can produce human speech without errors and are talented language learners."

"What can I say, Apasss? I really like what I see! Reinforce these genetic lines for future generations. By the way... I've wanted to ask for a long time, how is it going with the clutch of the former Swarm Queen Nai Igir? Are the Iseyek Prime larvae developing?"

Before answering, my First Advisor turned the upper portion of his body, as if feeling the air with his antennae:

"I have long wanted to speak about this with you, Crown Prince, but I haven't gotten the chance to do so privately yet. All Nai Igir's valuable eggs are alive and have reached the first branching point, where their development path can be selected. Now, I need to find out what you want to do with her descendants, Crown Prince."

"What are my options?" I wondered aloud, surprised at the mysteriousness that my advisor was using in reference to the clutches.

"Crown Prince Georg, all Iseyek Prime are, by default, rulers. Eight hundred forty-three new rulers, each of which is capable from birth of producing the language of gestures, speech and pheromones that control other Swarm individuals. All of the still unhatched descendants of Nai Igir are sure to find allies and form their very own clan, and are not even remotely guaranteed to obey the Swarm ruler. Each of them may declare their right to rule the whole Swarm in the future and defy the current ruler. I have ordered their growth artificially halted for now and want to get orders directly from my ruler on how to deal with them."

Ugh, as if I didn't have enough other problems. Eight hundred forty-three claimants to my throne were about to grow up? And what if...? I didn't say anything out loud, but my First Advisor still got my meaning.

"I could destroy the whole clutch, Crown Prince, but such an action will have a very strong negative effect. The loyalty of your subjects will decrease and, in some places, there might even be flare-ups of rebellion. Although I have no doubt in Your Highness's abilities to suppress any uprisings."

"That may be so, Apasss Ugu, but it is an incorrect move. Nai Igir, when transferring control over the Swarm, entrusted me with the life of her children, and probably had just such a possibility in mind. The most obvious solution is: no children, no problem! But she trusted that I would not do that. And she was not wrong. Let's look over other options. If the Iseyek Prime are good rulers by nature, let's make them into managers. Perhaps limit their lack of respect for authority and uncontrollability?"

The Beta Iseyek shifted his whiskers in confirmation. My suggestion was completely possible.

"Then we will prepare Nai Igir's progeny to be the

viceroys of planets, rulers of megalopolises and large populations. Talented, hard-working and absolutely loyal to the ruler of the Unatari State and, as a link in that chain to the Duchess of the Swarm. You can calculate the gender proportions yourself so the Iseyek Prime will be able to adequately procreate, but not grow out of control. But we will not make them all into managers. Iseyek Primes, by human standards, are quite beautiful. We should develop that quality. Separate off a hundred eggs, which we will give a special role. Particular qualities to develop: wide sectile wings with bright coloration, the ability to produce melodic trills that are pleasant to the ear, a talent for music and dance. And they must have the ability to fly! These individuals will become a new genetic line, the pride and of the Swarm, and a true treasure! I will give the ten best ones to the White Queen, I'm sure she'll appreciate them!"

My advisor told me that he had accepted my orders, and put them into action, then imitated a deep bow. Rosss appeared unexpectedly next to me and also bowed. The translator commented on their simultaneous and identical trill for me:

"Apasss Ugu and Rosss thank Your Highness for the good will you've shown to Nai Igir's progeny. They both admit that they had no faith that their new ruler would protect the clutch of the former Swarm ruler. Of course, any order from their ruler would have been obeyed without a second thought, but they are glad at such a wise and bloodless solution. Crown Prince Georg's orders have already been passed on to the Swarm at large and met there with approval and glee. The loyalty of the Swarm to Crown Prince Georg has never been higher!"

It was good that the First Advisor and I found agreement on such a delicate issue. Now I wanted to discuss other things. Above all else, I was interested in the Alien *Queen*.

"Your Highness, the Alien crew has already abandoned the massive starship. To do that, the *Queen* hovered approximately two hundred miles above the surface of the gas giant Hnelle-VI, after which an opaque column of light extended down into the cloudy atmosphere. It must have been some kind of elevator. In less than seven hours, all Alien individuals left the ship this way, some of them taking some kind of equipment with them. At present, our technicians and sappers are checking the *Queen*. But, based on what they've seen so far, the Aliens have fulfilled their promise. All the supercarrier's systems are intact, no surprises were found. After some cosmetic repairs, recruitment and training of crew, and also outfitting her with new combat drones, we can attach it to the Unatari Fleet. Approximate time needed to get the starship in working order: one month."

"Excellent! That's even better than I was hoping. And what are the Aliens up to on the planet?"

Apasss Ugu started moving his whiskers in a funny way, which, as I already knew meant confusion or lack of information.

"I see... Then I order a web of reconnaissance satellites put into orbit and for round-the-clock observation of Hnelle-VI to commence. We have no basis to trust the Aliens, so we must track their every move. What about the technologies?"

"Crown Prince, Unatari scientists are hard at work. The method of calculating coordinates for super-long jumps based on disruption points has already been worked out. This technology can be implemented on all of your fleet ships. By the way, very important information: the eleven-dimensional system the Aliens use could have not only local extremes, but also absolute ones. And it isn't necessary for the resolution of an eleven-dimensional matrix to be either a local or absolute extreme point."

"Wait, stop. Translate what he's just said into simple language for me, without all the complex spatial mathematics."

"Crown Prince, there are two different conclusions here. First: disabling a warp beacon doesn't always block the ability to move from one disturbance point in space to another. Our mathematicians are composing a resolution table and an accompanying travel map, showing which movements can be made, even if there is no beacon on the far end of the warp tunnel. The second conclusion is more clouded but, all in all, we have grown substantially closer to figuring out the Mechanoids' abilities to calculate warp jumps to a star system with no active warp beacon. In the fairly near future, our ships will be able to use old data about previous travel between starships without the Mechanoids to calculate travel coordinates. And in the distant future, it's not impossible that we could develop a fundamentally new method of moving between stars — practically instant and not requiring preliminary installation of warp beacons. In five to seven years, and perhaps even sooner, such technology is sure to appear."

The importance of what my First Advisor had just said was hard to overestimate. Limitless abilities for expansion in space, and no more need for long, many-year flights at sub-light speeds from star to star. All scout ships and the warp-beacon transportation networks would be made immediately obsolete... The race that was first to discover such technologies would get a colossal advantage over all others. The most radical change was that it would instantly eliminate the necessity for all warp beacons, and just one lone race would remain in all the nearest, known parts of the galaxy. All the rest would be locked into their isolated systems with no possibility to move or even communicate, after the warp beacons were destroyed. This was both something to think over and to be afraid of.

"All developments and research on this topic must be conducted in one place, and a regime of the strictest secrecy is to be observed there. If there are any important breakthroughs in their research, I am to be informed at once! And what of the technology for manufacturing antimatter? Any discoveries?"

"Unfortunately, there's nothing new there, Your Highness. However, we did manage to get the coordinates from former Gold House officers of the space factories where antimatter bombs and rounds are produced."

The gigantic millipede turned on the belt across his body and, very quickly flicking his appendages, so fast it was barely visible, brought up a hologram in the air before me. I studied the map and asked him to increase the scale. Apasss Ugu pointed to the supposed location of the secret manufacturing bases of the Antagonists near the fifth satellite of the third planet in a nondescript system.

"Perimeter Sector Eighteen, the orbital complex Oree-III-V, hidden from outside observers by a cloaking system. From what we know, it is the only source of antimatter the Grand Duchy possesses."

"Quite far away... Although, considering the new information about weak points in space, nothing is impossible... Set up a meeting for me with the very most experienced stealth bomber captains. I've got a job just for them. I need two separate groups. They will have totally different missions. And also... From what I understand, the Swarm Princess contest should be over. Have the results been tallied?"

"Yes, Crown Prince. All the star systems that participated in the contest have seen a storm of economic expansion, with intensive construction and growth in available jobs. But considering all factors, the commission of experts believes the most effective manager was Princess Astra ton Veyerde."

"Excuse me?" To be honest, that was the very last thing I was expecting.

"Yes, Crown Prince Georg. Her subjects love the White Queen and are jumping out of their shells to make sure their ruler wins the competition and becomes Swarm Duchess. By the way, the Red Queen was just barely behind in effectiveness. Your wife expended quite significant effort to determine and use the key growth points and achieved impressive final numbers. From what I know, the very powerful Truth Seeker used her abilities and even her students to find the most effective economic solutions. The other Swarm Princesses had noticeably more modest results in comparison with the victors, although they all showed that they are capable of serious work and management of subjects."

I thanked the First Advisor and hurried to breakfast where the others were waiting for me.

*   *   *

"Crown Prince Georg royl Inoky ton Mesfelle, it is a great honor for me to be invited to breakfast with your Highness's close family!"

Baroness Nicole ton Savoia was wearing a ceremonial space-major uniform and had all her regalia as well, making her look strange and even out of place on the backdrop of my older daughters, in light summer outfits, or Deia and Georg Junior in nothing but diapers and Ayna, the babysitter for my younger children, wearing a summer track suit. And also, the Crown Prince of the Empire himself was wearing nothing but shorts and a light cloak on his naked body, so no one there looked too snazzy.

"Nicole, we've been close for quite some time, so it's strange that this is the first time you've been a guest."

Just then, two of my guests came late to breakfast — Astra and Bionica. As if competing, both of the beautiful girls were wearing chic and obviously very expensive evening dresses, abundantly adorned with jewelry and cosmetics on their faces, and had complex hairstyles. I cannot say for certain what happened between my favorite and personal assistant that time, but the girls were sneaking dismayed glances at one another and nearly elbowing each other. The apotheosis of the conflict was when Astra, supposing no one would see, gave the android a strong kick under the table as she sat down.

It wasn't the first time there had been trouble between the White Queen and the Queen of the androids. I was reminded that they had even fought physically at one point. But still, with others around, and all the more so guests, they had never before allowed themselves to demonstrate their difficult relationship so flagrantly. But this conflict had gone on too long, so I decided it needed to end.

"Both of you, stand up. I have to admit, I wanted to announce the results of the Swarm Princess competition over this breakfast. My First Advisor got the results from a commission of experts for all of you and suggested that I, as Swarm ruler, appoint Princess Astra ton Veyerde Swarm Duchess. A few minutes ago, I was prepared to support that expert conclusion. But now, I see that my favorite is not ready to wear the golden ducal crown or shoulder the heavy weight of responsibility that goes with it. So, I'm changing my decision and declaring Swarm Duchess to be baby Deia! From here on and forever, Crown Princess Deianna royl Georg ton Mesfelle shall have authority over all Iseyek star systems and their billions of inhabitants!"

The dark-haired girl sitting on Ayna's knees clearly did not understand why the attention of all those present in the room suddenly shifted to her, and looked up at her nanny in fear. But, seeing happiness on Ayna's face and smiles from her older sisters, she calmed down and continued drinking juice from a bottle. Astra then, loudly sobbing and covering her face with her hands, ran out of the room. Georg

Junior threw on an unhappy face just after his mother, but still couldn't find enough reason to be upset and continued eating his oatmeal from a spoon.

"Now you, Bionica. Go and calm Astra. That is an order. How you do that makes no difference to me. But until you and Astra have made peace, I don't want to see either of your faces."

The light-blond-haired android beauty bowed in dignified silence and followed after her nerve-addled rival with a proud gait. I then then turned to the Space Major, who was somewhat shocked at what she'd seen:

"Nicole, please excuse that incident, but I just no longer had the strength to bear their mutual egging on. As the only man in this otherwise totally female collective, I have to maintain order so the family doesn't turn into a ball of poisonous adders. I'm impatient for my son Georg to grow up and thin out this division of ladies."

My elder daughters burst into laughter at my words, which immediately sapped all the tension.

But after breakfast, I managed to discuss serious topics with the Baroness. As it turned out, the Perimeter Sector Eight Fleet Commander was worried by the enemy getting ships that would be capable of taking or even destroying *Uukresh-* or *Quasar*-class carriers in just one volley. The *Executioner*-class ships of the Grand Duchy or the huge Alien super-battleships, which we had observed in Sector Seven really did cardinally change the situation on the battlefield and possible tactics.

While before we just needed to keep back a bit from the Alien *Behemoths*. The antimatter missiles they launched could be successfully tracked by our tactical computers, giving my ships several dozen seconds to make a dodge maneuver and avoid danger if necessary. But the *Executioner*, with its half-mile-long rail cannons could spit antimatter missiles with a speed near that of light itself, so it could easily hit large and slowly maneuvering targets, such as battleships and carriers at a distance of many thousand miles.

Against such titans, the best idea seemed to be getting as close as possible. The *Executioner*'s turrets had no tracking whatsoever and the huge cannons were not capable of hitting close fast-moving targets. But to do that, I had to enter the easy strike zone of other enemy cannons, those of the battleships and cruisers, which meant inevitable losses.

"Crown Prince Georg, I insistently advise Your Highness to change the Unatari Fleet's flagship. *Joan the Fatty* is known the galaxy over, so it's sure to be priority target in any battle. There is a *Mammoth* in the fleet, and two whole *Queens*. These ships are much safer, and can survive a shot from any ship. Use them!"

I smiled and, staring at the blue sea out my window, admitted to my assistant:

"Nicole, I already chose a new flagship for the Unatari Fleet a long time ago, but it's not any of those. Do you remember the private fleet commander conference, when we discussed the gigantic unused ship in Dekeye? It's the one the Iseyek spent many years building to evacuate their eggs, which is now unnecessary. Well, its dimensions are colossal and it's of a unique design, which promises the highest durability. It's warp drives are very high power and it has a huge energy storage capacity. The best thrusters, both cruising and maneuvering. It's energy shield is of heretofore unseen capacity... Are those not the required qualities for a ship that must survive at the very epicenter of space battle? I decided to take your advice into account and ordered the evacuation ship refit for military purposes. It now has super-heavy laser turrets, which once adorned the Dekeye orbital citadel, and also hangars for small ships and combat drones. *God of War*, which is the name I've given the ship, has more firepower than ten *Behemoths*, and without using any risky antimatter."

Baroness Nicole ton Savoia came up closer and chuckled, also looking far into the distance of the blue sea:

"Now I see where all the strategically necessary resources have been going these last few months — high capacity energy storage, produced by combat drone factories, tantalum composite armor... It's just that I've spoken a few times with Apasss Ugu or the admirals, suggesting various projects to strengthen the fleet. But every time I get the same answer, that the resources needed for my idea were being used in a different project."

"Nicole, that isn't all the innovations of *God of War*. I've spent a lot of time talking with the Mechanoids recently, because my fleet has often had to go into systems with disabled warp drives, or make sure I could get back. Along with that, the Mechanoids and I discussed some unrelated topics. One of their requests made an impression on me... For us people, it's hard to understand. We strive to gain more territory throughout the galaxy, and settle as many star systems as possible. But they, on the other hand, want to join together, unite all their separate spherical ships into one construction. The Mechanoids and I have found understanding in this matter. *God of War* will become a living ship, the chassis of which will have the unified Mechanoids built organically into it. Their consciousness will be capable of controlling the ship systems, at first just repeating the commands given by the crew, but eventually becoming the main command center. The ship now responds to captains' orders many times faster than before, and maneuvering and speed have made similar jumps, which is very important for such a huge and inert ship."

"But Crown Prince, there's no way to make another ship like that. We won't be able to just find more Mechanoids..."

"That's exactly right. *God of War* will be a unique starship. Only one can possibly exist in the galaxy. Calculations have shown that it will be capable of destroying a *Behemoth* in one volley, taking a *Quasar* out of commission in two or three hits and hacking down a *Mammoth* with around a half hour of intensive fire. And at that, it will be totally comfortable taking fire from twenty *Behemoths* and even an *Executioner* won't be able to get through *God of War*'s frontal shield. In five weeks, when the work is complete, the Unatari State will have a new flagship. And then we can begin our new military campaign and liberate the star systems of the former Red House, the last human systems occupied by the Aliens. We'll send the Aliens back where they came from!"

*   *   *

Astra knocked boldly on the door of my personal chambers in the deep of the night, having spent all day wandering the very most remote corners of the rocky island, skipping lunch and dinner. I had already begun to get seriously worried for the girl's mental state, seeing as she'd almost become Swarm Duchess and sent a couple chameleon bodyguards to observe the Princess unnoticed. But the White Queen had just been dancing, composing poetry, sunbathing in the nude and decorating the seaside cliffs with abstract patterns, using clumps of variously colored seaweed instead of paint. Now, my favorite was standing in my doorway, shifting nervously from one foot to the other, not making up her mind to enter my room.

"Tell me, Your Highness, don't you like me anymore?" there were tears in the beautiful girl's eyes.

I have to admit, such an interpretation of this morning's events, although it was totally in my favorite's spirit, had me at a loss. I had to assure Astra that she was mistaken, and that my warm feelings toward her hadn't changed one bit. At the same time, I chose my words carefully as not to provoke the Princess to another bout of wailing. I first tried to explain my difficult decision on her not receiving the title of Swarm Duchess, but she just waved it off carelessly:

"Crown Prince, you needn't worry like that! I never saw myself as Duchess of the Swarm. My grandma Fesilia predicted that it was fated for me to refuse a small crown and get a big one in exchange. I sincerely believe that what she said will come true! And if that's inevitable, I always did have one big crown in my dreams — that of a true Queen of the Empire, not some Duchess, Countess or Baroness, and certainly not of some backwards hole like Veyerde. And so, I never wanted to become Swarm Duchess, because I believe I'm fated for bigger things!"

"So then, why did you get so upset this morning, and run away?" I asked, once again not able to follow the freakish flight path of her bizarre logic.

"It wasn't the useless title that upset me, but the fact that Crown Prince Georg called me out in front of his daughters, my son, servants and a guest. Nothing like that has ever happened before! Every other time I did something wrong, my sovereign would tell me delicately one on one, and not put my mistake out there for all to see!"

So there it was... Astra gave another sob, preparing to burst into tears, but I had already figured out the fastest way to console the upset girl:

"Well, Astra, I ordered a gift just for you from the Swarm geneticists: the ten prettiest Iseyek Prime with huge and brightly colored wings just like a butterfly. They're intelligent insects that will sing, dance and fly in the air for you. They can accompany you everywhere, emphasizing your unique and beau..."

I didn't get to finish, because Princess Astra had thrown herself around my shoulders with a joyful cry. I couldn't stay on my feet and collapsed onto the sofa, bringing the girl, rollicking in joyful laughter, down with me. Astra got out of her clothes so quickly, I didn't even see, but I didn't do anything to stop her. The semi-transparent Alpha Iseyek Rosss appeared three feet from us, but immediately realized his master's life was not in danger, after which he decided to disappear, taking the rest of the bodyguards out of the room with him.

A little while later, satiated with affection and wiped out by the amorous frolicking, I fell onto my back. Astra, meanwhile, sat up next to me on the bed with a thoughtful smile on her face.

"Tomorrow I'll have to find Your Highness's new doctor. Otherwise, my sovereign will get a very interesting present for his fiftieth birthday..." said my favorite, referring to our shared carelessness.

"Come on, Astra, no need for that. I'd like any gift from you..." I said, in a very good-hearted mood and not wanting to fill my head with complicated issues.

Astra smiled thankfully and pressed her whole body against mine, like a little fluffy kitten seeking warmth and affection.

"Well, well, Georg... How easily you are prepared to betray our understandings. Tisk tisk. You That would not turn out well! It would mean I now have the legal right to rid myself of this new claimant"

Miya! There was the last person I was expecting to hear from. As far as I knew, the Red Queen had taken crystals after the successful return of my fleet to Unatari and was immersed in a deep sleep for a few days. That meant that the ruthless and very powerful Truth Seeker could converse with me even in her dream. All my relaxed good nature blew away like the wind. I distinctly sensed a set of icy fingers clenching around my heart, and at the same time saw an invisible blade hovering over Astra's head. I could hardly believe it was just my imagination. More likely, the Red Queen was showing me her abilities and letting me know that it was completely realistic for her to make these threats a reality.

But Miya surprised me:

"Alright, Georg, relax. You gave your daughter Deia a great present today in the form of the title Swarm Duchess, so me saving that life will be a certain type of compensation for the little girl. And, seeing how you like that airheaded doll so much, you can have a gift in return. The chance that you successfully conceived was just seventeen percent, but today everything will come up aces. In nine months, you'll have a strong and healthy son. I promise it as a Truth Seeker."

"But Miya, why are you doing that?" The Red Queen's behavior was totally uncharacteristic for her. I didn't understand my wife's motivation, which worried me.

"Alright, Georg, I'll be as frank as possible. Despite your exceptional abilities as a fleet leader, you're very inert on the political arena, and you need constant prodding. If not for my efforts, you'd simply have turned off the warp beacons around the perimeter of the two or three low-population star systems of the 'pirate dead-end' that you owned and sat like that with your legs crossed, thinking you'd achieved success. All these years, I've had to constantly push you, putting more and more new missions before you so you would keep moving forward. And now, the birth of a second son will force you into another choice."

"What choice?" It seemed I understood my wife's thoughts, but I still wanted to hear her say it.

"Either you leave the boy totally without rights like the first, and have to be ashamed to look your lover in

the eye or you take the situation into your own hands and become the ruler of the Empire in order to get the ability to hand out Crown Prince titles and provide power and a dignified future for both of your sons. Meanwhile, I'll achieve a very old goal, which I put before you long ago, and which I've been methodically aiming towards for many years — scrape my way to the very height of power, become the only and irreplaceable wife of the Emperor and rule all humanity together with him. We will be the ideal ruling couple. My abilities as a Truth Seeker will help you find the right decisions and achieve greater and greater heights, while I can continue to grow and become more powerful with the limitless flow of adoration of all the Emperor's subjects. I will provide us both with immortality. We will rule forever. And as for Astra... you can give your favorite another ten butterflies, that's plenty to make her happy."

My wife finished speaking her mind and told me she was going away. But I was lying in bed until sunup, unable to fall asleep and thinking over what the Red Queen had said. Many historical events and political processes that seemed random and unconnected began to look much less simple than they'd seemed. And also, the mysterious beginning of the war with the Blue House, it seemed, had found its explanation.

And my future looked utterly cloudy to me. Yes, her words about the eternal ruling couple of a unified Empire sounded tempting. Too tempting even, and I sensed a potential hidden agenda. After all, if I thought about it, the big war would end sooner or later, and the need for me as a fleet leader would fall away. Meanwhile, absolute power over the Empire was not the kind of trophy that could be shared with someone else. Miya had shown several times that, as a Truth Seeker, she was capable of surviving the death of a master fairly easily. So would a one or two year drop in her psionic abilities really stop her, if what was riding on that horse was absolute power? All my life experience was telling me that it absolutely would not. What was more, my wife had already killed me once and had certain experience in that matter.

Beyond that, in her Truth Seeker arsenal, there would be not only simple murder, but also violently forcing me to resign, or replacing the consciousness in my body with a more pliant and unassuming substitute. What wouldn't the Red Queen do in order to become sole Empress? And of course, the White Queen did not exist in her plans. What need did an Empress have for competition? Today, Miya had spared Astra's life out of her own selfish interests but, in the future, such humanity would be nowhere to be found.

There was too much that had to be thought through. It was very hard to resist a woman capable of reading your thoughts with ease. Miya was obviously on guard, if she had discovered my preparations for opposition. What was more, it was possible I was wrong in considering my wife selfish, and it was actually my actions provoking the worst of all possible scenarios. The reaction of the Truth Seeker, whose reputation was so dark, would be extremely harsh.

But it couldn't go on that way. I still felt that there was a set of cold fingers clenching around my heart.

Miya could hardly have wanted my death at that moment, because she still needed me. But the Red Queen had let me know distinctly that my life was hanging by a hair and could be ended at any moment. As could Princess Astra's.

Meanwhile, my wonderful favorite, not suspecting how miraculously close she'd just come to death, was embracing me and smiling idyllically in her sleep...

A Search for Answers

T HIS MEETING had been planned for a long time but, with the sudden flare up of war with the Blue House, then the movement of Unatari State ships to Sector Seven, it had been delayed several times. Meanwhile, all twenty-two nonhuman races answered the call of the Swarm Ruler and sent representatives to the Dekeye capital system. I suspect that this was exactly what the Dark Mother was afraid of: that, after the strengthening of the Swarm, all these space-faring races, many of which had had conflicts with humanity in the past, would not join that war as our allies.

There were just a few members of the A-ali race in Dekeye orbit, reminiscent of bubbles of glowing gas, the diameter of which could vary a huge amount — from sixty feet in the vacuum of space, to utterly microscopic dimensions at the bottom of the sea. Thin, but surprisingly strong, resistant to temperature and pressure changes, the skin of these spherical nonhumanoids allowed them to exist both in a vacuum and under water at a great depth. But the oxygen-rich atmosphere of the Iseyek homeworld was deadly to the A-ali, so they had opted to listen to a broadcast of my speech from orbit.

But even without them, there were plenty of unusual and exotic races: unhurried Crystallids, an organic silicon form of life; Pterans, the last timid and even skittish individuals of a race of intelligent flying creatures, which had practically been destroyed by humanity; Gygosians, huge and deliberate creatures that resembled walruses with disproportionally large heads and fantastic mathematical abilities; and Umibots, cyber-organic creatures reminiscent of small octopuses at one and a half feet long. They had resisted a human invasion for almost thirty years in their star system, but at the end of the day, they were subjugated and forced to sign a humiliating treaty with massive indemnities...

Accompanied by my foreign politics advisor Duchess Katerina ton Unatari, I looked through the pane of one-directional glass at all the diplomats who had gathered to hear out the Swarm Ruler. My advisor gave detailed commentary on every group of nonhumanoids, describing their abilities, strong and weak points, and also telling me the history of their relationship with mankind. In the majority of cases, my cousin's opinion of the race was disparaging and even pejorative. According to her, before us were either hopelessly technologically backward species, or the pitiful remnants of a once populous and strong race, left alive by humanity simply because they no longer represented a threat.

Hoping for these allies to give us any even moderately useful help in the upcoming war was simply naive. Especially if I considered the fact that many of the diplomats came from planets under control of the Empire or the Grand Duchy, so they simply would be unable to join my side because doing so would threaten their species with complete extinction.

"And what race is she?" I asked, pointing to a semi-transparent green-haired girl no taller than one foot, dressed in a short bright crimson dress with miniature slippers. Pretty, lithe and fragile, simply a doll come to life, she was the dream of any human girl. But for some reason, I couldn't remember anything about them.

"You don't recognize them? She's an Elvinian, refugees from Perimeter Sector Fifteen. But don't pay any mind to the fact that she looks humanlike, that's just for you. The Elvinians are a form of plasticine gel and can take any form they wish. They were discovered very recently on a Sector Fifteen planet. Initially, they were totally savage. But, in the fifteen years we've known them, the Elvinians have figured out the best way to look to catch humankind's fancy. The Elvinians are totally non-aggressive and live well in human company, especially that of teenagers and children. Red House aristocrats used to keep them in their palaces as servants and living dolls. Not long after their discovery, there were Elvinian populations on six different Sector Fifteen planets. Still, calling them a space-faring race is technically incorrect. They do not and never did have their own starships, people found them and brought them to new worlds."

"That's a sneaky strategy to settle the cosmos," Florianna stated. *"Elvinians are very smart and learn*

quickly. Their style is to not make a conflict with the leadership, but to use the stronger race for transport and protection, obtaining new knowledge and technology along the way. Just a year ago, it was impossible to see Elvinians outside of a few systems in the Red House. But they foresaw the threat of Alien invasion into Sector Fifteen and took measures in advance, including warning their masters and making sure the human refugees wouldn't forget to take them with."

An interesting form of coexistence. A small race, openly taking advantage of a stronger one in their own interests, but it still was not parasitism, more like a kind of symbiosis, with both sides benefiting. Then Duchess Katerina continued:

"I heard that, in the last year, there has been a popular trend for such pets in the Imperial Core. Children simply adore them. But getting your hands on one is quite the difficult task. Elvinians are very cantankerous and even capricious in their choice of master. And by the way, if you want, give this little Elvinian girl to Deia. I'm sure she won't refuse. Elvinians think that getting work with an aristocrat's child is the most respectable thing there is and, if that aristocrat is a ruler, all the more so. I'm sure your daughter will appreciate the living doll."

"No, Georg. I don't agree." This time, it was Miya jumping mentally into my conversation. *"I don't like the idea of an unfamiliar, crafty and guileful creature being near my daughter. Maybe the Elvinians are considered safe, but physical harm isn't the only thing I'm worried about. She might spy on Deia or control the yielding mind of my girl, inspiring freakish ideas and*

breaking the girl's value system."

Wait a second! There was something to that... something very important. I raised a finger, asking Katerina to be quiet and not bother me. My cousin had said that, in the Imperial Core, there was now a trend for Elvinian servants... And a significant number of them served as living, talking dolls, mainly for children of quite highly placed parents...

"Cousin, how many Elvinians are now embedded in high-society and influential human families, having become the best friends of their children? Totally approximate, just tell me an order of magnitude."

Katerina shrugged her shoulders unconfidently and threw out a guess of a few thousand, perhaps even a few tens of thousands.

"Sure, let's say that. And now let's suppose that these living dolls are capable of communicating between one another and exchanging information. In fact, that is probably the case. After all, Elvinians are sending their valuable experience to one another somehow, sharing successful appearances and behavior, thus also allowing their brothers and sisters to better fit in to human society. That means we have before us a network of agents already in place, which can be used for all kinds of different purposes. All we have to do is get control over it and use it to our advantage!"

"Espionage?" my cousin suggested.

"Yes, espionage is the first thing that came to my mind, but that isn't all. Public relations! It's one thing for us to deliver our point of view via data screens. Everyone is used to that, so it isn't very effective. But it is another thing entirely if the dear children of highly placed parents tell their parents, for example, that the Emperor is bad. Let them say he's decrepit, a mad old bat and at war with the good guys. What's more, lots of children of upper military, aristocrats and other influential figures have the implants to express their own opinion of various people and factions practically from birth. So, if their favorite toy, which they trust implicitly, explains in detail what they should do, what points of the internal menu to choose, what buttons to press..."

Katerina's eyes started glowing with a joyous flame, her lips stretching into a smile. My cousin was clearly imagining the possibilities of such an informational attack.

"Georg, you're a genius! But I have one idea for how to increase the effectiveness. Have you already seen the new season of *Jeanne the Star Traveler*? It's season forty-three. The first episode is particularly relevant."

"I haven't even seen the last forty-two seasons," I admitted, not totally understanding what my cousin was hinting at.

"It doesn't matter. Well, it's the first episode the animation studio produced with its new owner, Princess Astra ton Veyerde."

What?! I gave a drawn-out moan and covered my face with my hands. Why was I being punished like this?! Was the story of Astra's address to her subjects not enough...?

"Cheer up, Georg. You've got the wrong idea!" Katerina rushed to reassure me. "The quality of the new seasons is very high, and the plot is unusual: the traveling pink frog Jeanne comes into the real world.

Being intelligent, she sees a threat to everything alive: the overwhelming horde of ghastly Aliens. She immediately joins the ranks of the glorious heroes fighting bravely against the invaders. Overall, it's very naive and predictable, but children are sure to like it. The episode hasn't aired yet, but tens of billions of young viewers are clamoring for its release. My idea is this — what if we make a few little adjustments to the plot?"

"How do you mean adjustments?" I asked, not getting my advisor's idea.

Duchess Katerina explained readily:

"Let the brave heroes, who the main character Jeanne joins up with, be led into battle by the indefatigable Crown Prince Georg. And let the ultimate leader of mankind be an old, greedy and lazy guy, who puts a stick in the spokes of the heroes to keep his grasp on power. Such a character would make children feel a wild disgust, and the connection with the real political figure will be understood by everyone except infants. We can have the Elvinians and android servants give the children a very timely hint about how to punish the nasty villain from the cartoon and help their beloved pink frog Jeanne! Georg, if the Emperor's standing doesn't fall into the negative after such an informational attack, you can fire me as your advisor for incompetence!"

The plan my cousin had suggested looked not only realistic, but in fact guaranteed to succeed. I chuckled in satisfaction:

"Well then, Katerina, didn't you just say that all these races were totally useless? Brute force isn't the only thing we need..."

"That's exactly right!" Katerina cut me off, hurrying to say her fill and looking very animated. "If these pipsqueaks and androids loyal to Bionica kill the Emperor's standing, they will do more damage than a whole fleet of combat starships. Lowering the ruler's standing would mean reducing the flow of his subjects' admiration, which would weaken his Truth Seekers, who would then no longer have enough strength to monitor the situation in the whole Empire, or maintain the health of the three-hundred-year-old August... Georg, catch my meaning, this will not be just an ordinary informational attack. This will be something much bigger, never-before seen in history. Everything in the Empire that seemed to have a solid foundation may collapse!"

I wouldn't have made such categorical assertions, or hurried with the certain predictions. At the end of the day, one old ruler is quite far from the Empire as a whole. What was more, the number of star systems under Imperial control wouldn't fall with August's standing, and neither would the number of ships in his fleets. But still, I didn't scold my cousin, appreciating her sincere enthusiasm and desire to quickly implement the plan.

"Alright then, it's decided. Everything is clear with the Elvinians. I feel like we could also use those gigantic mathematicians. They should be directed toward reinforcing scientific groups, especially those working in the field of studying space and fast travel. So, call the Elvinian and Gygosian representatives here into separate rooms for private conversations. I'll talk with the rest of the diplomats now. I will not demand that they throw their species into the furnace of interstellar war, I will simply put a choice before them. They can help my state, which will cause their race to get a royal reward of money, resources, technology and seats in the future senate, or even new planets for them to settle. They can also stay aside in the forthcoming squabble, then no one will touch them. But if any of the races try to aid the Empire or the Grand Duchy, I swear that I will make their entire species extinct!"

*　　*　　*

It's very rare that I dream, and I never ever have nightmares. Perhaps, it is evidence of my age and life experience, which has made it practically impossible for anything to scare me. But maybe, my psionics were protecting their ruler's dreams very effectively and chasing off negative visions and emotions. So, when I saw an old lady in a black robe with a hood thrown down over her face and a staff in her bony hands, I wasn't scared at all, more curious.

I really wanted to look under her hood and see her face. In the end, it was my dream, so I made the rules! No sooner said than done, a gust of wind shot up suddenly and threw back the hood, revealing a wrinkled face, a nearly bald head with very thin gray hair and white eyes that could hardly see a thing.

"Greetings, Krista!" I said, immediately recognizing the galaxy's strongest Truth Seeker. I couldn't imagine why she'd be in my dream, but still I bowed politely to the powerful lady.

"For some reason, you aren't afraid of me at all..." she groaned out in dismay instead of greeting me, and

I heard distinct notes of disappointment in her voice.

I smiled happily at the very strongest of the Emperor's psionics and explained:

"You've got the right outfit, so if you had jagged scythe in your hands instead of a staff, you could have actually scared me."

But Krista obviously didn't get my joke. And it really was an obvious mistake on my part. In Perimeter Defense, *death was never depicted as a hooded figure with a scythe. In this world, it took the form of a glowing, semi-transparent winged spirit normally of a purple or blue color. At any rate, I moved past it and continued talking:*

"I'm not afraid of any Truth Seekers, even one so powerful as you. This is my territory, where billions of people and Iseyek adore me, so you are very limited in your abilities. What is more, your calling is as a teacher and advisor, not an assassin and, in case of danger, Miya and Florianna would come instantly to my aid."

"That is all true, Georg," the old lady said, easily agreeing and sitting down on a carved wood chair with creak. Where it had appeared from, I could not say.

I also decided I wanted one and was not even remotely surprised when a second chair appeared next to me, an exact copy of the first. Krista nodded in approval:

"Good boy, Georg, you're a quick learner. You have undoubtable psionic inclinations, and if you'd been born a woman, you could have become a Truth Seeker with time. But know this for the future: there isn't a single Truth Seeker capable of harming a person who has absolutely no faith in the psionic's abilities and is

fully confident in their own power. It's too bad August still hasn't figured that out..."

I didn't ask anything. Krista explained the last part all on her own:

"Every strong Truth Seeker can sense the coming of her death. And now, I can sense mine, as well as that of my master. I have no reason to feel pity. I've lived a very long life and have no fear of death. My time is at an end, and I must now make way for a new cohort. But August cannot understand that and make peace with the inevitable. The Emperor is lurching about like a wild animal in a cage, won't trust anyone and is prepared to annihilate anyone just to draw out his days. And now, he ordered me to use my psionic abilities to appear in your dream and kill you. I cannot defy my master's will, which is why I came. But I won't even try to kill you. I have neither the strength nor the desire..."

"Could I interest you in a glass of wine? I won't make it too strong." I offered. Krista was very well inclined to my suggestion.

A moment later, a table with a bottle and glasses appeared before us, and immediately thereafter came a dish of fruits. I poured some wine and Krista raised her glass.

"To the future of humanity!" I said, making a toast, and the old lady sipped the wine.

"I wonder, Georg, what do you think that future will look like?"

I just shrugged my shoulders ambiguously, because I didn't really have a firm grasp myself.

"You're the Truth Seeker here, not me. You should know. I can say one thing for certain: I will do everything in my power to fight back the hordes of Aliens from the systems they captured, and humanity will be unified one way or another."

"One way or another?" the old lady asked, mimicking me. "All I see for now is that you are planning to stir up some chaos in the Imperial Core by inspiring doubt in the power of August royl Akad. And though there is now relative parity between the Empire and the Grand Duchy, after your actions, the balance will be thrown brutishly in the enemy's favor. The chaos that follows that will allow the Antagonists to capture the Throne World relatively quickly..."

"That isn't at all certain! The Antagonists have plenty of their own problems. My sister, co-ruler of the Grand Duchy Violetta, using her desire to get revenge on my mother's killers as a basis, has begun a witch-hunt against the Lavaelle family. As far as I know, all over the Grand Duchy, they are arresting the ruling heights of the former Green House and all their allies, among whom are quite a few highly placed military figures. What's more, not today, but tomorrow, five star systems will be leaving the Grand Duchy for the Unatari State, because they're cut off from the main territory by the destroyed warp beacon in the Khell system. My diplomats are actively working on it, and progress in negotiations with the local leaders has been made. But if I think the Grand Duchy is starting to manage their internal chaos, believe you me, I have plenty more methods of throwing problems their way."

Krista finished her wine in a couple small sips, praised its complex flavor and set the glass aside.

"I'll admit, August and I seriously underestimated you, Georg. Right up until today, the Emperor thought *you could only act straightforwardly, counting exclusively on your fleet leading abilities and brute force. But you are trickier than that. You turned the main figures on the political arena against one another, yet managed to basically avoid any open conflict yourself. You declared yourself heir to the Antagonists, and also a pretender to the Imperial throne, and now you're just waiting for the most opportune moment to take those things from your enemies, who are tied up in war. You think you've got everything under control, and the situation is going your way. But don't think you're the smartest of all, Georg. You're also being manipulated, and have been for a long time, to great effect."*

"And who is manipulating me? Have you got any proof of that?" I asked untrustingly and Krista lowered her eyes to the floor.

"Georg, I'm not here to demand answers and explanations, I'm just here to suggest you think about one strange fact. During the joint mental attack of Truth Seekers on the second Alien Queen, she unexpectedly tried to speak with us. The Alien superconscience clearly recognized Miya and asked her just one question: 'Why?' Instead of answering that question, your wife instantly broke the psionic link and attacked my group, taking advantage of the concentrated force of her students. It was an unexpected strike. It took me great effort just to protect myself. I wasn't even able to save a few of my oldest friends... Ever since then, I've been wracking my brains over what her goal was, and what secret binds her and the Aliens?"

I understood that the Truth Seeker couldn't lie flagrantly, because doing so would mean being deprived of her psionic abilities. But what if, for a psionic, who already sees her death soon, losing abilities wouldn't be such a serious sacrifice, and the ability to cause a split in the enemy camp's leadership fully justified it? So, I answered quite neutrally:

"That isn't the way my wife told it..."

"I don't doubt that, Crown Prince. But you think here: it cannot be that those who sit in the Throne World are harebrained idiots, who also have such worthless military advisors that, during a serious conflict with the Grand Duchy, they would begin a second war and immediately call back a thousand starships from the front to guard the border with Unatari, right? Now, I realize that the conflict was a consequence of Miya's desire to hide her contact with the Aliens. But then, we perceived the attack on the Emperor's psionics as a declaration of war and were expecting a speedy invasion of Unatari ships into the Imperial Core."

I stayed silent. The things Krista was saying were very logical, explaining a lot of strange aspects of Imperial politics and truly giving rise to doubts in my soul. The old lady, meanwhile, continued her speech:

"Georg, there is another strange episode I suggest you think over. In all that tangle, someone killed Milena, Truth Seeker to your daughter, Crown Princess Likanna. But neither I nor my allies attacked the girl, I am completely sure of that. We had no reason to. But nevertheless, the girl died. Think for yourself: who could have profited from her death?"

"Only someone who wants to do harm to my daughter Likanna," I suggested, my teeth now clenched.

"That's exactly right. And there's one more thing you

should think over. Georg, the first time I saw Miya on the doorstep of my school in the Throne World, she was a young girl who looked to be sixteen or eighteen, and possessed an undoubtable gift for Truth Seeking. Even then, she already had the ability to create impenetrable defense against mind reading. It's been one hundred and fifty years since then, but your wife hasn't changed one bit. It takes Miya just a few minutes to rejuvenate herself back into the very same young and innocent-looking girl I first saw. And, as it were, while she was studying, several students died, and conflicts flared up between instructors. Three teachers committed suicide... Even the Dark Mother took part in the study of the tragic events. No connection between the murders was detected then, as was no ill intent, but the Truth Seeker school was closed down all the same. No one thought twice about Miya, though. An underclassman of little importance, she was too young and weak. But for a while now, I've been thinking — how old was Miya really at that time? What if she just seemed weak and young, but really was an experienced agent, embedding herself and successfully fulfilling a secret mission to destroy the psionic school and thus weaken the Empire?"

I didn't answer at all, and Krista didn't ask me to say anything in my wife's defense. The old lady clearly wanted to say her fill and, at the same time, muddy the waters in her opponent's ranks. The Truth Seeker sighed heavily:

"Ugh, I'd like to talk with you longer, Georg, but I have to say farewell. I can sense that you'll be awoken soon. You don't have to believe me, that's your right, but still think about what I've told you. And my advice

to you is to quickly find a new Truth Seeker for Crown Princess Likanna to replace the late Milena. It wouldn't hurt to protect your two other older daughters as well. Just don't choose one of the young girls Miya is training — her adepts are already fanatically loyal to the Red Queen. They will act as her eyes, ears and deadly hands. I hope you understand that such a Truth Seeker will certainly not protect your daughter and, if anything, will aggravate the threat. Astra, though, doesn't need her own Truth Seeker. Just keep the beauty near you, and her sister Florianna will protect you both. But I would still advise your favorite to carry a weapon, like a blade or a miniature laser pistol she can hide in her clothing."

The last piece of advice was so useless that I couldn't even hold back a chuckle. There were a plethora of the most experienced and reliable bodyguards surrounding me day and night, so I was sure I could manage without my favorite, of all people. And also, imagining Astra with a weapon in her hands was just as hard as imagining a ballerina with a set of plumbing tools, or a kangaroo in felt boots and a G-string. And it was with that image in mind and a smile on my face that I was awoken.

*   *   *

My cousin Katerina was in my bunk, shaking me by the shoulder, trying to wake me up quickly. From my very first glance at her rumpled hair and robe, hurriedly thrown on top of her pajamas, it became clear that my advisor herself had just jumped out of bed and hurried to me with a report.

"Georg, I have two pieces of urgent news. The first is that Duke Amelius royl Mast ton Lavaelle is on hold waiting to talk. He requests an audience with you and, what's more, says he wishes to discuss the capitulation of his fleet and Unatari State citizenship for him and his people."

"What?!" All remnants of sleep instantly flew out of my head. "Put him through! Actually, no. Wait! First tell me what the second piece of news is."

"Our cloaked frigates studying the Alien controlled systems of the former Red House have detected a large enemy fleet in the Oolaa system, Perimeter Sector Fifteen. They have more than five thousand Alien ships and another *Queen*!!!"

There it was, the third and I very much hoped last Alien fleet in human space! It was vitally important that we destroy it at any cost. But then the Alien problem would disappear! The only other Aliens in human space were scattered groups of three to seven Alien ships in Sectors Fifteen and Fourteen. They could be caught later, just as we would also clear all the planets the Aliens captured one after the next. The most important thing now was not to let the *Queen* and her armada go!

That news had complete possession of my consciousness. I immediately demanded detailed information be sent to my terminal about the composition and number of the enemy fleet, and began to go through the fastest potential routes for the Unatari State Fleet to reach the Oolaa system. What was more, I even forgot about the Duke waiting to talk to me. Only the fact that Katerina was next to me, clearly waiting for something, returned me to reality, and I demanded to immediately be brought some clothing adequate to my status as a monarch in order not to conduct the conversation with the upper aristocrat in nothing but my underwear.

Finally, I told her that I was ready for the conversation with the high-born aristocrat. The screen lit up and... at that very second Duke Amelius royl Mast ton Lavaelle fell down on one knee and pressed his forehead to the floor.

"Crown Prince Georg royl Inoky ton Mesfelle, I trust in Your Highness's just nature and request that you hear me out! I swear by my honor as an aristocrat that neither I nor those near me have ever even thought anything untoward against your dear mother, Grand Duchess Elisa royl Mesfelle-Lavaelle and that we had nothing to do with her death. I am prepared to undergo a Truth Seeker check to prove my innocence..."

Not hiding my surprise, I exchanged glances with my advisor. Katerina was also in shock and just screwed her face up in disgust. Once the proud and majestic head of the Green House, it was now painful and disgusting to look at him. A pitiful bald old man scared to death, who had burned through all his majesty and was now begging for mercy...

"On your feet, Duke. At least have the pride to speak to me standing!"

My words were intended to help the old man get himself together, but had the opposite effect. Amelius royl Mast ton Lavaelle's spirits fell through the deck of his ship. Not getting up from his knees, he moaned out in pain and hissed out, barely audible:

"I beg mercy, if not for me, then at least for the

members of my family... There are not so many of them left..."

Psh! A pitiful creature, he aroused nothing but scorn. All the same, it would have been stupid not to take advantage of the convenient opportunity to figure out all the details that weren't yet clear about the ruling heights of the Grand Duchy.

"Amelius, I need information on the Gold House Triumvirate and all the co-rulers of the Grand Duchy. Tell me their names and I promise to grant mercy to you and your relatives."

The old man, not standing from his knees, raised his head. Was it just me, or did I see on his face, beyond the distinct mask of fear, a shimmer of clear surprise?

"Of course, Crown Prince Georg, I'll tell you everything I know. During the celebration of her three hundred fiftieth birthday, the ruler of the Antagonists, Crown Princess Eleonora royl Akad offered power over the Gold House to her three closest relatives, the so-called Triumvirate. The first member of the Triumvirate is your late mother, the Grand Duchess Elisa royl Clement ton Mesfelle Lavaelle. The second is your sister the Grand Duchess Violetta royl Inoky ton Mesfelle Damir. And the third is... you, Crown Prince Georg royl Inoky ton Mesfelle."

The floor rocked under my feet. It cost me great effort to hold the unflappable expression on my face. Now that was something! My foreign policy advisor Katerina, who was standing inside the Duke's field of vision, even covered her mouth with her hand in order not to show her shock with a scream.

"Very strange, I don't remember ever meeting

Eleonora," I said thoughtfully. "My memories of her birthday are full of holes, because during the celebration, I was strung out on crystals..."

A toothless explanation, but I couldn't think of anything my cousin would perceive as more truthful. I do not know if Katerina believed me or not, but the expression of horror slid off her face. Meanwhile, Duke Amelius continued:

"They say that your elder brother Roben royl Inoky ton Mesfelle was also offered to become a shadow ruler of the Antagonists, but that he categorically refused."

"Now that I believe completely!" I said, now somewhat calmer, and even finding the strength to laugh. "Roben had no interest in politics in any form. In fact, he tried to stay as far as possible from any conspiracies or potential dangers. But that's all in the past. I need information on the co-rulers of the Grand Duchy."

Duke Amelius finally stood to his feet and answered with a deep bow:

"There are still three co-rulers from what I know, but I only know the name of one: Grand Duchess Violetta royl Inoky ton Mesfelle Damir. I tried to come to an agreement with your sister so I could also be a co-ruler, but she refused. Your sister told me that all positions were taken, telling me you were one of them. I'm afraid that I cannot help Your Highness in this matter."

It was a pity that the curtain of secrecy remained in this issue. Yes, I knew that one of the other co-rulers of the Grand Duchy was my mother, and after her death, Violetta had offered me the vacant seat. I had refused then, and now was wracking my brains trying to figure out the name of the mysterious third...

"Alright, Duke Amelius, you fulfilled your part of the deal, and I intend to fulfill mine. How many ships are in your fleet?"

"Fleet?" the Duke chuckled bitterly. "I have no fleet, Crown Prince Georg. All I have left is one cloaked cruiser, which is where I am now located along with the last few surviving members of the Lavaelle family. The captain of the cruiser is my grandnephew Crasav ton Lavaelle. The crew remained loyal to him, and only because of that fact did he manage to escape. A sick old man, a couple terrified women, an underaged great grandson and just one healthy man. That is all that remains of the once numerous and influential house Lavaelle..."

Crasav ton Lavaelle? That name was somehow familiar... I rooted around in my memory and, although it took some time, I did remember him. He was the haughty and self-assured aristocrat I had a conflict with in my very first days in *Perimeter Defense*. Holy shit, Crasav had survived and even become an authority to his crew and managed to evade my sister's agents. Clearly, the public loss of rank and being ejected shamefully from his ship, which I had subjected him to back then for delinquency and non-fulfillment of commander orders, had gotten through to the young man.

I listened to my senses and realized that I was not experiencing any negative emotions whatsoever toward the captain, although he had once been responsible for two of my people losing their lives. Our conflict was far in the past, and now we were in totally different political "weight classes," so it didn't make much sense for me to pay any mind to the mere junior officer or wish any ill on him.

"Duke Amelius, speaking of the pitiful state of your family, you are missing the fact that a fairly significant cohort of your ancient house live in Unatari State space. Among them are some famous politicians and military men. In fact, Vajek Lavaelle is Admiral of the Perimeter Sector Nine Fleet. I'll admit, I did once think of using them as a legal justification to declare war on the Green House. But the Green House has fallen into oblivion, and I think the time has come for your family to forget about the divide and reunite."

"I think the same, Crown Prince Georg. I hope that our relatives will be glad to see us. And if I am wrong, I do have something to placate them with." The old Duke replied, finally coming to his senses and even smiling. "I managed to keep control over all of the family bank accounts, as well as those of our family's corporations. Duchess Violetta's financiers will be quite struck when a trillion credits leave the Grand Duchy for the Unatari State!"

The old Duke laughed, bowed deeply again and signed off. My advisor Katerina, who had been hiding off camera until that point, stepped out in front and spoke with a nervous laugh:

"Now the main thing is for our financiers to also not have heart attacks when so much money comes in to the Unatari economy. I suppose I'll have to warn our economy minister so he'll be prepared. But I wanted to say something else. Georg, I must give your sister Violetta her due. She simply knows no equals in arranging the genocide of political rivals. The Purple House fell at her feet within ten days, and your daughter Joan is the only surviving member of their ancient dynasty. The Green House held out a bit longer, but also gave in to Violetta. The surviving members of the Lavaelle family can be counted on two hands, and they were forced to flee to foreign lands to save their lives. I hope these examples will serve as a lesson for you, if Violetta offers to let you jointly rule a unified government."

That was for certain. Duchess Violetta could not abide co-rulers. Every person that attempted to share power with my sister had met a horrible end.

FINAL BOSS

I HAD TO PUSH back the date of sending the United Unatari Fleet on its combat mission several times, and every time with good reason. Many ships needed to be modernized, and outfitted with drones, which took a long time to produce in such insane quantity. What was more, we needed to install new navigation systems, and train crews how to use them... All that took resources from factories and space docks and, above all, time. But at that, I had such fantastic trump cards up my sleeve that I didn't envy the Aliens, the Perimeter Sector Fifteen Fleet, or any enemy that might stand against me. For the first time in history, I was absolutely sure that I had the strength to handle the third *Queen* and her armada.

We didn't show our whole fleet to the cameras. But all the same, what the journalists were allowed to see — the disk-shaped twenty-mile diameter supercarrier *Red Queen*, the gigantic flagship *God of War*, and some other ships that got slightly lost on the backdrop of all that but were still impressive: a nine-

mile-long *Mammoth* and six-mile-long *Executioner* —
was more than enough to label this expedition
decisive and final. Eight *Quasar* carriers and an
Uukresh (two of the ships having just passed initial
inspection and joined the fleet). I also had two
hundred forty battleships, all totally modernized and
equipped with experienced crews, a thousand cruisers
of all kinds, and nearly five thousand destroyers and
frigates. All that made the Unatari Fleet a terrifying
force, commanding the respect of all fleets, both in the
Empire and the Grand Duchy.

Speeches by politicians and military figures of all
levels were now starting to reflect a general mood that
this military campaign was Crown Prince Georg royl
Inoky ton Mesfelle's attempt to win a crown that was
his by right, that of the whole united Empire, and that
it would not end with the defeat of the Alien armada
in Sector Fifteen, but in the Throne World. And
although I didn't officially confirm these rumors, I also
didn't deny them or give any speeches suggesting
otherwise. I had no doubt that the Empire and Grand
Duchy's spies were letting their masters know about
that mood, and I purposely didn't impede the spread
of this information, because demoralizing the ranks of
our opponents could only be to my benefit.

The first step of the operation was to jump directly
from the Hnelle system to Perimeter Sector Fifteen via
a disruption point in space. Oh, it was a grandiose
spectacle! Even I, having seen lots in my life, was
amazed at the endless rows of starships hovering in
space, awaiting my command to begin the attack.

But I waited, looking at the timer to synchronize
our arrival time with that of the second Unatari Fleet,

which was taking off from Swarm space. That was my ace in the hole, which no one even suspected existed, not my enemies, and not even my own troops with the exception of just a few particularly trusted individuals. And meanwhile, in the far off Uvi system, there were lots of other ships ready for the military campaign, not only *White Queen* (the second Alien supercarrier, now with a new crew), but also the remnants of the Alien armada, and several Grand Duchy ships, which had escaped the explosion of the Forepost-10 warp beacon. There were also twenty-four *Trias*, which was everything the Swarm had. Half of them had to be called back from many-year space flights to new unknown stars in view of the particular importance of this campaign. All landing ships were filled to the brim with Alpha Iseyek. We were ready for a harsh and uncompromising war.

And now, it was five minutes before we would jump. I took the place of the commander in the fleet headquarters, now transferred from *Joan the Fatty* to *God of War*. To my left, as always, was Bionica. My pretty assistant was concentrated and serious:

"My Prince, approximate warp time is one hour forty-seven minutes. According to recon data, in the system where we are going, Kness, there is just a very small Alien fleet: three *Sledgehammers*, three *Hermits*, and ten *Meteors*."

"That's barely even a mouthful for us," laughed senior tactician Max Gregor, sitting to my right in the place normally occupied by Nicole ton Savoia. The space major herself was undertaking a very important mission: leading the Second Unatari Fleet, which was taking a different route through Perimeter Sector

Fifteen to meet my fleet in the final system, Oolaa.

I chuckled to myself. Long gone were the days when a small group of Alien ships caused alarm in my subjects, and the appearance of just one *Sledgehammer* led to complete panic. Now, the situation was totally different. Absolutely everyone in the Unatari Fleet up to the very last robot janitor didn't doubt our victory for even one second.

But then...

Emperor August royl Toll ton Akad has died at the age of 340.

ATTENTION! The Empire cannot be without a leader.
Election for new head of the Empire will begin immediately.

You have the right to cast 32.7% of the votes of the Imperial Aristocrats.
Would you like to support the first in the line of succession: Count Julius royl August ton Akad, or would you like to vote for a different candidate?

Well, well, the decrepit old August bit the dust... What could I say? It was a totally predictable event. After Astra's studio released its episode about the pink frog's adventure, the Emperor's standing fell deep into the negative, which caused the flow of his subjects' adoration to dry up and, with that, the healing and rejuvenating abilities of his Truth Seekers.

But still, the death of the ruler had come a bit too fast. I thought the old man would putter on another month or two, realize the hopelessness of his struggle and, in the end, resign. In a month or two, perhaps no vote would even be needed. The war with the Aliens would probably be done by then, and my fleet would be orbiting the Throne World, indicating the right way to vote to all the citizens of the Empire with the force of its cannons.

Alright, I'd leave the dreams and return to reality. Voting for Julius, the Emperor's son, who hadn't accomplished anything at all was, naturally, not in the cards. What other options did I have? I opened a detailed list of claimants. Crown Prince Uvius royl Miro. Duchess Savuka royl Akad. Count Lestor royl Mesfelle. Who even were these people?

Obviously, the system was automatically suggesting the first people in the long line of claimants but, in modern reality, it all looked rather comical. These individuals were known only for their ancient families, and not for any present majesty or fame on the political arena. For example, fifth in line was Duke Amelius royl Lavaelle. The refugee aristocrat had lost a political struggle and been forced to leave the Green House to save his own hide. I mean, what the hell kind of Emperor would he make???

Eleventh was my sister the Grand Duchess Violetta royl Inoky ton Mesfelle Damir, and that was somewhat strange. She had announced the secession of the Grand Duchy from the Empire and, in theory, should have lost her place in the line to the throne. Although, perhaps I simply didn't fully understand all the complicated laws of succession and there were some separate paragraphs that governed this very circumstance.

I found myself twelfth in line. It was far down, of course, but we'd see... I tried voting for myself, but that was a no!

Action impossible
You have been declared a criminal in the Empire and have lost the right to vote for yourself until all issues have been normalized

Geeze! But at that, other people could easily vote for Crown Prince Georg. I watched as my percentage grew. While I just sat there batting my lashes, not knowing what to do in this idiotic situation, Bionica warned me:

"My Prince, the Second Unatari Fleet has already entered warp jump. In order not to ruin the whole plan of the military campaign, our fleet must start in forty seconds."

Ugh, I looked again with sorrow at my name in the list of candidates and chose the option "Abstain."

"We will not change our plans! All ships, prepare for warp jump!"

The new ruler of the Empire shall be Duke Julius royl August ton Akad (40.8% of votes)

Just for curiosity's sake, I opened the final results. Second was my sister Violetta with 24.4% of the votes. Crown Prince Georg was next with 20.2%.

How could that be? The total was more than one

hundred percent, considering the share I was unable to make use of.

"The final result shows the percent of those that actually voted, and not of all potential votes," Bionica said, having noticed my incomprehension and hurrying to explain. "But if Your Highness had voted for himself, you would have become the new Emperor!"

I didn't answer my assistant at all, although my vexation at the missed chance made me fit to burst. Just then, on the big screen, in the image being broadcast from the external camera, space darkened and rolled up into a tunnel. The stars grew dim and began to move across the monitor with greater and greater speed. The Unatari Fleet was going to war with the Aliens in Perimeter Sector Fifteen.

*   *   *

"What the heck was that, Georg?!" my foreign politics advisor shouted, tearing into my personal chambers like an enraged fury and demonstrating her disapproval with all her appearance. "Not enough fun? Wanted to finish your games? The Aliens aren't enough for you? Decided to show all humanity your power? Why did you abstain and not end this idiotic war?!"

"Do you seriously think I would have refused to become Emperor, if I could have?" It would seem that, due to my severe annoyance, I overdid the volume of my voice, because my cousin took a step back in fear.

I had to apologize, then tell her what happened in a normal tone. Katerina was very surprised, because she also didn't suspect the existence of such restrictions.

"Everything turned out bad..." she said with a dismayed cringe. "Understand, cousin, that if it was simply impossible to vote for you at all, you would have gotten no votes. But in that case, everyone in the galaxy would have understood the stupidity of such a result and doubted the fairness of the election. Now though, the result has been announced, and there is no chance to protest it. But, wait... But why didn't you just vote for one of your children? They're all underage, and you'd have become their regent."

"To be honest, it didn't even occur to me," I said, admitting my slow-wittedness, but Katerina had already done all the calculations and shook her head.

"Although... no, it wouldn't have worked. Practically nobody voted for your daughters, they all have a result close to zero, and Georg Junior wasn't even in the running. So, even with the thirty-two percent you were entrusted, they'd have lost. The Emperor's son had a few percent higher, and he'd have won anyway..."

"You should have voted for me," Princess Astra piped up, at the other end of the room drawing a new dress for her miniature Elvinian girl. "I got four and a half percent. And if Crown Prince Georg had additionally put the votes entrusted to him by the aristocrats into my candidacy, I'd have won and become Empress. Then, I'd have simply abdicated in favor of Crown Prince Georg or declared you my official husband. Overall, I'd have found a way to make my master Emperor."

While saying this sentence, my favorite didn't even

turn her head to us and continued drawing a design for some complicated skirt for her miniature servant on her touch-screen board. My advisor and I exchanged surprised glances, impressed not even so much by the method of victory Astra described as by the fact that Princess Astra, who no one took seriously, really could have become Empress.

"Your favorite is making me blush in shame yet again and feel like a worthless advisor," Duchess Katerina sighed. "How didn't I think of such a thing on my own? What's more, I have no doubt that Astra is not making things up. She really would have refused the throne in your favor, Georg."

"Yes, she is unique. Others would be tearing out their hair in annoyance at the missed chance. But in Astra's system of life values, a dress for her living doll is much more important than not getting the title of Empress. I wouldn't even be surprised, if my favorite thought the whole forthcoming campaign against the Aliens to be something totally pointless and dumb, that doesn't even need to be paid any mind. And maybe she even has her own way of solving the Alien problem, but isn't telling us because she knows we wouldn't listen to her advice."

I said that at quite a low volume, just to my cousin, which made it all the more surprising and embarrassing when Astra not only heard me, but answered:

"That's right, Your Highness. Why should I fill my head with the war in former Red House space, if no one has any doubt in Crown Prince Georg's eventual victory, even the Aliens. And although they are prepared to sign a peace treaty on certain conditions, the Aliens aren't even asking, because they think the ruler of Unatari would refuse no matter what. And I'm in complete agreement with them there. Why should my liege make an agreement for part, when he can take everything by force?"

"What?!" Katerina and I shot out simultaneously, shocked at Princess Astra's admission.

My favorite finally tore herself from the design and, taking her living doll in her hands, walked over to us. Placing the Elvinian on the table, Astra pointed at her servant:

"This is Maoya, she's a member of the Elvinian race, which we also call 'the Aliens.'"

The shock, obviously, didn't only strike me, but everyone else in the room as well. One of my ever-present invisible chameleon bodyguards couldn't even hold it together and fell off the ceiling, becoming visible in midair and breaking a chair with a crash. But the Ravaash individual's blunder was barely noticed, because everyone around had their attention entirely fixated on the miniature girl.

"Maoya, tell us about your race and about the conditions on which the Elvinians are prepared to sign a peace treaty," said Duchess Katerina.

I had earlier heard the Elvinian speak when Astra was playing with her living doll. In a very thin little voice, reminiscent of the tinkling of tiny bells, the doll confirmed that it was precisely her race, along with a few others that humanity collectively referred to as "the Aliens." She said that the Elvinians had obtained permission to settle human territory seventeen years ago from an authorized representative of humanity, and that they had paid a very high price to do so, giving technology and agreeing to perform a service for humanity.

"Was this 'representative of humanity' Orange House Count Inoky ton Mesfelle?" I clarified, already understanding that I could hardly be mistaken.

"Yes, Your Highness. The negotiations with our race were led by your father. The meeting took place in the Amati system in Perimeter Sector Seven. We told humanity about the idea of a unified consciousness — the greatest achievement in the evolutionary path of any race — and we offered our help train humankind in collective thinking. We were also interested in the possibility of settling in human space."

"What agreement did you reach? Or is that also secret information?" I asked, referring to my negotiations with the *Queen,* and her refusal to provide an answer to the majority of my questions.

"That information remains a secret, but the Elvinians have come to the conclusion that Crown Prince Georg is the rightful heir to Count Inoky and thus has the right to know that secret. The results of our negotiations are as follows: your father had no interest whatsoever in a unified superconscience for humanity. Count Inoky stated that people are individualists and rebels by nature, so they would never agree to live in a government with total mental control. Such a path would be unnatural to your race. But the Count's assistant expressed interest and asked a great many questions. In the issue of settling your territory, we managed to reach a mutual understanding. The Elvinians gave Count Inoky everything he asked for: ship designs, star maps, and technologies. Your father immediately sent the valuable data to his assistant on a yacht."

"Miya?" Katerina supposed, and the tiny doll nodded.

"Yes, that was her name. All communication was sent mentally with her participation, because we did not know the language of humans. Beyond that, the Count used his Truth Seeker to test our honesty. Miya told her master that the Elvinians would fulfill their end of the deal. After that, the negotiations were completed, and our scout ship headed back to our homeworld. Only later did we learn that Count Inoky died that same day. Anticipating your question, Crown Prince Georg royl Inoky, our race had nothing to do with your father's death."

"The Elvinian is not lying. She really is sincerely convinced that the Elvinians were not involved in the death of Count Inoky royl Mesfelle."

Florianna's hint came at a very good time and allowed the conversation to continue without getting hung up on the death of my father.

"Elvinian colonists appeared in Perimeter Sector Fifteen seventeen years ago, using a weak point in space in the Kness system. On the advice of Count Inoky, we didn't advertise our arrival and just quietly founded a settlement on the planet Kness-II. Fairly quickly, people discovered us, but considered us aboriginals. The contact went smoothly, and people had a patronizing and even good-willed opinion of the Elvinians. We then didn't advertise our past. Soon, Elvinians settlements appeared on other planets as well. But it was a whole twelve years before we were contacted through the old channels and demanded to fulfill our promise."

"Who contacted you? Miya?" Katerina clarified, but the miniature Maoya shook her head just like a human:

"Not at all. The signal came from Green House space. A whole group of military advisors got in touch with us, representing Duchess Eleonora royl Toll ton Akad, the ruler of the Antagonists. The Elvinians and other far-away races were told to play the role of ghastly invaders, destroying everything in our path and coming out of nowhere, like a boogeyman, inspiring horror in everything alive. All star systems we captured during that military campaign were promised to us for settlement. We sent these conditions to the interplanetary races we had long worked and communicated with. Other than the Elvinians, there were two groups that agreed, the Fetkhi, which you call the bush Aliens, and the Ehoki, which you call the jellyfish Aliens."

Well then, the prehistory of the conflict with the Aliens was now clear to me, just a few small details to settle. I asked the living doll about the instructions that were given to the "ghastly invaders." Maoya answered readily:

"Our priority mission was to completely wipe the Swarm off the map and destroy other nonhumanoid races. Our second-level mission was to weaken the Great Houses until they no longer posed a threat of any kind to central authority. It was forbidden to attack the Gold House or the Imperial Core, and later that rule came to also apply to the Green House. Also, we were forbidden from conducting any negotiations with humans or any other races until the end of the military campaign."

"I see. But now, I want to hear about the terms of the peace treaty Princess Astra mentioned."

Here, the miniature girl blushed and answered that it would be better for me to have that negotiation not with her alone, but with the unified superconscience of their race, given that the situation and terms might have changed. But it would only be possible to contact the unified consciousness after the starship left the warp jump, and I would also need the help of a psionic. What was more, the Elvinians knew the tragic fate of the Fetkhi race, which had lost its unified mind, so they said the psionic middle-man could not be Miya.

"The Red Queen knows better than all other Truth Seekers about the structure of collective consciousness and knows how to destroy it," Maoya explained.

"Crown Prince Georg, I can try to speak with the third Queen, but I'm not sure of my abilities. The last two were mortally dangerous. Only the presence of more powerful Truth Seekers in the group — the Dark Mother, Krista, and Miya — who took the brunt of the mental blow, saved my life."

I sensed clear hesitation and even fear in Florianna's thoughts. No, the girl was certainly not appropriate as a middle-man, because I could not afford showing any lack of confidence or fear of my opponent.

As if having read Flora's mind, the Elvinian girl offered her services as a middle-man for the negotiations. But here, my advisor Katerina started actively objecting, pointing to the high risk involved in using an unknown psionic. Also, Flora couldn't give an unambiguous answer on whether the upcoming negotiations presented a danger to me or not. We reached a dead end without having come to any decision.

"Seven minutes to warp jump exit," Katerina reminded me, glancing at the timer. "Georg, if you do negotiate with the Aliens, you should not delay, because the Unatari Fleet has to stay on schedule. Our courageous military will decimate the Elvinians in the Kness system, and the *Mammoths* with cruisers and battleships docked on them will not stop capturing neighboring Sector Fifteen systems. This could be the beginning of a great war, but it would be nice to avoid it, if possible."

*   *   *

Exiting the warp tunnel brought us the most authentic surprise.

The Empire and the Grand Duchy have concluded a peace treaty

The Empire and the Grand Duchy have concluded a military alliance

Duke Julius royl August ton Akad and Grand Duchess Violetta royl Inoky ton Mesfelle-Damir have announced their engagement
The marriage ceremony will take place on the Throne World at the same time as the coronation of the new Emperor and Empress

What a twist... The two largest political forces had united but, to me and my government, it was the most unpleasant way things could have turned out. What was more, after the wave of elation from billions of subjects seeing their new rulers end the bloody fratricidal war and unite the Empire and Antagonists after a two-century split, the authority of Julius and my sister would take off into the heavens. Also, the coronation ceremony and wedding would most likely be beautiful and pompous. The citizens of the Empire would like it, which would only add to the storm of adoration for the new Emperor and Empress. In the eyes of the Empire's citizenry, I then would have turned into a blatant outlaw, whose vile misdeeds had united two eternal enemies.

"Bionica, when is the coronation in the Throne World?"

The synthetic beauty closed her eyes for a second, after which she answered:

"My Prince, it will take place in forty-seven hours in the Silver Palace."

"Navigator, calculate the fastest route from the Kness system to the Throne World!"

Senior Navigator Mike ton Tir considered it for a minute, then lowered his eyes to the floor. But based on the way his face went dark, I could tell I shouldn't expect good news. And I wasn't wrong. In the best case, the Unatari Fleet could reach the Throne World in seventy hours, and that was if we managed to reach an understanding with the divisions serving on the warp beacons.

And then, in the center of the headquarters, the large hologram of the star map went out, and was replaced by a message:

"That isn't totally true, commander. It is true that there is no direct warp jump path from here to the Throne World, and that a traditional route would take too long. But we are currently in a weak point in space. And there is also a weak point in the Imperial Core we can move into. The uninhabitable YI-76R system, discovered by humans more than four hundred years ago, but declared uninteresting for either colonization or exploitation. The YI-76R star system is not included in the transportation network, there is no warp beacon there, but we could calculate coordinates for a jump to it. And from that point, we could open a normal tunnel to the Throne World, if their warp beacon is turned on.

Information communicated by the ship God of War.*"*

Ship? Ah! The unified body of Mechanoids sewn into the chassis of my huge flagship and plugged into all starship systems! I thanked my ship for the valuable advice. My advisor Katerina then noted:

"The Throne World warp beacon will most likely be constantly activated in the next few hours, because lots of guests will be arriving for the coronation ceremony. Georg, we can make it!"

Just then, Admiral Kiro Sabuto approached me. The gray-haired veteran bowed with dignity and asked me if we were really going to change the goal of our liberating mission just because of the ceremony in the Throne World. The admiral put it in even sharper terms, asking if my sister's wedding was really more important to me than driving back invaders from rightful human space.

Standing change. Empire Military faction

opinion of you has worsened.
Present Empire Military faction opinion of you:
+67 (veneration)

I was forced to reassure the famed veteran and tell all officers that the Alien problem would be solved in very short order, before the ceremony in the Throne World even began. Based on what I saw, my subjects didn't particularly believe me. But, with a smile on my face, I asked them all to hold their horses and not think me a madman, even though some of my actions might seem strange.

"Bring Princess Astra to fleet headquarters. And tell her to bring her doll with her!"

Complete incomprehension was reflected on the faces of my staff officers, although they were all intrigued by my behavior and no one dared make an inappropriate comment. Astra appeared a few minutes later and, on my request, placed her living doll on a stand in the center of the room.

"My dear officers, please allow me to present the most authentic representative of the so-called Aliens," I said, pointing to the miniature girl, and Maoya gave an elegant bow, confirming my words. "She is a member of a highly developed space-faring race, the Elvinians. Their homeland is located hundreds of parsecs from here. On their first encounter with mankind, the Elvinians politely requested the right to found colonies in our systems. But they had bad luck. Of all people, they chanced upon the Antagonists, who declared that the right to settle must first be earned, by destroying the enemies of the Gold House. And so, the Alien invasion and the bloody many-year war between humanity and its invaders is merely a consequence of those behind-the-scenes understandings. But now, the Elvinians have realized that the war would come at too great a cost, and would like to sign a peace treaty."

"I'm unaccustomed to the human perspective on it. However, there were no errors or omissions in Crown Prince Georg's speech, that's exactly how things stand," the Elvinian said, confirming my words.

"Respected officers," I said, taking the floor yet again, "I admire the artfulness of the Gold House agents, who very skillfully set humanity and the Aliens against one another. But still, I very much dislike the way the situation has turned out, given that the ruler of the Antagonists has eliminated her main political opponents with Alien hands and is now just about to come to power over a united Empire. And she will be doing so at our expense. After all, it is we who spilled blood and fought heroically in harsh battles with the ruthless space invaders. Many of our comrades gave their lives for victory in this uncompromising holy war. We fought very stubbornly, and I can also guess that the Aliens are also not happy at the deaths of millions of their compatriots. The Antagonists, meanwhile, who cooked up this porridge, have wiped their hands of the whole thing, just watching as we and the Aliens destroyed one another. Meanwhile, the problem of the Aliens could have easily been settled with diplomacy. And that is precisely what I am about to do — negotiate with the Alien brain center and determine the terms of a peace treaty that will be satisfactory to both parties. Friends, you know me well enough to be sure that I would never agree to any deals that are not in humanity's favor!"

Admiral Kiro Sabuto bowed to me yet again and then to the miniature girl separately, after which he wished me success in the upcoming negotiations. And meanwhile, Duchess Katerina walked up and whispered something right into my ear:

"Georg, it seems I have found a curious argument against the forthcoming marriage in the Throne World. We've just discovered Baron Juan ton Amolie, Duchess Violetta's fiancé, in a military hospital on Unatari. He suffered a great deal in the explosion of the battleship *Purple Star* — he's gone blind in both eyes, been badly burned and lost a leg — but he's still alive. So, your sister is technically still engaged. The medic says that the Baron's ocular nerves were not destroyed, so he will manage to restore his eyesight with cybernetic implants. His leg can be replaced with a similar prosthesis. It seems to me that now is the perfect time to send that information to the Throne World and brighten the beautiful bride's day."

"Oh no, dear cousin! I want to go to the Throne World and tell Violetta myself."

*   *   *

"Everyone to your places! Two minutes to warp tunnel exit! I demand complete composure from everyone. Reconnaissance is reporting a high concentration of Imperial and Grand Duchy ships next to the Throne World stellar citadel. For the first few minutes, the balance of forces will be simply monstrous. Whether we survive until reinforcements arrive will depend entirely on our professionalism and ability to work together."

My loudspeaker announcement was meant to get the crew of *God of War* into as serious a mood as possible. Unfortunately, I had cut some corners and was at something of a disadvantage. It turned out to be impossible to bring such a huge fleet to the Throne World all at once from such a nonstandard direction due to the abundance of military and civilian objects in space. The area near the star fortress with the warp beacon next to it was very crowded. My military advisors ran the numbers a few times, but they kept getting the same result: it would be impossible to guarantee sufficient space for groups of more than three hundred cruiser-class ships. Or forty battleships. Or two *Mammoths*. Or one *Queen...*

The time had come! *God of War*'s tactical computer froze for a few seconds from the abundance of ship markers and stationary objects. Then the sirens began to wail, informing us that there were enemy ships in the immediate vicinity our fleet. Finally, the computer sneezed out a three-dimensional image, and I managed to more or less get my bearings. Not long after, the tactics officers began to provide me with information.

"Fifty-seven thousand hostile-classed markers on the radar."

"Fifteen hundred markers classified as defensive structures."

"Over four hundred thousand nonmilitary objects."

"The nearest fleet is forty miles away and has been identified as belonging to the Throne World customs service. Thirty-seven *Flycatcher*-class destroyers. All of them are now in our ships' sights. I have confirmation that we are ready to fire."

I had to immediately intervene:

"Do not fire on customs agents, they are not our enemies! Attention, fleet! All ships begin acceleration toward the sun. Your speed must be synchronized with *God of War*. Form a dense core. Four battleships hold six miles behind the flagship. Cruisers another twenty-five back. Prepare to reinforce shields! Immediately inform me if we are targeted!"

I was ready for the star fortress's huge turrets to come into motion and open fire on my ships. But time passed, and no activity was observed. It looked like, due to the chaos of all the guests arriving for the coronation, our ships had yet to be detected. Admittedly, that could only be to my benefit. With every minute, the number of ships in my fleet increased. And in ten minutes, with the arrival of two *Queens*, my fleet would already be in complete control of nearest space. Then, even the devil himself wouldn't be able to scare me.

"Commander, a request has come in from the battleship *Conscience of the Nation*, which belongs to the Third Imperial Fleet. They want us to identify ourselves."

"Say whatever you can dream up, just to draw out the time. Tell them we are relatives of the bride, bringing a big surprise for the newlyweds."

To my surprise, it worked, and no one bothered us for the next two minutes. Probably, many people noticed us. No matter what, it is hard not to see a gigantic twenty-mile-long ship of unknown design, but they all thought we were supposed to be there. The second and third groups of ships reached us safely. However, the arrival of the fourth group of Unatari ships changed everything. The huge *Uukresh* carrier by the name *Joan the Fatty* was simply too recognizable. I suppose that my former flagship was entered in all existing databases, so it was spotted instantly.

My communications officers detected an explosive uptick in the intensity of radio transmissions in nearby space. Many red dots on the tactical map kicked into motion. We had clearly been noticed. There was no sense in continuing to hide, so I increased the volume of the microphone attached to my helmet and asked to be put through to the main open channel used for communication between the ships near the station.

"Attention, all ships! This is the Crown Prince Georg royl Inoky ton Mesfelle, ruler of the Unatari State and your future Emperor. Yes, I had to personally come to the capital of the Empire and declare my rights, because the so-called vote that took place was a total fiction. I should have won that election with fifty-two percent. The results you all saw were a sham, orchestrated to leave the crown in Julius's hands..."

Unfortunately, I was not allowed to finish speaking. A vile screeching and clamor rang out on the channel, some especially mettlesome person trying to drown out my speech. At the same time, a call came in from the planet. Grand Duchess Violetta wanted to speak with me.

"Katerina, arrange for the broadcast of my conversation with my sister on all the main news channels of the Throne World and the whole Empire!"

As soon as my advisor told me she was ready, I gave a wave, indicating she should be put through. But my sister did not appear alone on screen. Next to Violetta, warmly embracing the Grand Duchess by the waist, there was a tall dark-haired thin man, whose family resemblance to the late Emperor August was obvious.

"Crown Prince Georg, it's very impolite on your part to show up uninvited to our wedding," Julius said, beginning the conversation. I immediately interrupted the aristocrat and, parodying his speaking style, answered:

"Well Duke Julius, it was impolite on your part to fudge the results of the Imperial elections and try to take my crown for yourself!"

"How dare you throw out such unfounded accusations?!" The fop boiled over instantly, but I just smiled acridly and replied:

"What's the problem? Let's check right now before all the people of the Empire! Shall we use my Truth Seeker or yours? Or shall we take a neutral one, for example, Krista? You have my word as a Crown Prince, if the Truth Seeker refutes my accusations, I will personally beg forgiveness from you Duke Julius and swear allegiance to you as my Emperor. But, I demand you give me something back — if the Truth Seeker confirms that I really should have won the election, you swear allegiance to me as your legal ruler."

Julius began drawing air into his lungs, preparing to answer me with something hateful and emotional, but faded rather sharply and answered in a quieter voice, choosing his words carefully:

"I do not know how much the results of the Emperor elections correspond with reality, but I give my word as a Crown Prince of the Empire that I had nothing to do with any meddling that may have taken place!"

"And well done. Why should a future ruler blacken his own hands when the Imperial Secretariat and Secret Service can take on all the dirty work for him. Then answer me this control question, Duke Julius, but I warn you in advance — it will be evaluated by a Truth Seeker. So then, the question: if you declared new elections right now, who would win? I'm sure that you know the answer."

The man preferred to keep quiet, and that looked like an admission of defeat, which everyone understood at once. My sister, seeing how obviously the conversation was going in an unfavorable direction, hurried to intervene:

"Georg, let me be so bold as to remind you that you are a recognized criminal both in the Empire and the Grand Duchy. Obviously, you've forgotten that, seeing how you had enough impudence and thoughtlessness to show your face here in the Throne World. And what's more, to demonstrate the pitiful remnants of your fleet. What happened? Did the Aliens wipe the floor with you? Was the myth of Crown Prince Georg's invincibility left in the past?"

I smiled happily, as Violetta, despite not wanting to, had played right into my hand. Taking advantage of the opportunity, I told the whole Empire that the threat of Alien invasion had been totally neutralized. Two armadas of the ghastly invaders had been ground to dust by my fleet, and the third decided not to repeat the mistakes of its compatriots and capitulated. The Aliens had been left with six planets in Sector Fifteen where they already had colonies before the war even began. All the other systems would be liberated of Aliens within two months' time.

It was hard to imagine what happened after I said the Alien threat was no more. What could I say? Even Duke Julius and the bodyguards behind him couldn't hold back enthusiastic shrieks. Before my eyes, there began an unending series of standing-increase messages from all kinds of factions, nations and individuals. My fame reached +100 in less than a minute, the maximum possible, meaning that Crown Prince Georg was known by absolutely everyone alive. My global standing approached +200, and I now had a very weak idea of how a personage that was very nearly considered a saint could at the same time be a known criminal.

I was also overjoyed to see two new achievements in my personal profile:

Achievement unlocked: Savior of Humanity

Achievement unlocked: Drove Back the Aliens

When the flow of messages died down slightly, I turned to Violetta:

"My dear sister, you just mentioned the 'pitiful remnants of my fleet.' I suspect you were basing that on the very first messages about Unatari ships arriving to the Throne World. Ask your military advisors about the present situation in orbit and discover the true meaning of power. The gigantic *God of War*. Three *Queens*. An *Executioner*. Twenty-eight carriers, of which eleven are huge *Mammoths*. Two hundred *Behemoths*. Two hundred forty battleships... And I'm only telling you the part of my fleet that is already here. Thousands and thousands of ships are still on their way, just pouring into the system. By the way... as for the lost Blue House fleet, I found those bastards. They fled in their entirety to join the Antagonists. Now though, they realized that I am the legal ruler of the Blue House, and are asking to be taken back..."

Violetta shook her fashionable hair decisively and interrupted me sharply:

"That doesn't matter one bit, brother. In two hours, the marriage ceremony and coronation will take place, and I will be Empress. You then will be forced to either bow before me, or be branded a criminal for the rest of your days!"

"Is it really for you to judge who is a criminal? I was declared a criminal by the late Emperor August, who clearly didn't understand the situation and thought that the Unatari State was fighting on the side of the Grand Duchy. But I'm interested in whether your subjects know that you killed the ruler of the Gold House by refusing medical aid to a sick old woman, who just so happened to be your grandmother? That you killed every single member of the ruling family of the Purple House? That you murdered all Green House rulers you could get your hands on?"

"Georg, that was just a typical struggle for power. One might think you did otherwise," my twin sister snarled. But I shook my head judgmentally in reply:

"And they'd be right to do so, dear sister. I always try to act honorably. I have never killed without very good reason. I have never betrayed the Empire. Despite all my lovers and favorites, I have maintained common decency and never allowed myself to plan a wedding with one person while still engaged to another."

"What?!" Duke Julius pushed his not-yet-bride away scornfully and demanded an explanation.

And although Violetta tried to justify herself and say that it was all rumor and insinuation, I cut into their argument in elevated tones and said that I had fulfilled my sister's request and found her lost fiancé, the father of her future child.

That was the straw that broke the camel's back. The Grand Duchess lost her mind and, covering her face with her hands, ran off camera. An alarmed military man with space-major patches ran up to Duke Julius then and quietly whispered something, turning on the screen of his tablet and pointing at some data. The late Emperor's son's brows shot up in surprise. He turned toward me:

"There's an Alien armada in the Throne World system. Was it you that led them here, Crown Prince?"

"Those ships are no threat to humanity. I simply invited the Aliens to come to my coronation. Right after the end of the ceremony, they will fly back to their historic homeland. But just in case, there is a group of Alpha Iseyek on every starship high enough in number to prevent any potential excesses."

Duke Julius, now going a bit slower, said:

"The Imperial Fleet has made its choice. More than

half of the ships have already come to your side, Crown Prince Georg. Clearly, the time has come to recognize the obvious." The Duke went down on one knee and said in a ceremonial tone: "Crown Prince Georg royl Inoky ton Mesfelle, I officially recognize that the Emperor's crown should rightfully belong to you and swear loyalty to you as my future Emperor. The coronation is scheduled for two hours from now in the Silver Palace, and I suggest you not cancel it, simply change the schedule so Your Highness can make it on time."

"Two hours? Silver Palace?" I asked with a chuckle, remembering my first visit to the Throne World. "There's no need to reschedule anything. I've made it in less time before."

*   *   *

Nevertheless, the coronation was put off for a day. Time was needed to change the names on the signs and rewrite the poems and songs. What was more, my Butler Bryle demanded that all palace servants be replaced, as ancient custom demanded. Well, what could I say? There was a certain sense in that. Truth Seekers and security services wouldn't have enough time to check all servants. It would be simpler to just take people I already trusted, whose loyalty no one doubted.

The old man Bryle himself, abnormally proud to have the honor of being made official master of the coronation ceremony, methodically paced around the Silver Palace and fastidiously checked into every minute detail, forcing the servants to run their legs off correcting every little imperfection he pointed out so that everything would correspond to the highest Imperial standards.

I then, accompanied by my favorite Astra, looked over the rooms and corridors of the huge Silver Palace. To be more accurate, Astra showed me the wonders of the ancient Imperial Palace which, for seven hundred years, had traditionally served as a location for the most important ceremonies and receptions.

It seemed that Astra knew everything here. She told me the history of many pictures and statues. She commented on a luxurious malachite stairway to nowhere. It was a caprice left over from an Emperor who wanted to rebuild the north-west wing of the palace. He hadn't lived long enough to see out the construction, and his successor decided to restore everything to the design of the first palace architects. But the unfinished malachite staircase had been left as it was, as a philosophical symbol of the vanity of the path of excessive luxury, walked by many aristocrats.

There were crystal water basins in the internal garden. The amazing arboretum had specimens of plants from a hundred planets. There was a spire for watching the sunrise. A special room for solo performances of actors for members of the Emperor's family... The Silver Palace really was a sight to see. In the famed Nook of Kisses in the south wing of the palace, where Astra led me, we unexpectedly spooked a surprising couple. Duke Julius royl August ton Akad was standing in embrace with my tactics officer, Valian ton Corsa. I had no idea where and how the ravishing red-head had managed to acquaint herself so closely with the former Emperor's son, but we didn't stop them and hurried to get away.

In the space-history room, which contained rare artifacts from ancient, long gone civilizations and trophies from a great many of humanity's wars with other races, we met Bionica and Baroness Nicole ton Savoia. For the first time in my memory, the Queen of the androids was wearing a golden crown in her snow-white hair to symbolize her status. Nicole then was wearing a white ceremonial admiral uniform with gold epaulettes and so many military medals and orders on her chest that it looked almost encumbering.

"My Prince," said the android, addressing me, "we're having a disagreement we want you to settle. Nicole thinks that the political situation has reached a dead end and cannot stay like this for long. But I say everything will come together better than ever before. What is your opinion?"

The young admiral gave a slight bow to me and led her hand over the exhibitions in the room:

"Crown Prince, all of the history of humanity is one of ceaseless conflict. People are warriors by nature. We need an enemy to spur our progress. At first, we fought amongst ourselves. After that, humanity entered the cosmos and met an external enemy for the first time. We eliminated over thirty extraterrestrial races and subdued another twenty opponents, thus expanding our territory. The armed forces have always been honored. It was their blood that provided us with a secure future. But now, the wars are over and there are no enemies left. Yes, we are stronger than ever before. But why should the Empire have a huge space fleet of almost six hundred thousand ships that needs constant expensive upkeep, if it has nowhere to use them? A few years of peace will pass, then a voice will grow stronger with every year saying that it is an excessive luxury and the fleet must be reined in. What's more, a military that stagnates and does not fight actively and constantly will inevitably degrade. I think it was a very good decision not to stop the Grand Duchy ship group that fled The Throne World, taking Duchess Violetta with it. The Empire needs new Antagonists!"

I didn't have time to answer Nicole, because the room grew abruptly dark. Then, when the light returned to normal three seconds later, I saw Miya standing a few steps away. My wife was wearing the long bright crimson dress I often saw her wear, but the wide blue ribbon thrown over the dress was strange and went badly with the rest of the clothing.

The Red Queen didn't come alone, either. Twenty other Truth Seekers had come in a densely packed group and were standing in the doorway. What was more, though I had seen the group of her students dressed in black cassocks before, there were also four wrinkled old ladies I was seeing for the first time. In front of the group of psionics was Ayna, the nanny of my younger children. But recognizing her in the armored suit with laser assault rifle in hand was no simple task.

"What a smart girl!" my wife said, pointing at Nicole ton Savoia without any words of greeting. "She said the very thoughts that have been tormenting me so long. And what is more, she is also talented.

Becoming a famous admiral at such a young age must have come at a high price. Perhaps she'll come in use to me in the future."

I didn't understand how my wife did it, but Nicole collapsed to the floor senseless. Ayna walked up in silence to the body on the floor and unclipped the holstered laser pistol from the admiral's belt.

"Now for the guards and chameleons..." the Truth Seeker said, and at that very second, the two guards standing at the door had their guns torn from their hands and were being clenched by the throat. A second later, four chameleons appeared and collapsed onto the parquet floor, their appendages twitching in pre-death convulsions.

"The android is not dangerous, and neither is that dumb doll," Miya said, pointing at Bionica and Astra. "There should also be an invisible praying mantis milling about somewhere as well, but he has been removed from play. I stopped both of his hearts. Florianna is in a crystal dream and, unlike me, is not capable of sensing anything or acting in any way during it. But the paralyzed girl is the only one who will be able to recognize the consciousness substitution, so she'll have to be found and neutralized before the coronation is over. As you see, Georg, it is all very simple. Literally thirty seconds and your time will be over, while a person under my control will become Emperor."

The conspiratress really had caught a successful moment and removed all my guards quickly and effectively. I had no choice but to admire her efficiency. And although I was afraid of some dirty tricks from Miya before, I had no idea she could turn it around so quickly and flagrantly.

"Don't worry, Ruslan. It will all be quick and painless. Ayna will inject you with a sleeping medicine, and we'll trade out your consciousness in the usual way. The war with the Aliens is over, your goals have been achieved and the time has come for the true Crown Prince Georg to return to his body. I see you're surprised. Yes, Mr. G.I. is alive and well, exasperating me with his constant whining. He's suffering from lack of activity in the very same little pocket outside time that I showed you. You though, cannot go anywhere, because your body decayed long ago. But don't you worry, Ruslan. You will not die. Your consciousness will be kept alive. A brilliant fleet leader may come in handy one day. Humanity is on the doorstep of a great cosmic expansion and who knows what kind of difficulties we may encounter..."

Miya fell silent and looked attentively at me, not hiding her surprise:

"How can this be? I simply have no understanding of your emotions. You're ambivalent and calm? What? this doesn't worry you in the slightest? I guess I was expecting resistance from a fighter like you, maybe some foolish attempts to physically attack me or my companions... What is this? Have you made peace with it?"

"Nothing of the sort," I objected with a calm voice, not reflecting any emotions as I pulled a chair out of nowhere and sat down on it.

Miya didn't say anything and didn't express surprise in any way, but was still watching me with her eyes peeled wide. I then continued my speech:

"What's to worry about? Everything is going fairly

predictably. In any virtual game, there is a final boss, who must be overcome in order to achieve victory. I'll be honest. At first, I thought the third Alien *Queen* was that boss, and that I would have to take her down without your help or that of any other powerful Truth Seekers. A very serious opponent. But no, the unified superconscience of the Elvinian race turned out to be peaceable and a talented conversationalist. I learned a lot from our chat. I even gained some new abilities..."

I waved my hand and the four old ladies standing behind Miya in black clothing lit up like torches, turning to ash in a matter of seconds. I allowed the corners of my lips to curve up into a satisfied smirk, when Ayna went gray in fear, and the pack of student girls took a step back.

"After that, I thought a battle in the Throne World system would be the final test. The ghastly initial balance of forces, and also enemy space citadel with its gigantic deadly cannons... If my opponents from the Grand Duchy and Imperial fleets had been a bit quicker on their feet, the battle in the orbit of the Throne World would have been epic and found its way into the history books. I don't even know who would have won in the end of that meatgrinder but, in any case, it would have been a serious test of my abilities. But still no... Fifty thousand combat starships came over to my side without a fight. As the future ruler, I was very glad that I managed to retain such might for whatever trial the future had in store for me. But as a fleet leader and keen player, I was deeply disappointed that the legendary battle didn't come to pass. So that's why I'm glad that a real opponent has finally come to light. After Krista died, you became the strongest Truth Seeker in the galaxy, so you'll make a great final boss!"

I stood from the chair and turned to the girls, who were moving in fear toward the doors:

"Stay out of the upcoming battle, and you can keep your lives. My subjects will need Truth Seekers, and you're certain to find work."

"Yes, students. Don't intervene, this is my battle alone," Miya said, exchanging a conditional hand sign with Ayna. She then shook out her luxurious hair and cracked her fingers. My wife's eyes lit up with a magical orange flame. The Red Queen held her hands out to the side, and the world around us transformed.

* * *

We were standing on the top of a small barren rocky outcropping in the middle of a raging sea. There were slippery stones under our feet. The wind was cold and piercing. Waves were crashing on the stones, sending wisps of brackish water at our faces. The Red Queen slightly shivered in cold and threw a mantle over her shoulders. After that, she called up two identical chairs and offered one to me. We sat facing each other. Miya crossed her legs and called up a drinking bowl of deep red mulled wine.

"So then, Ruslan. You've come to the conclusion that the world around us is virtual. I wonder what the basis of your guess was?"

A somewhat strange question for a person making objects appear out of nowhere, moving things at faster-than-light speeds and basically not giving a damn about the laws of physics. Nevertheless, I answered seriously and in detail:

"I've come across some minor inconsistencies. The kind of stuff you notice with time. For example, the whole history of humanity begins from the Throne World and the development of civilization there. It's as if no one here knows about the historic cradle of humanity, Earth. They don't know about mammoths, coffee or all the rest. Nevertheless, you find ship names like *Thrush*, *Flycatcher*, and *Warhawk*, even though there are no such birds in the whole Empire. I checked."

Miya nodded thoughtfully, accepting the argument.

"Then you see the bugs in the implant system. Where is the server for such a system? The information would have to be stored somewhere and compared with something, otherwise the it would be too easily hacked to drive numbers up or down. Also, there were a few times when the system worked, even though interstellar communication should have been inactive. And the Voice of the Triumvirate getting the Pedal-Powered Tool achievement was also a glitch. I used that phrase in a private conversation, then it showed up in his profile."

"Is that all?" Miya wondered with a chuckle when I fell silent. "These things you call bugs can easily be explained with logic."

"No, that isn't nearly everything But I don't like the fact that our conversation has turned into a one-sided interrogation. I also want to ask you some questions. For example, the fact that you were an agent of the Antagonists for many years is obvious to me. When you destroyed Krista's school and also when you killed Count Inoky. But why did you wait twelve years to share the Alien technology with the Gold House?"

Miya was very hard to surprise. But this caught her so off guard she had to strain to hide her amazement. All the same, she quickly got her act back together and answered:

"Yes, I've been working for the Gold House practically since the splitting of the Empire, carrying out all kinds of missions for the Antagonists. The four Truth Seekers you turned to ash are my very old friends, through whom I exchanged information with the Gold House, and who would recharge energy for me. Yes, I am a very strong Truth Seeker all on my own but, in a pinch, I always had that backup source of psionic energy, which saved my life hundreds of times. They were Truth Seekers of a Truth Seeker, no matter how paradoxical that might sound."

"So, one of the very strongest Truth Seekers in the galaxy spent two centuries as a Gold House agent... Miya, you cannot seriously tell me you never wanted anything more than to fulfill orders, right?"

The Red Queen got embarrassed and shifted her gaze off me.

"Ruslan, I wasn't always such a strong psionic. Once upon a time, this life was perfectly acceptable to me. But my strength grew with time and, of course, I started wanting something more than to be an obedient instrument in someone else's political game. And one day, I truly got lucky. My master Count Inoky, returning from yet another meeting with some trollop, came across the scout ship of an unknown race. I wasn't with him at the time, because I was on crystals, but I had already learned to communicate mentally without leaving a crystal dream, and I helped the Count in the negotiations. I immediately realized the value of the technologies. It was my chance to change my life and catapult myself to the heights of power. But as for Count Inoky, he was not fated to return. Obeying my mental suggestion, one of the pilots turned off the emergency-collision warning system and slammed the shuttle into an asteroid..."

"You must have grown much weaker after that," I supposed and Miya confirmed:

"Of course. There was no way to avoid it. But I wasn't risking death, because I was being recharged with energy. It was worse that I was suspected. The death of Count Inoky was investigated for a long time, and I was one of the main suspects. My every step was watched, so the next few years, I stayed stiller than water with my head below the grass, simply living life frivolously and getting used to my new master, Crown Prince Georg royl Inoky ton Mesfelle, who did not have especially serious plans and lived the way that best suited him. And there was another reason for my inaction. I had already told the Antagonists about the treasure I had, and was carrying on long and difficult negotiations with them on my price. A girl from a non-aristocratic family without even a 'ton' attached to her name, I wanted to join the ranks of the upper aristocracy. My employers weren't sure, and the negotiations were difficult. But I was in no hurry. And then, one day, I was invited to a meeting..."

"Crown Princess Eleonora, ruler of the Gold House's birthday celebration?" I guessed, and Miya nodded in confirmation.

"That whole flashy party was planned just so the

daughters and grandchildren of the ruler could come visit her in Antagonist space. My traveling there as Crown Prince Georg's Truth Seeker didn't cause any questions. My master then got wasted at his grandma's birthday, drunk and high on drugs. I, meanwhile, made a positive impression on Duchess Eleonora royl Akad, but everyone particularly liked my trophies: designs for unique spaceships, advanced technologies, including for antimatter production and... contact with an extraterrestrial race. That was the very place where the idea of an 'Alien invasion' to weaken the Great Houses was cooked up, as well as that of creating a Grand Duchy to take their place. For my efforts, I was promised a reward. My child, who would be born in an official marriage with the ruler's grandson was listed as a co-ruler of the government before he was even conceived."

Here came my turn to get surprised. Deia?! My daughter, who wasn't even two years old yet, and who still had trouble speaking, was in fact the mysterious third co-ruler of the Grand Duchy?!

"Georg, at one point, you asked me if I was a member of the Triumvirate or a co-ruler. And I answered honestly that I was not. You must agree, it was an elegant solution! I was not co-ruler but regent to my daughter. And she, by the way, will inherit the united Empire if something bad ever happens to you. But I found an even more elegant solution and, after the coronation, decided to become Empress myself. Mr. G.I. has too weak a personality to rule. He will retreat from government affairs very quickly, immersing himself in endless entertainment and enjoyment. And if he tries to oppose me... Well, there's always a way to put someone more agreeable in his place instead. But just not you. You're too strong willed and will not submit to my orders. And... you're too powerful... I do not understand... and your new abilities... What the hell?! Are you invulnerable?!"

Miya started flailing her arms, and her face went red in strain. Clearly, the Red Queen was now testing out her whole arsenal of murderous abilities on me, hoping to bump me off. But I didn't feel a thing! Finally, Miya recognized the uselessness of her expenditure of force and lowered her hands.

"Well, Krista taught me how to resist people like you. Beyond that, unlike Count Inoky, I was interested in ideas of collective consciousness and the psionic abilities of the Elvinian race. I even learned to work with them. And right now, orbiting the Throne World there hovers a third *Queen*, where I have five million psionics backing me up."

I stood from my armchair and wiped away the illusion Miya created — the armchairs, the outcropping, the sea. We were then back in the middle of the space room in the Silver Palace, but the situation had changed.

A siren was howling and a great many soldiers with Unatari State emblems had filled the room. All Miya's students were lying on the floor with their faces down, and their hands bound behind their backs. Bionica, actively gesticulating with her hands, was explaining something to the head of my bodyguard Popori de Cacha. In the very center of the room, Astra was standing with a laser pistol in her hands over Ayna's corpse, which had been struck down by a well-aimed shot right between the eyes... I was not expecting such mettle from my favorite.

The second of general confusion passed and... Miya was left hanging off one of Rosss's razor-sharp appendages, having pierced her body straight through.

"How... can this be?" the Red Queen rasped out with her dying breath, sputtering the words through bloody foam.

Bionica explained readily:

"Well, Rosss is from a new genetic line of Alpha Iseyek, and doesn't have just two hearts, but four. And as for the blue ribbon... it was intended for Crown Princess Deianna, and absolutely does not apply to her mother. The Swarm language doesn't have such a concept as 'regent,' so the blue ribbon did nothing to stop the enraged praying mantis. And as for Astra... well, who could have known that she was the two-time pistol shooting champion of the Kingdom of Veyerde?"

Miya didn't even hear the last words. The eyes of the mighty Truth Seeker had gone dim and stopped moving. I walked over, crouched down and closed the eyelids of my dead wife. Tears started welling up in my eyes. Despite how complicated Miya's character may have been, she was still a remarkable person and an exceptionally beautiful woman. It was a pity that, in the end, she had chosen the weak-minded Mr. G.I., who was easier for her to manipulate...

"So, what now? Cancel the coronation?" Astra inquired timidly, having cast the pistol aside with disgust and looking in horror at the dead bodies.

Everyone around was silent and looking in my direction, waiting for a decision from their ruler. I stood up decisively and wiped away the treacherous tears with my sleeve.

"No, we will not cancel the coronation. What's more, put the marriage back into the program, as it was before. Today, old Fesilia's prophecy will come true, and Astra will be given the largest crown in existence! And yes... intercept Duchess Violetta's starships and bring my sister back to the Throne World. Now is not the time to let another Antagonists be created. Humankind is about to expand even further in the cosmos. Very soon, we will not have to crawl from star to star for decades just to install more warp beacons. Humanity will join the highest league of space-faring races, and the whole Universe will lie at our feet! Our Empire will need all its strength for that massive jump forward!"

EPILOGUE

Luna-34 orbital station
Laboratory of the Institute of Time

A PRETTY GIRL with a thoughtful look stands next to an open virtual reality capsule. Her session in the computer world had already been over for ten minutes. The equipment should have been deactivated and the sanitary UV cleaning procedure should have been started long ago, but the young beauty was delaying for some reason and nervously biting her lip. Finally, with a heavy sigh, she closed the lid of the virtual reality capsule, put on her work jumpsuit and, with a shake of her mane of stylish bright red hair, headed into the common room.

As she had supposed, her institute colleagues met her arrival with snickers and jeers.

"And, did number Forty-Seven surrender?" Crown Prince Georg would have instantly recognized the chubby man splayed out on the leather chair as his former employer Mr. G.I.

"But your said you had studied Georg in depth and were capable of predicting his reaction to any stressful situation. Your mission was to make him afraid, feign the capture of power, but not to die yourself. Not expecting such mettle from our client, eh?" The middle-aged head of the laboratory with face and voice of the Dark Mother was very upset, and didn't hide it.

The red-headed girl accepted a cup of hot coffee gratefully from the hand of an obliging android and took a seat in an armchair the robot pulled out accommodatingly.

"Yes, I was not expecting this," the girl admitted to her colleagues. "And really, who could have predicted that number Forty-Seven would obtain support from the Alien *Queen* and become totally immune to my attacks?! Such a thing wasn't planned for. It was wild improvisation on the *Perimeter Defense* algorithms."

The head of the laboratory wasn't at all satisfied by that explanation. She shook her head in reproach and began reading the notation with the prim voice of a strict teacher:

"Number Forty-Seven was supposed to resist with all his might, then realize the uselessness of all his pitiful vain attempts before your mental might and run away due to the imminent threat to his life. In the scenario, his consciousness would be saved by a miracle, shifting into the body of a low-level guard of the Crown Prince or the first android it came across. Knowing the character of number Forty-Seven, he would never have made peace with being deposed and would have gotten on a path back to the heights of power. Cautiously at every step, constantly worried about giving himself away, he would have captured the Empire built by Crown Prince Georg and crushed it under his boot. We managed to create the ideal warrior, a man who could defeat even himself! Instead of that, our object of study defeated you and became the sole Emperor... What a crazy damned ending! Just tell me, why do we need a ruler of a virtual Empire, when our mission here was to optimize tactical artificial intelligence algorithms for humanity's battles in outer space?! Tell me, do we have a backup of *Perimeter Defense* before you arrived on the Throne World?"

"Of course we do..." the redheaded beauty slowed down and spun over the consequences one more time in her head before risking making a suggestion to her boss: "But what if we leave everything as it is?"

"What do you mean?" her boss asked, now on guard and even more severe.

The girl hurried to expound:

"Well, we need battles with strong opponents, isn't that right? We'll have more than enough! According to the plot of *Perimeter Defense*, there will be a scientific breakthrough in the very near future. They are developing new interstellar flight technology, and humanity will fly off to explore the cosmos. That is a boundless field of potential for us! Why arrange for number Forty-Seven to battle old versions of himself, when we already know he will win? So, I say there's nothing for us to gain from resetting the backup. Instead, let's let him do battle with very strong enemies he's never met before! Number Twenty-Three is already ready. Number Five as well. And also,

Thirty-Two is very nearly at the necessary level. In all battle simulators, he now confidently defeats standard tactical programs Kiro Sabuto and Kheraisss Vej. So, we have worthy opponents for number Forty-Seven. We can gradually turn on more and more program modules and arrange encounters for him with new space races or alternate versions of human civilization."

The "Dark Mother" frowned and thought it over, but the fat man immediately supported his colleague's idea:

"I like it! There really is a kernel of rationality! Think of all the combat possibilities we could test! Although... I see a certain risk as well. With all these innovations, we might not see something in time, and allow discordance of different game modules or some other kinds of bugs, which would make our client realize that the world around him isn't totally real."

"He already knows!" the girl chuckled, showing a row of even, pearly white teeth. "Tell me, colleagues, who didn't clear the remnants of the older version from *Perimeter Defense*, and left the names of Earth animals? Hawk. Python. Thrush. Number Forty-Seven noticed that."

"And what was his reaction?" her boss asked, now alarmed and intrigued.

"Totally calm. It seems to me that he accepted my philosophy that there's really no difference between a real and virtual world, if everything there is good, and you perceive it as your home. Number Forty-Seven would tear anyone to pieces for his Empire, his children, his White Queen and his unborn son, his second cousin, and his friends!"

A long silence descended. Taking advantage of the pause, the youngest person in the room risked jumping into the conversation. She was a girl of thirteen or fourteen years with many differently colored braids.

"I am also in favor. Nothing needs to change. Number Forty-Seven has earned the Emperor's throne! How sincerely he loves me, how he protects Likanna from danger! Georg isn't pretending at all, and isn't playing. He really does believe in everything around him, and truly lives in *Perimeter Defense* with all his soul. It would be unfair to take away his hard-earned victory!"

"We have already given Georg a great deal!" the fat man objected. "In his original timeline, he was going to die very soon. He was too good at playing some online game and deprived his opponents of virtual property that they acquired for very great sum of money. In revenge, they hired an assassin who found and eliminated their offender in the real world. The person who ordered the murder was soon found, and the event was widely publicized. That was exactly how we tracked down such a great fleet leader from long ago, who you know as 'number Forty-Seven.'"

The redheaded beauty latched onto her colleague's story:

"We gathered information about him, and set up a meeting. At first, we checked his abilities with a short contract, then we took him on for the real job. As you know, pulling anything material out of the past is impossible, and changing a person's fate is also. But without breaking the physical laws of time, we saved the consciousness of the doomed man not long before his death..."

"Number Forty-Seven is nowhere near the only such person we rescued that way, simply taken from an older layer of time. He is from seven centuries in the past. Back then, there was no such thing as interstellar flight, nor the First Contact, nor the Sacred Defense of the Homeworld. People thought they were the only intelligent race in the Universe and naively believed it was enough to build a fast rocket, and the cosmos would unfurl before them... What a coup it was for humanity to discover that there had long ceased to be unsettled systems in outer space, and any territory needed to either be bought or conquered."

The laboratory head cut off her colleague's story. The old lady raised a finger, calling for quiet and drawing the attention of those gathered, after which she said:

"Alright, you've convinced me. We will leave number Forty-Seven as Emperor and prepare a scientific breakthrough in *Perimeter Defense* for reaching deep space and discovering true enemies. Prepare number Twenty-Three and number Five for the same. Send them technologies, and reinforce their fleets. The plot will be as follows: number Forty-Seven's scout ships will come to their worlds. Arrange for a conflict, and an uncompromising space war until one of the sides achieves victory. Only one may survive — the best of our fleet leaders. And he is the one who will be entrusted to lead humanity's space fleet on its first military campaign!"

END OF BOOK FOUR

About The Author

Michael Atamanov was born in 1975 in Grozny, Chechnia. He excelled at school, winning numerous national science and writing competitions. Having graduated with honors, he entered Moscow University to study material engineering. Soon, however, he had no home to return to: their house was destroyed during the first Chechen campaign. Michael's family fled the war, taking shelter with some relatives in Stavropol Territory in the South of Russia.

Having graduated from the University, Michael was forced to accept whatever work was available. He moonlighted in chemical labs, loaded trucks, translated technical articles, worked as a software installer as well as scene shifter for local artists and events. At the same time he never stopped writing, even when squatting in some seedy Moscow hostels. Writing became an urgent need for Michael, driving him to submit articles to science publications, news fillers for a variety of web sites and a plethora of technical and copywriting gigs.

Then one day unexpectedly for himself he started writing fairy tales and science fiction novels. For several years, his audience consisted of only one person: Michael's elder son. Then, at the end of 2014 he decided to upload one of his manuscripts to a free online writers resource. Readers liked it and demanded a sequel. Michael uploaded another book, and yet another, his audience growing as did his list. It was his readers who helped Michael hone his writing style. He finally had the breakthrough he deserved when the Moscow-based EKSMO - the biggest publishing house in Europe - offered him a contract for his first and consequent books.

Want to be the first to know about our latest LitRPG,
sci fi and fantasy titles from your favorite authors?

Subscribe to our **NEW RELEASES** newsletter:
http://eepurl.com/b7niIL

Thank you for reading *A Game with No Rules!*
If you like what you've read, check out other sci-fi, fantasy
and LitRPG novels published by Magic Dome Books:

Reality Benders LitRPG series by Michael Atamanov:
Countdown
External Threat
Game Changer
Web of Worlds
A Jump into the Unknown
Aces High

**The Dark Herbalist LitRPG series
by Michael Atamanov:**
Video Game Plotline Tester
Stay on the Wing
A Trap for the Potentate
Finding a Body

Perimeter Defense LitRPG series by Michael Atamanov:
Sector Eight
Beyond Death
New Contract
A Game with No Rules

**League of Losers LitRPG Series
by Michael Atamanov:**
A Cat and his Human

**The Way of the Shaman LitRPG series
by Vasily Mahanenko:**
Survival Quest
The Kartoss Gambit
The Secret of the Dark Forest
The Phantom Castle
The Karmadont Chess Set
Shaman's Revenge
Clans War

The Alchemist LiTRPG series by Vasily Mahanenko:
City of the Dead
Forest of Desire
Tears of Alron

Dark Paladin LitRPG series by Vasily Mahanenko:
The Beginning
The Quest
Restart

Galactogon LitRPG series by Vasily Mahanenko:
Start the Game!
In Search of the Uldans
A Check for a Billion

Invasion LitRPG Series by Vasily Mahanenko:
A Second Chance
An Equation with one Unknown

World of the Changed LitRPG Series by Vasily Mahanenko:
No Mistakes
Pearl of the South

**The Bard from Barliona LitRPG series
by Eugenia Dmitrieva and Vasily Mahanenko:**
The Renegades
A Song of Shadow

Level Up LitRPG series by Dan Sugralinov:
Re-Start
Hero
The Final Trial
Level Up: The Knockout (with Max Lagno)
Level Up. The Knockout: Update (with Max Lagno)

Disgardium LitRPG series by Dan Sugralinov:
Class-A Threat
Apostle of the Sleeping Gods
The Destroying Plague
Resistance
Holy War

World 99 LitRPG Series by Dan Sugralinov:
Blood of Fate

Adam Online LitRPG Leries by Max Lagno:
Absolute Zero
City of Freedom

El Diablo by G.Zotov
(a supernatural thriller)

Mirror World LitRPG series by Alexey Osadchuk:
Project Daily Grind
The Citadel
The Way of the Outcast
The Twilight Obelisk

Underdog LitRPG series by Alexey Osadchuk:
Dungeons of the Crooked Mountains
The Wastes
The Dark Continent
The Otherworld

An NPC's Path LitRPG series by Pavel Kornev:
The Dead Rogue
Kingdom of the Dead
Deadman's Retinue

The Sublime Electricity series by Pavel Kornev:
The Illustrious
The Heartless
The Fallen
The Dormant

Citadel World series by Kir Lukovkin:
The URANUS Code
The Secret of Atlantis

You're in Game!
(LitRPG Stories from Bestselling Authors)

You're in Game-2!
(More LitRPG stories set in your favorite worlds)

The Fairy Code by Kaitlyn Weiss:
Captive of the Shadows
Chosen of the Shadows

More books and series are coming out soon!

In order to have new books of the series translated faster, we need your help and support! Please consider leaving a review or spread the word by recommending *A Game with no Rules* to your friends and posting the link on social media. The more people buy the book, the sooner we'll be able to make new translations available.

Thank you!

Till next time!

www.ingramcontent.com/pod-product-compliance
Lightning Source LLC
Chambersburg PA
CBHW071636260626
47170CB00001B/122